The Space Between

Aligned Visions Publishing, Albuquerque, NM

ISBN: 978-1-952921-01-8

The Space Between

Book One
In The Series

Tales From The Convening Collaborative

C. J. Paloma

This is a work of fiction.

In certain parts of this book, individuals, institutions, and circumstances might resemble real life individuals, institutions, and circumstances on Earth. Hopefully certain words and certain forms of sentence structures will resemble good writing as well.

It's my stance that since we are all made from the same Debris, all art is derivative, and every aspect of life is interconnected. Therefore, individual depictions of things cannot be considered fictional or factual. It is all one. Nevertheless, this is a work of pure fiction as the word is more commonly understood.

Some really specific and yet totally random coincidences do happen in real life. And they might happen in this work of fiction. Or they might not.

Any resemblance to real public figures, institutions, physical locations, rich guy organizations, official governmental policies, global situations, colors of the sky, names of trees or planets, or references to pecan pie as something recognizable like pecan pie, are, yeah, COMPLETELY coincidental. They are just as coincidental as the police helicopters that now fly overhead for a few minutes throughout my neighborhood at about the same time, most days. I'll just keep blowing kisses at them. Or make other gestures, depending on my mood. Or perhaps I'll incorporate police helicopters into a work of fiction, we'll see.

Also, please note, I do not condone all of the ideas or actions that occur in this book, not by a long shot.

-CJ Paloma

For all CC Members and aspirants.
And, especially for all active CC Members.

Table of Contents

Compassion Is Terrifying   9

Bringing The Human On Board   13

Sharon Rubric's Initial Standardized Interview   27

Reporting Back To Cabeza   42

Further Suspicions and a Request   54

Highest Wisdom Has Almost Come   64

The Announcement   65

Catching Up Double Digit Dimensional Style   67

Interview With Petra—Socks Emerge   73

Blatherings   86

My Rage Is Grief   91

Learning From Hate   94

Armagettin'   95

Fun Facts And A Consult With InDepth   111
    It's The Trauma, Stupid   113
    The Old Stories Still Have Power   116

The Dream Doesn't End   126

Sharon Speaks With Sync   136

Sharon's Astral Spying   152

Fun Facts For Sharon   165
    Greetings Of The Day   168

Tribe Talkin' By The CC   179

I Hear You   190

SlipFreud, The Electri-pipe, Sharon And The BFD   196

What's Going On   209

Sharon's Morning Awakening   212

Purrfect Synchronicity   217

Highest Wisdom Actually Does Make An Appearance   225

Petra And Meg Discuss The Proposed Mission   228

A Convening Of Intentional Consciousness   233

Musings Start To Morph   246

Props—But Not In A Good Way   251

Mysterious Connections Of The Nefarious Sort   259

Meanwhile, Back At The Ranch   263

Murmurs   267

Preppers Gonna Prep   272

Denial Is Not A River In Egypt   275

Pathways to Cures   279

Consults With The CC, Or: It's All Up To Sharon   282

A Little Help From The CC   285

Representin' For The CC   287

The Saga Of Amy G Dala   296

Who Would Prosperity Harm?   305

On Earth Today   309

The Meeting Of Radically Different Mindsets   316

What's Next   333

An Urgent Communication From Other Beings In The Known Universes   336

Spell It Out: What About Sharon and Petra?   351

MMR Sucks—Also Known As An Afterword   352

Appendix 1   354

Definitions For Sharon's First Year   363

Miscellaneous As Neededs: 387

Compassion Is Terrifying

Compassion is terrifying. To truly be compassionate, people have to allow themselves the experience of being a little bit vulnerable.

Movies with dozens of gory deaths routinely become blockbusters, grossing far more money than utopic visions of worlds where kindness and love reign supreme. Sweet visions of life are generally confined to chick flicks, romances, and "love conquers all" tropes, where humans in the end "do the right things," and people go home feeling good. But they always seem to do so only after huge odds have been surmounted and/or horrific shit has happened.

We don't start with beauty, stay with it as it evolves, and then end with a somehow even better vision of the world that is also based in beauty.

I understand what the normal objections are: They have to do with tension. Where's the tension, where's the hook? How do you create suspense in exploring peace, love and understanding?

And I think about the crowds of people who go to see Matrix movies, Terminator flicks, or the throngs who watch *The Walking Dead* at home. They will say action shows are fun, exciting, and make them feel alive (by shooting, killing, or blowing up several folks during the course of the movie or episode). These audiences like feeling surprised and exhilarated by a sense of danger or excitement.

Millions of people say they like watching explosions, torture, and multiple killings or assaults on their screens. And these are often the same folks who seem to absolutely cringe at anything that's compassionate and gentle. They often become quite dismissive and condescending when it comes to depictions of kindness or explorations of tenderness.

Honestly, some days I think it's just too scary for people used to watching death and mayhem to sit in a theater and weep at the beauty of a butterfly's wing.

-Sharon Rubric, personal correspondence to the author, 2018.

Part 1

Bringing The Human On Board

"We have just had an accidental communication with a full manifestation! As you know, this is a highly infected planet. Repeat, the planet is infected, so we will board the human form, but will need to use strict quarantine protocols during retrieval and subsequent on-boarding to the ship. Duration unknown."

"Holy smokes, that's gonna be a bit of a bear, isn't it?" Shelley was looking grimly at her controls.

OT wanted to wince at the truth of the words. But the Chief Navigator calmly grunted and instead said, "Nah, we can handle it. We've done drills and practiced situations like this before. Just stay calm and worry not, Shells. It's just like another Capture Retrieval drill."

"Yes, ma'am!" Specialist Janus Shelley turned her attention to readying the retrieval scoop housed within the rover. Due to the delivery of some medicine, the rover had already been hovering in incognito mode several miles above the planet's atmosphere. And the quarantine dome was already in place around the scoop. Shelley made sure the dome opened and closed and then let out a loud sigh in an effort to release tension.

"Do you need to practice the whole sequence in space, Shells?"

"I wouldn't say no, ma'am," the Remote Transfer Specialist replied.

"Okay, I'll give you about twenty seconds, it's all we have. On my command," OT said.

Yes ma'am!" The Specialist was grateful for the practice. Senior crew members who were alerted to the incident were all either making their way to the deck, or tuning in to the ship's Navigation Deck monitors. Without prompting, those who were able sent positive energy to the area and to the Specialist herself. Soon

Shelley's shoulders relaxed, and she began to feel excited anticipation instead of worry about the impending maneuver. OT gave a mental thumbs-up sign to the invisible beings who were helping. She privately communicated to her co-workers, "Thanks, she needs that."

Specialist Shelley was still a bit of a rookie at her job, but she was the Remote Transfer Specialist currently on duty. Capture retrievals only occurred a few times a year at most, and the experience would boost her confidence if she successfully retrieved the human form without incident. If. The word should not be overlooked in this case. Retrieving beings who were Unaware of the gazillions of other life forms living in the known universes was always a little tricky, but it was a doable maneuver.

However, this planet was suffering from a serious infection, which made it much more difficult for beings to actually become aware. As a result, no one had been thinking there might be an accidental communication, much less a full manifestation. Generally, beings would be too sick to stay aware enough to engage in accidental communications.

And that meant the stakes were now a lot higher as well. In the past, incidents had been documented where infected (and thus malicious) entities had lured CC ships into retrieving them; the entities had then tried to spread their infection to the CC ship members. But there were also a few documented cases of authentic accidental communications on infected planets, just not in this quadrant of the known universes. Much extra care would be needed in this capture retrieval. But Janus Shelley had already proven to be a solid crew member, and OT was feeling confident they could pull it off.

"Ready, set...and...go!" OT said as the door of

the rover's loading area opened into space a few miles above the planet's atmosphere.

Janus moved the retrieval scoop and the quarantine dome out into space, and quickly opened the quarantine doors. Then she practiced scooping and closing the dome a couple of times. It was easier than she thought it might be.

"Looking good! Nice!" OT's comments were more effusive than her usual words of encouragement, but the move was complicated, and they needed this to be successful. Besides, Janus was doing a good job. A being with just slightly more Hubris would have passed on the offer to practice; so this would be a good write-up to once again show that taking advantage of extra practice was good…practice. Again, assuming the retrieval went smoothly.

"Just remember, Shells, the atmosphere will have more gravity to contend with. So you'll need to give both maneuvers more thrust to get the same motions. Also, when the rover is on the ground, I won't be able to move it much, so remember that when you are bringing the scoop back into the rover."

In this particular Capture/Retrieval situation, dinging the interior of the rover with the scoop was a small peril in the grand scheme of things, but it did bear mentioning.

"Yes, ma'am," Shelley said. She was in full concentration mode and sounded confident. She brought the machine back into the rover and continued to flex her shoulders in efforts to stay calm as OT closed the loading area doors. OT resumed the rover's course and then quickly and quietly guided it towards the surface of the planet.

Time was of the essence. OT's words were the only sounds on the Navigation Deck. "Going into planetside atmosphere in five, four, three, two, one. Entering planetside atmosphere…target area in four seconds. Three, two, one, and go!"

OT opened the doors to the rover again, and Shelley moved the dome-covered scoop to the area where the human was still tentatively tasting an ice cream cone. There was a slightly dazed look on her face. The scooping apparatus looked very much like a magic carpet with translucent cover on top. Overall, it vaguely resembled a personal sized flying saucer. It was behind the human, so she did not notice it at first.

Suddenly, Meg, who had been the one to accidentally contact and create a manifestation for the human, sent out another mind command, "Wait! She's going to ask to come on board, no need to use a capture sequence."

OT immediately replied, "Are you sure, Meg? This is an infected planet. "

"Ninety-eight percent sure, OT. I am in communication with the human's 6D element, who sees us and is asking to board. I have checked carefully. Neither she nor the human's other elements appear to be harboring any Ill Intent."

Specialist Shelley looked uncertainly to OT for her command. OT said to Meg, "It's an infected planet, so this needs to go smoothly. And, you know your 98 percent has always been 300 percent in my book. But you still need to convince me."

Meg publicly communicated back, "OT, ma'am, she asked for an ice cream, I heard it as a mind command, manifested it, and the human took it and began eating it, as you can see. She also said 'Thank you' out loud just before the rover entered the target area. Her 6D element is yammering in my ear, almost hysterically happy at being rescued. I know you can't see the 6D, but look!"

The human had just turned and spotted the retrieval scoop and was staring with surprise and curiosity. Then she held out the ice cream. They all watched as she said out loud, "Did you give me this? If you did, thank you!" It was clear to all who could read nonverbals in humanoids that this one was exhibiting no Ill Intent, or even Fear. Indeed, she emanated (emanated!) Goodness. Along with Goodness, curiosity was her primary response. She smiled slightly and cocked her head to one side, appearing to intently study the retrieval scoop.

Almost reflexively, Specialist Shelley dipped the retrieval apparatus ever so slightly in a gentle response. OT looked at Shelley and then at the human on the screen, obviously impressed with both. OT then communicated to Shelley, "Abort the Capture Retrieval plan. Slowly open the quarantine doors so you don't startle her."

The entire crew held their breath while Janus Shelley executed the maneuver. If the human ran, there'd be a messy chase, and the newbie Specialist might flub it.

The human stood still, intently watching as the flying saucer part retracted and somehow disappeared into the apparatus, leaving only a flat, floating platform. The human now looked up as if listening to someone. She smiled a little, still seeming to listen.

Meg said, "The 6D element is communicating with her human." Murmurs of surprise could be heard among the crew members.

"Consciously?" one of the crew asked.

"Affirmative, I can hear them both. The human is consciously communicating with her 6D element, asking for advice. And the 6D element is sending reassurances and encouragement to the human to approach the retrieval platform," said Meg. More murmurs from the crew ensued.

After a brief pause, the human said out loud, "I hope you're right!" to what seemed like no one in particular. Shelley again dipped the machine ever so slightly, as if in response. The human then seemed to become aware of her ice cream again, and she offered the ice cream cone to the machine in front of her with a friendly gesture and smile. This time the machine only dipped and moved back ever so slightly.

At that, the human said gently, "Okay, I guess you're right. I can't quite tell how we'd share this, anyway. May I approach?"

Shelley dipped the apparatus a little more deeply and moved the retrieval scoop platform towards the human ever so slightly. The human emitted a small smile in acknowledgement, but stood almost motionless for a few seconds more, only moving to take a bite from the ice cream. Then she shrugged and started cautiously walking towards the platform.

Meg exclaimed, "The 6D is encouraging her! She's saying 'Well, you don't know, what we can find, why don't you come with me, oh girl, on a magic carpet ride.'"

"Is that code for something?" someone asked.

There was a brief silence; then Meg said, "Most likely not. The 6D element is telling me it is a lyric from a song the human enjoys."

"Quick, manifest a comfortable seating area for her in the rover!" It was the Captain herself. The video monitors flickered for a couple of seconds, then the Captain appeared on them, looking on intently at the human headed for the retrieval scoop apparatus. Shelley lowered the platform, and the human scooted herself onto it without difficulty.

Meg cut in urgently: "Please do not use the quarantine dome, OT."

"I concur," Captain Cabeza said. "We will use the whole rover as the quarantine area. We'll follow usual reboarding procedures for the outer parts of the rover. We can then sterilize the insides of the rover after the human is successfully relocated to guest quarters on the ship. But we'll still need to use the quarantine dome once she's ready to go to her guest quarters. And let's ensure the human is made aware of the need for quarantine procedures."

OT nodded, knowing the Captain could see her, and waved a small command to Shelley. Shelley nodded as well, but her attention was focused on carrying the human slowly towards the rover as smoothly as possible.

Balancing the human on the platform was turning out to be one of the more difficult parts of the process so far. The human sat with her knees up and her arms wrapped around her legs. Looking down, she noticed some half-dried mud by her boots and brushed it off the floor of the apparatus. It fell to the ground noiselessly.

As the human did this, her weight shifted, causing Shelley to curse as the platform tipped a little. Shelley paused to regain balance. Then she slowly and very carefully continued to move the apparatus towards the rover. The human noticed the balance issue and said, "Oh, sorry!"

At the same time as Shelley was inching the platform forwards, OT engaged the rendering program for the rover, slowly moving the entire machine from the default of transparent to opaque. She then selected the program that would automatically analyze and then match the local atmospheric pressure and components, so the human would be able to breathe without having to be fitted to an apparatus.

Meg was wildly adding flourishes designed for humans to the rover's interior. She had already created a sectional couch, a flat-screen TV, a mini fridge, and some newly manifested lights. A couple of seconds before the human entered the machine, the 6D communicated with Meg and said, "Oh, thank you so much! If you add some flowers—purple irises—she'll be yours forever."

"Okay," Meg said breathlessly. She produced a bundle of irises and manifested a vase to go around them. The vase of flowers hovered at what would be about eye level to the human once she entered the rover. Meg lowered them a bit so the human would be better able to see the flowers.

Shelley stopped the platform once it and its passenger were within the walls of the rover. The human hopped off and stared around a bit. After a moment, her gaze landed on the flowers in the vase, still sort of hovering. The 6D said, "Um, maybe a side table for them?"

"Of course, sorry!" Meg muttered. A side table matching the general decor manifested, and the flowers lowered onto it slowly.

The human had been watching the whole maneuver with her mouth half-open. Obviously a bit overwhelmed, she still managed a somewhat playful, "How did you know?" Then she licked a drip of ice cream that was trailing down the cone and onto her hand. Meg didn't answer, but a napkin suddenly appeared, hovering within reach of the human. The human took it and bowed a little in several directions as a sign of thanks.

She stood in roughly the middle of the now transformed rover.

The doors of the rover still appeared open, but OT had used an old trick to return them to transparency mode while the human debarked from the carpet. She then had surreptitiously closed them. OT now asked if she could inform the human of their intentions to bring her on board the main ship.

"Wait." It was Meg again. "If I may, I would like to attempt to communicate with the human aspect, Captain."

"Yes, go ahead, Meg," the Captain said quietly. Her heads bobbed in the video monitors around the control room.

Meg thought for a second, then made a sound to mimic a gentle throat clearing.

The human said, "Yes?" in response.

"We would like to welcome you to our rover," Meg said. "And we would like to take you on board our main ship, if you are willing and ready, ma'am." She said it gently, emanating friendly hospitality, of course.

The human looked around the rover without saying anything. She eyed the seemingly open entrance and studied it intently, but said nothing. Various crew members observing from the Navigation Deck were busy studying, making notes, and analyzing the human's reactions. She emanated no Fear; no aggression, no subterfuge was apparent, or Ill Intent. Instead, she emanated Goodness and cooperative energies like a normally aware being. She appeared to be assessing her surroundings quite carefully, and her gaze went back to the entrance once more. The ship was abuzz with these quietly murmured observations. The human continued to eat the ice cream, and with a bit of pizzazz, wiped her mouth with the napkin.

She tentatively looked at her arms and legs and tested them out a bit. Then she said, "Well, nothing hurts, at least. I think I must have tripped or fallen somehow and am hallucinating. Like Dorothy in The Wizard of Oz." Her gaze now returned to the ice cream cone in her hand. She took a fair-sized bite of what was left and savored it before continuing.

"But it's definitely not a bad hallucination," she said shrugging a bit. "You gave me ice cream, you have my favorite flowers...I think that might be a sign of some sort." She took a deep breath. "The air smells fine." She paused, then said, "I don't see you, but you're talking to me in a kind voice." She suddenly scrunched her brow and looked towards the doors. "Are you friendly?"

"Very!" Meg replied with enthusiasm.

The human took another bite of ice cream and continued to look around. "Well, you sound friendly. And you sound female. Um, are you?"

Meg and the 6D aspect conferred quickly and quietly before Meg said, "Uh, yes, by your standards."

The human looked at the flowers again with some approval. But then she narrowed her eyes and asked, "Are your leaders male or female?"

At that, Meg spontaneously burst out laughing, as did the crew on board.

"Much closer to female, ma'am!" Meg said congenially.

The human laughed as well, and snorted happily. She finished off the ice cream, still considering the situation. "Most likely, I am lying unconscious somewhere on the trail, but... This place, this hallucination, or whatever it is feels safe, and I really don't get the sense that I need to wake up any time soon." She paused, looking around intently, searching for clues in the immediate environment. Then, quietly and more to herself, she said, "And really, I think Petra would tell me if I did…" She trailed off, still standing quietly in the middle of the room.

Meg realized she'd been holding her energies still, willing the human to come of her own accord. No one on board the ship seemed to be breathing either, at this particular point. All were intently emanating whatever good energies they thought the human could comprehend. The human deliberated a little longer. She tilted her head first one way, then another, her interior puzzlement and curiosity clear to any crew member who could read human body language. After another moment, the human nodded. "The ice cream was delicious, and it's been a pretty good hike so far, I must say." At that, she strode over to the couch and rather enthusiastically hopped onto it. Leaning back into the cushions, she said, "Yes! I'm ready to board your ship, that will be fine!"

Captain Cabeza, watching from her station, said, "Excellent," rather loudly, but the human did not seem to hear it.

Meg squelched her excitement, and managed to say with kind professionalism, "Wonderful. Welcome aboard, ma'am! Please let me know if there is anything I can get you, but this won't be a long ride."

Captain Cabeza smiled briefly, then gave the signal to OT, who now re-rendered the doors on the rover from translucent to fully opaque. The human noticed this detail, and squinted a little as the opacity filled in. The ship's cabin was completely silent for a second as they watched the human carefully take off her slightly muddy shoes and place them on the floor before she rearranged herself crosslegged on the couch. The Captain was aware that all eyes were on her and the human. She smiled briefly again and let out a long whistle, momentarily savoring the moment. The pregnant pause began to be punctured by excited sounds coming from the crew members. OT quietly checked her controls, conferred with Specialist Shelley, and then the rover left Earth. It appeared ship side in the safe area almost immediately, but stayed in dark mode.

The Captain swiveled her heads in the general direction of OT. "OT, why the delay?"

OT looked up. "Meg's asking for the delay, ma'am." Meg had to speak over celebratory whoops to reply.

Meg spoke up, saying, "Captain, if I may, this being is used to 3D time as it manifests on Earth. Her 6D element informed me that if she arrives instantaneously, it may be a shock." She paused. "But the aspect is also saying that a ride longer than ten Earth minutes …ahh…'May freak her out' is how the soul aspect is phrasing it, Captain."

"Ah, well, by all means, we'll stretch this ride out to about seven Earth minutes, how's that sound, Meg?" Before Meg could answer, another of Cabeza's heads said, "No, let's make it five. We will board the human in five Earth minutes. Great job, team!"

Meg emanated agreement. The Captain then graciously started applauding the crew members. The whole control room whooped back their relief and excitement. Shelley beamed and stiffly pushed back from the operating console.

OT began to tentatively maneuver dials and buttons to bring the rover out of dark mode in the requested amount of time. But she quickly looked a little puzzled. Shelley caught her eye and understood the issue immediately, as she also had the same question. Shelley cleared her throat and said over the rising din, "And how long is five Earth minutes in CC time, Captain?"

"Excellent question, Specialist Shelley," said Captain Cabeza. "Anyone know for sure?"

An engineer asked a nearby computer, who responded almost instantaneously with: "Earth's time measurement in this spacetimecontinuum is at a relatively slow processing speed. The easiest translation is that 33.3 CC minutes are equivalent to one Earth minute. This is using standard analog mathematics and physics, which are reserved for planets and beings with 3D processing speeds and capacity."

After the briefest of pauses, the computer offered further commentary, "Aside: Some other Earth spacetimecontinuums are even slower, clocking in (lol) at forty-five or seventy-eight CC minutes to one Earth minute."

Murmurs emitted from the crew. In the background, someone said, "Why do those numbers sound so familiar?"

But the engineer ignored the distractions and did a quick calculation. "That comes to approximately 166.5 CC minutes, Captain."

"Wow, that's slow," murmured Meg.

The 6D aspect piped up at this. "Oh Lordy, you have no idea. Things move really slow down there."

At that, Meg turned her full attention towards the 6D, whose presence was anchored in the rover. Meg made her energy deliberately and theatrically become apparent in a space near the 6D on the rover. She beamed friendly energy and communicated in her natural voice. "Welcome aboard, I'm Meg."

"Very pleased to meet you! I'm Petra," the 6D replied, her energetic presence dancing with obvious joy.

Much to Meg's surprise, the human looked in her general direction and squinted, trying to understand what was going on. Petra immediately said, "She can't grasp you fully, of course, but she can tell you moved your energy around."

"Wow," said Meg.

"Yeah, I've been very blessed," Petra replied.

Sharon Rubric's Initial Standardized Interview

The human was onboarded to the main ship without incident.

The 6D element, commonly known as a soul to humans in this spacetimecontinuum, helped facilitate the onboarding. Since 6D elements are known to be aware, and have either been exposed to or easily grasp the realities of the CC, Meg and Petra spoke freely, and Petra helped facilitate the on boarding.

Petra was a bit chatty, and exuded a good deal of nervous energy. But this 6D was clearly very competent, sensitive, and full of Goodness. In other words, she was a fine soul. Any human would be lucky to have her. She exuded a chipper kind of confidence to the 4D and 5D aspects of the human, and ensured they felt comfortable. Petra also periodically sent soothing energy to the 3D physical form of the human.

There had not been any stop planned to meet, greet, and assess the native life forms, as the ship's officers had assumed the planet only held Unaware life forms in this particular spacetimecontinuum. The retrieval and onboarding of this human—especially from such an infected planet—meant a lot of extra work, mostly having to do with setting up quarantine protections for both the crew and the human. Various crew members also had to familiarize themselves with, and provide basic life support features for, the human's needs. The 6D aspect helped by answering their questions cheerfully.

By CC law, accidental interactions (between previously unknown aware, Semi, or Newly aware beings) are to be minimized as much as possible until the official assessments are complete. Because of this, the researchers restricted themselves to observing the human by way of visual monitoring only. The human seemed to sense that this was occurring, but did not appear to be bothered much by it. Petra informed Meg that the human was used to being watched by cameras, as they were stationed all over Earth, and mostly networked so they could be accessed by "intelligence agencies." Petra snorted when she said the phrase. Meg was unsure what this meant, but made a note to pass this observation on to the ship's Senior Assessor, Senior Officer Sync.

Due to how integrated the 6D was with the human, Meg was tasked with asking Petra if it would be okay to pump a small amount of anti-anxiety medicine into the atmospheric mix for Sharon, to help her calmly transition to being on board a spaceship more easily. Petra agreed to this after being assured the medicine was not addictive or incapacitating.

From the human's perspective, she had travelled for just a few Earth minutes before the moving sensation seemed to cease. In CC time, the rover was immediately transported back to the main ship, where it stayed in simulation mode for about three hours. During that time, crew members scrambled to prepare for the human's arrival. Quarters in a 3D section of the ship were outfitted to allow the human to feel "at home" in them. Atmospheric gases were mixed and piped into the quarters to the proper pressurized levels, so the human would not awaken to find herself in a pressurized suit, which the CC had previously learned caused Fear in 3D life forms. The human would later be fitted with a suit and would need to wear it if she wanted to access certain areas of the ship. In consultation with the 6D element, the ship's crew determined the immediate disclosure of quarantine procedures might be Fear inducing for the human. So they agreed that the procedures would be explained to the human after the initial assessment, and during the initial orientation, both of which would occur during a sleep induced by Officer Sync. They would document the deviation from normal protocol, and the reasons for the deviation in the appropriate logs and reports.

When the rover finally "landed" within the ship, the rover's walls became translucent in a way that allowed the human to see what was happening. Now a little artificially calmed, the human again showed no fear, but still maintained an avid curiosity about what was going on. With little trouble the human indicated she understood she was now on the larger ship, and smiled when greetings were issued to her via a combination of her 6D aspect talking to her and Meg speaking to her warmly via a simulated loudspeaker. Since the human seemed to be taken with the "magic carpet," arrangements were made and communicated to the human that she would be moved to other quarters via the contraption. She was also told the quarantine dome would be placed over her to maintain air pressure—this was true—and to keep her safe from particles that her body might not be used to—also true. She agreed to this with no problem.

The human was then informed that the crew would like to transport her to quarters while she slept, so as to not overwhelm her. She hesitated a bit at this, and she and the 6D conferred privately for a couple of moments before she agreed. After a few more questions, all were satisfied that the human had arrived in good health and was sufficiently informed of what to expect. She was then very briefly introduced to Senior Officer Sync, who, after presenting as a friendly human hologram, promptly induced a sleep. Sync was able create this state in the human as easily as a mother reassures a child by hugging and showing love to them.

Sharon's eyelids grew heavy, and she was asleep within seconds.

Sharon's physical body was then moved to a comfortable room that could eventually become her quarters, should she decide to stay on the ship after assessments were completed. In a few minutes, and with the human deep into her sleep, Officer Sync would begin the CC-mandated assessment protocol. She would eventually talk with the human, but the first parts of the protocols were best done while the human slept. Sync could access the human's subconscious and unconscious mind in this state, and gather baseline information about the most important traits beings possess. After Sync gathered that information, she would then facilitate the transmittal of a very brief (two Earth hours) orientation, customized to address the needs and initial questions that this particular human might have—as best as the CC crew could predict.

> #
> ********************
> #

Officer Sync had been a senior crew member for the GSS Prosperity for the past seven CC years. The GSS Prosperity was one out of well over a thousand ships in this section alone. The Convening Collaborative, or the CC as it was usually called, is the governance entity for the entire singularity of aware beings in the known universes. It's a huge governing body, and almost universally loved by CC members. All aware beings are automatic members, which gives them certain rights and responsibilities, and all automatic members are invited to join as active members. The vast majority do. Active members pledge to strive for Goodness. Striving for Goodness is the main foundational reason for the existence of the CC and, not coincidentally, for its astounding success.

A very brief history of the CC is taught to all members of the CC as soon as they become aware of their membership within it. It goes like this:

"Membership in the singularity has grown into the gazillions (singularity—gazillions, lol, get it?). It is by now clear that Goodness is chief among the universal values needed to become aware, and then to function well among the cultures of the aware. Congratulations on your personal level of Goodness, and thus your membership within this group. Membership as an automatic member of the CC grants you certain rights and responsibilities, which will be explained in more detail.

We hope you will decide to become an active member of the CC. Active membership is always a voluntary choice, as long as beings are currently equipped with sufficient proportions of Goodness within their consciousnesses to be freely able to act in Good Faith. Active membership entails two things on your part.

1) You pledge to the CC to strive for Goodness in all situations and interactions, whether with other CC members or not, and

2) You agree to a full assessment of traits and functioning so that the CC and you will know about your baseline levels of characteristics associated with awareness, and especially Goodness.

All results of the assessment will be shared with you. The assessment will become a part of your official file, along with your CC number, date of birth, species, home planet, and any other relevant information you consent to having included.

The CC may use results of the assessment to offer suggestions to you or to request assistance from you as an active member. You may respond to any suggestions or requests in any way you see fit. All is voluntary. All is collaborative. All is cooperative in nature, and in good faith. All is rooted in striving for Goodness. All is oriented towards expanding love, peace, and prosperity.

Additionally, you may always and forever change your mind about whether or not you want to be an active member of the CC. But if you should decide to apply for active membership after any period of inactivity, a new assessment will be required.

Upon completion of the official Orientation to Automatic and Active Membership within the CC (also known as OAAM), you will be given your first opportunity to decide whether you would like to apply to become an active member."

These exact paragraphs of explanation are offered to every aware being when they reach the developmental level of being fully capable of informed consent. The only exceptions to this happen in cases exactly like the one now occurring. Mandatory attempts to complete assessments are required by CC laws anytime beings on official CC business and beings previously assumed to be Unaware accidentally communicate with each other. Incident reports of all significant accidental communications also need to be created. In point of fact, the initial incident report for this communication and manifestation had already been transmitted to CC Headquarters. Officer Sync's name would be on all four reports, and it was a duty she took seriously.

Finding new Semi or Newly aware beings through accidental communications is the second most common way that Semi and Newly aware species become known to the CC. As a rule, awareness levels expand roughly along with the contours of the known universes, which—as even Earth's primitive knowledge of astronomy can tell us—continue to expand. So membership in the CC keeps expanding.

Often individual members of species come into awareness within a very short time of each other, especially those in the eastern sectors of the known universes. Scientists have theorized that the ultimate orientation of the known universes allows for faster processing speeds within the animate beings that reside there. Others theorize it's the water. Some suspect the effect is just an elaborate illusion.

A few other species have longer periods of awakening. Humans are most definitely slow awakeners. The period between theoretical abilities for awareness and the actual awakening of the majority of the species is an especially dangerous time. All sorts of things can and do go wrong in this window of time, and in the five previous timelines known to exist on Earth in this spacetimecontinuum, humans had all failed to pass from nonaware to aware. No one knew quite why, but normal MMR developmental issues had turned into serious infections in each timeline.

While never completely routine, the GSS Prosperity had engaged in numerous accidental communications with Semi and Newly aware beings in other galaxies over the time Sync had been with the ship. Every being from those encounters needed to be assessed, then given opportunities to stay among the aware or be returned to their native habitats. As a result, Senior Officer Sync had (with Meg's help) created three "mini me" Syncs that conducted most of the easiest assessments so she could attend to her other functions on the ship. However, since this would be an assessment on a human from a badly infected planet, Sync would be doing the entire assessment herself.

MMR is a nasty infection, and one that by definition disproportionately affects the larger members of most of the species it attacks. Left untreated, almost all members of a species will become infected with MMR beliefs, and might live in horribly infected states for many generations until the infection resolves or brings the species to extinction. Early in her career, Sync had witnessed a small infection that had been quickly contained, but it was still a shocking experience Sync had not forgotten. The infection had spread due to a new Assessor (a friend of Sync's) not catching signs of MMR during one of her first unsupervised assessments. Now, official Best Practice protocol is to have the most experienced Assessors do any assessments whenever there was any chance the being might be infected. Sync, along with her friend and several other Assessors, had lobbied for this to become CC Best Practice.

In MMR, infected beings often resort to subterfuge, a fact of which Sync was well aware. She also knew that certain beings could often hide subterfuge fairly easily by being unusually charming. She'd already noticed how charming Petra was, and was aware that Petra could be infected and either not know it herself, or try to hide it. But her interview with Petra would take place later. For now, Sync was only going to assess the 3D, 4D, and 5D aspects during Sharon's sleep. She was prepared to take her time and added in two extra "reflection intervals" to the computerized protocol she'd use and make notes in. A set number of reflection intervals are built into assessments automatically to remind Assessors to periodically self-scan for biases and assumptions, but the best Assessors routinely added more for complex assessments. With her protocol personalized, Sync was ready.

She "entered" the physical quarters where the

human was. While the human slept, she stayed in her nonmaterial form and simply observed her for a few moments. Sync had a soft spot for humanoid types in general. Many *hybrid* humanoids were among the aware. But not many *purely* humanoid species were aware. None were known in this particular spacetimecontinuum on this planet, and certainly not in the timeline Earth had requested help with. Nor were any known from the genus "sapiens." (The obvious Hubris involved in naming your own kind "wise"! A propensity towards Hubris was known pretty much universally as one of the few negative properties beings could be cursed with.)

Since there were quite a number of obstacles stacked against them, the few successfully aware pure humanoids she'd encountered had been all the more beautiful as creatures. Kind of like the first of any kind to break a barrier, the first ones are almost always exceptionally good. Sync made a personal note that she knew would not appear (as such) in her final report. 'They are such simple creatures, really. I can see why some more complexly dimensional beings pick certain ones to act as their personal totems.'

Sync continued to observe the human as she went through the checklist of pre-assessment procedures. Standard protocol for humanoids is to first bathe the dreamer in sounds that soothe the body. Vibrational energy in the form of sounds are the closest any humanoids can get to consciously experiencing the electrical impulses that are the creators of all organic processes in the known universes.

Indeed, experiencing these energetic impulses in the form of music is the easiest way for most life forms who reside in certain dimensions to understand them. It's just a matter of arranging the impulses in particular ways.

As the sounds worked their ways into this human's deepest processes, Sync became aware that the 6D element was somehow watching her. She paused and asked the 6D to please integrate with the rest of the human for these first few assessments, and assured her that she was looking forward to talking with her on an individual basis. Petra complied without making any comment, but her energies seemed to consist of Goodness. Sync noted that rather striking anomaly in a special place on the assessment forms, and returned to the task at hand, sending the equivalent of musical sounds through the human's body. When Sync felt the human was ready, she did the rough equivalent of telepathically asking the dreamer to trust her. Sync's ability to access and manipulate electrical impulses extended well into eleven dimensional understandings, so she was quite skilled and quickly gained the trust of almost all beings she came across, including this human.

However, right after Sync asked and just before the human gave permission, the human's entire physical body seemed to flicker for a very small moment. The anomaly was so unexpected that Sync momentarily lost her focus. Startled, she even checked to ensure Sharon was not a very advanced type of hologram. She did not appear to be. She also made sure the 6D was fully integrated with the 4D and 5D aspects. Sync made note of the flicker on the same special place on the assessment forms. This was the exact kind of nuance that a less experienced assessor might miss. Sync took the equivalent of a deep breath and returned her focus to the issue at hand.

Sync thought the flicker might indicate some fear or hesitance, so she emanated goodwill and love towards the human for almost a full minute. By the end of that time, the human appeared to be in a very restful state, and Sync observed no further anomalies. Satisfied that all elements were in place for a successful assessment, Sync began to telepathically guide the human through what was called a Standardized Interview—Maximized for Efficiency—at the 3D level. The protocol is known as a SI ME 3D.

There are several Standardized Interviews, or SIs, all able to be administered at different dimensional levels. All CC members are assessed once every ten years. The usual Standardized Interviews are maximized for Goodness, as it is such an important quality to the functioning of ships. Goodness has an official definition among the ship's crew and, indeed, for all members of the CC, or Convening Collaborative.

Goodness is defined as the sum of a being's capacity for honesty, agreeableness, compassion, empathy, and ability to work collaboratively within a multispecies (Tribe) environment for the common good. On Earth, those that function altruistically or stay true to their roles as public servants truly invested in serving for the common good would be considered to have high levels of Goodness.

The usual SI also assesses for negative traits, such as Fear Based Thinking, Hubris, and the amount of Callousness the being appears to have.

All aware species born into aware cultures learn early that trying to rid themselves of vestigial negative beliefs and traits is counterproductive. It is the level of Goodness and the amount of awareness that matter most. Knowing your own attributes helps you get along in life, and knowing your own levels of less desirable qualities is really one of the only ways you can protect yourself (and others) from allowing those negative qualities to drive your beliefs and behaviors.

Further, Goodness is not diluted by petty PFFFs

of envy, irritation, or insecurity. Even fleeting bouts with Superiority do not dilute Goodness. Hubris does, however, seem to actively dilute how Goodness can manifest in a being. Fear-based thinking, Greed, and Callousness are the only other factors known to threaten the manifestation of, or in some extreme cases lower an individual's level of, internal Goodness.

Over time, and much to Sharon's benefit and the benefit of other Semi and Newly aware beings, the discovery had been made that Semi and Newly aware beings often could not tolerate the self-knowledge of being partly composed of less desirable factors. In trying to get rid of or deny parts of themselves, the beings inevitably slowed their progression to full awareness, often substantially, and usually with great levels of personal distress accompanying their efforts.

As a result, CC-authorized Assessors like Sync usually used a slightly different tool, maximized for efficiency. It was always, always, always used when retrieving beings from MMR-infected areas. Maximizing for efficiency rather than Goodness enabled the Assessors to deliver the results of the assessments to beings without unnecessarily burdening them with difficult information in the early days of their journeys to full awareness.

Sync had talked briefly to the ship's resident human expert, Professor InDepth, and read through the materials InDepth had suggested. What she found was shocking. The human's world was incredibly primitive. Almost unimaginably different from the environments most aware beings come from, Sync mused. Equally as stunning, this human had somehow become at least Semi aware while living on the same planet as those with the most extreme types of MMR type mindsets. Through her research, she had found that on this human's spacetimecontinuum, the most narcissistic and infected humans had actually harmed millions of their own species.

Humans had needed to actually create social movements to address things like slavery, labor exploitation, racial and ethnic segregation, and gender inequality. Meanwhile, incredible economic disparities had manifested, even as the humans made some strides towards equality in other areas. Support for social justice was moving humans closer towards awareness, but awareness for some in the species was still a long ways off, and all sorts of inequities were hampering the qualities of life for billions down on the planet. It was a real disaster zone. Earth had not been exaggerating about how ill her humans were.

Recently they'd had revolutions with hashtags in front of words. Quite truthfully, Sync was a little unclear on what they were exactly. She supposed the hashtag was part of the humans' efforts to create an organically arising universal language, after their perfectly reasonable attempt to implement something called Esperanto failed to take hold. As if anything of value could really take hold on a planet when Fear Based Thinking dominates.

Sync had also learned that Hubris was a shockingly common attribute. According to both Professor InDepth and the research she read on this specific timeline within the spacetimecontinuum of the planet, a fair number of humans actually thought of themselves as "rugged individualists" and "self-made." As if thousands of other humans and all the elements on the planet hadn't had large hands in educating them, keeping them healthy, feeding them, laughing at their stories while they were children, cooperating with them as adults, and so on.

But perhaps most barbaric of all, Sync had learned that humans still had (and used) militaries. How they'd survived this long was a mystery. In the rest of the known universes, aware beings could (and did in large numbers) major in Goodness at universities. It was a highly valued area of study. Active members of the CC could easily find quite lucrative work in the vast arena of Intentional Goodness that protected the aware throughout all the known universes. Over the years, Goodness had been very carefully defined indeed. Beings from all kinds of aware species wrote dissertations on it. Entire mind-command centers were filled with row upon row of information, poetry, and transmittals about Goodness in one form or another. After all, it was the main trait that kept the known universes humming along. All aware beings know they are all interconnected, so the active cultivation of Goodness is a major industry in all the known universes.

And, as every school child knows, Goodness is closely associated with quality of life in all quadrants, and it is one of the only universal values that aware beings share. This poor human had none of those advantages. The environment she lived within on the planetary level was absolutely appalling in its barbarism and backwardness.

Officer Sync noted that this human was still clearly able to become at least Semi aware, despite these circumstances. As Sync assessed traits the human seemed to possess, she noted several more surprising anomalies, and wrote careful notes on them. She left the "Special Impressions" section blank for the time being. Despite her gut instincts usually being spot on, the notion she was formulating was so unusual that she did not want to put in the assessment—at least not yet. However, she was eager to discuss her thoughts with the

Captain.

Reporting Back To Cabeza

Three hours later, Sync was back on Cabeza's command deck. Sync had accessed several spacetimecontinuums to study the information. So although the report was ready for Cabeza in three hours, Sync had done twelve full hours of work analyzing the information and taken another ten to sleep, eat, and play tennis in a vaguely humanoid form on a recreation deck. Then she had showered, a particularly lovely experience she liked to indulge in when inhabiting a 3D form. She silently entered. As usual, Sync felt the Captain startle when she comprehended Sync's presence. Sync emanated a rueful apology and wished she'd remember to emanate a simple bell signal more often.

The GSS Prosperity is a fairly large Matter=Not ship with almost seven thousand aware life forms attached to it as crew. Its cargo capacity can be enlarged as needed. Aside: The enlarging dynamic is an eleven-dimensional, physics-based technology—referred to in Earth's Harry Potter books as the "Extension Charm." As a result, the ship can transport cargo up to about the size of Mercury. But usually it only holds several warehouses worth of goods from various parts of the known universes. All ships routinely take on cargo to be distributed and bartered in different parts of the known universes. The GSS Prosperity also often carries up to three thousand more aware life forms traveling for a variety of purposes to other parts of the known universes.

Matter=Nots are a general style of ship suited for use in both Conventional and Dark Matter Dimensions. The Prosperity is composed of a core Matter=Not ship and eight smaller ships that integrate and divide off into fully functioning smaller delivery ships or recon/excursion ships as needed. Within those ships are smaller rovers and other technologies for transportation to different environmental and dimensional planes. In its three-dimensional form, the GSS Prosperity appeared as Oumaumau to humans living on Earth as early as 2017, easily cloaked as a large, inanimate bit of Debris.

The ship's interior consists of several decks, with some adapted to fairly specialized life forms, and in several cases, different dimensions. A good number of materially based beings live in the same gravity and atmospheric ranges with little assistive technologies or modifications, so several decks are calibrated to those conditions. Living quarters are designed to be comfortable and to please the occupants. Often mixes of elements that subtly reinforce positive psychological responses (to beget high levels of Goodness) are added to the decks. Beings needing fairly rare atmospheric conditions usually wear assistive suits tailored to their species' specific needs.

Beings aboard all CC ships are all used to living among other species, and significant inter-species differences are simply dealt with as the differences they are, and not feared or hierarchically arranged (lol, as if).

On the command deck, Sync's report manifested near Captain Cabeza. Instead of using a holographic As Needed, she elected to read a paper formatted version of the thing. Sync smiled inwardly; the Captain's 3D roots were showing. But she was brilliant and practical. Then Sync noticed two pairs of reading glasses had manifested and were hovering near the Captain's arms. That made more sense: she going to read the report with two of her heads, not just one. Sync watched with some intrigue as the Captain set the paper copy down. Several of her arms did some complicated maneuvers, and within a short time, two piles of paper appeared. At that point, a couple of Cabeza's arms simultaneously placed glasses on adjacent heads. Then, with simultaneous ease, the arms each picked up a stack and zoomed the papers in and out a little until the distances were at an ideal reading length from her eyes.

Cabeza's physical movements, and indeed those of Nervonians in general, often resembled a team of synchronized swimmers. The deeply saturated hues of Cabeza's dermatil added to the effect: bright-yellow necks, fading to an orange face and startlingly blue lips. Arms and torso were usually green but could change intentionally, or sometimes unintentionally in startle responses.

Sync, along with many others, loved to watch Cabeza change her dermatil during speeches. Nervonians all had a vaguely regal air about them. As they grew older, they often developed ridges along their spines and chins, so they vaguely resembled many-headed iguanas. But Cabeza's regal looks had begun early, a great quality for a Captain to have and one that inspired confidence in her crew and in the passengers on board during any given voyage. Cabeza's gracefully complex physicality helped almost all species relax, as Nervonians were able to emanate their own Goodness more easily than many other species.

While she waited for the Captain to read the report, Sync hovered unobtrusively in a corner and picked a memory to review. She dipped into a moment during a long ceremony that had been held deep in the Solarium of 13 Solstices.

Aware beings could intentionally (or unintentionally) request diversions during times of disinterest, and mind commands or sometimes even food substances would be discreetly supplied. Sync had no need for food substances. At this particular ceremony,

Sync had made an unintentional request and a small selection of mind commands had appeared. She was fairly new to the ship at the time of this ceremony and was eager to learn all she could about her Captain. So she had chosen from the "All About Nervonians" series. As a standardized mind command, it had first given "The Basics" level description of the physical attributes of the species at hand. The sections listed major organs, atmospheric and nutritional needs, developmental milestones, and timelines. Then there were the numerous sections that contained introductory level information about the species' cultural focus/foci, a brief history of how the species entered Awareness (if known), and its major strengths. It further discussed psychological dispositions, and included several other sections.

Sync had absorbed much of the information, then gone back to the IntraSpecies section specifically to see if a shrinking response she'd seen in other Nervonians was listed. It was. The information packet stated that Nervonians showed respect and deference to other Nervonians by shrinking and looking as deferential as possible. The information packet then specifically stated something to the effect that "although this posture may look like fear, it is not. Nervonians never fear each other. Recall that the Nervonian's fear response is the peculiar dermatil arm color and patterning changes discussed in another section."

Even now, three years later, Sync remembered with chagrin that it was at that point in her reading, when she realized other Nervonians were showing great respect to the Captain, that she had issued a fairly loud vocalization, which interrupted the ceremony's keynote speaker. It was the equivalent of a human saying, "Oh, of course!" absentmindedly. Except in Sync's case, the vocalization was more of a squawking sound emanating from all corners of the area she inhabited, which happened to be the largest auditorium in Pert on Perkey Island, a delightful area in the Solarium of the 13 Solstices. And of course, it was full of the aware species native to the area: Kangas and Wallerts. In fact, the Kangas and Wallerts were being honored for their dedicated service to the Convening Collaborative's "Tribe Cross-Cultural Exchange."

Unfortunately, both Kangas and Wallerts are fairly sensitive beings who startle easily. So her emanation disrupted the speaker and startled many in the audience. She then immediately emanated a quiet apology to the gathered beings, which further served to startle the attendees, although it did avoid a stampede of Kangas and Wallerts.

Sync giggled to herself (more or less) at the memory, then emerged from her reverie and continued to wait patiently as Cabeza read through the results.

"Oh my God, how has this person been surviving?" Cabeza's heads gracefully swiveled in Sync's general direction as she spoke; her eyes held concern and shock. In assessing the Captain's response, Sync could tell Cabeza was not doing this for theatrical effect.

"It's a good question, Captain. It's got to have been a tough situation for her, there's no doubt about that." Officer Sync looked calmly at the Captain.

Captain Cabeza returned her gaze to the report and continued to read. Sync noticed there was something peculiar about the Captain's demeanor, but she couldn't put her finger on it without delving into the Captain's auras further. As a professional, she avoided reading other officers in depth, but her curiosity was piqued. The vibrational energy she saw emanating from Captain's body aura was different somehow, but none of the

Captain's heads appeared to be aware of it.

As Captain Cabeza continued to read, Sync grew increasingly curious. The Captain's mind auras, usually very strong and confident, were showing signs of uncertainty, very rare for their leader. As Officer Sync continued to surreptitiously study the Captain, Sync recognized some common qualities such as curiosity and profound respect towards the human. These were not at all unusual for Captain Cabeza's 7D auras to emit. She was also observing shock and horror, which were completely understandable given the circumstances the human had endured. But along with those qualities, Sync was getting the sense that the Captain was feeling personal interest, personal intrigue, and…a sensuous attraction to the human. The thought hit her like a physical force. Sync quickly backed away from that area of the Captain's mind, even as she kept investigating the Captain's general reactions.

Sync and the Captain enjoyed a relationship that was convenient for both of them. They had profound professional respect for each other and shared many of the same interests. They also worked closely and intensely together. It was natural that eventually they had physical relations—well, it had certainly been natural for Cabeza, who was a materially based entity. Sync's concept of sensuousness was based in other dimensions. But when she was in a physical mood, she could enjoy intensities that would instantly obliterate 3D based beings, so she kept it very toned down for Cabeza. Nonetheless, she enjoyed their physical forays quite a bit. That had begun about a year into Sync's tour on the ship. Since then they regularly sought each other out for repeat and new explorations. They were not exclusive, though, as that would be a bit confining for both of them.

The realization that Cabeza had some sort of

attraction towards the human wasn't making Sync jealous, but it was unusual for Cabeza to be attracted to a one-headed physical entity. She generally was attracted to other Nervonians. And to beings that naturally existed in other dimensions.

Sync continued to study the Captain's auras and other emanations with interest. The Captain was reading the report with two of her heads and watching the deck with a third head. Her two remaining heads were dozing contentedly. They would take over during the quiet hours. These things were normal. But the Captain truly didn't seem to be aware that she was emanating any of the small emotions she was emanating. How unusual!

A lack of awareness about emotional states was something that Sync rarely saw among any of the officers when they were talking business. Officers were highly trained to be able to identify and then separate their personal feelings from the business at hand. They did not dismiss their feelings, but they learned to consciously access them and then categorize them as specific entities, as factors in the situation to remain aware of. The team's expertise in doing this was so ingrained that they'd again won the Convening Collaboration's prestigious Informed Awareness of Personal Feelings as Fluctuating Forms (CCIA PFFF) trophy a few months back.

As the Captain continued to read the report, Sync determinedly searched about for things to do that wouldn't intrude further into Cabeza's mind. She requested and then idly accessed some information about the history of the award they'd won that would soon take them on a trip to Zanand-Idu. The As Needed had this to say:

"The   Convening   Collaboration's   Ship

Governance Department created a permanent 'General Award Group.' The GAG is composed of statisticians, process improvement and quality control leaders, and at large and rotating public members. The GAG are loved by all who work on the ships."

That was quite different from the poor human's experience with similar groups as they manifested on Earth, Sync mused absently. With the Captain still reading, Sync took several moments to slow her own processing times down so she could stay in the same space with the Captain.

Sometimes working with materially based beings could feel pretty tedious to DDDs. DDDs (Double Digit Dimensional beings) could process information exponentially faster than materially based beings, and a large part of inter-species training for them was to remain patient with material beings and their incredibly slow processing times.

After making her way through the As Needed, Sync finally stopped reading and sat for a few moments, simply enjoying her feeling of contentment. Truly, the ship functioned well. Sync enjoyed reveling in the ship's success. Indeed, her own leadership in creating the EASE unit (Emotional Assessment And Support Entity) had been instrumental in the crew's consistently strong performance in this area.

Sync noticed the Captain was getting further along, so she accessed another As Needed. She chose the Captain's speech of thanks to the crew for their performance that won them the award. There was an option to choose to have the speech information transmitted via video. Sync chose that option.

"Greetings Tribe Members!" Cabeza said this with all five heads in unison. It was a neat trick that non-

Nervonian Captains could not do. The effect of five heads all transmitting information in a complex synchrony helped inspire confidence in crew and passengers alike.

The Captain went on to give a speech that managed to be heartwarming, campy, and dignified all at once. It lasted about three minutes, which like pop records on Earth, was considered to be in the sweet spot for maximum appeal. By the end of it, two of Cabeza's heads were quietly humming the most dramatic bars of the Tribe Anthem in the background. 'Nice touch,' Sync thought.

Sync had watched this video a few more times than she would admit to publicly, but always got the equivalent of a little teary at the last few lines, which had to do with Goodness levels and the Captain being in awe of the crew. These words were stock phrases, tools of the trade, Sync knew; but Sync also knew the Captain not only meant them, she lived them.

This year's PFFF trophy came with a two week stay for the entire crew at a resort planet. This was scheduled to begin in a little over a month from now.

The mind commands that she now saw appeared uninteresting, and Sync was again aware that Cabeza was still reading the assessment. Sync emanated a little to nudge the Captain. The Captain did not respond. Sync emanated with a little more velocity. Still nothing. Finally, she made a throat clearing sound. One of the Captain's heads looked around, communicated something to the others, and the heads all bobbed a bit back into awareness of Sync's presence.

"So, Sync, err, what's your impression?" Cabeza asked, a bit self-consciously.

"Well, the information from the assessment tool was a bit...complicated, which is, as you know, fairly unusual for a 3D species. And it gave quite conflicting answers. So I added a few thoughts after the tool did its own synthesis in the Interpretation Section. For this assessment, I collected the human's most significant unconscious and subconscious histories, and one of my main findings is there are delightfully complex discrepancies between lived histories and her emotional responses. They deviate substantially from the usual sorts of emotional responses that typically emerge from this kind of species during such experiences."

"What do you make of that?"

"The deviations are sometimes quite pronounced, to the point where the tool's analysis suggested the most likely answer would be some kind of a psychotic thought process." Sync paused, thoughtfully. "The second most statistically likely cause, according to the tool's analysis, would be some sort of impairment or limitation in normal cognitive functioning." Sync let that hang in the air, noting the Captain emanated protective auras about the human beyond what might normally be expected.

Cabeza was silent for a moment, and Sync noticed with some curiosity that Cabeza seemed to stumble a bit in her thought processes, which was also unusual.

"And what is your analysis of that, Sync?" The Captain sounded strangely formal.

"Well, I think the imaginal qualities of this human is much more advanced than 'the average bear,' as they say on Earth. And—"

"She's a bear? I didn't think they had any inter species kind of—"

Sync interrupted quickly. "No, no, Captain, it's an old Earth saying. English, I think. Sorry, didn't mean to obfuscate." Sync emanated "Goodness with affection, humor, and humility," along with a touch of "playfulness." But the word "bear" triggered another idea, one she would research a little more before voicing.

The Captain then face-palmed two of her heads and allowed the head attending directly to Sync to blush a little and give a sheepish smile. "I see, go on," she said unnecessarily.

Sync paused. "Well, this human—who appears thoroughly human, by the way—is very intelligent and creative. Her Reasoning Mind has a kind of mental flexibility that is not often seen in humans infected with MMR. I'd say that though her processing rate and capacity is in the top ten percent of her species, the other qualities she is high in—which include very high levels of Goodness, Openness to Experience, Fairness, and Emotional Accessibility—sort of...combine to become more than the sum of their parts. So the overall effect is contributing to her abilities to...transcend certain...limitations that are common to her species in the spacetimecontinuum in general, and in this timeline."

Sync paused, searching for the right words and tone. "Captain, I think this human is not only Semi aware on the 3D levels—and fully integrated at the 3, 4, 5, and 6D levels—which, as you know, makes her unusual for a human in this timeline, but she also appears to be matriculating to a 4D and 9D perception mode simultaneously." Sync's energies performed the equivalent of a gulp. "Which does add up to—you can check my math—uh, a 13D capability of sorts."

All three of the Captain's awake heads turned with unabashedly surprised looks on their faces to the eastern part of the room, from where Sync's presence always seemed to emanate most strongly.

"That makes her not only one of the very few Semi aware humans in this entire spacetimecontinuum to communicate with us, but the very first in this particular timeline. And, it, uh…also…makes her a candidate for…" Several of the Captain's heads all gasped in surprise as awareness dawned within her consciousness.

Sync made vigorous emanations that correlated to nodding her head in agreement. "Exactly, Captain."

Further Suspicions and a Request

"Okay, that's a very intriguing possibility, yes, but let's slow down for a minute, " Cabeza said, ever the pragmatic and logical being.

Sync nodded. "Of course. I concur, it's still just a theory. On the other hand, it certainly looks like a duck, walks like a duck, and quacks like a duck."

"How do you see her as a duck?" Cabeza challenged.

"I don't, Captain. It's a theory at the moment...um, Captain, the duck analogy is another Earth colloquialism."

Cabeza's more curt head said nothing but whirled in Sync's direction while the one that had been communicating continued. "Ah, I see. We are both thinking she is specific kind of 13D being, correct?"

Sync emanated agreement.

The generally curt head then winked in Sync's direction and turned back to its previous position, gazing out the front of the craft into the space beyond.

Sync was intrigued by the wink. "You are pretty sly, Captain Curt. Maybe we'll have to commune again...." She realized she'd emanated that out loud.

"Yes, maybe we will, but we need to focus, Sync. Tell me, what else has made you come up with this theory?" Cabeza said with the hint of a smile.

"Well, The flicker was the first overt clue. That was on board, though. I'm getting ahead of myself. I'll try to tell you in chronological order. For some reason the Terrapin Station's ghost story flashed in my mind as we were hovering above the surface. The lines are:

"The Ghost Witch Is was unable to know
Of the deep distress she had to show

And she screamed in a way that was misunderstood

As a request for something simply sweet and good."

Cabeza grunted thoughtfully.

"So, that happened first, I think. But really, I have random lines come up all the time, Captain; it's part and parcel of my being-ness, my Synchronicity. And the plight of humans, especially smart, female humans, is well known, so that could have just been percolating in the back of my mind. You know, a poor species caught up in the less than ideal circumstances of its environment and the infection we know exists on Earth."

Cabeza nodded again, pursing her lips a bit on most of her heads, a habit she did when listening intently.

"So I really had no idea when we picked the human up at first. She'd apparently wished for an ice cream; Meg manifested it, thinking it was a regular request from an aware being, and so that kicked in the accidental communication protocols. So, we got her on board, got her settled, and I went in to interview. I mean, that whole sequence was quite amazing in itself, of course; how it changed from a capture to a willful boarding—such grace! But nothing in that was syncing up for me then—and I know you see what I did there, Captain, lol. So at the time, I just thought 'Okay, ice cream, that's kind of fun,' you know?"

Cabeza inclined a couple of her heads in an easy gesture.

"Here is the thing, though. Right from the beginning, when I went into the room to begin the assessment, the 6D aspect was able to detach and watch me, while at the same time she was also integrated with the human's other aspects. She immediately left that mode of being when I asked her to integrate with her human, and we haven't had a chance to communicate about that particular thing yet. But a 6D aspect being able to do that is quite unusual. So that was one of the first things I could identify. But…also, there's this part I can't quite identify. I could sense something was different, but couldn't read it. Highly unusual for me with a 3D manifesting being, Captain."

"Yes, I'm aware," the Captain said drolly.

"So the 'Ghost Witch Is' story immediately popped back into my mind. And the human is there, sleeping, not knowing a thing. But in her dreams, I could tell she was looking around for me, so I manifested for her in a way I thought would be pleasing."

The Captain, remembering their last encounter, swiveled a head in Sync's direction, raised her eyebrows, and communicated an affectionate comment about being sure that Sync created a highly pleasing being since she was so good about knowing exactly what to do.

Sync stirred some playful sexual energy towards the Captain and continued with her recounting, "Right off the bat in the dream interview, both her soul and emoti said 'I scream' instead of ice cream when they were talking about the ice cream manifesting."

"Well, that's interesting."

Sync could tell the Captain wasn't quite following her so she recited the lines again. "And she screamed in a way that was misunderstood as a request for something simply sweet and good."

"Oh, I see what you're saying now," Cabeza said. "I'll admit that does align in a weird way with "The Ghost Witch Is" story, but on the other hand, it could be coincidence."

"True," Sync said.

Just then a computer pinged and announced, "Incoming request for a convening with Captain Cabeza from 10D Being Planet Earth."

Cabeza looked a bit surprised, but said, "Request accepted, please patch her through." Cabeza flicked on a monitor and waited for the video feed of the Earth to come online.

As soon as it did, Cabeza said, "Greetings, Earth. I am with my Senior Officer Sync. I assume her presence will be all right with you, but do indicate if you would like a private meeting."

An ethereal voice intoned, "Greetings, Captain, and Officer Sync. I am delighted to communicate with you both. Thank you for the swift reply to my request and equally swift ability to convene with me. Goodness be upon you all."

"And you as well, Honored Earth. What do you wish to convene about?" Cabeza asked.

"I am so grateful for the medicine you brought to me. The decision to ask for it was difficult, and yet once I made the decision, I felt an ease and serenity I had not known in quite some time. With this particular timeline, I had hoped the humans could evolve, but alas, a critical amount remain badly infected in some quarters. I have been ill due to the pollution the humans have created, the fires and floods. It seemed like I had just gotten done recovering from the hole in my ozone layer that they caused, when the cumulative effects of some of their other antics have caught up with me. I have been running a fever, my ice caps are melting, I am releasing much more gas than normal, having animal die-offs, etc. I'm afraid I'm pretty sick with this thing. It was not a decision I made lightly to ask for enough radiation to eradicate the humans, but it seemed like the only recourse."

The Captain nodded gravely. "MMR has been a particularly difficult infection to eradicate wherever it erupts throughout the known universes. We can only hope research breakthroughs will soon lead to more effective antidotes or vaccines for it. We all share your wish to eradicate MMR without having to eradicate the species that unfortunately become…problematic carriers of it." Cabeza was looking quite regal, kind, and wise. Sync was openly admiring her materially based presentation.

"Yes. I was going to commence with the radiation protocol within the week, but as I was observing your ship leave, I also witnessed the extraordinary manifestation and the request by the human's soul to board your ship, to be rescued from the planet, from me, her mother."

Earth paused here for a moment, appearing to choke back some emotion. "While I assure you, part of me cannot help but feel deeply hurt by that desire, I also know it is not me, but the MMR the human and her elements wish to escape. And I find their reaching out and trusting that aware beings will help them to be a most extraordinarily courageous act."

Cabeza and Sync could see a very large winter storm brewing over half of North America. Earth was clearly ill.

Nevertheless, she persisted. "Given the circumstances on the ground here, millions of my dearest and most aware humans are in deep despair. They are not afflicted nearly as badly with the disease as some of the others, but they are floundering as much as I am as they try to stop the madness down here. I love them all the more for their awareness and compassion for me, and each other. The particular human you boarded is one I have personally watched over. She and her elements are Good beings, Captain, and I do not say that simply because I am their mother. They are truly good beings and…"

She paused, appearing to succumb to a blizzard attack.

After it subsided, she continued. "They are Good and truly aware beings. They know things. But they have not been listened to down on the ground because they do not speak in the ways that the infected speak. Seeing that they were able to catch your attention and come up with their own intervention of boarding your ship, well, I realized they were quite innovative and brave. I got to thinking. And my idea and request is this."

She paused again while she released a large bit of CO_2 into her atmosphere. "Rather than immediately use the radiation, the thought came to me that maybe they and you—with the help of the CC—could…develop and implement a different kind of intervention for my illness. So that I won't have to use the radiation."

All of Captain Cabeza's five heads were now alert. Five pairs of eyes solemnly blinked in unison. Five heads simultaneously took deep breaths. Otherwise, she was still as she contemplated the request. Sync unobtrusively swirled some optimistic energy around, which seemed to break the spell.

"Do you have a specific intervention in mind, Honored Earth?"

"No, I honestly don't. At this point, the specifics of MMR—and how it so badly infects some of my humans—eludes me, as it does everyone else. As you are no doubt aware, the vast majority just want to live in safety, peace, and prosperity, but some get so utterly infected…" Earth belched up another large cloud of CO_2

before continuing.

"However, I do think that the human you have aboard is pretty wise. Somehow she along with many others really do seem to be fully aware on this planet; they just generally aren't listened to. Because she is human, and a psychotherapist as well, she may have more insight into the disease that could help the CC in its research, if nothing else." Earth indicated she was done speaking.

The Captain nodded a couple of heads and said cordially, "I see. This request will be taken under immediate consideration, but please allow my Senior Officer and myself a moment to communicate privately, Honored Earth. We will resume contact in approximately one minute."

"Of course," Earth said.

Cabeza flipped the monitor off and all five heads swiveled around to where Sync's energies were gathered.

"Wow." Sync spoke first. "I wasn't expecting that!"

"You seem to be excited by this idea," Cabeza said.

Sync swirled energies around thoughtfully. "Not sure if that is my true response yet, but I am most definitely surprised. And you?"

"Yes, I am also surprised. But now that she's made a request for help, it's practically out of our hands, of course." Several of Captain Cabeza's heads vigorously nodded as another one said this point. "CC expectations, ethics, and law are quite clear on the matter. So obviously we have to consider her request first and foremost according to the Golden Rule. We need to ask ourselves: How would I want to be treated, were I in her shoes? And the answer to that is really simple: If I ask for help, I would like to receive it."

She added, "So that is my first inclination. Your thoughts, Officer Sync?"

"I concur with the Golden Rule, of course. And I know that should lead our decision-making process. My other thoughts are more about strategies Earth may have been thinking about that led her to make this request. Earth knows that these beings have been down on the ground, living within the infection. As such, they do know about the infection far more intimately than we do. Even our refugees from other planets are not human refugees, and species-specific issues and timeline-specific issues are important to consider. They may have some ideas on how to address it. We've also never had the opportunity for human survivors to have a say in planetside interventions before, so on those merits as well, it's a good idea. Earth is considering them to be fully aware beings, and from we've seen so far, they may be even more aware than they appear to be if our hunches are correct. I definitely think it's worth a shot, if they will agree to it."

"I concur," Cabeza said. And with that, she flipped the monitor back on and told the Honored Earth they would be happy to do their best to try to create and implement different solutions, and would ask the human and her elements to work with the ship and the CC to help. "We can use persuasive strategies if necessary, but hopefully they will willingly help us," she said to Earth.

"Wonderful. Thank you so much. Goodness be upon you," Earth said.

Just as they signed off, one of Cabeza's heads whirled around as OT entered the room.

Cabeza smiled. "Ah, OT. We've just had an auspicious communication with Earth, so I am running a bit late. Let me get your update after I finish with Sync. I will be just a moment more with her. In the meantime, please arrange for a quick DDD and Senior Officer Stand Up meeting in, uh, forty-five minutes. Oh and invite InDepth. Ask her if she has suggestions for any other crew members who have MMR expertise. Oh, and ask her about any other hominoid experts as well, yes. Then make sure to invite anyone InDepth suggests."

"Of course, Captain," OT said, already walking towards a computer to generate the alert.

Cabeza turned her heads back towards Sync. "You can either attend the Stand Up or not, of course."

Sync nodded. "I'm going to do more research on our theory, and my guess is Meg will be coming to see me with her report soon."

"Good, Sync. Very good. She'll be important to have at the Stand Up, though, so some part of her should attend that as well. Keep me apprised of anything you find that is pertinent." More quietly she added, "Oh, and, uh, are you free tonight?" One of Cabeza's heads smiled wolfishly.

Sync emanated some flirtatious energy and said, rather loudly and theatrically, "Boom chicka, boom chica, yow yow yow. I sure am!" With a bright emanation, she (more or less) winked at OT and said, "See ya later, sweetie!" to the Captain. Her presence left, but she let a soundtrack go on for a few seconds, fading it out gradually.

OT looked back up from the computer after making the alert. Her trunk looked a little retracted somehow, but she was smiling broadly. She half sang, "Love is in the air, there they go without a care." Then she cleared her throat in mock seriousness. "The soundtrack was a pretty nice touch, huh?"

Cabeza sighed and mock frowned at OT. "Are you prepared to give me a status update or what?"

Highest Wisdom Has Almost Come

After leaving Captain Cabeza and the control center, Sync retreated to a place (ha) where she liked to study. She then asked one of her computers to research a particular poem with the term 'unable to bear' in it. If her memory was correct, this auspicious event happening with the human was even more auspicious than any auspicious event she'd ever witnessed on the auspicious event-prone GSS Prosperity. The computer seemed to stall out and began to slow, significantly. What gaseous bits of Uranus was this about?

Eventually the computer pinged a signal, indicating it had not found the requested information. This happened so rarely Sync didn't recognize the ping tone and had to ask the computer to explain itself. Then she ran the query again, with slightly different wording. This time the computer found some relevant lines of poetry from the Solarium Nativitatis. But a split second before the information appeared on screen Meg cleared her throat, startling Sync a bit.

The Announcement

Back on the Captain's deck, Captain Cabeza quickly contacted and relayed Earth's request to the CC's southwestern quadrant headquarters. The leadership there immediately concurred that the crew of the GSS Prosperity should indeed try to help Earth by exploring other possible treatment options. Captain Cabeza then immediately called her senior speech writer to craft an announcement outlining the change in plans. Within a few minutes Cabeza and her speech writer, a Wintonesian, had written the following:

"MMR, though thankfully not very common, is a serious illness that entities infected with it have struggled with for eons. It is a known fact that among 3D-based beings, the most dangerous time in a species' existence is the relatively short time during the transition between the state of being Unaware to the state of being Semi aware or Newly aware. This is true for any species, but seems especially problematic for humanoids. When transitioning to universal awareness, infection by MMR is one of the few really tragic illnesses known to afflict a species as a whole. Indeed, though it usually only infects one species, the fallout from that infection routinely causes problems among many, if not most, of the planet's other life forms. For these reasons, as most of you know, there is an active effort within the CC to find more effective ways of managing MMR, and to help find a cure for it.

Crew, we now have an assignment that can possibly help the CC learn more about and maybe even find a cure for MMR. Earth has requested our help –in conjunction with the human we just boarded, to find another solution to her infection. While completely unexpected, I am truly excited about this opportunity to help the planet Earth, and the CC in this endeavor. And I hope you are also as enthusiastic about this new assignment as I am.

It will delay our fall off however, because the assignment is currently expected to be at least two months in length. Additionally, it is quite possible there will be extensions beyond that time. The CC has already agreed that generous amounts of extra life points will be awarded to the crew for this two month inconvenience. Arrangements have also already been made so that any crew or passengers with disinterest in the new mission or with pressing issues to attend to will be able to transfer to another ship in three days' time. As usual, all crew are free to choose to take or decline this assignment."

During the Stand Up, the announcement went over well, without any problems with key staff, as Cabeza had hoped it would. She put Professor InDepth in charge of coordinating the actual planetside interventions, whatever they would be, and was pleased to note the genuine buzz of excitement that seemed to rise up within the group as a whole, with various crew members already volunteering to support the new mission.

Cabeza asked the crew to form various committees (lol), and then made arrangements to do a live, ship-wide announcement about the change of plans.

Catching Up Double Digit Dimensional Style

"Hey girl!" Meg's energies became present.

Sync created a reminder flag on her computer screen and turned her attention away from it as it went dark. "Hey, yourself!" Sync said, then added, "Girl."

They both laughed, more or less. DDDs are not materially based, so they are not gendered in any traditional sense, other than some of them having the ability to create other life forms.

But they—like the majority of aware beings— value and express compassion and empathy consistently and intentionally. In all of Earth's known spacetimecontinuums and timelines, the CC had noticed that, within humans, females tended to embody these qualities much more consistently and intentionally. So while Meg had been momentarily thrown by Sharon's question on gender and the gender of the ship's leaders, she was not bothered in the least that she had sort of fibbed when she had said she was more or less female and that their leaders were female as well.

"Nice job with getting the human to board, by the way," Sync said. "That was one of the more amazing capture retrievals I've witnessed. And what was with that voice you used? It was lovely."

"Yeah, thanks. It's based on a human from the Honored Guest's timeline, a great singer named Gladys Knight. My physical presentation is going to be a sort of updated version of her as well. It's kind of fun being in that body. I've never had any occasion to manifest as a human before! They have lovely little ranges of emotion. But, Sync, I wanted to come and discuss this with you, because it is just crazy to me that I didn't recognize that the requests for manifestations were coming from unknown beings. I figured they were crew members, you know?"

Sync smiled. "Yes, yes, the antecedents, good!" She accessed a log that would be part of another report to the CC on the unintentional communications and the results from the assessment. Then she added, "I know what you mean about manifesting a human body. I took on a human form during the dream state assessment I conducted with her last night. I based mine on a human female I saw in her home city. 'I like her accent,'" she said, mimicking it playfully. "But tell me more about the requests you got. You know that's what I need to know."

"I will. But I also just needed to be in the vicinity of another DDD for a while. It gets a little tedious down there on the materially based ship decks, with their slow, slow, processing speeds, doesn't it? And, at the same time—this communication with the human and her elements—you'd think I was as slow as a bison or something! I'm actually a bit embarrassed about it, because now that I recognize the requests, I realize I've talked with them several times. As in maybe eight or nine times."

Sync threw energies around in surprise as she simultaneously took notes in the log and fished around for something in the dark matter realms.

"I know, I know!" Meg said, responding to Sync's surprised and somewhat distracted energies. "The communications were mostly with the 6D one, but I have talked with the mind and the emoti as well. You know I would have reported them had I realized they were from unknowns."

Sync waved energy around, dismissing Meg's concerns. "Of course I know that. Just tell me what you've got." Sync finished setting up the quantum particle based dice game that she'd been looking for and gestured for Meg to take a turn. Both of them needed to relax a bit, and this would do it. They picked up a game that had been in progress for several CC weeks. Meg companionably threw the dice before she spoke again.

"Honestly, I am not sure when it began. I think after we were in Marukesh, for the fall out a while back," Meg said. She then moved energy around based on the dice roll.

Sync stopped, startled. "Meg, I'm sure I don't need to tell you.... I mean you do realize that in human terms that was... almost a full decade ago, right?" Sync took her turn and threw the dice while her puzzled energies swirled around.

"I hadn't really noticed until now, no. Time just sort of slipped by, I guess." Meg thought for a moment. "Yeah, I guess it really is pretty spectacular, isn't it?"

Sync didn't bother to emanate agreement. It was sent in another mode.

While the higher dimensional modes of communication are vastly quicker, and more elegant, there is one drawback. The vocabularies in these dimensions are vast (as in billions and billions of words worth of vast). So DDDs who do not know each other well have to spend time defining unfamiliar concepts and dimensional interpretations for each other. Meg and Sync had known each other for eons and had long found ways to easily communicate using shared concepts and frameworks.

Single D beings could comprehend that DDDs were varied; they knew they could be planets, dwarf stars, black holes, or red giants, but it made no real sense to them. It was much like a human and a lizard regarding each other on a sunny afternoon. The human, like DDDs, could see so much more of the larger landscape and comprehend more. The human could know concretely that the lizard's entire world was comprised of a couple of square miles of desert outside of Santa Fe. But the human could not know how the various grains of sand felt on the lizard's underbelly, how its tongue smelled the air around it, or how it perceived the ultraviolet colors that wiggle through the flowers in spring. And the lizard could not know much of the human's life; it generally would only know that the human was a big alive thing, much like some of the other large, often four-legged living things it sometimes encountered.

Meg and Sync talked and played dice for quite some time in a space outside of conventional time. During the last part of their conversation, Meg said, "Gotta go soon, got an errand to run before the Stand Up. But I've got a couple other things to run by you: After you do your first in-person rounds with Sharon, I'd like to go and talk with her about our past encounters and see what she knows. I'm also planning to personally attend to manifestations for her. You okay with all that?"

"Of course," Sync said conversationally.

"Oh, and I need to tell you about some stuff Petra said. She is a kick in the pants. Have you talked with her yet?"

Sync studied Meg's energies, and then confided in her. "No, but she did this unnerving little thing during the dream state assessment. I could feel her watching me. She was both inside and integrated with Sharon, and outside her, watching me. I asked her to go and stay inside and integrated, which she did, but I can't remember if I've ever run across a 6D who could do that."

"Wow," Meg said. "That's wild, but it doesn't surprise me all that much. She is razor sharp, that one. I mean, look what she was able to orchestrate from an infected planet! So far I really like her. Funny, gracious, playful. I've sensed no Ill Intent whatsoever, and I have been looking for it, Sync. I remember the story you told me about your friend. I sense no subterfuge or egoic reactions from that one, just a lot of wit and kindness."

"Good to know. What did she say that you want me to know?"

Meg threw the dice one last time. "It was a comment about something she called 'intelligence agencies.' It was clear she didn't think very highly of them. It was when we were noticing that the human wasn't upset by being watched. Petra said that Sharon 'was used to that,' that 'intelligence agencies' watched humans all the time. The way Petra referred to them seemed like…it was clear she found these agencies offensive in some way. Just thought I should let you know." Meg picked up the particles from her roll and swirled some energies around playfully. "Yes! Now that I'm finally back in the lead on this game, I'll get going. I've got a message that a personal BFD is not working optimally over in a Snooglist's quarters."

"In a Snooglist's quarters, huh, imagine that." Sync and Meg both chuckled, more or less.

BFDs often malfunctioned for Snooglists. The species is carbon based, semi humanoid, and 3D, but Snooglists also have an apparently unique feature among 3D beings in the known universes: certain patterns of dark matter continually orbit around individual Snooglists, starting when they reach maturity. Each Snooglist has a pattern that is slightly different, like a fingerprint or any other variation that makes individuals different from each other. These orbits of dark matter often affect how all kinds of things work in their presence—sometimes for the better, and sometimes for the worse. Their ship's main navigator, OT, was a genius at upgrading and fixing all sorts of ship functions willfully, but many Snooglists were not as adept. Certain kinds of devices, portable BFDs among them, tended to befuddle almost all Snooglists when they malfunctioned.

Meg said, "Yeah, one day we'll understand what gives with their dark matter entourages, but for now my BFDs are woefully under-engineered for the poor Snooglists who have to use them."

Sync chuckled good naturedly. "Well, good luck with that, sweetie. See you later!"

They exchanged energies and Meg vanished. Sync tossed the dice into the box and watched as the particles rearranged themselves back into their regularly spaced distances. She admired the way they danced with each other for a little bit. Then she turned her attentions elsewhere.

Interview With Petra—Socks Emerge

After the Stand Up, Sync came to see Petra as part of the official assessment. "I'm Officer Sync, the ship's main Assessor. You can call me Sync. What should I call you?" Sync asked.

With a friendly swirl of energy, the 6D soul said, "My name is ET Petram. But please, just call me Petra. I am so excited to be here; you just can't imagine!"

Without prompting, the 4D and 5D elements also emerged briefly from the sleeping human and introduced themselves.

"I'm Emma," the 5D emoti said quite warmly.

There was a slight pause, then the 4D mind element briefly said, "Just call me Sharon, same as the 3D human form. I am pretty freaked out with all this, as you might imagine, so I'm gonna go back to sleep if you don't mind."

"Of course. Nice to meet you both," Sync communicated gently in her singsong voice.

As 4D Sharon receded, Petra emanated fond energy towards her and said, "Good night, Sharon. Just remember they brought you irises, they are friendly." Sharon grunted and was gone.

Then Emma said, "Thanks, Petra, we'll keep remembering that, and the ice cream they gave us when we asked for it. Nothing much better than ice cream when I scream, right?" She giggled nervously.

"Uh huh!" Petra said.

Sync emanated a polite smile, and noted the play on words again without fully understanding what they meant.

Emma then said to Sync, "We're all a bit overwhelmed. But we trust Petra. So we'll let her do the talking...Plus, I'm also exhausted from all this...newness... but it's very nice to meet you, and thanks so much for the flowers, the comfy quarters, and the ice cream."

Sync graciously moved energies about. "I understand completely. Enjoy the rest of your sleep, and really, it's quite lovely to meet you all. We'll talk later!"

"Bye-bye, sweetie!" Petra said.

In addition to the two ways of communicating ice cream, Sync had immediately noticed the connectedness between the three elements, and how they had responded so immediately when Sync had asked the 6D what to call her. Sync was amused by their names as well. Of course, the 4D mind element would name herself after the 3D Form! That was a logical thing for a human mind to do in the absence of any other role models. The mind element must have had it really tough as she became aware on a planet in denial about awareness itself.

Sync immediately noted this in the "Relevant Environmental Factors" section on the assessment. She noted the 'ice cream versus I scream' word play down as well, in the "Noted, but Not Yet Understood" section. This was all done in less than the blink of an eye due to her processing speeds. Sync then shifted her energies back and emanated hospitality towards the 6D soul. "You all seem lovely. And Petra," she said, "thanks so much for being so willing to converse in this format. You must be aligned with the Lunctus?"

"Yes, I am Lunctus, and it's been a hell of a ride down on that Earth. You have no idea. Sheesh!" Petra replied. "I'm really starting to like it here already."

Sync was amused with this soul's colloquial speech. She'd rarely encountered souls who'd been on planets such as Earth, simply because most of those souls were attached to bodies and minds that were Unaware, so the soul only communicated with the self it lived in. If the soul was Lunctus, it could also connect with others of its kind.

"Yes, I can imagine," Sync said, then retracted the thought and added, "Actually, I don't know what it was like at all. I'd like to learn more about your experiences on Earth, and how you connected with others of your kind down there, but right now, we need to follow protocol and find out how long Sharon has been able to manifest."

"You mean wish for things and make them appear?" the soul asked. Sync nodded some energy around.

"Well, it's been happening for a while, actually, but the 'I scream' incident was the first time Sharon's 3D and 4D had seen it happen in the moment. Same with Emma, come to think about it."

Sync again noted how Petra had pronounced 'ice cream' as 'I scream,' and put another note under the note she'd just made. There would be time in the protocol to ask about anything "Not Yet Understood" later.

Sync emanated interest and said, "So there have been other communications?"

"Yes, Meg and I have been in contact irregularly for years, although I didn't know her name until now."

Sync emanated a little surprise. Petra apparently knew she'd been contacting Meg for quite some time. In her experience, and in the general understandings from the larger research into the phenomenon, unintentional contacts usually only began a few weeks prior to the actual manifestation event. She put that bit of information in the "Not Yet Understood" section as well. At this rate, she figured that would take up a much larger part of the assessment than usual. But she simply said, "Tell me more."

"Well, I guess there were actually two kinds of

contacts or manifestations as you are calling them. The 'in home' ones didn't happen very often at all. Maybe once every year or so. Or, sometimes there would be three things in a short period of time and then nothing for months."

"Okay, why do you call them 'in home' manifestations?" Sync asked.

"Well, you know Doc, they only happen at home, and they are full manifestations that stick around, at least for a while. So in our case, occasionally extra socks would appear in the laundry, or Sharon would think she'd bought a tablet of paper, and when she went back a few weeks later, there'd be three tablets instead of one."

"I see, you call those in home manifestations, okay." Sync was engrossed. These were common types of unintentional manifestations, so this was matching up with her research.

"By the way, please feel free to call me Sync," she communicated.

Petra responded with, "But I want to call you Doc, because I know you're the ship's shrink. Is it offensive?"

"No, but you don't need to—we are equals here."

"Ha, yeah, good one, you're what, 13D and I am 6D. Thanks, but you know waaaay more than I do," Petra said easily. Then, with a twinkle, she added, "Doc."

They both chuckled. Petra continued. "Uhh, I don't know what to call the other thing I did. I usually asked to manifest things Sharon might interpret as signs. For a long time I'd manifest things like half a bouquet of flowers, or a small camera part, usually in odd places, like on an otherwise clear sidewalk. Sometimes, a couple of magical-looking rocks. One of my favorites was part of a smashed dish with a half-eaten bagel—with cream cheese—right in the middle of the street." Petra danced a hearty laugh. "That was funny. Sharon puzzled over that for a long time. The china was really good, and she just couldn't figure out how it got there."

Sync emanated a question.

"Oh no, Sync, they were never scary, not at all. But I see, now that you mention it, the bagel thing could sound fear inducing, but no, it was not meant that way, nor did she ever take it that way." Petra paused for a moment, figuring out how to communicate it. "Sharon would know there was something going on, but she just couldn't figure it out."

"Okay, I see. What was the wish for that one?" Sync asked.

Here for the first time, Petra's energy took a dive, and a wash of grief emanated from her. Petra shook her energy around and said, "Well, it's complicated. The short answer was I was frustrated. It was a pivotal point, and Sharon didn't pivot. It happens." Petra sounded glum, so Sync emanated sympathy and waited while Petra put the issue back to rest internally.

After a moment, Petra shook her energy again and went on. "I was just playing with the techniques. Mostly because I was a bit bored. Honestly, that planet is a dump. Most of the other beings are great, but some of those 4D human minds, oh my God. They were so tiny and yet so full of hubris and ego." She made an exaggerated eye roll energy movement before continuing. "So much of what happens on that planet would make for a great sitcom, really. But I digress."

Petra smiled, seeming to will herself back to a perky state, and her energy danced a little. "Sometimes the wishes were pretty far removed from the actual thoughts Sharon had. For example, with the 'in home' manifestations, I'd ask for socks once in a while—cuz I know that's a thing on Earth. Anyway, I'd ask for them when Sharon would get lonely, trying to show her that she wasn't alone. It was really difficult, because for a long time her 4D, Sharon…wasn't aware at all, so I'd be doing it all by myself, or sometimes with Emma."

"You figured out how to ask for these manifestations on purpose? And by yourself?" Sync was impressed.

"Well, yes and no. For the 'in home' manifestations, I could only reach out to Meg once in a while, and only when I wasn't trying at all. So I'd be in sort of that nice Rest Mode. I don't know exactly what you'd call it, but that's sort of how it feels, you know? Anyway, when I was in that mode, and Sharon and Emma were in similar modes, I'd kind of take their energies and ask for things, ya know? They wouldn't fully know it, but we'd be sort of communicating somehow. I don't know, it's hard to explain."

Sync said, "Don't worry, it's fine. Words are frightfully limiting sometimes."

"You're telling me." Petra made light of the issue and also communicated relief by swirling her energies around a bit. "Well, anyway, it was sort of like that dozing state that 4D minds sometimes have. You know, the states where they are able to connect with other parts of themselves—and us—and figure out something cool? It was me in an equivalent state, I guess."

Sync emanated warmly. "How old are you?" she asked.

"Forty-two." Petra laughed. "Oh, I know, right? It's rich. The answer to everything is forty-two, but I really don't think I have the answer to everything." She grinned and swirled some bits of mischievous energy in the air around her.

Sync, meanwhile, had taken the equivalent of a

sharp intake of breath, and then asked, "Light years in CC time or Earth light years?"

"I'm strictly an Earth light years kind of gal, as far as I know," the soul answered. "But it feels like I've been on that planet for eons and eons of CC years."

Sync noted the nondefinitive answer and changed course abruptly. "Sorry, I got us derailed from the manifestation protocol a bit. Can we go back to the wishes themselves? You don't have to tell me about painful ones at all."

Here again Petra's energy sunk a bit. She sighed. "Honestly, Sync, I don't want to be a downer, or talk bad about Earth and the 4Ds there, but it was bad, I mean really bad." She sighed again. "The 4D minds, it was like most of them were infected or something." Her energies stole a shy glance at Sync before she went on. "So I would be bored, no Lunctus souls for miles around. I'd witness the 4Ds being just…jackasses…sorry to use that kind of language and insult jackasses, but they were…lacking in Goodness and overstocked in fear and hubris. You know, life in a dysfunctional system of oppression. It was so out of balance. Incredibly out of balance. Man, it was ugly sometimes."

She paused, a pensive energy surrounded her area. "So, Sharon 4D is sharp, no doubt about it, the girl is smart. Anyway, she would see patterns, heartbreaking patterns, but we could only talk on certain levels. She wasn't super aware of me, nor did I know how to connect with her very well. And Emma would also be overwrought sometimes, ya know, just so sensitive to the problems of the planet. So those things were going on. But Sharon, she isn't like most of the 4D Minds, she's limited of course, but she's also confident enough to try new things, ya know? She'd let go once in a while.

"She would let 3D Sharon take the lead, and 3D Sharon would take us out for bike rides or hikes, and we'd all be freely connected in some ways for a while. It was cool. And Emma, she could summon up exquisite kinds of compassion and warmth—for being in a human of course—and she would listen to music and be so moved by it. Sharon knows how to play a couple of instruments, and of course we all got to feel connected by that. So we'd all play together. Oh it was great. All of us in harmony (lol). So we tried to take turns. Sharon's 4D superpower was writing and learning new things. She's an idea person, big time. She'd get Emma all excited about some new idea, and then I'd join in and we'd write clever things." Petra paused, smiling.

"My superpower has been the ability to do these little manifestations. So when Sharon and Emma found them, we could all ponder them and have hope of being rescued. Eventually we learned to consciously connect, mostly out of desperation. Really, we were all hoping to be rescued from that planet." At that, Petra was still for a minute.

Sync solemnly nodded energy around, indicating she understood their distress. "I hope this will be of some comfort to you, Petra, but the particular timeline you've been in *is* infected. You are spot on in your assessment. Spot on. We can get you up to speed on what we know about these kinds of infections, of course. There's plenty of information we can share."

Petra nodded and seemed to relax a bit. She also allowed herself a brief, satisfied emanation, then quashed it. Then, clearly for Sync's benefit, she cocked her energies a little, sensing there was more that Sync needed to say.

"So that means that we have to think about the safety of the ship. We'll have to carefully monitor you for hidden infection. But it's clear that with the amount of Goodness you allow to shine, any hidden infection from the MMR disease or its mutations and offshoots should dissipate rather quickly since you are now in a safe environment. But..." She paused and cleared her throat. "We'll need you and your 3D, 4D and 5D cohorts to refrain from solo excursions, and I'm going to ask you to stay fully integrated within your 3D human form unless senior crew members like myself ask to speak with you directly. Will that be okay?"

Petra was listening intently. She began to exhibit a reaction, but said, "Wow, wait until the others hear about this, they will be so relieved. 4D Sharon has struggled so hard with not knowing how much to believe Emma and me. I think we'll all want to stick together right now, so the other parts will be fine with that. But let me make sure I understand—you want me to refrain from being Lunctus with anyone else besides you and whoever else is on the par—" She stopped herself. "You want me to not connect with anyone except those on the, um, authorized list?"

Sync emanated sympathy and communicated, "Please don't try to censor yourself, Petra. I love your sense of humor. No need to be formal. You can call it a party list if you want to."

Petra danced a little. "Okay, let's make it so!" Then her energy settled, and she said, "But seriously, Sync, how do I know who is okay to talk to? I mean, I've already heard others here."

Sync emanated a question to her.

Petra said, "Oh I can hear them at random times, like out in the halls, or when they're really happy or upset. I heard Meg when she was manifesting that seating area for us, cuz she was kind of stressed. I mean, it was just reflex to talk with her." Petra flitted energy around and said, "Tis a blessed thing to actually be able to communicate with someone just living life, rather than to just reach out to nothingness!"

Sync asked, "Are you able to hear others on Earth?"

"Yeah but I try not to. So I usually only hear others when they are reaching out in either desperate situations, or sometimes…in super connectedness…if ya know what I mean." She swirled energies around a little mischievously.

Sync moved energies around, indicating her understanding and humor.

Petra said, "But aside from a few really beautiful connections, the calls were mostly for help and were…I guess I'd call it work. Not that they were penance or punishments or consequences for me, but it was hard work to listen to and then try to soothe other souls reaching out." She saddened again, but shook her energy around, and pivoted it to beam towards optimism. "And I've got to tell you, it's gonna be a little difficult for me to abstain from connecting with others who I can share with on a real peer to peer level. So how will I know who is okay to talk to?"

Sync emanated reassurance. "You've got excellent instincts, Petra, so do not be worried about anything you overhear, as long as it doesn't arouse Fear in you. We are a clean ship. If you overhear and respond accidentally, you don't need to really worry about it. But as soon as you catch yourself, please just try to leave the conversation as soon as you can. No need to report any small instances—unless you become Fearful. If you sense Fear, I want you to immediately call for help from whomever you most trust, whether it's me or Meg, or someone else. So what we will do for now is I will introduce you to those who you can talk to, and then you can talk all you want to them. If you have questions or need help, you can always ask. Some of us may not know the answers to your questions, but we won't hide anything from you. That's not our style on this ship, or on any other in the CC, actually."

'Why am I getting nervous?' Sync wondered to herself.

"Maybe because you can sense I'm able to hear you as well as you hear me? I don't know for sure, but I was just able to hear you when you asked yourself that question." Sync's energies froze for a brief moment as she took in Petra's communication.

Petra moved her energies around in a sort of self-effacing and apologetic way. "Sorry, I don't mean to do that most of the time. Well, not most the time. I, I, I did just then, I won't deny it. But…"

"In general, you don't try to hear thoughts, but you do?"

"Correct," Petra said out loud with a quiet seriousness. "Not that I want to, Gawd, some of the absolute bull widdle I've heard! Mostly when there are hubristic bores, or drugs, or trauma involved. I have to remember, those that think such ugly thoughts really are not happy creatures, and for that, I pity them."

Sync's mind was racing, but she only said, "That sounds like a good attitude. I'd like for you to meet with Professor InDepth next. She is intergalactically known for her work studying humanoid forms, and I think you'll like her. Either she or I will get back to you about a good time for the two of you to talk."

Sync moved energy around gently before conveying the next part. "Your ability to read my thoughts is…highly unusual, even among aware beings, so I'm frankly a bit startled by this information. But it does mean we can freely communicate, so feel free to do so with me if you have questions or anything. I will ask you to try to refrain from reading my thoughts as much as you are able though, okay?"

"Of course. I'm sorry, Doc. I don't mean harm, and I'll try to not do it." Petra swirled some sheepish energy around a bit. "And please know that I am so excited about being among aware beings that I'm sure I'm acting out a bit, maybe even showing off a bit...please forgive me!"

Sync moved energy around warmly and laughed. "Apology sincerely accepted." She added, "I think we're going to become good friends, once I get used to these talents that you have! But for now, please try to remain integrated with Sharon and not access anyone's thoughts unless they invite you to do so. And when Sharon's form awakes, could you let me know? I'd like to talk with her. I'll make sure I don't frighten her or Emma."

"You got it, Doc," Petra said with a wink.

"Oh, and I have another thought—feel free to turn me down on this, but I was intrigued when you said you all wrote clever things sometimes. Would it be possible for me to see some of those writings? I am trying to understand as much as possible about you all and wonder if reading the writings could help me." Sync noted Petra's hesitancy. "Truly, it can wait until Sharon and I have talked, but we are sort of working in a bit of a time crunch—I'll explain why later, I mean what the crunch is, when you are all awake."

Petra said, "Doc, the only reason I hesitate is because some of the writings are pretty, uh...harsh. Sharon was pretty angry down there a lot of the time. Kinda nuts, even. I'm not sure how she'd react."

"No worries, then. We'll just wait," Sync said.

"No, Doc, hold on, that's not my final answer. I'm just weighing the pros and cons. You have a different mastery of time, right?"

Sync was surprised Petra had guessed this. "Yes. I can go back and forth in time, and access lots of extra time before Sharon wakes up if I need to. I do have other written materials to access, though. It's not a problem to wait."

Petra threw out some energy. "Nah, Sharon will get all shy, and hem and haw, and get embarrassed if you ask her. If the deed's already done, none of us will have to go through that song and dance. She trusts me, and I trust you, so yes, I'll get you a bunch of our writing to go through. But let's go through the first couple together, if that's okay."

"That would be fantastic!" Sync said, and meant it.

Blatherings

The universe has so much to offer.

Everything I know I learned from my experiences as an individual bit of consciousness. And what if it is all wrong? By now, I'm sure it is. We need these individual bits in order to learn and experience in a way that expands the knowledge of everything. But it's folly to think that humans, born of tepid levels of heat and water, are the height of life in the universe.

It's utterly laughable once ego is put away.

We are just a few inconsequential steps along the road to understanding a universe that is way too vast for us to really fathom. We are lost toddlers in the universe, just trying to find our way as a species. We are able to discern a few letters in certain alphabets, but the amount of information we are not yet able to grasp takes up the space of entire galaxies.

Our visions about our blue-green algae beginnings may be correct and wondrous to us. They are wondrous! They are utterly inspiring!

But we must be willing to understand, and also somewhat ruefully admit, that we are born of tepid, bland, safe, room temperature concepts and ideas.

The lack of passion in our existence is mundane when compared to the birth of a star. So we come into awareness in a vast universe with the passions and level of sophistication of children. Our sciences are child's play kinds of thinks/kinds of things. Born of mothers too vast, compassionate and loving for us to fathom, we create our own gods, and see cotton-candy treats as the heights of wonder. And they are, in the moment. We must never forget the wonder that cotton candy brings to a child.

Love of and from the universe encompasses all, we believe and maybe even know that much. Our cotton-candy wonders and crude material bodies must be included in that love, surely, as are our human families, and our ultimate and unfathomable mothers and sisters.

But our most advanced sciences are crude, homemade parodies of tools. We know that. We only need the intellectual and emotional agility to accept the certainty that we are much like lost toddlers. Some, or possibly many, of our kind can't even jump that short of a distance. Hubris shackles more than a few humans to their laughably primitive and Fear-based delusions of superiority.

For the rest of us, those of us willing to be humble in order to be wiser: This world is obviously an experiment of sorts, at least to us little humans living in it. We may be like strains of beneficial penicillin, or we may just as easily be more like an Ebola or some other nasty bug.

It's all relative, we know that. From an Ebola's perspective, it's just about the greatest thing around. Who is to say we are the beneficial beings we think we are? Really, we're just bumbling along: naive, unsophisticated, immature. Maybe like gazelles on good days.

What if we are existing in numerous worlds at once? We are conscious, but collapsed and expanded all at once into everything. And everything together means nothing is separate and therefore cannot be experienced as different. So we must find ways to be separate, to differentiate, in order to experience.

Then again, if we think in terms of dark

matter…can we? If we think in terms of dark matter and tremendous temperatures of millions of degrees…and those flaming masses of debris we call stars in the universes of matter. Energy expends itself and goes back to the dark matter realms? I certainly do not know. But it's possible.

And what about deep freezes so cold that matter ceases to exist, the other end of it…? I cannot begin to imagine it being so cold that things cease to exist… Yet this can be a reality somewhere, somehow. The mere thought is poetry, as frivolous and as all-encompassing as poetry.

My eighty years on the planet as a little bit of consciousness is an infinitesimally small fraction, a tiny bit of the entirety. I am less than a fraction of a blink of an eye. I'm okay with that.

Self-important men, focused on their own egos, their own survival, their own legacies, are often not. Those focused on profit and caught up in competition against others are often not okay with that assessment. They laughably try to prove their might and that their might makes right. As if. As if.

Fathoming the gap between my bit of "time" and an ant's conception of time is instructive. Five days signifies a block of time from my perspective. But my yardstick and an ant's are completely different. An eon to an ant might be the length of my lifetime as a human. And an eon to me might last the length of a yawn for a nebula's consciousness—and I know they have them. My soul knows they have them. So the differences in perception, maybe the key is in the 'all is one' approach. In other words, a nebula, a human, and an ant walk into a bar. Someone asks them, "What time is it?"

"What's the difference, it's all relative," they say in unison.

#

Sync felt compassion welling up as she read through the human's writings.

"They are just blatherings on a page," Petra explained. "This one we wrote when she was super tired. She just kept writing, ya know? And we made a running joke calling them blatherings. We all knew they didn't make perfect sense and that they weren't complete, but we also knew they made sense in some realm, in some time or dimension. They're sort of fevered first-draft-y type things. I have trouble understanding some of it myself, Doc—"

"Like I said, you can call me Sync, please, no need for formalities. Lol, see what I did there, form-alities!" They both chuckled, more or less.

"Seriously," Petra continued. "Sometimes when we write, it feels like it does for me when there 8Ds or 9Ds around. I can sense them, you know? But I can't talk directly with them. Yet somehow their thoughts come out in the words, they just appear. I swear Sharon is able to speak with them somehow, and I know her emoti Emma has something to do with it, though she'll never admit to it."

Sync was excited to hear this, but tried to appear neutral. "You say 'we' when you're talking about this. And you say she had conceptions of other dimensional entities. When was it that she became consciously aware of you?" Sync asked with genuine curiosity. She was also purposefully switching to another point of interest, away from the topic of the emoti.

"Hmm, must have been around 2000 or so, after I saved her a couple of times. You know, humans call them premonitions? Yeah, I told her to watch out. The first time was us almost getting hit by some kids on a runaway sled, of all things! We lived in Pittsburgh at the time. The second time, a car running a red light at about fifty miles an hour got my attention, and I made her stay stopped at a green light. Someone was honking at her to go and everything. Then this car goes flying by and hits the light pole. Dude was killed instantly, but Sharon—and the cars behind her—were fine. Anyway, after I saved her bacon that time especially, she believed in me. And in the past few years, we'd really developed a trusting and conscious relationship. I was about the only soul she could talk to— ha, see what I did there?"

Sync did the equivalent of chuckle with her energies. Sync was really taking a liking to Petra. She hoped the human mind and emoti would be as engaging.

"This is really interesting stuff. Do you have more?" Sync asked.

"Yes, I can gather a bunch up for you. But I've also got to say, some of the writings are pretty…rough," Petra said carefully.

My Rage Is Grief

The rage I feel about YOUR loss of humanity is horrific. My rage turns to an immense grief about you when I am at my most honest, when I am my highest self. I hate your stunted vision of what humans can and should be. And I am deeply saddened by it. I both hate and am so deeply saddened by this: It is clear you cannot not even comprehend what people like me are saying because you are so stuck inside your hubris and your delusions of separateness and hierarchy.

Your ability to unthinkingly hold beliefs about certain kinds of supremacy, your beliefs about the so-called 'human nature' of war, your beliefs about 'might makes right' that are so utterly inculcated into your being that you can only view beautiful and compassionate expressions derisively, as 'saccharine' bits of unimportance. As 'girlie' and somehow lesser than. You do this unthinkingly, routinely, with no insight, and with great defensiveness when someone dares to call you out on it.

But part of you senses that I can see your fear, even as the rest of you simply tries to dismiss me and others like me who know the world can transcend these ugly hierarchies. I know that you see me as lesser because I will not resort to violence, and because I don't fit your idea of a wise person. And I grieve knowing that you will never be able to really understand larger, much better possibilities for this world as long as you continue to live from your hubris-filled, small, and profoundly fear-based worldview.

You attempt to oppress and control others in your misguided ideas about what life should truly be about—we know this. And you will deny it, but we both know this is true: your need to control comes from your fear.

Full stop. And I am legitimately justified in hating those small minded parts of you that harm us all. Full stop.

But what gets lost is this:

My rage is more truly a profound grief. Grief about the utter injustice you inflict on yourself. I witness people making themselves small and mean enough to become stunted visions of what humanity can be on this planet.

My rage comes from witnessing human energy become so twisted and thwarted and small. Irony abounds, you who view yourself as superior in so many ways, do this only because your views are so very, very small.

Tl;dr: Just like Rogers and Hammerstein said in South Pacific, you have to be carefully taught to hate. And I grieve for you that you were.

Will this confession help us come to a merciful understanding? I doubt it, but it's worth a try. It's what my heart says must be the next step in trying to communicate to you. My sisters and brothers keep saying that peace and understanding is right here, if you and I just live in peace and understanding. You have trampled over my rights, and the rights of my brown and black sisters and brothers. You have trampled our rights and abused the entire Earth for hundreds and hundreds of years. You are fear made into action. You are hubris, desperately trying to cover your own fears, desperately denying your own fear's existence, but you are made almost entirely of fear. And for that, I profoundly grieve for you, even as I want to stop you and kill the parts of you that appears to be fear-ridden bits of cancer. It is your very smallness and meanness that I grieve for. It's that I see you infected by a cancer of small-mindedness. That's what I grieve for. May we all grow.

Learning From Hate

We can learn from anyone, even those who see Others as dangerous or lesser than themselves—we can study their fear-based actions and learn to more deeply understand the places where they get stuck. They are the same places where all of us get stuck—at least some of the time. We all act with hubris and the short-sighted certainty of mistaken righteousness in some ways. Most of us have learned (directly from the haters) that this keeps us small, keeps us in pain, but we all still fall victim to our own demons from time to time—we do so even in staying stuck in hating the haters. The key is to let our sense of mercy stay front and center. And that's a difficult thing to do.

Armagettin'

An explosion in the atmosphere, some weird waves in the sky for several hours, and poof, 539 million souls departed this Earth. Hundreds of millions watched in horror as their coworkers, neighbors, bosses, relatives, people at the gym, people at tables in restaurants, those shopping in boutiques, and strangers in the cars next to them simply started to fade away. Airlines reported that the loss of weight on some flights from the disappearance of so many passengers had caused near crashes. Numerous one-car crashes from cars hitting poles or guardrails happened. In all cases the people just started to gradually become…transparent, and then faded away completely within the span of a minute.

The people this happened to didn't seem to notice. In fact, if anything, they'd become a little more relaxed and calm while the process was happening. But the witnesses who saw them fade and disappear in real time were stunned, of course. Those who witnessed strangers disappearing were the most frightened. Interestingly, the majority of those who witnessed the fading of people they knew were puzzled and frightened, but not many were truly aghast—at least not after the initial shock wore off. In the literally thousands of studies and articles that followed the disappearance of the 539 million souls, people reported very similar stories.

The people were just gone. Poof. Roughly seven percent of the world's population. Gone. And it was over in an instant.

How the planet responded in the aftermath is the most important part of the story.

#

Petra explained, "I think she was trying to

channel her anger at some corporate foul up with insurance or something when she began to write this. I wasn't right there for most of the first draft. The first draft's tone was a little more...uh...passionate." Petra giggled a little. "It's still very much a work in progress, of course."

Sync nodded some energies and went on reading without comment.

#

Real life before: 70 percent of the workforce was indifferent or disengaged from their work. Only 20 percent of the entire population was flourishing, thousands were dying on the planet every year due to completely avoidable issues. Violent crime was at appalling levels in many countries; in the United States, avoidable deaths were at utterly sickening levels from crimes named and from other crimes passed off as policy.

The planet was polluted in places to the point where many people got sick and thousands died each year from poor air quality or dirty water. The planet was heating up to the point of all kinds of flora and fauna were going extinct. Many people living in first world nations could ignore these realities, as the loss of life generally happened to poor people in faraway places. Many others were heartbroken.

After the event, there was chaos, complete and utter chaos, of course. How could there not be? But even in the chaos there was another kind of immediate change. Those who had known the Faded as fathers, husbands, wives, coworkers, bosses, church leaders, and customers all shared similar stories about the characteristics of those who had Faded. In many cases, some who only superficially knew the Faded grieved, while others who knew the Faded in different capacities

stayed respectful and hid their true reactions from view.
#

Sync said, "I'm guessing that Sharon saw some statistics that moved her to write this?"

Petra laughed. "You've got it, Doc. She thinks that reason and facts are the most important parts of any arguments. She often forgets that for many people, things as harmless as facts sometimes…uh…back people into corners. Sometimes facts make humans double down on their old ideas because they are frightened of having to change their minds. Certainty is so important to most humans down there."

Sync nodded.
#

Because of the hundreds of millions of eyewitnesses, it was clear that no governmental claims could be made to discredit the event or downplay it. But the reality was that most governments had functionally ceased to exist at the public leadership levels, due to the numbers of Faded that had been claimed. Certain sectors of society had been affected much more than others. This had become startlingly clear within hours of the Fading.

In some cases, it initially appeared that some very nice people had gone missing. But along with them, entire blocks of the most corrupt senior-level politicians also simply vanished. With only a few exceptions, vast numbers of executive-level political leaders had Faded from the world. Entire swaths of military leaders and the majority of their underlings vanished. Not a single CEO of a Fortune 500 company was left anywhere in the entire world. A-n-y-w-h-e-r-e. Most senior officers in these firms had also Faded. And senior leaders in many industries were greatly afflicted.

Other industries were fairly unaffected: The

majority of social workers and teachers were accounted for throughout much of the world. Entire Fire Departments and hospitals were left largely intact, with the exceptions of some doctors and hospital administrators with certain reputations. Many police departments had seen their numbers halved, a few had not been affected much. Certainly militaries had been stunningly affected.

America's political landscape was changed. The current administration and his entire cabinet had gone missing, as had dozens and dozens of appointed and senior staff. The vast majority of politicians in the federal levels of Congress—and their staff members— had Faded. Appointed judges at the federal level Faded in alarming numbers; many locally elected Sheriffs, AGs, and judges also Faded. The vast majority of senior and mid level military officers had Faded. Most lobbyists Faded. Entire swaths of defense contractors in DC and around the globe: Faded. Virtually all intelligence agencies had only low-level administrative staff left. The vast majority of survivors in all fields set to work immediately to ensure the safety and well-being of those around them.

#

Sync said, "Intriguing. That part reads to me like you all had a hand in it."

Petra eyed the hologram of the document critically. "Yeah, we did, but I can't say as it was one of our better efforts, really."

"Based on some of the poetry you've showed me, I'm inclined to agree; but as Sharon alluded to earlier, it's the ideas that are the most important part of the story. At least they are to me." She paused and added, "I can see why you didn't think it was ready to publish, though. I imagine this could be seen as pretty extreme stuff to other humans."

"Actually, Doc, it isn't that far from many humans' thoughts and intuitive understandings. The thing is that humans are repeatedly taught to believe that their systems are good and fair and just. The propaganda machines are absolutely relentless in feeding the humans the line that all these business leaders and politicians are out there fighting for the common good, when clearly – at the higher levels- they are mostly power hungry, cynically corrupt, and selfish opportunists. Without the propaganda machines, many more people would continue to see right through these people's motives, like their guts tend to do at first. But the many, many bits of cultural propaganda keep them uncertain about their own abilities to think things through and make their own decisions. Like most religions have done." Petra sighed heavily.

Sync nodded. She sent compassionate waves of energy to Petra. "I can't even imagine how difficult it must have been," she said quietly.

Petra recovered and flitted her energies about before replying, "Oh, and the super ironic part of it all is that Sharon's living in a time when things are so much better for people in general. Women and men. We often joke that our problems are first-world problems. When we read stuff about current people in poor parts of the world, or black females living two or three hundred years ago, Emma gets so depressed, she can barely drag herself out of bed. We can't imagine how people could have ever been so brutal towards one another." Petra continued solemnly. "And when we see how it was—all over the world—for everyone, but especially women…hell, I get so depressed I want us to stay in bed all day as well! But we have all agreed we have to keep making things better—for all of us. All the humans and the planet. Because it also hurts the stunted little men, when they get to act like such...idiots." Petra laughed nervously at her last sentence. "Sorry, it's sometimes really hard to stay compassionate for the dumb shits, ya know?" Now she was grinning sheepishly.

Sync said nothing, but nodded her energies in agreement while trying to suppress a smile.

#

The first theory indicated that what was targeted was greed. Others then refined the idea to assert that a combination of belief in the value of being ruthless, greed, callousness, and hubris was targeted. This second theory appears to have been more accurate, based on the reports of millions of people who weighed in on the characteristics of Faded people that they had personally known. Some have recently postulated that the origins are somehow related back to trauma, but this line of thinking needs more research.

Regardless, people would almost uniformly report the Faded person was—at the very least—self-centered, and in many, many cases downright oppressive and/or abusive, and treated people around them badly. About 75 percent of the Faded were males. It was quickly determined this was not due to innate differences but because males had been socialized in different ways. In short, males behaved much more badly than females (on the whole) due to the differences in how they were generally expected to behave as humans.

Within a couple of days it became apparent that the approximately 7.3 billion left were frightened, yes, but they also had only compassion to share with each other. Helpers have always emerged after a disaster. But in this case, the people surviving the disaster had apparently been spared precisely because of their capacity and willingness to be generous and helpful in the face of danger or uncertainty. This apparent fact soon became readily apparent to most survivors. Once this was determined or intuited by individuals, they then— almost universally—decided to show even more compassion and generosity towards others. Because of that difference and accompanying dynamic, there were serious and far-reaching repercussions.

#

Sync nodded excitedly. "Petra, this is really interesting! Something very much like this did happen on another planet with human-like life forms. It's very similar. They were also struggling with the same kind of planetwide infection as Earth. I'm very impressed!"

Petra looked both pleased, and a little uncertain, maybe even troubled somehow. Sync went back to reading.

#

Almost immediately, people arranged to keep basic infrastructures up and running. While certain media outlets had been severely affected, others were not. But within the major media outlets, almost all of the senior editors, writers, and the most well-known news personalities had Faded. That there was such a universal Fading across all the news outlets, not just certain ones known for bias, was a shock to many of the survivors. But without the noise of the greedy and selfish, consumers were able to listen to the remaining staff explain that there'd actually been a pretty fair amount of institutional bias and outright cover-ups over the years. Those now left within those mainstream organizations stepped up to transform the outlets into true public service communications outposts. Many news websites transformed into public bulletin boards.

Open source sites quickly reconfigured as well and became valuable assets in the rebuilding that followed. The people left within telecommunications industries quickly granted everyone free internet access, and programmers found and shut down surveillance programs that infringed on the rights of consumers.

Many policy changes adopted by governments actually originated on social media comments under articles about the issue at hand, such as how to ensure trucks with essential cargo had enough fuel to get to their destinations.

Immediately after the Fading, reports about peace-making and infrastructure issues began to dominate the public communications. People showed up by the dozens or even hundreds to utilities and community events over the next few weeks, to offer their services and give workers a break. Electricity immediately began to run free, as did water, natural gas, and internet service. Solar-powered innovations immediately scaled up, while drilling for oil and coal slowed vastly in the weeks after the Fading.

#

Petra seemed a little nervous by this point. When Sync asked her about it, she shrugged good-naturedly. "I guess I'm a little sensitive about how simple we handled the money part. I know the biggest tangles are located in this area.

"Surviving humans would generally know what to do to be kind and compassionate towards each other. But the economic systems we've been using on Earth have been so brutal and are so complex, I'm afraid we've sort of oversimplified how many tangles might happen."

"Ah," Sync said. She wasn't surprised Petra was expressing some insecurity about how their story handled capitalism, but she was startled by Petra's use of the word 'tangles.' She carefully chose her next words.

"The most amazing thing here, so far, Petra, is this: On Beneficus, the planet where something similar happened, there were similar worries about how things might turn out, as you can imagine.

"And," she drew the word out, "despite a whole lot of concern, when their equivalent of...something very close to capitalism started to 'wither away,' it went so smoothly that their inhabitants ended up calling the demise of their system the 'No More Tangles, No More Tears' event. They had this—"

Petra excitedly broke in. "Yes, yes! 'No more tangles, no more tears!' We had that saying as well! It was from an ad for baby shampoo. Ha!" Petra laughed. Are we somehow...parallel...to this planet, Doc?"

"I really don't know. Let me finish your article, and then I'll do some research on it." Sync was excited as well. Synchronicity was definitely in the atmosphere, and Petra's energy was infectious.

#

Stock markets around the world closed voluntarily, as their senior staff had been greatly affected. The markets closed first for three days, then two weeks, and then four weeks. There were astonishingly quick worldwide agreements made that individual investors in all the markets could withdraw a small amount from their assets per month for the first six months if they needed to. But in general, the largest bundled assets were immediately frozen. A wealth tax was immediately imposed on billionaires (or, usually, their estates) to cover emergency expenses for millions of poor and working class people. Minimum wages were universally boosted to create living wages throughout the world. In many countries, Basic Universal Income laws were enacted. Similar measures were imposed around the world, with very few problems. Many jurisdictions immediately enacted 'no forced work' laws to ensure that people could attend to their families and their own basic needs without then experiencing negative repercussions from their employers.

The largest banks in the world understandably had no senior-level leaders left to speak of, so the leaders that did emerge from their ranks reached out to community-based banks and credit unions for developing common sense continuity plans and rules that governed how individuals could fairly access their more liquid assets. Owners of small businesses were exempted from these regulations for payroll purposes, if truly needed. Corporate taxes were immediately enacted, and most military funding, especially in the US, was diverted to true peace promoting projects, such as to ensure employers would be able to succeed in supporting their employees. Immediate shutdowns of the hundred most polluting companies were enacted, as were their counterparts in other places in the world.

It became clear that some extremely wealthy enclaves had experienced large numbers of Faded casualties. But what was also clear was that there were no looters haphazardly breaking and stealing from these areas, or any others. Instead there were armies' worth of helpers who went around in self-organized groups, looking to help keep the peace. That turned out to be a surprisingly easy endeavor overall.

#

Petra said, "Yeah, that whole section all sounds a bit too…uh, neat and tidy to me, if I'm gonna be completely honest, Doc. We all agreed that part needed more work. And Sharon wasn't happy with the pace or tone of the whole thing." She flitted a bit of energy around again. "But this last idea we felt was pretty important—and hard to express. You can't imagine how ugly it gets down there, and we all know that some of it is completely orchestrated. But other humans...they think we're a bit paranoid about how much freedom of expression is suppressed or manipulated, so the last part was something we were really trying to make super clear. Tell me what you think, okay?"

"Of course, I'm honored to. Let me take a look," Sync said.

#

The freedom of speech the internet had once promised began finally to be realized in many places around the world within a few short weeks after the Fading.

There was a tremendous drop off of divisive and mean-spirited rhetoric. Before the Fading, public comments on the internet were routinely infected, to the point that many people refused to engage in any discussions at all in the online comments sections.

Comments designed primarily to sow the seeds of dissent had not just been written by immature thirteen-year-olds. No, it soon became quite clear that there had been quite a network of groups and 'sock puppets,' at work that were no longer in operation. The Fading had taken with it thousands of people who had been paid by their militaries or greed-based corporations to write comments as if they were just Regular Joes. Crooked PR staff had often taken on online personas as if they were regular people just writing their own opinions. The tactic of divide and conquer by sowing division had been "upgraded" by online sock puppets very effectively. Sock puppets had learned very potent ways of diverting attention from corrupt actions.

Before the Fading, propagandists learned that dropping a bunch of nasty comments into a comment section would result in most people not wanting to engage or comment. So they paid people to pose as regular citizens commenting. The paid commenters would then deliberately dump the equivalent of raw sewage into the public waters. Sincere and informed people then didn't refute lies because they were too disgusted by the rhetoric to want to respond. Then those infected by hate, the naive 'true believers,' and other ill-informed people, became emboldened by the sock puppets' offensive tones and divisive drivel. These people would then (knowingly or unwittingly) carry on in much the same styles as the paid commentators, causing more divisiveness.

The vast majority of the content polluting the ether had been written by those who Faded, of course. So after the Fading, things changed substantially. There were no comments from Regular Joes claiming that global warming was a hoax, no dudes hysterically claiming that feminists were evil, shrill, feminazis, or that racism didn't exist right after a racist article or comment was planted. Defenders of violence by corrupt law enforcement dropped off immensely. The people who had authored those kinds of comments had all Faded. The amount of hubristic pomposity from callous and under-informed 'splainers' of any stripe went down exponentially. Inflammatory videos trying to bait people into becoming fearful were no longer uploaded to media sites, especially as it became clearer and clearer that people with the highest levels of compassion had been spared.

Imagine the pure bliss of those reading and interested in the subjects at hand who no longer had to wade through juvenile and stunted idiocy. In a short few weeks, it became very clear how much had changed. People could actually post their true thoughts without fear of being attacked. And they could get real and insightful feedback on those thoughts. Yes, of course there were disagreements, sometimes significant ones, but discourses stayed overwhelmingly civil.

Very few had really understood how well the sock puppets had stifled real, productive free speech until their comments were gone, and the stench from them faded from the ether in much the same way as the producers of the vile comments had.

\#

Petra's energies emanated embarrassment as she remembered how graphic Sharon's original language was. She hadn't read through the document in a while, and though the rage had been tempered a little, she worried it was still too much. But Sync's comments were surprisingly positive.

"I think you guys were super clear here, but you might want to—"

"Tone it down a bit, I know, I know," Petra jumped in.

"No, that's actually not what I was going to say," Sync replied. "I was only going to suggest that in the second to the last paragraph you might want to change the wording from 'a short few weeks' to 'a few short weeks,' that's all. I think your use of the metaphor about certain forces deliberating dumping raw sewage into public waters or swimming pools is unfortunately quite apt. So no, I don't think toning the whole thing would be helpful. The metaphor works here because it helps illustrate to what lengths people were willing to go to, and how sickeningly ill the whole propaganda machine was...uh, is? What is the proper tense here, Petra?" Sync emanated a sympathetic smile.

"In The Fading it was, but on Earth it still is, I'm afraid," Petra said with a sad laugh.

Sync acknowledged the point and continued.

"And I again want to thank you so much for being willing to share these writings with me, Petra. I truly appreciate your honesty and candor about them as well. This has already helped me understand humans with quite a bit more detail, and these writings are going to be super helpful to us in helping Earth come up with a plan for her recovery."

Petra stirred around some sheepish energy. "Ah, you're welcome, of course, Doc," she said. "But, Sharon's, ah, not necessarily a completely typical human, so that might be sort of important to remember. Many people don't think quite like her. And the infection is pretty bad down there. I don't know that it's worth it, quite honestly. I'd probably just opt for the radiation cure myself, if I were in Earth's shoes."

Sync moved energy around thoughtfully for a couple of moments before responding. As far as she knew, no one had told Petra about the radiation, and she had purposefully used the phrase 'come up with a plan for recovery.' Yet Petra clearly knew what Earth had originally planned. It seemed as though Petra had overheard the thoughts of the 10D Earth herself. She'd never run across a 6D who could do that.

Finally Sync said, "I wasn't going to mention this yet, and, I'm not sure how to tell you this exactly, Petra. The thing is, uh, Earth, she was 100 percent ready to use the radiation we brought, right up until the ice cream incident. Now she's asking for help, and in specific, uh, she wants you all to help plan planetwide interventions with us."

Petra's energies see sawed wildly in response to the information. "Us?!" she fairly spluttered. "The Earth is delaying using the radiation because of us?! Why? What on Earth (lol) is she thinking? We don't have any...special powers..." Petra's energies trailed off as she realized, that just by virtue of being aware, they probably did possess special powers compared to others on that infected planet.

Sync emanated some calming energy. "Here's the thing, Petra. You guys were able to contact us even though we have assumed your species was Unaware- that's not easy to do on a good day in a supportive environment, and yet you were able to do this while living on a highly infected planet. Your elements are integrated in the exact way needed for a species to become aware at a time when many others on your planet desperately need guidance from others like you. You're aware, even if you don't completely realize it, lol. Earth knows you, and thinks you all might be able to help."

"Sync, those are just..." Petra trailed off, confusion evident in her energy.

"Really?" Sync made her response sound a little indignant on purpose. "Petra, it's not that big of a stretch to think you could help, and I think you know it. And, besides." She paused. "Earth is ill. You know it, I know it, Sharon knows it. I would imagine that 7.6 billion out of your 7.7 billion humans down there know it. Earth has had the courage to ask that we try something new. She asked specifically for your help. Are you going to deny her?"

Petra took in Sync's argument. "No...of course not," she said quietly. She did the equivalent of a hand wring. "Okay, we'll help, but Sharon's gonna freak out! She will see it as a big...a big..."

"Burden? Obligation?" Sync asked.

"No, no, not at all. She'll sign on willingly, but she will worry like crazy that she'll screw it up. Of course we all want to help! That's just who she is, who we are. But both Sharon and Emma will get so worried that they're not doing enough or that they're doing something wrong. I just know it's gonna be exhausting having to reassure them all the time. But...I trust you, and who am I to argue with a 13D?"

Fun Facts And A Consult With InDepth

Sync left Petra to her thoughts after Petra gave Sync access to more writing. Sync quickly read the gist of one Petra had laughingly said she starred in. She then went back to Petra to ask her if she could share that piece with another crew member. Petra seemed pleased and easily gave permission, although she was still a bit distracted by Earth's request and said she was trying to figure out how to preemptively stop Sharon and Emma from worrying. Sync thanked her and took the writing immediately to Professor InDepth.

#

The world did end; we just didn't notice it. Way back in the twentieth century, and we are now a few decades into this new world. It's an exciting time or transition. But a very dangerous one, as well. Millions of us know this. The work is to figure out how to leave our Ptolemaic visions of reality behind.

We need to let our souls lead the way. We need to let love and compassion guide our actions and explorations. Profit should be way down on the list of priorities. Pretty freakin' simple, right? But apparently way too complex for many corporate, political, and military "leaders" to handle.

In aiming for individualism, we have been a bit immature, it seems. We've pushed ourselves away from our Mother Earth, like teens push away from their parents in order to form their own identities. We've been like young teens trying to prove ourselves—with precious little skill or grace.

And we've created dangerous situations—quite

like teens involved in high-risk behaviors, not fully understanding our own actions. Trying to live with the unprocessed, dimly recognized traumas of the wars and disease and disasters that preceded us. We do this in typically unaware ways: we replicate our traumatic experiences, mistaking our own actions, made in unaware reactions born of fear, anger and grief, for how life should be. Thus we create needless wars and suffering and ridiculous ideas about power and status. And we recreate trauma for others in the process.

These are the lonely, twisted beliefs of an abandoned species trying to grow up. Our documented history shows us we've experienced childhoods chock full of traumas, and we've had to deal with those traumas alone, in the best ways we could. So we developed gods in our own images and superstitions to make meanings of our circumstances. It didn't matter that they were false. Ptolemaic Theory worked fine for hundreds of years, thank you very much. And so have our current fictions. Fictions about status and power being more important than love and compassion, sad as they are, still seem quite important to those in power.

We fought others, believing it was the only way to be safe. We blamed victims and created truly ridiculous stories about our own superiority vis a vis "Others." We slaughtered or enslaved Others who had cultures full of knowledge that we can only now guess at. We eradicated their knowledge because we were afraid. Simple as that. We were afraid.

Those who still oppress are still horribly—often hysterically—afraid. Simple as that.

Fearful people are like wounded bears—quite dangerous and more than a bit irrational. And the fearful necessarily take up most of our attention as we defensively try to (ha!) reason with them. But we can't reason with hysterical men. We must render them harmless, or they will be the death of us all. This is becoming crystal clear.

These are the truths of our history. The evolution of people cannot continue until we awaken from our childhood beliefs. These beliefs are understandably entrenched. These are beliefs modeled on our only experiences of how life can be. Think of a child growing up isolated in a violent home. They see the world as violent. They cannot know there are other ways of being until they reach a certain capacity in their imaginations. As youngsters they learn how to cope with the material lives they are thrust into. To a child in survival mode, life can only be absorbed; certain ideas cannot be questioned until the child is in a different time and place.

So, for the millions—maybe billions—of awake among us, the time has come for questioning. Re-evaluating our beliefs about who we are and how we are supposed to live has become necessary. For those of us who are aware of the needless adherence to outmoded systems based on trauma and fear, this particular moment of time is absurd to the point of farcical.

We are living in times that are absurd to the point of farcical.

It's the Trauma, Stupid

Yet we don't quite know how to escape the material world's realities. Those in power still believe we must live within the constraints of how we've currently arranged our material worlds. We've created a material world stacked with obstacles born of primitive cultural systems: Corporate capitalism, with its huge monopolies, firmly entrenched in obtaining and retaining 'power over' the marketplace; a military presence—which gets funded at absolutely ridiculous levels—to ensure political 'power over.' We developed caste systems, and patriarchy. And the caste systems and patriarchy themselves? Born of fear and trauma. The very idea of 'power over' is rooted in fear and trauma.

That is the main point. Not the patriarchy, not the capitalism, not even the militarism, but the trauma. Trauma is what causes obsessive quests for power over.

Regaining a sense of power by any means necessary is the first thing survivors focus on in the aftermath of trauma. In survival mode, no one is focused on fairness or the rights of others. No one.

Humans suffered through millions of bits of traumas even before we started inflicting them on each other. Trauma raised our Fear Based Thinking to absurd levels. We acted accordingly, colonizing, enslaving, and proclaiming dominion over everything we encountered. We've never returned to normal. Simple as that.

Fight, Flight, Freeze. Those are the only options available to humans in the immediate face of danger. And so we created a division of labor to handle those reactions. Males were expected to act with aggression. Males were expected to act tough, strong, shoot first, ask questions later, and take control of situations—typical reactions to trauma—try to fight, try to regain control.

Females were socialized to be small, meek, frightened, subservient. These are also typical reactions to trauma. Trying to hide, not be seen, escape, or at least avoid more harm. These reactions were encouraged by cultures sickened from and overwhelmed by the traumas that happened to their people.

And it went on—oppression in a hundred different forms for hundreds of years, even while humans were creating better worlds in other ways. The trauma born obsessive quests for 'power over' created hierarchies of oppression. And, like cancers, those cultures went out and conquered and colonized others.

But oppressed people, even in their fear, spoke up and pointed out the truths of the oppression all around them. And eventually, enough compassionate people were able to listen without the shackles of unconscious, trauma-based reactions blinding them. So the worst of it stopped—legal forms of slavery ended. As oppressed people kept fighting, labor and the civil rights movements happened.

Then feminism happened. Feminism helped to free women from their socialization. We know that part of the story about feminism. But what we do not consciously realize is that feminism also freed women from their gender's typical ways of expressing trauma symptoms. Simple and as complex as that.

Our males have not been awakened by a similar revolution in nearly the same numbers, and so many of them are still trapped in acting out symptoms based on traumas that happened long ago. Simple and as complex as that.

It gets even more complex. Obviously, males still hold and continue to manufacture the bulk of 'power over' cultural norms. With about five percent of females taking on CEO positions, and the larger cultural norms still operating on assumptions that hypermasculine traits and attributes are to be aspired to, we are collectively imprisoned by these beliefs, attitudes, and norms. They infect all of our major institutions, our economic systems, our assumptions. All these assumptions about the importance of obtaining and consolidating 'power over' others are rooted in fear. Simple as that. And that fear? Born of trauma.

The Old Stories Still Have Power

Many still feel the need to dominate and control, even as the more conscious among us recognize these kinds of actions are completely…primitive.

Religions were developed to codify the spiritual impulses of humans. Religions were meant to be languages for our souls to communicate their most beautiful thoughts, ideas, and divine concepts. Yet time and again, religions were exploited by the fearful, to the point that many religious dogmas severely limit many (most?) humans in our quests to experience the spiritual. Is it any wonder we find it hard to listen and heed what our souls tell us?

With a few exceptions, the religions that survived did so due to conquest. In most places and for most of recorded history, forced or culturally coerced conversions (to a monotheistic male god and/or a male son or prophet of a male god) were the norm. Think about that for a minute. What kind of gods do that? Gods created by people with huge power and control needs (formed by trauma-based reactions). No devils needed.

How can one truly believe Another is equal to him if he believes that only his religion is the one true way? When he believes only those who follow his religion's doctrines are living correctly, how can he not feel somehow superior to Others who don't share the same beliefs? It seems, at this point, that monotheism only serves to reinforce an 'us versus them' mentality. Except our souls know there is no 'them.' Not when we all live on a single planet. Not unless we continue to kill off all those we consider to be 'them.' It's as simple and as complex as that.

'Us versus them' is a Fear-based and primitive mindset, and undeniably harmful to the survival of the species at this point in our history.

All institutions created by 'might makes right' mindsets contribute to and reinforce these same, dangerously hubristic hierarchical values. So easy to see when one is not imprisoned within the confines. So hard to see it when one still lives within the confines.

Put another way: People living in the Anthropocene need to do better than to try to stuff themselves into the cramped and suffocating kinds of 'might makes right' primitivism that currently infects so many of their cultural constructs.

We've all been here before. And we need to do better or we will perish. Some part of me knows we've tried and failed before.

\#

"She wrote this?"

"Yes. Tell me, does this look like other human writings you've studied, Professor?"

Professor InDepth took a deep breath. "Well, yes and no." She walked to the window and looked out before continuing. The Earth was in view; they were only a few thousand miles away from it. "Yes, in that this particular piece appears to be something called cultural analysis." She studied the writing for a few more moments.

"Okay," Sync said, indicating she was following so far.

"But the qualities of this writing are frankly surprising to me..." Professor InDepth appeared deep in thought.

"How so?" Sync asked.

"Well, first off, humans aren't generally aware of other timelines. That's one way."

Sync's energies immediately relaxed from a tension she had scarcely been aware of. "Right. That's exactly how I see it, too. This is almost an exact replica of their fifth timeline, the one you told me about with all the pyramids. So, my main question, I guess," Sync said, "is how do you suppose this human is able to…know this reality?"

Professor InDepth sighed. "That's unclear to me."

"But…do you have any theories?" Sync asked.

Professor InDepth nodded. "I do. In her timeline, there were supposed to have been numerous oracles, fortune tellers, soothsayers and the like. But most of them lived well before this human's time. There was a fairly long period of time that modern day humans call 'antiquity.' But it appears that even then, the known oracles were completely infected with ideas born of MMR.

The professor trailed off. Then she shook her head and said "Supposedly, a main task of some—if not most—of these oracles was to predict which wars would be won, what regions would be 'conquered,' and by what means money was to be gained." InDepth looked in Sync's direction pointedly.

"You're kidding." Sync was honestly shocked; she'd heard the infections were pretty bad, but this was ridiculous.

"I wish I were kidding, Sync. This was not completely universal, but for the majority, it appears that making predictions about war, money, and power were their main jobs. It happened often enough that— obviously—we can start to see the extreme levels of sickness in the society, and how pervasive the sickness was. When they weren't being asked to predict the outcome of wars, oracles would sometimes— sometimes—foretell of years of prosperity or hardship. But as far as we can tell, they were never asked about larger concerns. Often the futures humans appeared to want to know about would be small issues of personal gain, you know, typically selfish egoic concerns."

"When did they ask about—did they even learn about Compassion and Goodness?" Sync was fairly incredulous.

"No, not often. Remember, all these timelines that have failed have been badly infected with MMR. So values of competition, status, typical symptoms of might makes right, the use of coercion and often brutal uses of outright force, bribery, corruption, denial, the inability to see others as equals, all these things were believed to be okay or even good! Sync, the beings in this timeline are so filled with Hubris and disease that less than two hundred years ago some humans actually owned other humans. And it was perfectly acceptable for people to believe certain groups of humans— including women— inferior. I mean, talk about projecting your own fears outwards!

"In these timelines, all these kinds of things— and more—were at least tolerated, and many of them were actually venerated, as was war and conquest, which I know is hard to believe. The humans infected by the disease were all focused on dominance and naming themselves as the superior groups, assigning labels of inferiority to anything and anyone that wasn't physically strong. They were so Fear ridden and Hubristic, they could not see that proclaiming themselves to be superior to others based on their ability to use brute force was laughably stupid."

Professor InDepth's gaze was focused on a nebula to the east. She was silent for a moment, then spoke with more optimism. "Considering the state they were in two hundred years ago, they've actually made a lot of progress. But, obviously they are still reeling from these beliefs, and the beliefs are still locked into the cultural norms of their institutions. Many humans still hold some of them. Worse, those who are the most severely infected with MMR are the most consumed with having power over others. So they use fear, lies, and force to continue to try to consolidate power around themselves. And it often works."

Putting a hand up to the window, she paused in thought before adding, "Ruthlessness is seen in some quarters as heroic! They still value—and use—military might over diplomacy on some parts of their planet! Can you even imagine?"

InDepth shook her head sadly. "Just think of all the beings who have had to live on that planet with that infection. What a waste, what a horrible waste. Instead of those with Goodness being able to develop higher levels of it, they've had to fight against infected 'leaders' and the policies they try to implement."

"What do you make of this idea of trauma causing the MMR to hang on so tenaciously?" Sync asked.

InDepth turned and smiled. "Ah, that's the second way these writings are different to me. Quite frankly, I think it's absolutely brilliant. I think we may have actually found causality for the entire illness! We know humans suffered innumerable trauma while both their cultures and their brains were in a certain evolutionary phase, so it explains why quests for power and control have become so important to them. As you know aware beings don't place nearly the premium on having power and control, and certainly not "over" others. That's a pretty insecure way to behave, as we can see. But trauma changes how humans view life. It makes power and control become super important to humans. And it's interesting how their 'fight or flight' reactions became so gendered. It's incredibly obvious once you see it. Males got angry and fought to control and dominate everything around them, and females got frightened and tried to placate or hide!"

Sync nodded thoughtfully.

"And," InDepth drew the word out, "when you are in that fight mode and you believe that being strong and dominating everyone and everything is your best reaction, consider how much distaste you would have for anything you see as weak, or even compassionate." The Professor pushed her glasses back up excitedly.

"Um, I'm not quite following," Sync said. Sync had some understanding of the psychologies of millions of aware species. Though she had a soft spot for them, pure humanoid psychology was not one of her many specialties.

"Okay—when you're a traumatized human stuck in MMR kinds of thinking, you see the world as a place to dominate or be dominated by. Because you are so thoroughly stuck in this way of thinking as the only way life is or can be, you'd see running away or avoidance as a 'weak' response, right? So if women were expected to be weak…they would be seen as, you know, really less than."

Sync nodded her understanding at that part, but moved energy around, asking for just a little more explanation.

"To someone stuck in a MMR mentality, more harm, or even dying, is not the worst thing that can happen. Refusing to fight is. That is seen as a retreat from life, therefore supremely weak. Life is: either dominate or be dominated—there is no sense of living peacefully among equals or of fair play, because in that completely Fear-based way of seeing the world, somebody has to dominate or else they will be dominated.

"So, refusing to play the MMR game is even worse. If you fight and lose, at least you understand what the game was, and you show 'bravery' by participating. But ignoring or dismissing the entire game as irrelevant or unnecessary is…I think they call it sacrilege, although that might be a little harsh. I'm not an expert in this timeline.

"Even if it's not sacrilege, not playing by the rules of MMR is clearly transgressive—after all in MMR, rules are authority, and authority is might—therefore it is right and not to be questioned. So breaking the rules by having the presence of mind and bravery to show compassion, or refusing to engage in hierarchal thinking, appears to be sacrilegious, or at the very least, a show of weakness—of all things!

"And also, from a MMR perspective, the person responding with compassion—our best quality!—is engaging in dangerous behaviors, and signaling to the infected that they are not playing the MMR game correctly.

Sync indicated some understanding. "Oh, wow. Talk about gaslighting! So, women, being conditioned to be both compassionate and meek, were seen as both dangerous, and as basically shameful. And then later, when they, along with many men, saw past the lies and began to question the need to even play the MMR games, they were seen as heretics by the infected. You're saying that to the infected, those who don't believe in MMR as a good system are somehow shameful, by default. "

"Right! They were seen as "uppity" or as damned hippies or some such nonsense. And since women in this timeline were allowed to use compassion more often, the infected felt extra threatened by them. So they reacted strongly. To me, it helps explain how misogyny got so ingrained," InDepth said, nodding her head vigorously.

"Ahhhh, that is a good point," Sync said with some surprise in her tone.

"And, this trauma idea helps us frame MMR a little differently." InDepth looked excitedly towards the area where Sync's energies were located. "Think about their victim blaming. They blame the victims because in their minds if the victims had been right, they would have used strength and brute force and wouldn't have been victims. Enough brute force would have solved everything!

"It's absurdly simplistic thinking, but it is also how humanoids react when they are in difficult situations—they simply don't use all of their brains when they are reacting to trauma. They can't! Their brains shut down to better focus on essential functions of figuring out fight or flight strategies. That's a physiological fact that even they have grasped down there on the infected planet.

"It explains other things too. Think of all the violence in their entertainment, their beliefs in the inevitability of war, and of vengeful gods. It is so very typical of trauma survivors to see the world as a dangerous place!

"The correlations are everywhere. They are afraid of people they see as Others, afraid to have certain people in positions of authority! Then there are their ideas about scarcity. I mean, most of them don't feel safe enough to really pursue their passions. The focus on 'obedience' by some folks, coupled with their incredibly primitive concepts of 'power over'—and their profound unease with vulnerability!

"These things are all typical reactions that grow out of trauma for humanoids. Oh, I'd say this linking back to trauma reactions is pretty convincing stuff, yes."

"Huh. It really is kind of an elegant explanation, isn't it?" Sync said admiringly.

"Yes. In fact, I think we might be able to help Earth based on this new way of thinking about the MMR issue. Certainly the high levels of testosterone are problematic, but as you know, lowering testosterone hasn't worked in the past, nor has eliminating males from the human populations, so I think this idea is extremely exciting. I'm going to take it to the intervention team just as soon as I can call a meeting together!" InDepth pushed her sleeves up and strode over to a computer.

Sync marveled at the apparent synchronism at work in the choice of their reading these particular writings. Then she wondered if Petra had mentioned this particular piece of writing with a bit more insight than Sync had given her credit for.

Part 2

The Dream Doesn't End

The dream world was real? No, that couldn't be. Sharon wondered how long she'd been out. She imagined she was lying somewhere along the trail. She worried that she'd bleed out or get too dehydrated or some kind of predator would find her. She worried that some bass-ackwards sketchy dude would find her while she was apparently immobilized, unable to wake from the wonderful dream she was having.

"Why can't I wake up?" she asked aloud.

She had just emerged from a sleep of some sort and found herself still in the dream world. She was stretched out in the supremely comfortable bed in the quarters she'd been given on the GSS Prosperity. She was wearing unfamiliar but comfortable clothes, a green teeshirt and a pair of sweats. She blinked hard and willed herself to wake up on the ground somewhere along the trail. It didn't work.

She tried quieting her mind to see if she could summon Petra. Petra would help her figure out how to awaken. After a short time, she could sense that Petra was around. She called out with her mind, "Petra, can you help me wake up? I'm worried! I've been dreaming too long!"

She immediately sensed reassuring energy being sent towards her, and she heard a voice that seemed to be Petra's saying: "It's all right, this is real, we are finally safe. I'm being serious, you are not dreaming, dear one. You are awake and safe—feel it for yourself!"

It sounded just like Petra. But the words couldn't be true.

"Yes they are! This is true!" Petra sounded a little impatient.

Sharon shook her head. In all her experiences with listening to her soul over the past few years, she'd never known Petra to steer her wrong. Petra always had Sharon's safety and well-being as her highest priority. If she suddenly heard the little childlike voice tell her to not make the lane change, she listened, trusting the voice more than her "logical" mind. It had saved her more than once. She thought of Petra as her guardian angel. But right now, her logical mind was fighting against the words this voice was saying.

Sharon heard what sounded like a bit of a harumph, and then she felt a whirl of energy come towards her. She'd felt this energy a few times before, usually when she'd been pretty upset about things. The effect of it was comforting, a sense of being hugged by her soul. At the end of the hug, Sharon could almost physically feel a playful push. "It is me, silly! I'm right here, same as always!"

Petra sounded happy and excited, more so than usual. This was saying a lot, since she was usually quite upbeat and playful. Right now she sounded close to giddy. Sharon shook her head a little and said aloud, "Aren't you worried?"

"Not at all! It's so exciting to me that we are here. I swear to you, you are not in any danger here or back home. And we have not fallen into a cactus filled ravine, I promise. Nobody mugged us, and no, you did not have an aneurism. We are both super, super safe here. Really!"

Sharon knitted her brow. "Where are we then?"

Petra actually tsked at her a little. "Dear one, it's like you were told during your sleep: We are aboard a ship, we are in space, and we are finally, finally among aware beings. I swear to you, this is real!

"Look, I know it sounds crazy, and it's a shit ton to digest, so why don't you just stay in bed and think it through for a while, okay? I'm actually talking to some folks in another part of the ship—they want to know all about us. Oh, and that Officer Sync will be coming to talk to you soon…I'll be around, though!"

Sharon frowned again. But she took the words on faith. Petra's suggestion to "think it through" was practical, she could try it. "Okay," she said out loud. "I'll try."

"Good! Petra out!" That was their standard reply to signal they were signing off. Sharon heard something like a flutter of energy receding.

Sharon knew she was alone again. But somehow that was okay. The short talk had calmed her, and Petra's reassurances made sense. Sharon wondered if she was somehow on some drug, maybe like psilocybin, because she realized she actually felt pretty good. She felt safe, like she knew she was in a comfortable place. Well, even if she was on some drug, so what? She knew some self-defense moves.

After pondering for a moment, and rehearsing a few defensive moves in her mind, she looked around. She was in a room of…some sort. She couldn't tell how it was lit, but it was light and cheerful, and safe. The plastered walls were clean; the furnishings around her bed were in a vaguely southwestern style, and in good condition. She realized the room, and its furnishings, though unfamiliar, somehow looked very much like her own home. She was in a nice, safe, cozy, and comfortable king-size bed. She decided she was not ready to get up. Maybe she'd try to doze back off. Yes, that might work. She'd think about events calmly and hopefully fall back asleep.

So she turned on her side and started in earnest to recollect the events that had led up to this point in time—whenever that was. It started with the ice cream appearing out of nowhere. She'd been hiking. "Okay, that's when the hallucination started. So what could have happened to me?" she asked out loud.

She'd been up in the Sandia Foothills, hiking on a section of a trail that she'd been on a few times before. The trail had been relatively easy, and she'd been going at a fair rate of speed even trail running in a few places. The terrain and plants were familiar. Typical high-desert vegetation dotted the landscape: small to medium-size junipers and pinyons mixed in with various brushes. There were some yuccas, a few cacti; there were large boulders in a few places. There was no snow on the ground, but a dusting of it a few hundred feet up. Her intent had been to go up a little past the snow line and turn around. She had no uneasy sense that there were big animals out and about. She'd seen smaller scat, but no sign of bears or cougars, and it was far too late in the season for snakes. What other kinds of danger could there have been?

She ticked off as many possibilities as she could think of: There were no overgrown branches to trip over. She'd eaten nothing weird, no wild mushrooms. She couldn't imagine she had accidentally ingested LSD or MDMA or anything like that. There hadn't been any iffy-looking dudes along the trail. Two women about a mile back, and before that a male and female, both friendly enough. There'd been four cars total in the parking lot, and her own truck had been the only car even close to being sketchy. There was some irregularity in the trail itself of course, but she wasn't on a steep grade, so skidding or tripping wasn't much of a risk at all. She had felt fine, she had enough water, she wasn't hungry, she was completely acclimated to the altitude. What could it have been?

The day had been beautiful for hiking: low to mid 60s, no clouds, very little wind, just a beautifully sunny early December day in the southwest. She'd worked up a little bit of a sweat and was in the sun, ascending up the southern side of a small rise.

With a start she realized she had actually made a wish for the ice cream. Her exact thought had been, "This is perfect, but now I'm a little hot. I wish I had some ice cream. Wouldn't that be nice?" And then damned if an ice cream cone hadn't appeared right in front of her.

"Okay," she said, drawing out the last part of the word. "That happened. Then what?"

Sharon scrunched her brow as she tried to remember the exact unfolding of events. Her first reaction had been surprise, then amusement. She'd looked around, and realized there was no one else there, no one else to witness this event or offer explanations for it. Then Sharon remembered that the sense of Petra had become very strong right as the ice cream appeared. Sometimes that happened. Out of nowhere, Petra would just sort of be present and start telling Sharon something or showing her things to notice. But that usually only lasted a few seconds, or at most for a couple of minutes. Sharon remembered Petra "appearing," then laughing at the ice cream, and saying with delight in her childlike voice, "Take it!" Because Petra had laughed, Sharon had immediately felt at ease and knew she was safe, even if things were really, really weird. She'd taken the ice cream cone out of the air, and then tentatively tasted it. It was delicious, and she'd begun to feel a little... playful...at that point. Why not? Petra was happy and enjoying the situation, and Petra had excellent judgment.

Sharon realized another unusual thing about the situation had been the constant sense of Petra being right there. It was as if Petra had become an almost physical companion while the events were unfolding, rather than the occasional ghostlike muse who made brief appearances and said a couple of sentences before disappearing again. Petra had been there almost as solidly as if she had a physical body—and that had helped to sort of normalize the situation, weirdly enough. It made Sharon feel more secure, kind of like how you just feel more at ease with a friend around when you meet new people. Petra had ascertained the situation was safe and friendly, and Sharon had realized—as friends do—that Petra wanted to stop and chat with...them...for a minute, and then for longer. And...who were they, again?

She recalled the scene. The voice on Earth had been wholly disembodied, but also somehow attached to a concentrated bit of energy swirling around that made the air thick and somehow animated. The voice was kind, and rich, and utterly beautiful. It had seemed to be female, but also androgynous. The voice had sounded like...Gladys Knight. So much so that Sharon had wondered if the Pips would appear as well. Then Sharon remembered that she had asked if the being was female. The being had sort of been puzzled about what gender was, before Petra said something to her. Sharon could guess what that was about. Petra had told Sharon several times that she wasn't gendered, but she appeared female because she was made of sugar and spice, and all that. So when Petra and Gladys Knight had conferred for a moment and then Gladys had said, yes, she was female, Sharon had sort of guessed that was not entirely accurate. Despite these strange happenings and bizarre thoughts, Sharon had just accepted this as a normal interaction. Like you might in a dream. So weird!

Still laying in the nice warm bed in the ship's quarters, and not falling back asleep at all, Sharon continued probing her memories, trying to reconstruct the events as precisely as possible in her mind. During the whole encounter, she had felt mostly...curious, happily interested in the weird things that were happening. The whole thing with the magic carpet appearing and bowing to her and then giving her a ride to that rover thing... It had all been quite interesting, really, and she had felt very much at ease—again, mostly because Petra was there. She had been alert for danger, of course; she always scanned for danger. But she at times she had felt...delighted. That was the word. She'd been kind of delighted by the surreal turn of events.

Not the whole time. She'd gotten a teensy bit worried.... When was that? She remembered being introduced to these strange beings after they'd landed. But that was maybe just a little sense of shyness. It was the thought of going to sleep in front of strangers—that was it! Sharon didn't nap in public places easily. That is what had been a little nerve wracking. But Petra had said it was okay. And she fell asleep immediately after meeting another one of the crew members. That had been Officer Sync.

So then Sync had told her told a bunch of things while she slept. This seemed perfectly natural at the time, and it actually still made sense to her, weirdly enough. They'd talked for hours. Sync's voice had also been so easy to listen to, in part because it had a light, singsong quality to it. But unlike Gladys Knight, who'd first talked to them on Earth, Sync seemed to have a slight Indian accent. The way her energies concentrated in the air in a certain place were also a bit more delicate, and somehow colored sort of differently. Where Gladys

Knight's energies had a deliciously warm and sweet quality to them, Sync's seemed to be just a bit more peppery, but just as kind and friendly.

Sync had told her about the ship and about her being among "aware beings" that weren't humans, and that they could talk via "mind commands" or out loud, whichever felt more comfortable. Sync had reminded her she was asleep and had asked her permission to "run some tests" that would help the beings understand her, and humans in general, a little more. Sharon had been okay with that. Then Sync had asked her about herself. Sync had seemed so nice and smart, and Sharon trusted her almost instantly. And so she had told Sync stuff that seemed relevant. Sharon now remembered that she had felt a sense of relief and some excitement talking with Sync, as if she had just returned home from a big trip and was telling a good friend, or maybe her mother, about it for the first time.

But that telling was hours ago. Sharon had no idea what time it was, but sensed she'd been asleep for some time. And now it was just feeling a bit weird and overwhelming. She hadn't fallen back asleep or wakened up from this…whatever weird thing this was.

She sighed and decided to sit up in bed. As she began to wiggle and reach around for the pillows, a thing that looked like a control switch materialized nearby. Sharon jerked her head back in surprise, then picked it up. Clearly the thing was a control switch for the bed. Thankfully the arrows and buttons were quite intuitive. Sharon tentatively pushed a button, then another, and found herself in a very comfortable, upright seated position, with the bed covers and warmth still surrounding her. She now saw a large mirror directly across from her. Her hair was sticking up a bit; she smoothed it down and stared at the mirror. Her very familiar-looking audience of one stared back, expectantly.

"Wow. This is weird," she said out loud. She shook her head in disbelief for a few seconds before again realizing she felt pretty good. Deciding she must be on some sort of psychedelic trip, she consciously chose to just go with it. Freaking out would be about the worst thing she could do. So she resolved to not freak out. It was surprisingly easy.

"All right, let me summarize so far—just like Petra suggested." She said the last part loudly and with a bit of playful sarcasm, as if Petra might be listening.

"Okay, first off there was ice cream. It appeared because I asked for it. And it was good." She ticked the sentences off in a factual way, noticing as she did that the words she said aloud sounded normal to her. She then looked at one of her hands for a moment, then opened and closed both hands, studying them intently. It appeared she did have control over them. She looked at the walls, they did not appear to be morphing into any weird shapes. So she wasn't having the same kinds of hallucinations she'd remembered from her few forays into mushrooms. Everything around her looked normal, if more cheerful. She shook her head.

"A magic carpet appeared. Petra told me about eight times that everything was safe, and wasn't this just a fantastic opportunity, and we should go with these creatures. No; she called them beings, not creatures." Sharon paused, thinking for a moment. "I trusted them. Even though I couldn't see them. Weird. But…okay, what next?" She looked at herself in the mirror. She gazed calmly back. "Well, we went with them, and Petra was super excited. Petra *is* super excited now that we're here." Here Sharon frowned slightly. More quietly she said, "I am referring to Petra as if she is a different being from me and not a part of me. That's weird too. But they tell me she is a different being who lives in a six-dimensional world." Sharon guffawed.

She again peered at the mirror and said theatrically, "Clearly, I have fallen into a science-fiction matrix of some sort." Dropping the theatrics, she went back to just enumerating facts: "But it's safe and pleasant here. And though I have no idea why, I actually feel really, uh, good. Let's see, what next? Oh, yeah, I came aboard ship and agreed to go to sleep for a few hours. Before I fell asleep, I met Sync. I liked her very much immediately. She talked to me in my sleep and told me all kinds of incredible things about this being a ship full of 'aware' beings. And she went on about Goodness. It all made sense. It made a hell of a lot of sense. And everyone's been kind…and now I'm still here. Okay…so me wishing for ice cream started it, maybe. Or maybe it started earlier? Let me see, what went on earlier in the day?"

She opened and closed her hands a few more times, slowly shaking her head.

Sharon Speaks With Sync

At this point, Officer Sync quietly slipped into the quarters, and with something that sounded like a little bell tinkling, made her presence known to Sharon.

Sharon said, "Yes?"

Sync answered with what Sharon dimly remembered was called a mind command. It wasn't a command at all, but a communication. She identified herself: "Hello, it's Sync, the one you've already been speaking with in your dreams." The communication was unmistakably friendly, and Sharon trusted whoever was talking to her without question.

Sharon said, "Hello," in a friendly way.

"Greetings, Sharon!" Sync continued. "I'm sorry to impose, but I first want to make you aware of my presence. Then I would like to talk with you. Petra indicated you'd probably be 'thinking about things.' I can wait until you're done with that. If you have questions, I can probably help. I can leave and come back, or you can continue to complete your thoughts— either way is fine. But, I need to tell you, I cannot help but hear pretty much anything you consciously think when I'm in your presence…while I am in this particular mode. Would you like me to leave or stay?"

"Uh, you can stay, I guess?" Sharon's voice rose on the end of the sentence, indicating her uncertainty.

"And would you like to continue your thoughts? Or talk now? I can wait a little while if you want to finish thinking things through to a natural stopping point. But I'd like to talk sometime soon."

Sharon started to weigh the options. Before she could answer, a memory flooded her consciousness and she fell deeply into it. It was the news. She'd been surfing online. The articles and videos were all so hideously depressing, about violence, inequality, the corrupt and brutal who occupied positions of great political power. She'd read about billionaires who made fortunes at the expense of others; she'd scrolled through videos of protesters in what seemed like every part of the world. Everyday people risking their safety, even their lives, in support of basic human decency. They had to protest against those who were making food inaccessibly expensive, or authorizing the use of force against their neighbors for profit or to stroke their own egos. Hundreds of thousands of protesters were demonstrating against oppressive governments who had colonized them or had taken their country hostage in coups or corrupt elections.

Sharon had been sent over the edge by the unrelenting cascade of dystopic news. She had felt attacked by the now familiar combination of profound grief, anger, and frustration at the state of the world she lived in. The relentless repeats of militaristic men in suits loudly proclaiming they wanted to bomb places they couldn't even locate on a map. These men being interviewed by other men in suits who—without irony—called them "war heroes."

Fringe groups of two hundred protesters trotted out as if they represented millions of people's thoughts. The deafening silence of the corporate-owned media whenever it came to what the most popular grassroots leaders called for as they tried to win back political power from corrupt cowards. The platitudes of bullshit the corporate media spewed on an hourly basis as they spun a reality out of carefully curated bits of half-truths. Finally, she recalled shouting at the computer when a video of brainwashed fundamentalists spouting stupidity about their righteousness and the evils of women got to be too much for her. "Fucking morons! You utter fucking idiots!" she'd yelled at the screen.

Remembering this moment very clearly, she said, "Damned right I scream. Any aware being might do the same!" She said this aloud, using the same term, 'aware,' she'd learned about from Sync, who had spoken with her earlier... And who, she suddenly realized with some embarrassment, was right here, in her quarters and overhearing everything she thought. The memory had only taken a couple of seconds, but it was so deep and vivid! In her mind she dimly registered Sync's profound sense of sorrow for her before her mind dipped right into another memory.

This one was of Sync introducing herself, just a few hours before, telling her she was surrounded by compassionate beings. It was so lovely, so calming. So validating. She remembered telling Sync about Earth, and being deeply heartened that Sync had not given her a rueful smile or a response along the lines of "it's like that here, too." Instead, Sync had looked at Sharon with a deeply sympathetic kind of sorrow. She'd somehow conveyed a deep, compassionate sadness for Sharon's experience, as if she was very sorry that Sharon had been living in horrific conditions. Sharon had that same sense now. She felt grateful for the sympathy. Then her mind stopped producing thoughts for a moment.

Sharon was not sure how much time had passed. But she immediately sensed Sync around her.

'I don't want to wake up,' Sharon thought.

'What do you mean, wake up? You are fully awake right now. This is reality.' Sync's calming communication came into her head. The same lilt was there—yes, it was definitely a soft Indian accent.

Sharon's heart was heavy from the memory of Earth's problems. Sync seemed to understand this. 'You're saddened and upset by the memories. Let's get your mind a little calmer, okay?'

Sharon nodded. She was still sitting up in bed, her hair starting to stand on end a little again.

Sync took Sharon's hand telepathically and led her mind to a warm, sunny day in a beautiful landscape. As they traveled, Sharon could see Sync more clearly for the first time. She was translucent, like a hologram, but this did not seem strange at all. Sync appeared as a friendly, wise, sisterly or motherly type woman. Her appearance matched her voice; she could be Indian or Pakistani. She could be in her 30s or 40s or so, but she also appeared ageless. Dark hair, lovely, smooth brown skin, white teeth, and a ready smile. She was very attractive and full of life, and deeply present with Sharon. Somehow it was clear to Sharon that this form was not Sync's natural state, but one she chose simply to help Sharon feel more at ease, to give her an anchor to focus on.

They were somehow floating over a series of grass-covered hills dotted with large oak trees. They glided a little above the landscape, over the rolling hills for a few minutes in a companionable silence, just taking in the beauty of the land. On several hills there were wild irises in bloom. Sharon dimly thought it must be spring. It looked familiar, like the oak and grass covered hills in northern California. Sharon felt a bit of a sense of homecoming. Eventually, they landed on a hilltop with a territorial view spanning miles in all directions, the sun warming them. Sharon could hear birds and the rustling of grasses in the small breeze. She could see, hear, smell, and feel a sense of abundance and…love…around her. The very light seemed to have a friendly cast to it.

Sync eventually broke the silence. "We strive for Goodness here. This is a taste of what comes from that striving. Beauty, peace, prosperity, and love. Feel the land speak to you of these things. We have sorrows, we have suffering, but we don't have much of those things. Aware beings truly know how to flourish, and we know how to create cultures that nurture Good and healthy ways of living. This is our reality, right here, right now. I am creating it for you as a natural landscape, because Petra told me that is how you feel most at home, but we create these same experiences in our relationships with one another. When aware beings interact, we strive for the same kinds of feelings this landscape creates in you—to emanate love towards each other. You know the world can be transformed by love, by compassion for all beings. You know this is what we are all really meant to strive for. And here, aboard this ship, and in the known universes, we are able to spend most of our time doing just this. We believe—we know—we are meant to create love, and experience it. In our worlds, in the known universes, this is what aware beings spend hours creating, experiencing, working at, sustaining. We thrive because collectively, we live as love manifested, as difficult as that may be for you to believe.

"You are not living on a planet that is able to consistently manifest this right now. But aware beings have realized worlds of beautiful, compassionate, loving kindness in more parts of the known universes than you can ever imagine.

"We have been living in this way for millions of years. We live on different planets, in different parts of the known universes, and in different dimensions. But we live in beauty, and in acceptance—you might call it peace—and with generosity towards all beings. We treat each other with loving kindness. And you found us! You contacted, us Sharon! With just a sweet wish for ice cream!

"And we were close enough to hear you ask for

it. How marvelous is that!" Sync's voice and her singsong lilt carried real affection and kindness. She shook Sharon's hand back and forth a little between them as they stood side by side on the hill. She continued. "Truly, it is an auspicious sign. We welcome you. Our worlds are many, and you are welcome to explore any of them now. You can come with us and live among us! Welcome home, my friend. Welcome home!"

"Oh my God," Sharon said. Her eyes had involuntarily started welling up. Two tears escaped down her cheek, and she quickly wiped at them. To cover her embarrassment she half-heartedly swatted at a butterfly near her head and said rather gruffly, "But, this can't be right. How can I even hope to live among you like this?" She stretched her arms out wide to encompass the beautiful landscape in front of them. "I can visit these places, yes, but I live on a polluted, warring world where brutal men run amuck with fear and greed. Where millions of people have to protest against things as basic as not killing people just trying to live their lives."

Sync said nothing, but her eyes were full of solemn compassion.

Sharon continued, "The world I live on has people so intent on becoming kings that they don't even notice that they create only stinking piles of utter shit around them. They chase after 'power' and 'money,' they don't care at all about running over people or destroying the world. They just want 'power.' As if the kind of power they desire is worth anything at all.

"Any show of kindness or compassion is seen as weakness. Some people oppress anyone they think they can get away with oppressing. I hate it there, but it's where I live. It's where I'm from."

Sync's energies were infinitely compassionate. Sharon's eyes welled up again as Sync said, "I am so sorry, Sharon. These experiences sound awful, they would wound anyone. But you have a place here. You belong here, you belong to everything good, you belong in environments of grace and compassion. Everyone does. It's clear you come from a very mixed up planet, but you belong in the peace, prosperity, and the compassion of loving kindness. Everyone does."

Sharon's voice broke with emotion. "But these people believe in things that are just infecting everything. Everything! It's all about fucking might makes right. And it's ridiculous. Even letting a car in in front of you on the fucking freeway is assumed to be a sign of weakness by some of the humans I have to live with."

Sharon sniffled loudly, not trying to hide her emotions anymore. "And don't even get me started about the military 'might makes right' idiots. Or the horrendous rape culture we live within. Or religious nuts who think God is on their side when they kill or condemn other humans. On our planet, certifiable warmongers are seen as national heroes. Seriously. My country is just in-fucking-fected with these idiots. A few hundred utterly slimy and greedy defense contractors— and the weasels in Congress think we need a fucking military budget of just obscene numbers. Most of the rest of us don't, but the weasels just make up shit to justify their greed. And all the while kids don't have enough to eat, and people go bankrupt—seriously—from medical bills thanks to our fucking for-profit medical models. And other idiots, oblivious to these realities, put assault rifle cartoons on the backs of their cars to show how 'cool' they are, even though there's another mass shooting every fucking day. What kinds of blinded people do that? We are a planet of utter idiots."

Sync said quietly, "Yes, we've been watching

your planet for a little while now. We can see the mess you're in."

Sharon continued bitterly. "Yes it's a mess. It's a world where war is peace, and chasing money is valued far more than nurturing the planet and its inhabitants."

Sync said nothing more. She simply stood next to Sharon as she continued to sniffle and wipe at her tears. Inwardly, she was amazed at how utterly terrible Sharon's experience sounded, and how Sharon's use of words like 'infection' and 'might makes right' matched up so closely with the CC's assessments and understanding of what had happened on the planet.

Eventually, Sync said out loud, "The beauty and peace and loving kindness are quite a lot to get used to. And you have a lot to be legitimately angry about. I don't know what else to tell you."

Sharon laughed humorlessly. "Well, that's honest. I'm sorry to dump on you like that. This hill— it's beautiful, and this is all so lovely. I'm sorry."

"No, no, please, you've been living in some extremely difficult conditions. I understand—we all understand—that you've got a lot of things to process. We've been doing some research on your planet, and it's clear that there are a lot of very serious problems there. Your planet has asked us to help, and we want to help. But we need to know more about how things work, and that's going to take a little time. That's partly why I wanted to talk with you today. We actually don't know much about humans in your...uh...we don't know much about humans in general. So when you're ready, I'd like to ask you some more questions. But I don't want to upset you, and I want to make sure you feel safe. Please, take in as much of this as you can, and please, try to take solace from this." Sync's free arm arced widely to indicate the landscape surrounding them.

Sharon again reminded herself that if she were on some sort of psychedelic trip, she might as well make it a good one. So, wiping tears from her eyes, she indicated she would do that. Soon enough, she dipped fully into the beauty, and this time she let it feel spectacular. Colors exploded. She felt the warmth of the sun, the very aliveness in the air. She and Sync first stood near a magnificent oak tree and took in its immensity. Then, as they both crouched to gaze at a butterfly that had landed in the grass, she wept again, this time from being touched by the beauty.

Sharon was not sure how much time had passed, but she heard Sync ask, "Are you ready to go back to your quarters, Sharon?"

Sharon felt curiously refreshed. She thought about asking Sync whether she was on a hallucinogen of some sort, but decided against it. Instead, she sighed, and looking around a little wistfully, said, "I suppose so."
#

Sharon's next awareness was of being back in the ship's quarters, sitting up in her comfy bed with her hair standing up on end a bit.

Sync made excuses that she needed to retrieve her notebooks and would return in a few minutes. Before she left, she suggested Sharon get dressed and go sit in the living room. Clothes that looked very much like the ones Sharon had been wearing during the hike suddenly appeared on the bed next to her just after Sync uttered the suggestion. Sharon consciously told herself to accept these things as pleasant, and realized it was actually pretty easy to do so. She found the clothes were slightly different from ones she owned, but they fit amazingly well.

As she wandered into the bathroom in a bit of a daze, various items manifested right after she thought about them: a toothbrush, toothpaste, a comb, some soap, towels, and a washcloth. Perfectly warm water came immediately out of the spigot, so she splashed her face and combed her hair down. She looked in the mirror and touched her face, wondering if she would ever wake up, pondering how this all felt so real. But she wasn't too worried about this strangeness, somehow.

She wandered back out of the bathroom and noticed a galley kitchen area to the left of the bedroom for the first time. Two cups of coffee suddenly appeared on the counter. Sharon was still thinking about the problems she had relayed to Sync, so she said, "Thanks!" out loud with a bit of forced cheer, and took the coffees out to the living area.

The living room was not large, but it was well appointed, with a coffee table situated between a tasteful and surprisingly comfortable couch and love seat combo that faced each other. There were a couple of wing-backed chairs against a wall, making a U-shaped sitting area. The chairs appeared to change shape and morph into a more casual southwestern style as soon as she eyed them critically.

"Thanks," she said again, this time with more sincerity. As an experiment she toyed with the idea of different fabrics on the chairs, and they obligingly changed a couple of times. Sharon then asked for a couple of side tables and flowers, which all showed up as nice configurations. Nothing to fear from these kinds of hallucinations, she decided.

She also noticed a lack of windows, but the lighting was somehow bright enough, that wasn't oppressive. She then realized from the light appeared to be coming from the walls themselves. She looked closer, there were no canned lights in the ceiling or overhead lights that she could see. As she was vaguely pondering this, a cat appeared. Sharon hadn't realized she's asked for that, but it made a certain amount of sense. The big, fluffy, dark-grey creature was dozing peacefully in the middle of the couch. Sharon set the cups down on the table and took a seat next to the cat. It woke up, blinked at her a couple of times, and then rolled onto its back. The cat began stretching a little, and was obviously inviting Sharon to pet it.

Sharon had known a good many cats before and so was quite cautious in accepting this invitation; but the cat seemed content and placid as it accepted Sharon's tentative caresses. A bit of purring began.

Sync tinkled a bell, then slowly manifested as the same Indian or Pakistani female human in the love seat across from Sharon. Sharon motioned towards the coffee. "I would say I made it for you, but it actually just appeared on the counter—I hope you like it." Sharon smiled with more confidence than she would have thought possible, given all the strange things going on.

Sync privately but playfully cursed Meg for manifesting coffee for her. 3D forms were hard enough for her to manifest, but to pretend to eat or drink was a real trick in this form.

"Thanks, I'll try not to spill this as I drink it," Sync said with some humor.

"Are you an actual being right now or a...hologram?"

"More of a hologram, really," Sync said with a laugh, noting the human was really quite gracious, given all the strange things she was experiencing.

Sharon looked at her with a hint of a smile. "You're not joking about spilling the coffee then." It was a statement, not a question.

They both chuckled as Sync said, "No, I'm not. I might try to drink it, though—I do love a challenge."

There was silence for a couple of minutes while Sharon continued to pet the cat.

"Sharon, your planet's problems are...complex. Do you know how your bodies get ill?" Sync was aware of the immense pit of anger and grief the human was trying to avoid falling into. She'd be angry too. And utterly grief stricken. These beings had...militaries...and killed each other, over differences in ideas. It was utterly barbaric.

"Yeah. And I imagine you're gonna tell me the Earth has some disease that she is fighting. You mentioned that while I was sleeping. And you know, I've thought about it that way myself lots of time—back on Earth." Sharon paused. "But I have been trying to live in that shit pile. It's been willfully created by some of those dumb shits."

Sync's hologram gave Sharon a sympathetic look and then sighed loudly. "If I may, I'm going to throw a lot of information at you right now. I am appearing here as a human so you'll feel as comfortable as possible. But I am thirteen-dimensional being, which means I can think and create in dimensions you cannot even conceive of. I have been to many places in the known universes, and I'm telling you all this so you will understand this next fact: I can go through time, once I am zeroed in on specific locations. Just as I can read minds, once I am in a certain mode."

Sharon nodded, trying to appear casual about it.

Sync went on. "And time is already different here on this ship compared to Earth's time. So while it may seem to you that we've just met, I've actually had the equivalent of several days to study your real life conditions down there. I've also had two separate conversations with Petra, and she has, well, shown me some of your writing, which is beautiful overall, I must say. I'll stop there, for now. What do you think of what I've just said?"

Sharon appeared thoughtful as she replied. "I'm not sure actually. On Earth I'm often appalled by how ignorant some people can be. Seriously. Most people on Earth live within cultures that I consider to be quite…uh, primitive, I guess." She looked at Sync's form. "So part of me is thrilled to not be the smartest person in the room, and that's the truth. Another part of me is kind of nervous about that, but Petra is so thrilled to be here…so that's how I know somehow that all of this is a good thing," she said, sweeping an arm around. "I would trust her with my life. And I'm doing that right now, as far as I can tell."

Sync nodded. "How do you feel when I tell you I've looked at your writing without your permission?"

Sharon's expression rapidly changed from thoughtful, to concerned, to embarrassed. "A little upset. But Petra gave you permission, so not too angry…more embarrassed, really. I've written some horrible things about…how stunted things are down there. Kind of like the stuff I said a while back."

Sync nodded again. She flashed a fierce smile. "Let me be serious here. Sharon, if I were stuck down there in your situation, I doubt I would feel any less vindictive and angry towards those I thought were at fault for perpetuating the problems that you all are dealing with. But the anger is blocking you from acting in positive ways."

"I know, I've felt stuck for a long time," Sharon said quietly.

"And I can see in your writings that you certainly have conceived of your current cultural norms and values in terms of illness. That's really exciting to us because that's how we on this ship see it, too. So you're definitely onto something. But as you note in some of your writing, the disease is not willful. It's the equivalent of an autoimmune disease, or a cancer. It perpetuates itself by creating conditions that helps it thrive, in the same way as any other disease. So while many behaviors appear fully willful to you, there are, in reality, only a very small percentage of humans on your planet who are fully aware of what they are doing. And they are also infected."

Sharon paused for a moment, half-angry, half-mournful, still wondering if she was dreaming all this. She was aware of the types of things Sync might have read. The litanies of criticism against other humans on her planet. The blind rage she felt towards some that made her curse their existence.

"Okay, I'll bite, what is this disease?" Her tone was wary, half-hopeful, mostly just curious. But at least she was distracted. Sync's hearts went out to her.

"We call it MMR. Let me be clear: In many nonaware forms of being, MMR is a legitimate developmental phase. But it cannot coexist with awareness. Beings who can conceive of life beyond themselves have to grow out of it. And for some reason, your humans are having real trouble with that. I'm getting ahead of myself. MMR stands for 'Might Makes Right.' Does that ring a bell for you?"

Sharon's eyes widened. "Uh, that's…ah…something I've…theorized about."

Sync looked at her meaningfully. "Yes, I'm aware of that. Petra pointed it out to me right away. Your ideas about Might Makes Right and Patriarchy springing from it are quite intriguing. We've come up with pretty much the same theories, and we've tried to develop vaccines, treatment protocols, and antidotes to the disease based on those theories. But we're missing something, because we haven't been successful yet." Sync debated and then decided to very casually mention that Sharon's idea of trauma triggering the problems with MMR was new to them.

But she didn't get a chance because just then some donuts appeared on the coffee table with a little thump. Sync stopped, theatrically looked around, and then appeared to get information from some invisible source. She nodded her head as she gestured at them. "Rumor has it, they should taste great, but they are healthier than your Earth based ones, so you shouldn't have a sugar rush after eating them."

Sharon politely looked impressed, but her mind began racing again. Sync noticed the shift, and immediately sent some calming energies. Within a second or two, Sharon remembered her vow to make the best of this trip and told herself to just go with the flow as best she could. As soon as she did so, she found it was surprisingly easy to just relax.

Indeed, the last few hours on this spaceship seemed to feel safer and more normal than the sometimes very surreal events of life on her troubled planet did. She allowed herself to be distracted by the donuts and idly tried to figure out how old Sync might be.

Keeping the tone light, Sync tried and failed to drink some coffee, spilling a bit on the table. They both giggled. She explained that while ingesting food or drink was difficult, she could move some things around materially, and then demonstrated she could use a napkin to clean up the spill. They both chuckled in amusement.

As Sync was nodding and wiping up the spill, a small flapping sound announced Petra's arrival. Sharon was finishing her donut and looked in the general area where Petra's presence seemed to be. On Earth Sharon was not in the habit of speaking to invisible beings in front of others, so she said nothing, and waited expectantly for Petra to speak.

"You two getting acquainted okay?" Petra asked, with just a hint of wariness in her tone. Sharon was quite relieved to realize that it was clear that Sync also heard her. Sync smiled innocently and said, "Oh hi, Petra! Yes, we're doing fine."

Sharon smiled widely. "Yes, we've been talking a bit about some of the problems on Earth. And Sync's been showing me how this place is different from Earth. So far, you're right about this place, Petra. I figure I must be in some sort of dream or maybe on a mushroom trip. But I'm determined to have a good attitude and a good trip. So no worries." She paused. "The food's delicious."

Petra ignored the reference to being on a trip. "Good! I just wanted to make sure you were doing okay. Call me if you need me. Petra out!" A small flapping noise indicated Petra was gone. But before she left, Petra privately asked Sync to refrain from talking about the trauma MMR connections at all right now. Sync indicated she would respect Petra's wishes.

Sharon's Astral Spying

After they finished the snack, Sync told Sharon a little more about the CC. She explained how they had scheduled a trip to visit the Earth for business purposes, but had not been expecting to meet a person (or any being) who would be aware. Sync carefully left out the medicine delivery issue, as there could easily be complications from Sharon learning too much information about the contents of the medications at this stage.

Sync also again explained the need for assessing beings when they accidentally communicated with CC crew members. She went over the importance of Goodness and briefed Sharon on the preliminary assessment findings, congratulating her on her very high Goodness levels. Sync was also careful to further assure Sharon that she would be free to return home at any time if she so chose, after they were done with the full assessment protocols. Then Sync asked Sharon more about her life and how things worked on Earth. Sharon really liked and trusted Sync, and time went by quickly.

By the time they finished with these topics, Sharon's stomach was growling a bit. Sync walked Sharon through the process of intentionally conjuring up a lunch of avocado toast, some quiche, and a delicious juice that Sharon couldn't quite identify. Sync also encouraged Sharon to try to stump the as-yet-unseen 'Bio Fuel Dispenser' with an unknown dessert. As a result, Sharon had to explain what a small slice of pecan pie might be like. The manifestation of the pie was very well done, and she eagerly ate everything.

During lunch, Sharon said, "You know, I feel like we've only been talking an hour or two since I ate those donuts, but man, my stomach says it's been hours since I last ate. What time is it?"

Sync looked a bit thoughtful. She cocked her head. "Time is...uh...variable in general. I think that would be a good way to describe it. Time moves a bit faster on this ship than you are used to down on Earth. But honestly, time is...well, it's just a construct, it's not fixed. Time is a way of measuring things, and all measuring systems are a bit arbitrary."

Sharon scrunched her eyebrows together. "It matters, though, because if I'm gone too long, people on Earth will miss me. My family, my friends...I don't want them to freak out!"

Sync said she would explain about time differences in a little more detail soon, but that technically, it was as if she'd only been out on "a three hour tour" so far. Sharon laughed. "Fair enough."

Sync added that the ship had technology that helped all sorts of animate beings adjust to the ship time. "Your body should fully adjust in a week or so to this ship's time. But right now, you'll need to nap a lot. Like a toddler." She said this part cheerfully, like friend might speak playfully to another friend who was sick and needed to rest.

Sharon noted this, and consciously willed herself to keep on with the positive attitude, so she would stay in a good space for the duration of whatever the heck psychedelic trip—or three hour tour—she was on.

After lunch, they resumed talking about a whole range of subjects. Sync was interested in human psychology, and asked numerous questions about human-based emotions. Eventually, the subject turned to the differences between being observant and being paranoid.

Sharon said, "I think that the concepts are a bit more complimentary than people realize. The more observant you are, the more likely you are to see connections between things that others miss. But yeah, I'm also a bit paranoid."

"Why do you say that?" Sync asked, genuinely curious.

"Well, on Earth I sometimes have these ideas that people are watching me."

"Can you tell me about them?" Sync's tone was kind, and her attitude was deferential, which she knew would help Sharon feel comfortable. She could easily make the atmosphere even more appealing so that Sharon would tell her everything she wanted to know. But that would likely backfire in the long run, as the human would then feel intimidated by Sync's abilities to so thoroughly read her. Most humanoids, even those from safe and open planets, became quite uneasy when other beings were able to read them too easily. It had to do with humanoid propensities towards egotism and the insecurities that produced. So Sync had been purposefully using a complicated technique of timing her questions so that the Sharon would feel comfortable, but not later feel she'd overly confided in Sync. It was a complex dance of intimacy and distance, and much harder to do than just getting and staying in tune with beings from different dimensions and safer climates who could better handle a purely compassionate and empathetically knowing connection.

Sharon looked at Sync's manifestation and seemed to consider something before she spoke. Sync couldn't quite make out what it was. She could hear Petra briefly conversing with Sharon. But the content was not something she was in the proper mode to discern. Sharon was listening for Petra's response.

"Okay, sure," Sharon said almost to herself. Then she fully returned from her conversation with Petra. "I suppose I'll just…never mind. Anyway, what comes to mind is an experience I had recently while mountain biking along the Santa Fe Rail trail. It was fairly recently, and I ended up writing about it right after the bike ride, so it's clearer in my mind than many of these kinds of experiences. Writing helps me remember things."

She paused and smiled at Sync, almost playfully. "Of course, you probably already know that."

Sharon's smile unnerved her. Part of this human was genuinely calm, like some part of her knew she was a conduit of some sort. It went beyond the calming medications in the atmosphere, Sync thought, as she felt an involuntary tingling of her own energy.

Sharon had begun speaking. "Anyway, there's this great bike trail, maybe thirty miles long right outside of Santa Fe, and I'm biking it. From out of nowhere a 'random' helicopter comes along and went over me. From the angle it flew, I could tell whoever was up in there was looking right at me. I could hear the pilot and passenger in my mind. It was as if I was seated right behind them in the helicopter, complete with the din of the engine and the horrible electronic headset communications."

Sync emanated an appropriate bit of encouragement. Sharon said, "So the one guy says…" Sharon stopped. "It might be easier to explain this if, maybe, you just get inside, as if you are remembering with me. That would be easier, I think."

Sync was genuinely taken by surprise. "You want me to 'get inside'?"

"Yeah. I'm not sure what you actually call it, but I don't think I have to relay this the way I would to another human. Petra said you can 'get inside' while I just roll my memory, and that you will experience the whole memory pretty much exactly the way I do. She said it's easier for you than pretending to be human, and I should just trust and let things unfold. So I'd like to try it, if it's okay with you." Sharon looked at Sync's manifestation calmly.

Again, something about the human's calmness deeply surprised and therefore unnerved the 13D being. But Sync emanated assent in energy forms and made her 3D manifestation nod and smile.

"Okay, here we go!" said a communication that sounded distinctly like Petra. Then Sync was watching Sharon's actual memory of the incident.

#

"So these targets are chosen at random?" The ginger-headed newbie asked the pilot flying the helicopter.

There was a small guffaw. "That's what they told you?" the pilot asked conversationally. He looked forward and spotted the target easily on the trail. She was wearing a bright-yellow biking shirt of some sort and had a bright-orange bike. She appeared to be stopped along the trail, regarding something. With one hand he zoomed in a camera mounted on the outside of the helicopter. It appeared their target was peering at a lizard.

"Well, not exactly, but they made it sound like the targets were randomly chosen for our exercises."

At that, the pilot made a noncommittal noise. He was three months from finishing this assignment and wanted to keep his doubts about the work he had been doing to himself. He'd recently met a girl and wanted to get back to thinking about a particular way he'd like to screw her after dinner, and he didn't know if he wanted to get into anything deep with this guy. He also didn't know if the guy was a true believer, an internal spy, or a

Regular Joe.

After a silence, he decided to veer more towards the truth. "I've tracked this bitch a few times before, so I doubt there's anything random about her. In fact, other guys have tracked her as well. I have heard rumors, but really I have no idea why, based on what I've seen and what the other guys have said. She just rides that ugly bike or is out doing yard work or whatever, mostly hiking or biking. We track her when she's out in the middle of nowhere a lot. We only track her when she's alone. That seems to be a pattern—all of these targets, we track them when they are alone. Have you noticed that? Well, anyway, this particular dyke…never does anything…suspicious." There was silence, then: "Looky there! Whoa, she's only done that to me one other time." He felt a mixture of anger and a tinge of guilt.

They both watched the bicyclist intently as she looked up with an exaggerated grin and gave them a middle finger salute along with a clearly mouthed "Fuck you."

"So she knows we're tracking her?" The ginger turned in his seat to continue to stare at the bicyclist.

"Either that or she just doesn't like the noise we're making for her," the pilot said. He continued to fly straight on, as per protocol, to make the tracking seem as unobtrusive as possible.

"So why her?" the ginger asked.

"Why not? I really don't know what the deal is, but rumor is she went to UC Berkeley. Super smart. You know. Marxist commie lesbo, at least that's what I heard."

"Oh, well then fuck you, too, you little commie bitch. That's probably why we track your sorry ass," the ginger said without much malice before he turned to face forward again.

"Yeah, I don't get many of them flipping me off, but she's done that to a few guys. They've had her in their sights for a long time. Not sure why, she clearly isn't plotting anything, at least not out here. Rumor is she used to be pretty hot, so they just kept tracking her. But whatever, I don't really see it."

The ginger was satisfied with the level of accuracy they'd attained on the exercise. Photos had been taken as requested. The ginger made a note that indicated the target had been very easily located from her cell phone. He studied the information he had about his next target. "Okay, next one is—get this—a bleeding heart fucking immigration lawyer. He should be on I 25, about 7.5 miles north. The predictor algorithm says he will turn off on St Michael's. Prediction is he will then head west at the stop light, towards town." Static noise took over for a couple of seconds. "We should aim to intersect at about 11:19 AM according to this latest version of Finderfeed," he said cheerfully, referring to the locator software they were testing.

#

Sharon said nothing. The playfulness she'd been displaying just a few moments prior was gone. Sync scanned her for other reactions. There was no fear, only a sense of frustration and disgust manifesting as nausea.

Sync felt great sympathy for the human. It was clear that the recollection was spot on, and the ability to hear the humans in the helicopter was real. Sharon could somehow astral project so that she could see and hear other humans who were in the general vicinity. This ability was generally only known to be present in beings who could consciously access eleven, twelve, and thirteen dimensions. Yet here was a human from an infected planet with ability to do this. Who characterized her own abilities as proof that she was paranoid. Sync would share this new bit of information with Captain Cabeza as soon as possible.

In most parts of the known universes, Sharon's abilities would be a great blessing. But Sync immediately saw that because Sharon had been living on an infected planet, it was instead a nightmare for her to have those sensitivities. Sync had studied the planet's local ground norms and cultural contexts and knew that in this scenario, a few people might wonder if they were being tracked by military helicopters. But with these abilities, poor Sharon knew beyond a shadow of a doubt that she was being tracked by military men 'just following orders.' And yet people would label her crazy if she actually relayed how she came to this conclusion to other humans.

The callous disregard the soldiers had for the implications of their work was evident in their banter, and simply stunning to Sync. Clearly, the men did not care about anything other than the task at hand. It didn't matter to them that they were invading people's privacy, spying on citizens. They were just following orders. In fact, they seemed to feel superior about spying. As if they were doing something brave, not inherently shameful. Such a primitive response, so obviously born of Fear, and yet these humans were so turned around they managed to feel superior about it.

'The human ego, infected with this MMR strain, can rationalize almost anything.' Professor InDepth's words came back to Sync.

"Wow, that's horrible," Sync managed to say out loud.

"Yeah," Sharon said. "They don't see what they call 'targets' as fully human. They've been thoroughly trained to not access any emotions for others while they are working. That's how they can do what they do."

Sharon said this without emotion, just a tinge of sadness in her tone.

Sync was appalled. "They try to rid them of emotion? But what about...compassion?" Her voice trailed off.

Sharon laughed bitterly. "That's actually the very first thing they try to train out of them."

Sync looked at Sharon in horror.

Sharon registered Sync's shock and said, "You're surprised? No, I'm serious. It's actually a pretty foundational part of military training. The military branches try hard to make machines out of humans. They train them to make it so their natural empathies and sympathies, and their compassion disappears and...uh...doesn't get in the way of following orders to use force or otherwise violate people's rights."

Sync, stunned, continued to look horrified.

"Yeah, it's absolutely horrendous if you really think about it. Problem is, many people don't really think about it. They just sort of accept it as part of life. As if it's natural, and not a supremely twisted bit of cultural illness, like slavery or witch burning was. It seriously makes me nauseous if I think about it too much. But yes, they honestly do try to train compassion out of humans. Specifically and precisely so they can be good soldiers who can use force and kill others when directed. Which is how these 'good guys' win 'fights for democracy.' Sorry, that last part, though true, was a bit sarcastic," she said quietly.

Sync's energies were still frozen in shock. Sharon, used to the defensiveness of other humans, looked at Sync curiously for a moment. Then she grimaced in sympathy as she realized Sync was truly horrified.

"It's sick, and people don't really see it clearly

down on Earth. Or they'd stop it," Sharon said patiently. "But obviously, if a soldier were to think compassionately, they wouldn't kill anyone or invade their privacy, or consider them as 'less than' or anything. So, yeah, they actively try to train these humans to become less compassionate.

"And the training works. Most of these guys really do see themselves as honorable. They are oblivious to the fact that the end game is always focused on accumulating more power over others, rather than promoting prosperity for all. They don't think about how sad and…they don't think about how stunted what they do really is."

Sharon stopped here and looked with some pain in Sync's direction. "The 'leaders' must know. But they are so greedy and fucking power hungry, they keep tracking pacifists like me, and training soldiers to become less than human, so they can kill people…to keep the peace." Sharon shook her head.

"Again, apologies for the sarcasm," she added.

Previously, Professor InDepth's assessment of how twisted military thinking was had seemed like hyperbole to Sync. But, if anything, InDepth had downplayed how destructive the military tactics really were. Training to lower compassion amounted to this entire—very powerful—industry actively working to make awareness as difficult as possible, if not impossible, for humans to attain. Sync mused that this bit of cultural illness was very much like an autoimmune response. The normal protective functions had gone completely haywire.

Because somehow on this planet, objectifying others and actively trying to decrease human connection between soldiers and others was seen (by some, at least) as a good thing! How stunningly misguided. Sync could now see how those who had compassion for Others would be seen as…traitorous…in this kind of "thinking."

Sync then remembered InDepth's comment that the soldiers were repeatedly told that they were heroes. Heroes! InDepth had insisted that throughout the known universes, when MMR had been found, embedded in the entire worldview of the afflicted were ideas that normalized and, even worse, actually celebrated violence and militarism, painting these things as brave and courageous, not shameful and primitive!

Sync had intellectually understood this must happen, but could not fathom how the soul and emoti elements in humans could have been so ignored. She had thought the Professor's interpretation must have overlooked something, that the 5D and 6D elements simply could not have allowed such utter barbarism.

But Sync had forgotten about the role of Hubris. It was Hubris that really allowed such foolishness! She'd just witnessed a stunning level of Hubris in both of the men in the helicopter. Now she could see how humans like them, stripped for generations of their personal senses of natural wisdom, would start to believe anything authority figures told them. Especially if those in authority then stroked their egos and told them they were heroes when they acted according to plan. These humans would naturally become hubristic about their worldviews—so righteous and defensive about their beliefs that they couldn't be open to receiving messages from their own souls or emotis, much less Others to whom they felt superior. The absurdity was truly sickening.

"Would you like to take a break? I'd like to briefly check in with a colleague, if that's okay with you," Sync said. She needed time to digest what she'd seen. She also needed to talk with InDepth again to better understand how these beings got so badly off track.

"Yeah," was the only reply. Sharon emanated sadness, and Sync could see energy drain from her as she tried to suppress her feelings.

Sync said, "I really don't know in your case, but it might make you less tired if you just let yourself emanate the emotions for a few minutes."

Sharon responded with a nod. "I honestly don't know if I can do that...I think I've forgotten how. You have to understand, guys like those two seem to be everywhere. Just everywhere. Probably because they follow me, but still." She laughed humorlessly. "And often with guys like those two, it's a super ugly confluence of people who are caught up in religiosity as well. I mean some of these people actually believe they are acting according to God's will, that it is God's will that they be 'heroic' and 'protect' America...by killing people when necessary."

She emitted another strangled little guffaw. "I, uh, really don't go over well with those types—you know, being a Marxist commie lesbo, and all—so I try to stay under the radar as much as possible, unless I know who I am around. Because in some cases, uh, it can get potentially dangerous. Being a smart woman down there is hard enough, but you can just forget about getting any unconditional acceptance if you're also a smart, loudmouthed, leftist, lesbian pacifist. It just brings out the worst in the brainwashed military types." She smiled wryly. "I am white, though. It's probably the only reason they haven't offed me already."

Sync emanated sympathy. "Yeah, I can imagine you wouldn't want to attract much attention from people like that."

"I try hard not to 'tread on them,'" the human said with some hint of sarcasm. "They are far, far stupider than rattlesnakes, and more angry and righteous, too. Any nine-year-old can see the flaws in their logic, but they sincerely can't. Jesus!"

"Are you going to be okay?" Sync asked. It was clear that Sharon's anger was gathering steam.

Sharon tried to reel herself in. "Ah, shit, I'm sorry. This is…this is what happens when I let emotions flow."

Sync murmured something about accepting the emotions as being there and being valid, but not trying to express them.

Sharon paused thoughtfully, then said, "Okay, yeah, good point. I forget that. I'll try." She flashed a sad smile. "I've got to remember to find the graceful responses. It's so easy to lose sight of them, you know?"

"I can't even imagine," Sync said sympathetically. She sent calming, soothing, and most importantly, *belonging* energy to the human for a few seconds. Then she started to fade out slowly. "Like I said, I'll be back in a few minutes, okay?"

Sharon forced another smile. "Okay." Then she got up and went into the kitchen area to get more juice.

Fun Facts For Sharon

Sync quickly found Professor InDepth who had, along with a couple of other crew members, just finished creating a quickly compiled and nonnetworked version of the Basic Newbie Fact Packet. She also got an update on the progress on Sharon's Tribe Talk device. Sync and InDepth spoke for a few minutes about the stunning things Sync had seen and heard from Sharon. When InDepth took on Sync's usual role and asked Sync what she needed, Sync allowed her most sensitive aspects to feel a deep sadness and grief for the plight of the humans. She wept. It was really was what needed to happen. It helped.

A few minutes later, Sync tinkled her bell and slowly manifested back into the living room area. She was happy to see that Sharon's mood had lifted. Petra was flitting in and out of the room, and let Sync know she had told a couple of small jokes that seemed to cheer Sharon up. Sync consulted her internal "clock" (lol) and was surprised to find the afternoon had flown by. She checked in with Sharon briefly. Sync then suggested they were at a natural stopping point for the day.

Sharon agreed. "Yeah, I am actually quite tired, but this—being able to talk freely to you—is so…refreshing. I mean it's extremely odd and weird, and surreal, and I'm sorry I am so critical of the humans down there, but it's such an overall good thing to be able to talk about it, I can't even tell you. I really have appreciated your listening to me very much. It makes me feel less alone."

Sync was touched and said so. Then, after a small pause, she deliberately changed her tone. "Look, I know I'm throwing a ton of stuff at you right now. I can't imagine how strange all this must seem. But there are several things I want you to know. The first and foremost is that we are very excited to have you on board, and we want you to feel as comfortable and safe as possible. That's always going to be the first priority for us.

"Second, we have a kind of manual for newly aware beings. It's tailored to you as best as we can tailor it right now. This is a nonnetworked version of it. The online version will have much more information, but I think that it might be good for you to spend the rest of today just accessing this manual, and maybe doing things you enjoy, like getting a little exercise, or watching videos...or something." Sync was grasping a little, not quite knowing how to help the human feel comfortable. She also really did not want to bring up the option of Sharon going home to Earth after the end of the assessment period—which would conclude after Sharon met with InDepth, so she avoided any mention of that.

"We're also working on a device that will allow you to understand other beings. Right now I am speaking to you in English because I can, but normal ship interactions are done via a device called a Tribe Talk, which needs to be fitted for each species. Because humans in your...uh, circumstances haven't been aware in great numbers before, we are having to create a specialized one. It should be ready tomorrow."

Sharon looked puzzled. "Are you talking about a...oh, what's it called? Petra?" She called out loud for Petra. "Petra, can you hear me? What's that thingy called? You know, the Douglas Adams thingy?"

Petra's energies whooshed about, and she supplied the term 'Babelfish' out loud.

"Yes!" Sharon looked triumphant.

Sync looked surprised. "Oh, I'm afraid I don't

know that term. What's a Babelfish?"

"A kind of fish that slips into a person's ear and translates, so different species can understand each other. But it exists only in science fiction, as far as I know," Sharon said.

"Babel Babel Babel," Petra said playfully. Her response seemed to tickle Sharon. Both were suppressing smiles.

Sync chuckled at Petra as well, and then turned her attention back to Sharon. "Yes, I suppose it's very much like that. We are creating kind of Babelfish for you, but it's not animate, per se. We call it a Tribe Talk."

Sharon looked a bit overwhelmed briefly, but nodded. "Cool," she said.

"Tomorrow we'll introduce you to Meg, and other crew members, including the Captain. In the meantime, feel free to access as much information as you want to, but please do try to pace yourself. If you feel any sense of anxiety, or worry, or fear, please stop and reassure yourself that you are safe here with us, because you are. And, because it's our way to be completely honest, I must tell you, we are mixing in a small amount of calming compounds into your atmosphere, so please don't worry about how you are reacting to things. You are indeed underreacting, but it's okay. We are sincere in wanting you to be safe on this ship and in these quarters. We cherish you."

Sync watched with interest how Sharon's heart seemed to receive the love she sent with the last words and then immediately turn from it so she could remain composed. How primitive and unnecessarily complex!

Sharon swallowed. "Thanks, Sync. I really appreciate that. And, yeah, I kind of suspected I was on some...medication or something." She paused, then apparently deciding to leave caution behind, went on.

"Really I thought, and I do still think…uh, anyway, I thought I must be on mushrooms. And quite honestly, between you, me, and Petra, I wish this medication could be piped in all over that planet. Especially into certain places where certain types of people gather, like war rooms and places where politicians make back room deals. But, uh…anyway…thanks for telling me."

She began to turn away, but stopped and added, "You know, this is all very strange, and it may be the meds, but it's…" She searched for the appropriate word and finally settled on, "…weirdly delightful. Yes, this whole experience is extraordinarily weird, but it's also delightful. So thank you!"

\#

Greetings of the day

from your friends at the CC, Sharon!

We will start today's information transmission by introducing you to your Basic Newbie Fact Packet. Because it is still being developed and still nonnetworked, it will be a highly abbreviated transmission, but we figure, it's better than nothing, right?

First Fact:

There is a rather large Standardized Template called the 'Basic Newbie Fact Packet,' which houses lots of cultural information and facts about the types of entities, beings, species, and modes of aware animation that reside within the Convening Collaborative's boundaries. You won't be receiving the Standardized Template, no one does. This is because the Standardized Template is absolutely humongous. To try to explain exactly how many topics are included within the ST

BNFP would make your head explode, and we will never ever put you into known danger, especially not of that magnitude. There are numerous safety precautions in place!

But just so you know, we will be using a personalized version of 'ST BNFP 3D, Intell-3,' which is average. And that is something to celebrate! The majority of individuals from your planet, in your spacetimecontinuum and timeline, would have their Fact Packet personalized from 'ST BNFP, 3D, Intell- (arrested at) 2.5- blockages due to cultural MMR infection' version. The vast majority of your current leaders (lol) would need to be supplied with personalized variations based on the 'ST BNFP 3D, Intell- (arrested at) 1.5- severe blockages due to cultural MMR infection with additional Special Needs due to: 1) Generalized Fear Based Thinking; and 2) Dangerously high levels of Hubris; with clinically dangerous levels of Acquired Greed and Acquired Callousness (both acquired issues resulting from Hubris and Fear Based Thinking).'

General Asides to the First Fact:

Newly arrived entities and/or beings are analyzed on several levels to ascertain what they already may know or intuitively understand about the known universes within the CC. Things like the dimensional level(s) they naturally exist in, the number of dimensions they are aware in and can perceive in (which are often different), their species' processing mechanisms and capabilities, and their own individual processing capabilities vis-a-vis the averages of their species. A large part of the assessment is about their ranges of emotions, with special emphases on their baseline for Goodness, and emotions known to inhibit Goodness, as well as a few other things.

The Basic Newbie Fact Packet is then

customized for the entity or species. In most cases, like yours, Sharon, the Fact Packet is personalized down to the individual level, rather than the species level. The appropriate information packets are then transmitted in a format that is comfortingly familiar to the species/individual (which from here on out known will be referred to as 'you,' 'Sharon,' or 'Doober') to support a sense of security in a transitional time we know is fraught with uncertainty, confusion and fear—much more on the fear aspect later, we promise!

Here is an example that will attempt to illustrate how the Standardized Template and your Basic Newbie Fact Packets differ. The first quote below is the literal English translation of the entry for the number of known facts in the known universes. It reads as follows:

*The known facts of the known universes number well into the 999***9^^N 3*555&&&& Septi-teraed quintupled cubed mega gazillion million, and counting as of <fill in today's date using species specific calendar notation here: **December 5, 2019**>. When the number reaches 9999***9^^N 9*998&&&& Octo-teraed octupled cubed mega gazillion million, the CC will begin to develop (by committee, of course, lol) another term for the new category of number. The last committee took <fill in with species specific calendar units here: **60 Earth years**> to decide on a new number. It is anticipated that due to <fill in species specific generalized equivalent, if applicable, here: **something very much like Moore's Law**> this time will be reduced due to our abilities to comprehend new facts. The new committee will probably work faster! Lol, lol, lol. As if!*

Our official translation for your Basic Newbie Fact Packet reads:

The number of known facts in the known universes, Sharon, is well beyond your comprehension of infinite. We know lots already, but we are still learning. Do not be afraid, we will not harm you.

We sincerely hope we've done a Good job in our translation efforts, and if you ever feel like your perception of an experience is drastically different from your personalized version of the Basic Newbie Fact Packet, please communicate this to Meg—don't worry, we'll formally introduce you to her soon. But it may be comforting to know that you two have already met! Anyway, from here on out we will refer to your Basic Newbie Fact Packet by its official name or by the acronym, 'BNFP.'

When you need to use the BNFP for 'on the fly' learning—and you will!—your spoken or outgoing mind commands to manifest it will need to include the officially recognized names for it, or a readily inferred reference to it, such as: 'The Fact Book,' 'That facty thing,' or 'The book thing, dammit.' Other variations may be added as the AI self-learning components responsible for your (networked) BNFP updates get to know you better.

Second Fact:

Our Auspicious Beginning:

The Convening Collaboration's birth is commonly referred to as Year 3 in the common Tribe Communication calendar. Please note however, that the full calendar notation is for the birth is: ALL D; ALL ST Cont; ALL tl, graft 3.

In the full calendar notation:

ALL D means 'All dimensions'

ALL ST Cont means 'All spacetimecontinuums'

ALL tl means 'All timelines'

Graft refers to standardized CC year equivalent. Please note, the CC's counting system is not a base 10 system. Trust us when we say it is too complicated to explain here, but our counting system is based in several dimensions you are unaware of, and tangentially because of this, the system is based on what you humans call pi. We are in 'graft' 3.1415. Your universe is around 13 billion years old, but the CC's age of 3.1415 is exponentially older, which makes sense given that there are an infinite number of universes. The next graft will be 3.14159, of course.

Earth has existed in five (known) spacetimecontinuums (excluding of course, the literary excursions found in many of your excellent sci-fi books). You live within the fourth one.

Here's how today's date on Earth looks in the official calendar notation: 3D; 4ST Cont; tl-6 (unknown); graft 3.1415; (U) = Most countries: 5/12/2019; Chinese: 2019年12月5日; In Sharon's American style: 12/5/2019.

Notes: We do not know for sure if there are only 6 timelines, so '(unknown)' is added for informational purposes. Next, '(U)' refers to the term 'Unaware,' which tells the reader that the majority (or all) of the life forms found in this ST Cont and tl are Unaware. Finally after the '=' sign, the planet's main current calendar notation.

On Earth, where the majority of beings are Unaware, there are several ways of notating the same date! This needless confusion is usually due to the stunted egoic states of the beings, and the Hubris they possess that disrupts and displaces understanding.

In places where there are (a majority of) aware beings, a planet wide or entity wide notation is used, and it usually includes the CC's system with a local time added at the end. In fact, the CC's notation system is used exclusively by all entities and beings at and beyond 6D.

Aside: On planets with other aware species, there is usually just one language. Aside to the aside: Many planetwide languages contain millions of words. For contrast, English contains about 171,476.

Third Fact:

Well, let's quit with all that talk of numbers, shall we? One of the main differences between aware beings and Unaware beings is the understanding and use of Fear. Fear causes insecurity, insecurity causes defensiveness, defensiveness causes...a bunch of things, but the bottom line is that Fear gets in the way of understanding, big, big, big time. All of awareness is about understanding at different levels. You are in a completely unfamiliar place and we understand (see what we did there?) that this will—at times—be frightening and overwhelming, as well as being incredibly interesting and exciting! This is true for all Newly aware or (as seems to be in your case, Sharon) Semi aware beings.

We created this teaching song for you. It is adapted from a song taught to the relatively few and unlucky CC members coming from areas where there are diseases born of Fear. Well, it's probably more accurate to call it a ditty. Please note, Sharon, the verse at the end is included for a specific reason that is a bit out of place here, but we want you to be exposed to this verse as soon as possible because there could be times when you may be—temporarily—thrust back onto Earth or some other unfamiliar Unaware environment without warning. Try not to be alarmed by that sentence. No, really, try not to be alarmed by it. Focusing on the song will help. We promise.

Amygdalas in Overdrive

Amygdalas in Overdrive
Will not ever let you thrive!

Amygdalas in Overdrive
It's when our IQs take a dive!

Amygdalas in Overdrive
Produce xenophobic little hives

Don't be Over active!
Don't be Over active!

Amygdalas in Overdrive
Is when we act like we are five

Amygdalas in Overdrive
That's how the hateful thoughts survive:-(

Amygdalas in Overdrive
The only time war arrives!

It's way better to think it through
Than believe the silly lies are true
Don't be Over active!
Don't be Over active!

Amygdalas in Overdrive
Will not ever let you thrive

Amygdalas in Overdrive
It's when our IQs take a dive

Amygdalas in Overdrive
Make us fearful and connive

I am able to stay real calm
When I sing this little psalm,
Don't be Over active!
Don't be Over active!

When…my…Amygdala's in Overdrive
My IQ takes a humongous dive
When I'm calm and think it through
I'll know more than I ever knew!

****

Don't be a stupid* pig
Calm down your brain and eat a fig
The natural fruit that's good for you
They taste great and steer you true
Full of wisdom and compassion
The time for figs is always in fashion
After you eat a fig, go ahead and say "Ta Da"
Because they will surely calm your amygdala!

*The words 'sexist,' 'racist,' 'homophobic,' 'classist,' 'ageist,' 'status monkey,' 'elitist snob,' or 'general dickhead' can all be used interchangeably here as needed.

Aside: Technically, in Earth's most proper English, the plural of amygdala is amygdalae, but within the CC we prefer the more common way of pluralizing nouns. Sounds a bit less pretentious, we think.

Aside: For a 2D video of Nervonians singing the first few verses of this Reducing Fear Song, please access here. We'll wait.

Aside to the Aside: We chose to include a video

of Nervonians doing this classic song for two main reasons:

1) They have five heads, so their choreography and harmonies are spectacular, and

2) The Captain of this ship is a Nervonian. Research on other humanoids has given us the knowledge that when humans first become familiar with other kinds of beings in situations that feel fun and playful, they tend to generalize their attraction to the whole species. When you meet her, we're sure you will agree: Captain Cabeza is a wonderful Captain!

Fourth Fact:

You have your own bathroom in your quarters, of course. If you need to use the bathrooms while on the main parts of the ship, you will need to request one to manifest. They do not actually exist on most of the ship. This is because many beings do not need to eliminate waste at all, and others only eliminate but once a year or so. Most beings that need to, void into their ship suits directly, which have built-in, species specific mechanisms to handle any waste products. Since that is a very foreign concept for you, and does involve a little potty training, your ship suit will not be fitted with this feature until you've thoroughly acclimated to ship life. Instead, please just ask for a 'restroom' to be manifested with a mind command. One will manifest very quickly.

Please remember to make this request using the wording 'restroom' or 'bathroom.' Please do not mistake any rooms marked WC for water closets. That would be bad. WCs are rooms for spiritual contemplation. WC stands for Wisdom and Compassion. You will find lots of yoga equipment and lovely, tranquil environments within these rooms. Please, under no circumstances try to use any bowls or sinks or ponds in a WC as a toilet. Thank You.

Aside: You may of course, enter WC rooms at any time once you are authorized to roam freely about the ship.

Fifth Fact:

This is actually advice, not a fact: Remember to pace yourself and not fill your head too full with new information all at once.

Sixth Fact:

Uh, the algorithms indicate it is time for a break.

Seventh Fact:

You are already aware of 'mind commands,' but we are adding this section to your nonnetworked version of this BNFP. It will be modified in future versions you receive, but we know you like to read, so we added it here.

Mind Commands How We Communicate (3D Basic):

Introduction: Mind commands are the usual form of communication among aware beings. Ideas, concepts, energies, and utterances sent through telepathic modes are the most common forms of mind commands. However they are also found in written form and in holographically available forms as well, called 'As Neededs.' Mind commands can range in complexity, from 'Tonight's special is our award winning winter squash and portabella mushroom loaf, drizzled with a sesame ginger sauce,' to 'Stop On Red,' to dissertation-length packets of information, complete with <shudder> complex statistical analyses. Mind commands come in two broad forms: accessible mind commands (often in the form of As Neededs), and incoming mind commands.

The terms are not capitalized except for As Neededs.

In Brief: Accessible mind commands are the

rough equivalent to the signs, printed matter, and prerecorded information you are used to accessing on Earth. Incoming mind commands are the rough equivalent of speech, and are mostly used between a few beings, although senior crew and Captain Cabeza will occasionally issue widely distributed incoming mind commands in the form of requests or, rarely, orders from a Centralized Mind Unit Channel.

History of Mind Commands: Mind commands were first developed by Wintonesians. It may interest you to know that the plurality of species aboard this ship are Wintonesians—they are fabulous communicators!

Aside: Wintonesian poetry is beautiful.

Aside to the Aside: Wintonesian communication architects consider your Emily Dickinson's short lines, with their innumerable interpretations, to be pretty cool work, for a human. And bonus: it appears she was Semi aware, although she never communicated with the CC, since no CC ships on official business were in the vicinity during her lifetime.

Eighth Fact:

Boundaries of the Convening Collaborative change daily, but in general, Sharon, anywhere you go will be within its boundaries and you will be afforded all rights, privileges, and protections as member of the Collaborative as a courtesy. We do hope you will decide to join as an active member. We can tell you have a lot of good things to offer.

Tribe Talkin' By The CC

Might Makes Right
We've come to fight
We've made a blight
Of everything in sight

Might Makes Right
We'll prove our right
By starting fights
Both day and night

In a world of Might Makes Right
The grip on power is tight
By those who reach the height
In the matrix of which I write

But it's clear to all who have eyes
That the world is causing its own demise

The old world is dying
And there is no more denying
That when we realize we are all part of one
We'll know real civilization has finally begun.

We'll reach another dimension
Some might call it an ascension
But I see it more as awareness
Simply more awareness.

The poetry, such as it was, was being projected
onto a screen that the participants were peering at as
Professor InDepth read it aloud. It was clearly still in
draft form, as there were many crossed out words, and
the handwritten words 'the whole thing is shit' were

penciled into the right hand margin.

InDepth paused and shook her head somewhat sheepishly before continuing. "Our Honored Guest's communications are not all like this, thankfully. But it's a simple level of language we can use as a minimum baseline in the Tribe Talk device." She shuddered theatrically. A few chuckles erupted in the room.

She moved on to the next slide. "What's interesting is this human actually uses terms like 'awareness,' 'Might Makes Right,' 'spacetimecontinuums,' and the phrase 'all is one and one is all.' She also wrote a story that very much mirrors the 'No More Tangles, No More Tears' event on the planet now called Beneficus in the Solarium Congiarium."

A couple of committee members expressed some surprise. Others furiously took notes. InDepth looked over her ocular enhancers and paused to let them finish.

"And a little earlier today, Officer Sync shared with me some other bits of our Honored Guest's writing. I have to say, the sentiments in that piece are quite advanced for a human in this spacetimecontinuum. In fact, we may be able to use some of her ideas to design new interventions to try to combat the MMR in some places that have the infection, and on Earth. Speaking of which, as all of you are aware, we now have a new mission to help Earth try to recover from MMR without resorting to the radiation cure. I've scheduled an intervention team meeting for later today with a large invite list. If you somehow did not receive an invite, please do come anyway. As many crew as we can have actively involved will be a blessing for the mission. At that meeting I will brief you all on the ideas that have recently come to light from her writings. They are really quite promising, and I hope you'll all be there." InDepth flashed a serious smile.

"Now, let's return to the topic of this meeting." InDepth used a pointer to direct the group's attention back to the rhymes on the screen.

"All right then. I hope you all are at least somewhat familiar with human anatomy by now, but here's a short summary. They are pure humanoids, with the classic five humanoid senses available to use in their quests for awareness. And like other pure humanoids, they have two arms, two legs, a torso, with one stomach and various inner organs. They have one head, and a basic brain. They have no extra brains." There were murmurs at this fact.

"Yes, they are quite simple in their processing capacities; their brains are fully within their heads, and they are as yet unable to modify their capacities. In the very recent past they have created devices they call smart phones—which are multifunction devices they carry with them that need…uh…an eternal source of electrical energy to function." At that, there were murmurs all around the table about the crazy inefficiency of devices needing external energy.

InDepth held up a hand. "Yes, they are wildly inefficient, but humans do not yet know how to use their own life energies to run these devices. In actuality, these phones are, of course, rudimentary extra brains, but most humans do not seriously see them as such at this stage in their development."

A new slide went up: a simple drawing of a human head, with various parts labeled. The slide also contained an inset depicting the inner workings of the human ear. InDepth immediately zoomed in on that.

"Humans have ears, located quite near their brains, as most other humanoids do. And, as you are undoubtedly aware, Tribe Talks are inserted into humanoid ears—usually. We are assuming this will be best for our Honored Guest as well. We'll be using a generic humanoid Tribe Talk device as a basis for building our Honored Guest's device. Any questions so far?"

There was a pregnant silence as the committee members shook their heads and looked attentively at each other. Professor InDepth paused for a beat before concluding with the standard meeting prayer lines. "May we work well together and prosper. May we find meaning to better all our lives. May we become aware of the answers we are seeking and better all our lives. May we be guided by Goodness. May we always find wonder in the singularity." She bowed her head slightly as she intoned the last sentence.

Besides Professor InDepth, Sync, several Wintonesians, and the main Apel were all gathered in one form or another in a conference room. The materially based members all performed the customary head nod of agreement as InDepth finished her last line. Then they all replied more or less in unison, "Praise Goodness!"

Apel's bodily presence was actually a very sophisticated hologram that could move fairly heavy objects and feel things on a bodily level. Her brain and real body were in what was commonly called a communication bath on another Solarium, light years away. The technology was advanced, but these baths were able to induce a state very similar to dreaming in the being who was teleporting. In many ways, Apel was dreaming her way through the meeting. The major difference between humanoid style dreaming and hologram teleportation is that beings are able to recall the interactions they have during baths with markedly better detail and accuracy than they normally recall normal day to day interactions.

All Apels called themselves Apel. It had to do with how they conceived of their interconnected consciousness as a species. And although it sounds confusing, it is surprisingly easy to figure out differences between each Apel. When talking about them, other species simply attached traits to the name to help distinguish between them: Funny Apel, Apel with the expertise in Chi, Tall Apel, Super bendy Apel, the dog-loving Apel, etc.

Some of the Wintonesians were a little wary or unsure about how to respond to Apel today. The species had very recently come up with technology for communication that appeared to substantially improve upon the universally used Tribe Talk technologies that Wintonesians had contributed eons ago to the known universes. Apel's undeniably superior technology was being rolled out in new Tribe Talk devices. But all beings in the meeting were Goodness based beings, with egos well in check at this stage of awareness. They were—as always—committed to working collaboratively.

This Apel was super smart, very gracious, sleekly designed, and sexy, to boot. Though both Apels and Wintonesians are humanoids, Wintonesians tend to be rather grey and...utilitarian...in appearance. But Wintonesians as a species were quite secure in their Goodness and the ones at the meeting were drawn to and admired this Apel's sleek body. Of course, it was possible the hologram was adding a few flourishes to her appearance. Even aware beings were known to throw in a little physical enhancement to their appeal here and there.

Truthfully, a few Wintonesians also felt a little competitive and intimidated by Apels. Certainly the touchscreen communications installed on all GSS craft now were based in part on Apel innovations that Wintonesians had initially ignored. But the standard working through of ego-based emotions was understood to be a process of growth throughout the CC. After all, this is exactly what PFFF training is about and where it comes in handy! No one was in denial or protective of their reactions. Still, for most humanoids, it takes some effort to keep primitive egoic reactions in healthy check. Especially in the case of newly arrived refugees. And there was one refugee among the Wintonesians at the meeting.

She was from the most problematic area in the known universes, which consists of four planets in the Solarium of Onychomycosis. Among those planets, MMR manifests more or less as it does on Earth, complete with extreme economic inequality, pay gaps, domestic violence, militaristic mindsets, and something that closely resembles Corporate Capitalism. In other words, the Apels and Wintonesians living on the four inhabited planets there are all ruled by fear and violence. There are militaries there (sic!). Dissent is quashed in some areas of the solarium by any means necessary, and large propaganda networks had devolved to farcical levels. 'War is necessary for peace keeping, and we must keep creating weapons to ensure a peaceful future' their politicians would say without an inkling of irony. None!

In this sad area, Wintonesians and Apels are mostly Unaware, and still engage in terrible power struggles with each other. They are infected with MMR and have very little awareness that they are infected. There are aid groups from the CC, but they can only help in limited ways. Primitivism such as sabotage (sic) and Winds of Ill Intent course through the entire fabric of spacetime and matter in this area. The sicknesses of

Greed and Callousness, as well as Fear and Hubris are still pervasive, leading to the deaths of millions of beings every decade. Still, some manage to become aware, resulting in a steady stream of refugees from the solarium. The CC welcomes and supports all refugees for several months, while they acclimate to life among the aware in the known universes.

The refugee at the assembled meeting was named Intra, and she was a talented engineer. She and her family had escaped fairly recently, and Intra was still in the later stages of acclimating to the high Goodness levels prevalent on the ship and in the known universes in general. As such, Intra was also still shedding her fears. It can be quite a shock to live among aware beings whose compassion and generosity consistently stays in the front and center of all their interactions. Wonderful stuff, but a bit overwhelming.

The lack of a need for Fear takes several months—sometimes years—for refugees to get accustomed to. It was a challenge for Intra to be in the same room with the hologram, at this meeting, but strangely liberating as well.

Apel, born in a Solarium among gazillions of firmly aware, longstanding members of the CC, was graciously deferential to Intra and the other Wintonesians. But the Wintonesian device they were modifying was a bit clunky, and if the human could rapidly advance in her awareness, the device they proposed would be outgrown very quickly and they'd need to make another one within as little as a few weeks. Assuming the human chose to stay, of course. All in the room were aware that the human had just come on board. But they also knew about her soul's request to be rescued, so there was really no reason to think she might want to go back to an infected planet, from their perspectives.

Apel spoke up as diplomatically as possible in the graceful, almost poetic way the Apels have. "As you just pointed out, Professor InDepth, the human's words range from incredibly sophomoric to quite graceful. And as we all know, being able to practice gracefulness in challenging situations is a strong indicator of a being's propensity to grow in awareness. So, since she presumably has this capacity, and is already settling in, I propose we build in room for as much growth as possible."

Intra sniffed. "And that would mean integrating your technology into the device, I assume." As soon as she said it, she felt a mixture of contrition and satisfaction. The other Wintonesians looked sideways at her and then quickly back at Apel. Sync was quietly observing from her area, ready to jump in if needed, but she assumed the materially based beings could help this refugee through her discomfort.

Apel smiled broadly at Intra and said, "I am aware you are newly from S.Ony, and I hope you are finding peace and solace here. I can't imagine having to live in an infected solarium and am very grateful for my luck to not have had to experience what you must have experienced living there. I bear you no ill will."

Intra was completely taken off guard by the reply, and her bravado left her immediately. All her desires about wanting to live in a world full of peace and prosperity came back to her in a flash. Her embarrassment over her actions was clear to all. "I apologize, that was out of line," she stammered almost immediately, her eyes welling up a little. The other Wintonesians cooed a little and emanated goodwill towards both Intra and Apel.

"Your apology is quick, sincere, and to the point.

I accept it with a heart full of goodwill towards you. I hope we can be friends," Apel said, steadily smiling at her.

And, as sometimes happens, the goodwill that results from beings understanding each other was hard to decipher, and Intra took it to be attraction. She blushed slightly, and looked away.

Sync stifled something like a smirk of energies, and spoke up. "Very good. Let's please reflect on the fact that our chief communications officer, Dos, has requested Apel be present due to the value that Apel technology can add to the already miraculous Tribe Talk technology that has existed for eons."

Communications Officer Dos nodded. "Very true, Sync. Apel, I think that it's a given that your interface technology is a good idea to allow for just such growth —and of course, this is growth that we hope will occur. I would like us to just move forwards with how to combine the technologies immediately. That is, unless anyone has any merit based objections," Dos added.

Various murmurs of agreement to move forwards emanated from the beings in the room, and they set forth to combining the technologies from the almost finished prototype the Wintonesians had already created.

Intra cornered Apel at the next break and apologized again. She then heard herself offering to be the test subject for the device once it was ready. She wasn't sure exactly whether it was due to feeling contrite, or wanting to prove that she wasn't boorish, or, if it had to do with perhaps wanting to know Apel better. Apel looked at her for a moment and then gave her a warm smile. "Okay. But I want you to know, I really do understand that your circumstances may have you feeling mistrustful of the intentions of someone like me, an Apel.

"And I wish to assure you, I am not, nor will any of me will ever be attempting to harm or block you——or any other Goodness motivated being—in any way. I speak of course only for the parts of me that live without the infections from which you escaped."

"But I escaped from the planet in order to not do the very thing I just did back there." Intra's communication was plaintive.

"We all realize that, Intra, and I assure you, I am—and all who witnessed the event are—heartened by your ability to immediately recognize your reaction, and own it so completely.

"This is, as you know, the hallmark of an aware being, to not cover up or remain stuck in mistakes. Awareness allows us to instead to acknowledge them, own them thoroughly, and above all, learn and change course due to learning from them.

"You reacted in an ego-based way, recognized it, and then you strove for Goodness. What else can anyone ask for?

"I know you are on a journey. We're all on similar journeys, although thankfully not as difficult as having to endure the hostilities of an MMR-infected planet.

"Do not be too hard on yourself. And please know you are surrounded by beings who wish to support you." With that, Apel gave a little bow and said, "I must be off to talk with Dos about a couple of logistics for combining our technologies."

"Thank you…" Intra said weakly.

"Oh!" Apel suddenly turned back around and addressed Intra again. "I think you will be a perfect test subject due to the similarities Wintonesians share with humans. And, most especially since you share a particular cultural experience with this human around enduring the MMR infection." Apel bowed again. "I anticipate that the committee will be happy to take you up on your offer!"

Intra looked pleased. Sync had been casually paying attention to the interaction. She had not been focused enough—until Apel mentioned it—to notice the happy coincidence of the team now having a test subject who recently left an environment where similar levels of Fear and mistrust were found. Excitedly, she informed Captain Cabeza of the newest bit of synchronicity, lol.

"There's been another small incident that lends support to the theory, Captain," she communicated to Cabeza, who was a full kilometer away in her command center on the vast ship. "I'll tell you about it later."

"Great!" Cabeza replied. Sync then turned her attention back to the committee and began urging the participants to return from their break.

Fourteen Earth hours later (about four hours and forty minutes later in CC time), the prototype was ready to test. The committee broke for a quick meal, but everyone was excited and wanted to get back to testing, so the BFD manifested food right in the conference room, and orderlies bustled in and out to clear dishes and feeding implements. Captain Cabeza herself had briefly appeared on video screen to offer her thanks and encouragement to the committee.

I Hear You

They were ready for the first test fitting. Sync moved energies around and suddenly the new device was floating near Intra. As Intra gazed in the corner where Sync's energies were strongest, and the rest of the committee looked on, Sync said, "Please give us honest feedback about all aspects of the experience. You may recall from your own fitting that there are standardized questions. Which reminds me, how was your initial fitting, Intra?"

"It fit perfectly," she replied.

"Well, good! So I assume you only were asked four or five questions, and calibration was not necessary?"

Intra nodded a little uncertainly, not understanding what Sync meant by calibration. Then she spoke up and said exactly that, instead of trying to play along. She was aware that she was holding some fear of being judged, but decided to risk the question rather than stay silent like she would have back on her planet of origin. To her deep surprise and relief, the entire room enveloped her in love and compassion, and many of the committee members, including Sync, were communicating energies as if they were extremely proud parents.

"Wonderful! That's your authentic truth, this is exactly what I meant," Sync said. Then she switched back to the subject at hand. "Often there are some minor glitches in the levels of…stuff." Sync faltered a bit. "When that happens, the levels of…stuff need to be calibrated manually. It usually only takes a couple of minutes when known beings are being fitted, but it can take a bit of time when less common beings are being fitted for the first time."

"Oh, you mean administering the being's proper ratios of selenium to molybdenum and manganese—the latter needed to protect and soothe the human's mitochondria. If those ratios aren't correct, then the appropriate amounts of topoisomerase needed to unwind the new language related bits of DNA are not produced." Intra face-palmed herself and said, "Well, duh, every Wintonesian knows that!"

Sync communicated a chuckle. "Yes, I suppose that's what calibration really consists of for this device."

The Wintonesians on the committee smiled good-naturedly at Sync's rather sheepish communication. Sync's knowledge of the chemistry-based components needed for each device was not deep by any stretch of the imagination. Her contributions to the committee were centered around the wearer's subjective experience and being able to quickly assess the linguistic, emotional, and semiotic accuracy of communications the wearer was creating in their own mind. She would then relay the findings to the Wintonesians mixing the chemicals, who would adjust the hormonal and other substance ratios as needed. The chemicals were absorbed in a time-released manner by an osmosis process near the being's processing center, so the communication would feel as natural as possible. Most beings left their devices in for months at a time. Some beings did like to turn the devices down if they were in particularly loud environments, or if the communications were not particularly interesting.

"So, again, it's quite likely we will need to calibrate, and please realize that there may be a substantial number of questions based on any discomforts or difficulties with comprehension or transmission from you to us."

At that point, Sync moved her energies around to

signify closure of her communication. Apel immediately stepped forwards, took the device from the air, and said, "May I?"

"Yes, by all means," murmured Intra, a bit smitten by Apel's piercing ocular devices.

Intra took her own Tribe Talk out, and Apel gently inserted the device in its place. Intra's world then got excruciatingly quiet for about ten seconds, as there was only silence at first. The volume on the Tribe Talk was set to zero upon insertion. Gradually Intra began to hear communications, and at the fifteen second mark, she solemnly put a finger up to indicate when it was at a comfortable level. The possibility of communications being far too loud were real, and no one wanted to shock the little mitochondria that had such important roles to play in receiving the signals from others.

At the sixteen second mark, Intra's finger was still raised. It was as if she was suddenly in a trance. Sync immediately told Apel to be ready to remove the device. She detected Fear. Intra was tensing up. Sync let it go to almost the eighteen second mark. By that time, the fear in Intra's eyes was easy enough for all to detect.

For Intra, it was as if she was in a dream. She couldn't understand what was being said. Quickly Apel pulled the device out from Intra's ear. She emanated reassurance as she handed Intra's own device to her. Intra's body language relaxed instantly once the device was out of her ear. As soon as Intra put her own device back in, she said, "Okay, whoa, that was scary."

Sync's attention was fully on Intra. "What's going on right now, Intra?"

Intra breathed in and out deliberately as she shook fear from her body like a dog might shake off water. "I was flooded with dread. Not sure why. Just sort of a bodily response."

"Are you feeling okay now, though?"

"Yes, yes, I am. Wow."

Sync emanated an apology and more reassurance.

"It's okay, I'm okay," Intra said.

Sync's energies continued to emanate concern and reassurance towards Intra. "Any ideas why the fear was so strong?" she asked of the group at large.

The Wintonesian responsible for mixing the elements and enzymes immediately spoke up. "Yes. I am really sorry. In hindsight, I should have let you all know this prior to the start, but I was torn between wanting Intra to have her own experience and not wanting to implant ideas of what might happen. I humbly apologize, Intra. The bodily fluids I was given to work with were chock full of cortisol and adrenal, human hormones that are secreted when the being is 'stressed out,' as they say on Earth. The levels were really high. So high, I thought somehow there was an error in the results, but the computer triple checked them for me.

"Due to the presence of those hormones, I needed to keep the input of the hormones high in the chemistry so the effect would feel familiar to Our Honored Guest Sharon. If we change the chemistry too much, beings spend too much available cognitive energy on trying to figure why they feel differently, and this significantly lowers their ability to comprehend what is being said. In short, we have to keep differences in hormones to a minimum or the experiential differences get in the way of the device working."

"You mean that amount of fear is normal for her?" Intra asked.

"Afraid so…er…no pun intended, sorry," was the response. The Wintonesian continued. "What we do with new species is to start with their current hormonal states, then as the being is able to understand communications, and their brains acclimate to the new inputs, we ask them to come in to adjust the hormone levels—as needed. For many aware species, we don't need to adjust the hormonal levels. But for refugees and new arrivals from infected environments, we do it all the time." The Wintonesian shook his head. "I am so sorry, Intra. No one meant to scare you."

"Oh, yes, of course. I remember going back and getting my levels adjusted a few times, that's right!" Intra said brightly. In a more scholarly tone she continued, "And I appreciate the efforts to not create a placebo effect by mentioning possible reactions ahead of time."

Intra bowed formally, a recognized communication of sincere appreciation and respect within the Wintonesians. Intra then publicly responded to an inquiry Sync sent her way via a private mind command. "I think the reason I was so affected is that it felt like I was back on the planet I came from. I sort of had a flashback."

Sync again emanated reassurance and gave the equivalent of a hug to Intra, who surprised herself by really allowing herself to feel comforted by it.

"Oh you poor thing," a committee member said.

Another Wintonesian angrily said, "That damned MMR. It needs to be eradicated from the known universes—and fast!"

Murmurs of agreement rippled through the committee. Apel looked forlornly at Intra and communicated as much reassurance to Intra as she thought the being could handle.

Intra felt it and gratefully looked up at Apel with tears in her eyes.

A few minutes later, Intra insisted that she could use her acquired stoicism with awareness and for the greater good in order to finish the testing. The committee members agreed after some discussion, and the testing continued. Luckily, a good fit was found rather quickly.

As an aside to readers of this tale: Apel admired how Intra handled the whole situation and asked her out for coffee after the meeting.

SlipFreud, The Electri-pipe, Sharon And The BFD

The next morning—while the Tribe Talk prototype was still being refined, in fact—there was a knock on the door. Sharon's quarters were located in the main D3 cabin area for passengers, but Sharon's had its own keyed entrance via a private hallway. Most GSSs (Government Space Ships) had several suites like this for passengers who needed more privacy, or who were in some sort of quarantine status, like Sharon was. The orderly was fairly used to dealing with Hermetic type species. The extremely introverted or shy beings who rarely wanted much contact with anyone were common enough. And he had—of course—been well trained in quarantine procedures, but this was the first time he was actually using them. And he had never encountered a human at all, as aware ones were quite rare. He wasn't sure what to expect. Meg (in her nonmaterial form) was keeping a very close eye on him to ensure things went as smoothly as possible. She felt a peculiar protectiveness towards the human and had taken quite a liking to Petra already.

The orderly immediately noticed that Sharon's eyes were wide as she opened the door. He knew this was a startle response from the packets of information he'd been perusing about humans. As a Sidi, he was perceptive, but a bit limited in the modes of perception that were available to him, much like the human. But he did have a high Goodness level, and was accepting of feedback and amenable to learning. He bowed graciously and was mimicking something called 'friendly, calming eye contact' to help the human feel more at ease. As a fairly young Sidi, and with Meg's coaching, he had been able to transform his facial features so that he appeared convincingly as a humanoid.

Sidis in their natural state look much more reptilian. However, residual camouflage functions in the species had evolved into a sophisticated ability to mimic many kinds of animated presentations. Some Sidis were so adept at mimicry that they accrued LifePoints by putting on shows where they transformed into completely different species. They produced award winning shows where they went from Centrails to Apels to hummingbirds to Nervonians to Wallerts to ferns, and finally to dolphins. Those who could transform into dolphins always closed their shows with deep bows and the line, "So long, and thanks for all the fish!"

This particular Sidi had been chosen to help with the Honored Guest today due to having a great gift for mimicry of sounds, and therefore, spoken language. His English mimicry was pretty darned good. He was unobtrusively wearing a quarantine suit. He also, of course, had access to his own personalized Fact Packet to help him if the human said or did things he did not understand.

He had spent half the night accessing all the information he could possibly stuff into his extra brain so he could be as prepared as possible to accommodate this unusual guest. The orderly had read that humans were primitive, but it was a different experience entirely to physically knock on the door as a way of announcing himself. What he'd been told was that Sharon Rubric had no way to access As Needed mind commands currently. None! He was here to help her learn how to recognize and access the various As Needed commands within her quarters. She also had not been fitted with a Tribe Talk device yet, so he needed to actually speak with her in English!

The split second after she opened the door, he noticed her wide eyes, as had been expected. But quite a bit of the human's short hair was also standing on end. It looked silly to him. Mentally kicking himself for reverting to egotism, he hid a smirk that had almost manifested and instead doubled down on presenting 'friendly, calming eye contact.' He knew 'smirking' could easily be perceived as rude or condescending, which he really did not want to be. He had a complex hormonal imbalance, for Uranus's sake, his was not willfully egoic behavior! He began to berate himself very briefly, but then remembered his training and quickly emanated Goodness. He was getting better; his therapy was paying off.

Back in discerning mode, he realized right away that she must have stood in the middle of the electri-pipeline. But how? It was clearly marked. Then he mentally face-palmed himself. That's exactly why he was here! She currently was limited by the blasted inability to access simple As Neededs. He marveled at how incapacitating that limitation really was. It was already manifesting (so to speak) in a physical way!

"Good morning, Honored Guest Rubric," he said in a very good imitation of English. "I am SlipFreud. I am at your disposal as a materially based guide or concierge. I'm here to help you manifest things, if you need assistance with that. Is there anything you want for break fast?"

Sharon smiled. He pronounced the word break-fast. She surreptitiously rubbed sleep out of her eyes as he spoke, as she immediately took in his beautiful, friendly, and somehow calming eyes. After he asked the question, she realized she was starving.

"Good morning. Please call me Sharon." She smiled at him. "What time is it?"

Rather than starting off with a complex and disconcerting explanation about the nature of time on the ship compared to Earth time, he rapidly searched the databanks in his extra brain and found the response he thought would be most appropriate. He smiled winningly and said, "Does anybody really know what time it is, does anybody really care?"

She looked at him with surprise and immediately relaxed. "I love that song, I'm surprised you know it."

SlipFreud allowed himself a small, self-satisfied grin, and then put on an attentive face for the human. He patiently explained that she could have just about anything she wanted for break fast, but she may need to describe substances in some cases.

Sharon smiled politely, but since Sync had helped her figure this out yesterday, and the BNFP had also explained this, she only half listened as he kept going on about it.

He was saying, "New substances are added all the time, and if you request a certain kind of substance, er, food, and the BFD does not produce a satisfactory substance, please feel free to reject the substance and modify—" He stopped in midsentence as he noticed her quizzical expression. "Where did I fail to communicate clearly, Honored Guest Sharon?" he asked kindly.

"BFD?" she asked, eyes still wide.

"Oh, in this case it means Bio Fuel Dispenser, so sor—" He stopped in midsentence again, and put his hand to his ear rather theatrically to indicate he was listening to an incoming clarification from his extra brain. He then politely willed his face to rapidly change expressions, and ended with a laugh and an apology. "I see, BFD translates to an inadvertent joke that might be considered rude to some. I am sorry if my reference to her—the dispenser—offended you."

Sharon laughed and said "No, no, the abbreviation just caught me off guard is all." Sharon privately thought it was a delightful mistake that the orderly had made by referring to the dispenser as a her, as if it were an animate being. She also again noticed how beautifully expressive his eyes were.

Meg, who had manifested the ice cream and spoken with Sharon already, and had taken the time to do more research on a certain human named Gladys Knight, had been listening with interest to the human's thoughts. As she absorbed Sharon's thoughts, she said to no one in particular, "Wow."

Sharon had already ushered SlipFreud in. Now, glancing at a mirror, she caught a glimpse of her hair. Horrified at its antics, she wondered what she had been exposed to. She had no idea she'd left the electri-pipe on full blast all night. She had also stood right in the middle of its projecting path for several minutes. She only knew that the blowing air in that particular space seemed to smell…no, smell wasn't quite the right word, but the air just seemed…healthy or nourishing somehow. If that was where they were pumping in the calming medications Sync had referred to, she was just fine with it. She'd inhaled deeply. Oh yes, she'd inhaled.

SlipFreud tried to ignore the Honored Guest's curious head patting while he patiently explained that her quarters had numerous embedded mind commands called As Neededs for various housekeeping issues. He explained there were As Neededs for how to use the physical BFD. Sharon had not noticed the physical BFD until now. It looked like a large toaster oven. In point of fact, it had not been there yesterday. Professor InDepth, an expert on humanoids, had thought the human might be more comfortable with a physical BFD, but now it only served to confuse Sharon a bit. She wasn't sure if it was just for creating food or for manifesting everything she asked for. Meg, watching from a corner of the room, couldn't resist the equivalent of an eye roll as she noticed Sharon's confusion.

SlipFreud further explained that As Neededs were forms of accessible mind commands. He said accessible mind commands were bits of information that beings accessed of their own volition. They weren't commands in the human sense of the word at all. They were simply bits of energy converted into information that were strategically placed to be accessible to the being to use as needed, hence the name.

"Incoming mind commands are slightly different," SlipFreud continued. "The being receives information somewhat involuntarily, but again, not necessarily as a command. I understand that for humans, Incomings are very much humans speaking out loud to each other. An Incoming could be from an orderly like me," he puffed up a bit, "informing a passenger that an art reception on D3 will commence at 5 P.M."

For what seemed like eons, SlipFreud explained how to summon toiletries and entertainment programs; he went on about summoning various forms of animated comfort, such as cats, or more passionate, ahem, aids for physical amour. He said As Neededs could be accessed to take in entertainment videos or to learn about certain technologies, or for almost any other items passengers might have questions about. As a special nicety for this unexpected passenger, the BFD had even manifested an old-fashioned waffle maker. It was only as SlipFreud pointed it out that Meg realized the waffle maker lacked an As Needed. She quickly manifested it as a semi-opaque floating screen with the words 'As Needed' in large font and 'Touch here for further instructions' in smaller font underneath it. Both SlipFreud and Sharon said, "Thank You!" simultaneously. At just that point, Sharon's mind grasped that the BFD was indeed quite animate somehow. She sent apologies into the ether.

Meg smiled and said to no one in particular, "Apology accepted, Honored Guest."

Sharon nodded her understanding of As Neededs in general. SlipFreud then further explained "Then sometimes you'll hear the word 'Aside,' which is, uh, an aside to the main bit of information." He thought Sharon looked a little puzzled. "They are little extra bits of information such as, 'Aside: If you get there after 6-ish, the artist may no longer be available.'"

"Ah," Sharon said, wondering why he was going on and on about things that she'd already figured out. Sync had been super intelligent, but this guy was...a bit slow, clearly. He did have kind eyes, though.

"Incoming mind commands can also be requests, such as the 'Please do not allow sound emanations to exceed forty decibels in the library.' Or they can be from beings not in the immediate vicinity, such as when there are 'All Ship Incomings' telling all on board that we have docked, or that we've...uh...won a GAG award."

SlipFreud looked very self-satisfied as he added that last part. Sharon decided not to ask him anything about that right now. God only knew how long he would talk.

Meg had customized Sharon's quarters for humanoid 3D Species and had obliged happily when Sharon experimented with manifesting requests yesterday to redesign the chairs. The quarters were unusual, though, due to the sparse numbers of As Neededs at the moment. Other quarters were generally prestocked with a great variety of topics, including entertainment stories, trivia games, and interesting or mostly relevant facts.

SlipFreud explained that after Sharon felt confident about her ability to access As Neededs, more of them would be installed in her quarters by Meg, the ship's main BFD. This would be done at a rate that did not overwhelm the human. He further stated this was standard Best Practice for acclimating newly aware or Semi aware beings. Complex algorithms had been created to ensure beings had enough information accessible to them but not so much as to overwhelm them—or clutter the quarters unnecessarily. The algorithms would be minutely adjusted to Sharon's specific needs as more was determined about her processing capabilities and preferences.

SlipFreud did not mention that the first human beings CC ships had ever taken on had been rendered useless from the information overload. Due to the aware having naturally high levels of curiosity, their newly forming awareness had quickly turned to run-of-the-mill human psychosis due to the terrifying amount of information suddenly available to them.

Luckily for this honored guest, the acclimating process had been refined. Since she was one of the first known humans to become aware in this particular spacetimecontinuum, special care was being taken to introduce her slowly to the new environment and monitor her carefully for signs of overstimulation, Fear responses, or other undesirable states that could lead to what the humans so quaintly called 'decompensation.' As if the poor things were ever really fully psychologically healthy coming from the environments they generally had endured.

Sharon understood the packets of information to be very much like the books and magazines usually available at hotels or resorts on most versions of Earth. The concept was easy enough to understand, and Sharon was becoming quite befuddled by SlipFreud's continued yammering on the subject. But what she did wonder about was SlipFreud's ability to speak with her in her native language.

"SlipFreud," she interrupted, "your English is so very good, do you practice with other humans?"

"No, Honored Sharon, you are the first human I have ever encountered. My Tribe Talk device has been temporarily set to a special mode. I am thinking about what I want to say in my language, and my Tribe Talk device is then sending me audio signals in your language, which I am then mimicking as 'speech.' I have no real understanding of the sounds I am making, but I am very good at mimicry of all sorts. It's a skill point my species possesses."

Sharon stared at him, not fully comprehending what he'd said. "Wow, the inflections are fantastic. I understand I will be fitted with this Tribe Talk device later today. Sounds like quite a feat of technology." Then she asked, "Is it polite to ask about what species you are?"

He laughed. "Of course! All is one in the Singularity of gazillions, but differentiation makes the known universes go round, Praise Goodness. I am a Sidi. We originate from the Solarium Contento, far, far away from here, in the eastern quadrant, and we still inhabit a planet there called Indus. It's much like your Earth in many ways. Like you, I am a three dimensional being, with four and five dimensional thinking elements. I also have a 6D soul element. I am male, full of Goodness, and skilled in mimicry."

He did not add that his own species had survived similar problems with MMR. Nor did he mention that those MMR problems had been brought by humans from another spacetimecontinuum, causing pain and suffering to all of his kind for several hundred years. Nor did he mention that many Sidis still privately thought all humans should be exterminated, since they seemed to bring so many problems with them wherever they went.

Instead he smiled winningly and said, "Would you like to practice finding and accessing As Neededs?"

"Sure!" Sharon said gamely.

SlipFreud quickly realized he had underestimated the Honored Guest, and said as much in an apology after Sharon flawlessly found and accessed several As Neededs, and then asked for and introduced SlipFreud to several delicious foods. She said the items were called coffee, Eggs Benedict with green chili, and 'Impossible pork sausage.' She also conjured up some apple juice and a small fruit salad. He wasn't exactly sure which items were which, but the whole experience was intriguing. He especially liked the way she looked at his eyes when he mimicked 'friendly, calming eye contact.'

After he apologized, she looked at him blankly for a minute and then simply said, "Thank you SlipFreud. I appreciate your apology and accept it."

SlipFreud thought he heard a small rustling sound, but he saw no one, so he figured it was Meg moving something about. He got up and began clearing away the dishes.

It was actually Petra, who had rushed to Sharon's side and was flapping nervously after Sharon had said, "Holy Shit!" very loudly in her mind.

"What's the matter sweetheart?" she said.

Embarrassed, Sharon said, "Nothing. I was just surprised, that's all."

Petra's energies turned curious. "Why what happened?"

"It was nothing."

"No, tell me," Petra persisted.

"Well, he apologized!"

"What?"

"He actually apologized. He's been mansplaining for, like, forty minutes, and not only did he just realize it, but, he also…he apologized!"

Petra scoffed. "Sharon!"

"I'm serious, it surprised me! Come on, Petra, you know that is not something you can expect to have happen! So I was surprised…quite happily, truth be known. Can't you at least forgive me for being happy about something a male does for once?"

Petra thought earnestly for a moment, then giggled. "You're right. I told you this place was cool!"

"And he has really lovely eyes."

"Oh, Sharon, don't go switch hitting on us. At least not anytime soon, okay?"

"Yeah, I know, he's just being nice, but Geesus, if more guys acted like that when they make mistakes, I probably would be much more inclined to switch hit. Just sayin'… Sharon out!" she said, trying to regain her dignity.

SlipFreud was carrying the last of the dishes to the sink. He needed to get going, but the electri-pipe issue had not yet been discussed.

"Honored Sharon, I have one last topic I'd like to explore with you," he said.

Sharon looked at him. "What's that?"

"Are you aware of the electri-pipe and how it functions?" he asked.

She shook her head.

"Come with me."

Sharon followed him to the place where the air felt really good. "Ahhh, I knew there was something about this area. It feels really…healthy here."

"See if you can find the As Needed," he said, determined not to act like a pompous, ego-ridden being again.

She watched him carefully and nodded. Noticing his more companionable and less guide like demeanor, said, "SlipFreud, I can't tell you how much it means to me that you first noticed and then apologized for over explaining things to me. And I love that you are being a true gentleman right now."

He said nothing, but bowed and gave another of his winning smiles. His therapist would be so proud of him!

"Ah, here it is," she said. She touched the screen and read out loud as she skimmed through the screens until she found the right information. "Operation, General Warnings... Ah, Functions!"

"Find health, renewal, and refreshment from this electri-pipe. This specific electri-pipe, constructed for the GSS Prosperity, consists of positively charged ions and a higher than normal concentration of chi and electrical impulses associated with flourishing. These items in these combinations have been found to boost energy levels in virtually all animate beings."

The section went on, but Sharon flipped back to the General Warnings section and read that out loud.

"General Warnings. There are no known adverse effects of the use of the electri-pipe. Static charge, and in rare cases susceptibility to small static shocks, can occur with prolonged use (over three hours at a time). Hair can be managed by applying anti-static hair conditioner to either wet or dry hair. Please ask for specially formulated hair conditioner to be manifested. Please ask for an anti-shock block to be manifested for you if you become susceptible to static shocks."

Meg had hastily added the parts about asking for anti-static hair conditioner and anti-shock block just a couple of seconds before Sharon got to it. It had made the whole As Needed flicker a little. But if Sharon had noticed, she didn't say anything. Instead she just looked up around the room, asked for the items, and gave a small smile of thanks. Then Sharon looked over at SlipFreud and giggled. "That's what is up with my hair! You're a genius, SlipFreud, thanks!"

"You are most certainly welcome, Honored Sharon," he replied. "It is my pleasure to assist. I have now discharged my duties, but if you require further assistance or anything at all, please do not hesitate to contact me using the wall bell near the BFD in the kitchen." He smiled and bowed deeply.

Sharon somewhat awkwardly did the same and walked him to the door.

What's Going On

"When did you notice the deviation?" the Captain asked.

"Right before I called you. It appears we've now been off course for about forty-five minutes," OT said in a vaguely Scottish brogue. She was looking ruefully at the control panel. "The computers don't seem to know that we are off course, that's what worries me, Captain."

"That I don't doubt," the Captain replied. One head was engaged in conversation with OT while another read a report of some sort. Cabeza had physically traversed to the Navigation Deck for their daily Stand Up meeting as there was—in addition to the unusual new passenger—this small anomaly happening with the main navigation computer.

Two more of Cabeza's heads were studying the controls while only one head dozed, a little unusual for this time of day. The head focused on OT noticed the angle of her nose. Its normal shape looked much like an elephant's trunk, with a languid and undeniably sensuous spiraling curve, as the artificial gravity on the ship pulled the end of her trunk downward. Today, however, her trunk was noticeably retracted, giving an appearance more like a sort of fat, terraced, football-shaped snoot in the middle of her orange face.

Her head tentacles were retracted as well, a rather odd occurrence that Captain Cabeza had never seen before. Cabeza wondered at the significance. A thought occurred to her. According to an old mythic power poem from an inhabited orb within the Solarium Navarro, when the physiology of Snooglists contracted, 'something mysterious will concur.' No one knew exactly what that meant. Not wanting to stare at OT too long, Cabeza turned her tertiary head back towards the space in front of them.

There was a small silence as the pair stared quietly into deep space together, trying to fathom what the navigation system was avoiding. OT glanced down at the path for the forty-second time in the past hour. What had started as a tiny deviation, so small as to be almost unnoticeable, was now turning into a rather large curve in the trajectory path on the big picture navigational screen. They were in a wide orbit within the Earth's solar system, but the ship was deviating from the course they'd originally set. The navigational computers, usually so chatty as to be annoying, were in this case completely silent about the purpose or cause for this detour. Even when asked directly they had answered with "Still formulating a response." In this case it was as if they did not have any awareness that they were deviating off the originally projected course. The new trajectory route had no explanation of 'Unanticipated Debris,' 'Dark Matter Related Issues Ahead,' 'Gravitational Fluctuations,' or any of the other common culprits for mid-course deviations. OT tsked through her mouth, which was situated above her nose, and then said, "I just can't figure it out, Captain. The sensors are not agitated, but there is definitely a strong sense of avoidance in the path the ship is taking."

"Could the ship be just navigating around some entity we can't see?" the Captain asked.

"It would appear so, but the sensors, ma'am, they just do not give me any sense of what the entity is. Except there's no Fear, agitation, or other undesirable sense that I can detect."

"Well, it certainly is a mystery," Captain said bemusedly as her heads shook in a complicated synchrony. Just then, the ship herself erupted into a sound not unlike a purring cat. Captain Cabeza's heads stretched to their full heights. The primordial startle response is a trait common to many species. However, the trait is more noticeable in Nervonians, due their five heads. At the same time, OT's nose retracted even further into her face, in a not unpleasing, but highly unusual, way for a Snooglist. She was beginning to look like a clam somehow. How was that possible?

Then, time seemed to stop.

As she came back into awareness, Captain Cabeza immediately seized the all-ship speaker and announced, "Crew, we don't know what is occurring. Remain clam, er, calm. Ensure you are safe and assist any others around you. If you are able, induce supportive electrical impulses towards crew, passengers, and the main operating system." She added, "Report any injuries to the Health Deck. Additionally, please monitor all systems for anomalies and report back via the Central Mind Unit. Repeat: report any anomalies back to the Centralized Mind Unit."

OT's trunk had resumed its normal shape and she looked with surprise at the sensors, then at the navigation plan. The ship appeared to be returning to the route she had requested.

Sharon's Morning Awakening

"Good morning!" The voice was cheerful and friendly. Sharon was startled. SlipFreud had left a few minutes ago, and she had barely made it out of the bathroom.

"Uh, good morning. Who am I speaking—er, communicating with?" Sharon unselfconsciously stood in the pathway of the electri-pipe in the hallway, and her hair immediately began to stand on end again.

Meg chuckled. "I'm Meg. I was the one who welcomed you on board our rover. No worries if you don't remember. I am quite aware of how many unusual things you have experienced in the past few hours. But I'm at your service."

"Oh, okay, thanks." Sharon's response was uncertain. She looked around, searching for the source of the voice she was hearing so very clearly in her head. She recognized Meg's voice; it had sounded much like Gladys Knight.

"Here, let me manifest a target for you." A hologram of an attractive Black woman in jeans and a sweater appeared near the dining table and motioned for Sharon to come nearer. As Sharon walked the few steps, Meg pulled out a chair and sat on it. She had chosen to manifest as a hologram rather than as a fully embodied being, so Sharon would begin to think of her as the ethereal being she really was. That way the human might get the idea quicker that she didn't have to see Meg to be able to communicate with her. The toaster-oven-sized BFD was still in the corner of the kitchen. Even though its placement had confused the human, it was a point of pride in her work that Meg's creations, once manifested fully, stayed solid and worked completely on their own for many years. Meg looked at the creation she had manifested. She drew confidence from her own skillful bit of work, and took a deep breath. This could become a complicated conversation.

Just then, the ship's gravity fluctuated wildly for a moment, and the chair Meg had been sliding away from the table for Sharon started to levitate. Meg had not actually been touching the chair—she had no need to touch anything to move it. But she had been directing it, and now it was moving of its own accord.

Meg was as surprised as the human and immediately scanned for danger. There didn't appear to be any. She then almost reflexively emanated high levels of trustworthiness, calmness, and protectiveness towards the human. That worked. Sharon's surprise did not turn to fear, and she looked from the chair to Meg quizzically. "Do you want me to try to sit in the chair?" She asked the question earnestly, ready to attempt to do so, since she assumed Meg was somehow levitating the chair.

"Uh, no. Please stay calm. The chair floating like that is not my doing, and I'm attempting to find out what is causing it." Meg started the response tentatively and ended authoritatively, feeling this would help the human. To her surprise, Sharon shrugged, and still watching the chair that was now dancing a little as it levitated, she went to the other side of the table. She pulled a regular chair out and brought it closer to Meg. Then she sat down, all while continuing to watch the dancing chair. Meg tilted her head a little as she noticed how transfixed the human was. A thought occurred to her. "Sharon, what do you think is going on?"

"Well, it's friendly, that's obvious." She paused a moment. "I can't quite make out what it's telling us, but it is sharing some good news. What a fun thing." She sounded genuinely delighted. Meg made a verbal "hmm" kind of grunting sound of agreement.

"Ohh. Look at that! " Sharon said it as if she and Meg were watching a live play or musical show. They were silent for a moment, then Sharon started nodding her head a bit. "Okay, yes, ooooohhh, that's spiffy!"

Meg asked, "Spiffy? What is it saying?" but got no response. Instead, Sharon looked at Meg for a moment with a playful smile on her face, and then turned her attention back to the chair. Later, no one could really say how long the spectacle of dancing objects— happening all across the ship—lasted. Some species watched and became engrossed in the dance, like Sharon. Others watched with some curiosity, but also with curiosity at the responses the dancing objects elicited from their shipmates. It was later confirmed that almost all of the intact males on the ship were aroused. After the event, there was a noticeable difference in their demeanors. Later research confirmed that everyone, but males especially, had been inoculated with more Goodness. The research would show long-lasting positive effects and fewer sad fits of egotism among crew and passengers.

A few moments, or hours, or maybe even eons later, all the levitating objects ended their dances and the beings that had been transfixed came back to consciousness; most a bit dazed, but curiously calm and sort of satisfied. Observers also seemed to emerge from slightly different spells and were mostly unaffected other than extreme puzzlement at what had happened. The timekeeping devices all indicated no time had elapsed at all, but this was contradicted by the experience of all aboard the ship.

The Captain issued another order. "All senior and

Double Digit Dimensional crew members, please gather in the Main Auditorium. Repeat: please gather in the Main Auditorium. Urgent Stand Up meeting begins in five minutes." With this announcement, overhead monitors in all occupied rooms had manifested of their own accord, as per the ship's design when the Captain or other senior crew members wished to give an all-ship command. All five of Captain Cabeza's heads communicated the order in unison. Meg's hologram looked at Sharon and said, "So sorry, I have to go. I was looking forward to talking with you, but I'll find you later, okay?"

Sharon's face betrayed a mixture of disappointment, puzzlement, and some intimidation at realizing Meg, this nice hologram in jeans and a sweater, was actually either a senior crew member or a Double Digit something or other. She also registered shock at the sight of the many headed Captain Cabeza giving orders for this meeting via a screen that had suddenly just appeared in the corner of the room. The screen was now displaying a calming screen saver of some sort.

"Don't you worry about anything. I'll be back in just a few minutes," Meg said on her way out.

"Okay" Sharon said. She sat and thought warmly about the dancing chair for a while.

She looked around, and then walked closer to inspect the screen more intently—it was solid, but appeared to hang in mid air, unlike the more translucent As Neededs that sort of hovered and then faded from view when they weren't needed. Suddenly she became sleepy again. She could hardly keep her eyes open. It was a deep, relaxed state, and it was about sleep, not being tired. She looked around her quarters and decided to lie down on the deliciously comfortable bed. In twenty seconds she was asleep and dreaming about Yeti showing her the spaceship they'd known was going to arrive at a secret airport located out in the forest. Sharon floated above the ship and could see that the flight attendants were deer, or maybe gazelles. They were friendly and efficient, and moved around on their hind legs, using their front hooves as hands. The pilot was a domesticated turkey, not very bright or quick, but steady, practical, and kind hearted. And even though pretty obvious things needed to be pointed out to the turkey by the gazelles, the turkey exhibited good judgment. She wondered what the dream meant even as she was dreaming it.

Purrfect Synchronicity

The ship's purring and the events that ensued during the purring caused quite a stir.

The crew soon determined that there was a common condition for the suspended movement of the items that had 'danced.' Any items that had been in motion due to the actions of an aware being had been affected. They had first stopped in their trajectories and then begun to dance. This included eggs in mid break, papers tossed, footballs in motion, and even bedsheets thrown aside for changing or during other activities. Within a short time, the crew also determined that since the ship was fueled by life energies and was defined— and most importantly defined itself—as partially animate, it had alternated between being affected and not being affected. Thus the purring sound was due to the rapid succession of the engines dancing for a millisecond, then being overridden by safety measures.

The science-oriented beings on board began pursuing more answers as to exactly what had happened to affect things in this way.

On the main deck, Sync tinkled a bell, she remembered finally! And Cabeza said, "Yes, Sync, just thinking of you. This is indeed an auspicious signal, is it not?"

Sync said, "As you said earlier, Captain, it could all still be coincidence, but it is another factor that appears to support our theory rather than disprove it."

Cabeza was a little surprised by Sync's response. Surely Sync would see the animate/inanimate ship purring in response to motion as significant. And without a doubt, the Snooglist's bodily changes were significant. The Captain wondered why Sync wasn't more convinced. Then she realized Sync may not have witnessed the Snooglists' transformation. The Captain, like all SDDs (Single Digit Dimensionals) had a hard time remembering that Sync and the other DDDs on board were not always present during events. DDDs like Sync did have boundaries, and although they could often spread over extremely large distances, their conscious attentions were generally limited to only a few places at once.

The DDDs' abilities were kind of like a human's foot being tickled by a particular blade of grass. If the human were engaged in other pursuits, it would not notice the blade at all. However, if the human's attention was brought to its foot, it could zero in on the event and focus rather intently, and then be able to assess what was going on from a much more comprehensive perspective than that of the ant below saying, "Hey, you, big being! Check out the blade of grass tickling your foot!" SDDs regularly had to help DDDs focus on particular events in much the same way.

Now, like a human paying attention to an ant that was going about its business foraging (or whatever), Sync was aware that the Captain's inner minds were working and having their own thoughts, but she could only "hear" the specifics of them when she was fully inhabited in the Captain's mind. Since this was rather intrusive, she refrained from doing so in most circumstances outside of her official assessment duties. Just like with any other materially based beings, the Captain would need to formulate the communications and then direct them out towards Sync before Sync could fully understand what she was thinking. To Sync, this materially based mode of communication could take the equivalent of several minutes if she stayed in her native dimensions, and so DDDs often lost track of SDD thoughts as their attention wandered in and out of other dimensions.

Sync was still a bit distracted when she realized that Captain Cabeza was explaining what she'd witnessed right before the Purring Event. "OT was on deck when the Purring Event happened. Her trunk retracted!"

Sync was at a loss. "I'm afraid I'm not following, Captain."

Cabeza's curt head cocked almost sideways and said, with more surprise than anything else, "Really?"

Another head said, "Well, let's bring up some information. I'm pretty sure my memory is correct, but possibly I've confused it with something else." As this head spoke, another head queried a computer nearby.

She turned a head back towards Sync's general direction. "I had gone to do our daily briefing on the Nav deck, because of that weird course deviation we were also experiencing—which has been righted, by the way. Anyway, we were in the middle of our briefing, trying to figure out this course deviation. Then OT's trunk somehow retracted, so she looked like a sort of cross between a kind of furry slinky and a football. I don't think she noticed it, but it was definitely a different look. Her head tentacles also retracted, producing a gloriously textured round dome that makes material beings just want to reach out and touch. Such great art," Cabeza mused. Regathering her focus she continued, "Are you familiar with the mythic power poems?"

Sync emanated some vague familiarity. "Not very intimately at all. They did not yet exist during my time of intensive studying."

"Oh, of course, that makes sense. By the time

they originated you had probably seen half of the known universes. I was a, well, a materially based kid, just being exposed to worlds beyond my own Solarium. Ah, it was an exciting time. Well, the mythic power poems are lovely, but quite puzzling as a group. I memorized several for a performance piece I did while studying. The piece went over very well indeed, thanks to all of these." She pointed to her many heads, who each rather theatrically took mini bows.

"The poems originate from the Solarium Imbibo, and they are said to be prophetic poems and 'among the most important communications to sentience's sentience.' And they are ordered very carefully, so the mythology goes.

"But no one from the Solarium, or anywhere else, is really sure what the poems mean, not at all. They sound beautiful, and they certainly consist of elements of love poems, but their structure is also in a kind of riddle form." Cabeza cleared a throat. An eyebrow arched and her other heads all gave attention to the one speaking.

"It begins with a few stanzas about love, the universe, and everything, and then:
'Snooglists come from way afar,
Their grace begotten from another star.

We know their love and compassion,
And their sinuous trunks are quite in fashion.

But when comes the day their trunks fall inward
Then the time will be that we can infer

Something mysterious will concur.'"

Cabeza's eyebrow again went up meaningfully in Sync's direction. "And…that's the end of that poem," she said.

"You meant to say something mysterious will occur, right?" Sync corrected.

Three of Cabeza's heads shook vigorously. "No, that's part of the mystery. It is most definitely that 'something mysterious will concur.'"

"Huh," Sync said.

"So, right as we're working on this course deviation, the ship started purring. And as that happened, her trunk retracted even further. I mean, Sync, she looked very much like a clam. It was that retracted."

Sync snorted. "That's why you said 'Keep clam,' instead of 'keep calm,'" she said, laughing out loud.

All five of Cabeza's heads looked a little indignant. "Well, yes." She said it somewhat sternly, but within a moment a couple of heads were also chuckling, and only her curt head still looked a little put out by Sync's amusement.

"I'm sorry, Captain Curt, but it's funny," Sync said, addressing the head known for handling the fussier sides of Cabeza's personality.

"Oh it's fine, you know me, but what I make of this is that it is pretty significant. Not to say…I don't know exactly what this all means, but I do believe that what happened and the human's arrival and profile are all very mysterious."

"I concur, Captain," Sync said without missing a beat. Privately she noted Cabeza's use of the term 'belief.' Cabeza rarely framed things that way, and Sync puzzled at it.

The computer pinged. The AI features on Cabeza's Command Deck only pinged in that particular tone when they felt there was something important to relate to the query at hand.

"Yes, computer?" Cabeza said loudly.

The computer replied, "Captain, this stanza may also interest you. Its origins are...debated, but it is thought to be from a powerful collection of writings called 'The Oracle Poetry Uncensored Series.' It originates from the Natavitiatis Solarium, which is near the first Interstice and the Imbibo Solarium...again, the writer is unknown. But it's a stanza from a longer poem quixotically called an 'Ode to Successive or Perceived Singularities.' This is the fifth stanza. Its placement as the fifth stanza may be significant, but that is only a theory at this point.

> Another dream world perhaps.
> ..Where no time has ever elapsed
> ....Not of our place, not of our time,
> ......Not of known dimension
> Yet there is sweet ascension
> ......Around us winds of change
> ....And our futures rearrange
> ..Winds blow us to a different space
> When Snooglists appear with flattened face.'"

"Wow, how many stanzas are there in total?" Cabeza asked. She shivered a little from the synchronistic signs, all pointing directly to "The Ghost Witch Is" story.

The computer answered: "There are three more stanzas, totaling eight. And please remember in this base ten counting system, the number eight sometimes represents a sideways way of saying 'there are infinite numbers.' The Original Imprints of the writings are kept in The Museum of Magic in the Imbibo Solarium on the planet Defixio."

"Put it on my bucket list, computer," Cabeza said. One head grinned in Sync's direction. " A museum of magic on a planet named Defixio—how wondrous is that?"

"Sounds like a magical place all right. Might be quite enchanting, actually. I think I'd like to come with you when you go," Sync agreed.

"It's a date then!" Cabeza was in fine spirits. Sync moved energy around in a frolic-like motion.

There was a small silence, then Sync asked, "And this poetry, computer, what magical powers does it possess?"

"The mysteries of love," the computer said almost coyly.

"Really, now that is intriguing, isn't it? All the more so due to the negativity you've found in the human's writings," Cabeza said, gazing in Sync's direction.

Sync moved energies around thoughtfully. "Well, yes, some of the writings contain very negative thoughts towards other humans, there's no denying that. In a few places she even compares some humans to cancerous growths, so obviously our Honored Guest herself has some growing to do with how she handles anger issues. You should see Petra when she talks about the regressed parts of Sharon, she's so saddened and embarrassed. It's adorable."

Sync continued, "But the negative thoughts clearly exist only as a response to her personal pain, not as an exhortation of any sort. And these writings have never been published; the human has no desire to share them. Petra said Sharon just writes them to keep from exploding, basically. So I don't really see a contradiction in that. It's not like Sharon is aware of all her writings being scrutinized like, I don't know, someone like their Dalai Lama. If she were a well-known public leader, I doubt very much she would have ever written some of the things I've read." There was a small silence. "Petra brought this issue up spontaneously when we were talking. She said Sharon sometimes even uses a pen name called Cassandra Dimstar, 'a prophet no one ever listens to, from a far-away solarium.' Petra said she tries to talk Sharon out of writing really negative things because it depresses them both and doesn't solve anything."

"So sad. They are really struggling down on that planet, aren't they?"

"It appears very bad." Sync's voice was full of sympathy.

Highest Wisdom Actually Does Make An Appearance

Sync returned to her studying place (ha) and was momentarily puzzled by the lines of poetry that greeted her as she fired up her computer to write more notes. The query! With all the hubbub from The Purring, she'd forgotten all about it.

She accessed the information and consumed it in a split second. It was as she had suspected.

Highest Wisdom has come to share
Even more Love and Peace upon the aware

She is coming, days of love are coming

In a certain time and place—
And the flattening of a Snooglist's face

Yes, it matters where
In a place of too many cares
The fruits of the universes will be shared

She is coming, days of love are coming

Out on a lost planet's thin thin air
On a world with too many cares to bear

All is one and one is all
When we know how to hear the call

For the thriving of love and peace
And for a time they will not cease

She screamed for fear to be turned to sweet

Into Something good to eat
And licked the cold to beat the heat
An amazingly simple little feat

Fear be gone within a year
No more tangles, no more tears

Love will thrive
Will stay alive
When the Sharings arrive

To share that's right, to share
And live where peace is just not all that rare
We Connect and boom, we become aware

A planet still unjust and unfair
With far too many cares to easily bear
Her request leads us back to the simple dare

To live in days of love, they are coming

We will live in the days of love
Justice is sweet, it will be fair
It will be ever so completely shared
Share On
We will live in the days of love

"There are too many coincidences for this all to just be chance. Even her name matches up," mused Sync.

Part 3

Petra And Meg Discuss The Proposed Mission

Instead of returning to Sharon directly after the Stand Up, Meg went to speak first with Petra. During the emergency Stand Up, the Captain and crew agreed that the Purring may have had something to do with their Honored Guests' arrival, and that instead of visiting with Sharon as planned, Meg would instead talk with Petra first about how to approach Sharon and Emma to enlist their help with combating MMR on Earth. Meg sent SlipFreud to let Sharon know she'd have to reschedule their visit.

Meg located Petra, and cleared her throat. Petra did not seem surprised by her presence, and emanated a warm and cheerful greeting. Once they got settled, Meg started in, somewhat inelegantly.

"What do you think will be the toughest part of the decision, or toughest thing for Sharon to understand?" Meg directed the question at Petra, trying to sound casual.

Both Meg and Petra knew she was doing a pretty bad job of hiding her true intentions, but Petra graciously avoided making any comment on Meg's intense interest, or on the implication that Petra would think of herself as completely separate from Sharon's 3, 4 and 5D elements.

"Well, I do think she's going to feel she's in a really tight spot."

Petra paused a split second, then amended her statement emphatically to acknowledge the point. "Currently, we are in a really tight spot. We know there are literally billions of humans back on the planet who are in danger of extinguishing themselves due to the idiocy of a small number of badly infected 'leaders' and their minions. And quite frankly, since we've been living on that planet we also know that virtually all of the humans on Earth have been infected—to varying degrees—with the disease as well. But, more importantly, we also know that all of those beings have—at their core— lovely 3, 4, 5, 6D, and 7D elements who did nothing to deserve life on a planet infected with MMR. We also know that there are billions of other life forms, and their corresponding elements, who are in danger as well. And we know that it's possible...no...probable that we have somehow been asked to try to help eradicate the infection."

Meg did not bother to make any comment on how Petra phrased that last part, but she was puzzled by it. She knew Sync had explained to Petra that Earth specifically requested their help.

Petra had paused and moved her attention momentarily towards the color-enhanced view of Earth in almost full sunlight, magnified and radiantly beautiful. Meg got a vague sense that Petra was waiting for her to understand something, but she wasn't sure what it was. This was highly unusual for an 11D being like herself.

Petra then emanated kindness and continued. "And I know Earth herself currently has what she needs to cure the infection. I also get that she is trying to find other ways...and she doesn't really want to use the radiation—since using radiation would mean the death of, well, all the humans, as well as...millions of other life forms. I mean the sheer numbers of birds alone fly up into the gazillions. Fly up, get it? Birds."

Meg groaned a little at her pun. Petra laughed. "I gotta tell you, though, Meg, Sharon's gonna have some real mind explosions in that big head of hers if she thinks about the Earth requesting help directly from us." Petra shuddered involuntarily. "Emma will, too; she's so sensitive. It's likely to slow things down, a bit, I'm afraid."

Meg moved energy around in a question.

"Well, she'll just freak out. It's a human thing. It'll be like stage fright. Some humans—Sharon's one of them—get really anxious when they feel they are being closely watched about something they care about. They get nervous and worry they will mess up or fail. It's a basic unaware ego thing."

"Oh, okay, I think I get it," Meg said conversationally, trying to hide that she was once again a bit shocked at the primitiveness of human minds.

"But..." Petra started, then brooded for a moment while she continued to look out at Earth. "We have developed a good conscious relationship, so they truly understand and trust me." Then she more playfully added, "I mean look how they took to the electri-pipe so easily."

Petra and Meg chuckled a little, both simultaneously conjuring up visions of Sharon's hair standing on end.

Petra went on. "Anyway, I know that the Earth herself will be okay in the long run. I mean, even if we try and fail to eradicate it, and the infection gets worse...once Earth uses the supplies, she—at least—will be okay."

Petra interrupted her stream of thought to direct what Meg assumed was a thanks to Captain Cabeza for bringing medicine. Petra then resumed her thoughts about the subject at hand. "And for us to be asked to work directly with Earth on this proposed mission is not something we are likely to turn down. I mean, we also try to live by the golden rule. And I love how the CC has elevated it so much. It's so very clear to me that we belong here," Petra said with feeling.

"But we—and I do mean we, Meg—are also

truly in need of recovering from the infection ourselves. I worry about Sharon 4D and Emma. And I feel a bit affected sometimes by Hubris, too. For months now I've noticed that I regress to rage and bitterness on a regular basis. Me!" she chirped. "It's not healthy for any of us down there. And that, quite simply, is the true issue."

Meg murmured sympathy. Both were silent for a long moment, gazing out at the Earth's physical presence, a few thousand Earth miles away.

"I don't suppose you could shield us somehow, Meg?" Petra asked suddenly.

Meg was surprised by the question. "What do you mean?"

"I'm wondering if it is possible for you to shield us from the infection itself, so we can just focus on implementing whatever steps we need to take?"

Meg paused for what turned out to be several moments. During that time, Petra watched with interest as tiny sparks swirled around in the ether in weirdly pleasing patterns. She realized this was Meg thinking deeply. "Cool data visualization, Meg," she said drolly.

Meg playfully shifted energies. "This is how my deep-thinking mode naturally manifests, Petra. BFDs like me burn a little hot."

Petra suppressed a sheepish grin, knowing Meg was flirting with her, but not knowing how to respond. She'd been stuck on Earth for so very long.

Rather than try to say anything, Petra just watched the sparks flit about while the Biological Firmament Designer did her thing. The tiny bits of energy followed a pattern somewhat like sparks from a fire might, but with a more controlled and graceful way of flying or gliding. Like they were purposefully driving themselves through the ether. Petra wondered if they were some kind of fireflies, but then thought with a start that these sparks were analogous to human synapses firing. She could not see anything that looked like neurons, just the sparks. Was space a humongous neuron in and of itself? Or was it a huge brain? Or maybe the sparks were some physical form of Patterned Chaos? Petra wasn't sure. She'd never seen the phenomenon before. She thought briefly about trying to tell the 3 and 4D Sharons and the 5D emoti to come to the deck where she and Meg were gathered, but then realized they could not manifest at all on this primarily 6D deck. Hell, Petra mused, Sharon still thought of Meg as "simply" a Bio Fuel Dispenser, not as the fine, fine Biological Firmament Designer she really was.

A Convening Of Intentional Consciousness

The meeting room was bright and comfortable and all the beings looked intently interested. The energy in the room was palpable and infused with kindness. Such a nice feeling, really.

"We've been asked by Earth to help her address the MMR problem down there. And since you are a native Earthling, we'd really love for you to help us help Earth. We'd like for you to act as a consultant." Cabeza said the words with a casualness that belied the importance of her formal request.

Sharon immediately cocked her head slightly and squinted a bit at the beings gathered around the room, but she nodded without saying anything. Petra conferred briefly with her.

Within a couple of seconds Sharon waved a hand and said just as casually, "Of course we'll help. No problem. But what I really want to know is what do you mean by "Intentional Consciousness? I've heard you bat this term around, but I don't quite understand what you mean."

"Well, it's just another kind of tool, you know, like a spoon, or an electric motor, or a silicon chip, or your various forms of propaganda. You've actually already used this tool throughout your time on Earth, and in many variations." Meg said this in an equally casual voice. She was delighted that Sharon had agreed to help the crew so readily. Now she, along with the other crew members, would try to move the conversation into the next phase, which was to come up with some sort of plan to try to stop MMR.

"We have?" Sharon, Petra, and Emma said all at once.

"Of course, we're using it now! We're

exchanging ideas, engaging in intentional consciousness, right now," Meg said. Feeling she'd explained the concept, she went on, "In many ways, your kind are so advanced—you can fly halfway around your world in a few hours. You are much like magicians when you talk to people in real time on the other side of the world. You have figured out how to venture into space, a little. You've got the capacities!"

There was a small silence.

Sensing Sharon was still a bit confused, Sync spoke up, "Intentional consciousness can take several forms, but in this instance, it is pretty much like problem solving. And that is what we are here for. Problem solving around technology is much easier to achieve than intentional cultural change, especially with the MMR infection. So there are some pretty big challenges ahead, but working together, we can handle this. So, let's get started!"

Captain Cabeza nodded all five heads gracefully.

Meg continued, "MMR is a pretty…uh, unrefined tool for dealing with relational issues. It's primitive and highly dangerous. But it's also difficult for those infected by MMR to think 'outside the box' of it."

Professor InDepth then spoke up. "Your writings have helped us see several interconnected reasons why your MMR-infected people try to trivialize the importance of relational concerns.

"We now understand that it is genuinely difficult for them to see how… uh, messed up their thinking is. The folks in charge like to believe things are just fine and dandy the way they are; and why wouldn't they? It's working out for them. They understand 'power over' and unconsciously assume that's the way things have to be. And not only do they have a harder time understanding 'collaboration with'—it also scares the bejeezus out of them! MMR-infected folks fear being vulnerable in any way, shape, or form."

InDepth paused. "I've made a couple more conclusions based on Sharon's writings. May I?" She looked at Captain Cabeza.

"Certainly!" Captain Cabeza said. She was pleased with how the meeting was proceeding, both with the reactions of Sharon and Emma, and with how her crew members were seamlessly moving forwards based on those reactions. However, she knew it was going smoothly because she had framed the request as the crew wanting their help as beings with direct experience in living on Earth, never mentioning that the Earth had requested help from this particular human. Petra knew, of course; she'd been the one to ask Cabeza to avoid mentioning the request.

Cabeza had not issued an order to withhold that information from Sharon and Emma. That was something she could not ethically do as the Captain of a GSS vessel. But Cabeza had a sharp crew and was sure they had noticed how she had avoided mention of the specific request Earth made. She hoped they would follow suit, at least until the mission was finished.

"Okay. Well, let's start with the idea of collective trauma reactions," InDepth said. "Human history is just chock full of traumas—from floods, fires, and famines, to diseases, epidemics, and predators. We know they were just inundated with trauma. That was long before they started inflicting traumas on each other on such vast scales, via militaries. And we now know that trauma makes people

- hyperfocused on power and control,
- avoid vulnerability, and
- naturally want to avoid negative

emotional states reminding
them of trauma.

These things are absolutely key to understanding *why* humans still struggle so mightily with the MMR infection.

"We can readily understand the quest for power and control in a straightforward way. But it's also present in the fear of vulnerability, and the avoidance and denial. Fears about being vulnerable lead directly to humans acting with such Hubris. After all, certainty is the opposite of vulnerability. And avoidance at lower levels leads to humans habitually turning to Hubris in order to avoid dealing with painful truths.

"Avoidance of vulnerability can also be seen as fueling Callousness, since being able to take on another's perspective, sympathize, or empathize with them is impossible if you don't allow yourself to feel some level of vulnerability."

Heads were nodding in the room. Professor InDepth finished by saying, "So right there you have a kind of 'germ theory' that ties together the symptoms with the causal agents. It's the piece that's been missing from how oppression, or MMR, keeps happening on your planet, and probably on other infected planets, as well."

Sharon tried to suppress a smile. She was aware that her heart was full of happiness at the recognition. With some surprise, she realized she was pretty optimistic. She reflexively tried to shush the optimism, then caught herself and tried to stay in it.

Meg added, "True, and very important. But despite the infection, humans are on track with other developmental milestones: they have put on their first pair of space boots and started to explore their front yards, and they have actually done a great job at really grasping there is more to the known universes than matter-based stuff."

Sync took the counterpoint to Meg's obvious cheerleading. "But as we know, with the infection of MMR at such an uncontrolled stage, the technological abilities humans have right now are dangerous. It's like giving a group of troubled teenage boys unfettered access to a muscle car and a bunch of alcohol…and then telling them to go drink it while they drive. Bad things could very easily happen."

Sync paused for dramatic effect, then directed her next comments at the human and her elements. "And obviously they have: MMR has led to all kinds of oppression and colonizing and empire building and needless competition. The use of military might still persists. Worse, many—maybe the majority—on your planet truly believe the Ptolemaic vision that militaries must exist, which, as you know, is inconceivable to the truly aware.

"The other dangerous issue you all face is the continued willingness and ability of the humans who are most infected with MMR to exploit any avenue they can for their own selfish ends. This has resulted in complete infections in many political arenas and many business arenas. Somehow, we need to target this."

Many heads nodded at this.

Meg shook her head. "Right, but I'm gonna keep saying it, because it's important: the progress is there, too. So maybe that could help us somehow. MMR has infected various parts of your planet in your timeline for at least five thousand years, and probably longer. It's a bad infection, there's no doubt about that. The easiest way to see it is through the existence of slavery and the subjugation of women. Both those atrocities had been around for, what, five thousand years at least, right?"

Sharon nodded, sadly. "Yes, and culturally for women and many other groups, there's still a ton of inequality, and don't get me started about wealth inequality."

"Yeah, I'm not disputing that at all. It's clear there's a lot of work to do, but look at the changes: in less than two hundred years, you've gone from being so immersed in MMR that humans owning other humans was completely legal. Now the practice is outlawed, and the groups who were once owned have made substantial progress in attaining an equal footing in society.

"The other thing these groups have done is they have helped awaken the vast majority of your species to how bad the inequities really were, and are."

Meg tossed some enthusiasm around as she made her next point. "Yes, these groups still struggle to be seen and treated justly, obviously, but they have inspired others to see other forms of MMR as the primitive and destructive force it is for your species.

"Two hundred years is not a very long period of time to go from 'ruling' by brutalizing and killing other humans on a regular basis, to having the worst of the activities legally vanquished throughout the world. We believe the levels of violence are diminishing overall, and the unfairness and realities of inequities are being seen and understood by more and more people. In other words, things are slowly, but generally getting better over time."

Sharon, Emma, and Petra gave each other shyly optimistic looks. Sharon shivered from the goosebumps making her head tingle.

Professor InDepth took up the thread. "Meg's got a good point. Your planet has made lots of changes in a relatively short period of time. And a good many humans down there understand that it's actually those who do the discriminating and do the oppressing who are acting in primitive ways.

"Obviously, you all have significant problems down there, and are—uh, you may very well be at the brink of extinguishing yourselves, but you have made great progress."

Meg felt compelled—was it coming from Petra?—to keep pushing the positive. "One of the things your BNFP will tell you is that as beings become more aware, their sense of time expands, and that appears to be happening on your planet, as well."

Sharon's brows knitted as she tried to understand what Meg was saying.

InDepth noticed. "So what Meg is pointing out is that when people who are concerned with social equality complain that change happens so very slowly on your planet, it is yet another manifestation of how they are already able to process ideas faster, like other aware species do. That, in turn, gives hope that your species will truly become aware, once they jump these last hurdles of inequity."

Sharon didn't trust herself to talk right then. She was exhilarated due to both the beings understanding her ideas about MMR, and her new way of seeing time. So she simply nodded, sporting a bit of a goofy grin.

Meg continued. "We can also see from here that one problem is that many of your majority group members get stuck thinking that rights issues are just for minorities. They fail to frame these human rights issues as the *main* way y'all are becoming better humans. Sharon, you said it best, so I'm just going to read it back for us all, right now.

#

Some are afraid to see the full picture because they still feel separate. They don't think to look at the world in other ways. Some are afraid—it's that simple. But some don't get the full understanding of 'we are all one.' I'm not talking about the haters here. I'm talking about those that see equal rights for everyone as only benefiting the oppressed. The still privileged folks who think they are doing okay, and who kind of understand and agree with the idea that equal is good, but don't really, don't truly get how—much—their own souls will be enriched by living in a world where there is prosperity for all. They can't yet conceive of how better off everyone would be, including every single person who is currently at the top of the heap.

#

Sharon said, "I wrote that? Well, I certainly agree with it, I just don't remember writing it."

Petra said, "We really have written a lot of good things, Sharon. That one you wrote after a trip somewhere, but I can't quite remember where."

"Oh, I'm vaguely remembering that now, but damned if I know where it was, either."

There was a short silence and then Petra said, "MMR creates an interesting problem really: it creates people who have convinced themselves they are the cat's pajamas, yet they are flat out afraid of meeting others on equal footing. It creates 'leaders' who hoover up more money than God, but who are still so insecure that they can't stand the thought of anything approaching true opportunities for others.

"And these types aren't really happy. Sure, they are smug, self-satisfied, hubristic, and arrogant. But they are not happy or truly content. True happiness is about love and compassion and trust and cooperation and connection and belonging, not having power over."

Heads nodded all around the table at what to them was a ridiculously obvious truth.

After a silence, Meg spoke: "Anyway, there are millions of humans who are close to becoming Semi aware. And there are tens of millions of other people who already know that humanity's diversity and all the wonder than comes with that is just a microcosm of more universal variations and wonders. That's awareness. And between the two groups, billions of you intuitively know that wonder, awe, and curiosity are much more natural responses to variation than fear. Billions are also coming to recognize that there are far, far more variations than there are hierarchies. But so far, this knowledge has failed to…" She paused, searching for ways to translate this simple concept into terms humans could understand.

"Your most infected folks continue to think of diversity as a scary thing. They are afraid of the unknown, they are afraid to accept Others as parts of them they have not met yet, but y'all are spinning around in space on one little planet right? One boat, one people, right?"

"Of course, we know that," Petra said. "But like you said, a certain percentage of people really don't seem to. And they are ready to use violence to ensure they stay in power—"

Sharon cut her off. "Because they are more obsessed with it. Power, I mean. Healthy people simply aren't all that obsessed with having power over others."

She looked around the room for confirmation. InDepth said, "That is correct, of course. Obviously, the more aware a being is, the less need the being has for something as primitive as having 'power over' others."

Sharon snapped her fingers and pointed at InDepth. "Right! But those obsessed with power and also obsessed with keeping MMR alive because they are so deeply afraid of not being in control. And that's not healthy. So what causes them to not be healthy? Well, like we've said before, trauma causes people to want to stay in control."

InDepth raised her eyebrows as she looked at Cabeza who nodded approvingly.

"And so maybe the best way to think about the MMR mindset is to imagine it is like a person stuck in PTSD or something. Only it afflicts the whole culture, not just a single person. MMR exists because collectively, people are stuck in fear that originally came from old, unprocessed trauma. It's clear some of those most afflicted didn't even personally experience trauma, but everyone on the planet has certainly seen the threat of trauma happening to them if they didn't grab up as much power as they could. It's pretty clear that even just witnessing or hearing about trauma that has happened to others can profoundly change people's behaviors."

Cabeza said, "This seems like an important point to incorporate into our interventions. Do you have ideas for how to use that information?"

Sharon shook her head.

"Well, let's keep the idea firmly in mind. Keep going though, I can tell you have more to say."

Looking down at her notes, Sharon saw: 'Knowing that really bad things can happen when we don't have control often makes us pretty unwilling to allow ourselves to become vulnerable. But it is only through some level of vulnerability that we can experience things like trust, love, and the ability to truly understand others.'

"Okay. I'd like to go back to how threatened some humans are by the idea of vulnerability."

Cabeza inclined her heads, indicating Sharon should continue.

"Almost all of our English synonyms for

vulnerability are associated with negative things. Vulnerability is tough for all of us. But men, as a whole, are still socialized—" she stopped in midsentence and looked around the table. "They are actively socialized to not be vulnerable. And as you all can imagine, that cuts them off from so many other emotions."

"Uh, wouldn't that would include making it harder for them to experience virtually all of the life affirming emotions humans have?" A Centrail asked incredulously.

Sharon grimaced and nodded her head solemnly.

There was a silence. Several CC crew members were truly shocked by the level of dysfunction. Sharon was reminded of how shocked Sync had been when she had explained how the military actively trains soldiers to not access compassion.

Grimacing again, she said, "And along with that, in certain quarters ruthlessness is seen as a legitimate tactic to use to gain power. So when those types feel threatened, they can become dangerous. A lot of them just double down on Fear-based reactions, or MMR." She sighed deeply. "Quite frankly, I just wish we could create a Fading for them."

Cabeza spoke up at that. "Well, that's a fine wish, truly. And the Fading makes for a good story because it helps illuminate certain concepts. But we do not know how to target the needed elements with enough specificity, not currently. We have tried lowering testosterone levels and eradicating males in the past, but it just hasn't worked out. Obviously, now we know it's not males or testosterone, or at least not just testosterone. And we might be able to come up with effective anti-MMR medicines in the future, but we certainly don't have the time to create that for Earth in this timeline."

Sharon blinked. "This timeline?"

"Yes. I know we've sort of mentioned it in passing…" Cabeza paused. "It's in your BNFP, but I don't believe anyone has actually discussed this with you. We call it the known universes for a reason, Sharon. Sync tells me you are a big fan of The Long Earth series. The authors weren't far off on it, although the multiverses in the CC are more like bubbles from a huge pot of boiling water, all existing at once on an impossibly large, uneven burner. Some places have many more bubbles and some places have fewer. We only know of five spacetimecontinuums for Earth, and you live within the fourth. Each spacetimecontinuum can have multiple timelines. We know of five previous timelines in your spacetimecontinuum. You are living in the sixth timeline. The previous five timelines all correspond to your 'mass extinction' episodes."

Sharon blinked again. "Oh, yeah, I remember the calendar definitions in the Fact Packet Thingy. The mass extinctions, that makes sense, I guess." After another blink she asked, "Wait, did you kill off males on Earth in another timeline?"

Sync jumped in rather nervously. "No, no, that was an entirely different solarium. Nope, we just arranged for some asteroids and helped Earth with a few massive volcanic eruptions, things like that. Earth has always used them of her own free will, no one has ever pressured her one way or another."

Sync knew the Captain had somehow brought this topic up on purpose, but she wasn't sure why. For now she wanted to ensure Sharon didn't get overly anxious; she was after all, just a one-brained being. Sync read Sharon's reactions carefully. Sharon, in turn, was focused on Petra.

And Petra was watching Captain Cabeza carefully. One of Cabeza's heads looked back in Petra's direction and raised an eyebrow archly. Petra flapped a little and then quipped, "Sharon, I'm sure all that stuff will be in the sequel, so let's get back to work on the plot for this little adventure, shall we?"

Musings Start To Morph

The next day, a larger group hunkered down in a conference room on the 3D main deck. The room was a bit too small, but no one seemed to mind. The atmosphere was electric with energy, and thick with the thoughts of well over two dozen experts in various fields.

They'd spent the last two hours discussing and exploring the ways trauma could be contributing to the MMR infection, and were now trying to figure out ways to lessen the grip of 'power over' that a small group of the most infected seemed to have on how things continued to operate on the planet, and specifically, in America.

"Well, one strategy we might think about is to seriously disrupt the proceedings at something like the Tri Lateral Commissary. Or, we could try infiltrating an intelligence agency—that might be easier, actually, given that spies from different countries seem to do that to each other all the time," Professor InDepth said.

Petra snorted, but said nothing.

"What's the Tri Lateral Commissary?" OT asked.

"It's a group of rich, white men who meet to come up with plans to control the world, so they can continue to hog all the riches in the trough they continually eat at!" Petra said with an uncharacteristic tone of sarcasm.

Sharon ignored Petra's vocalization. "Like many of this kind of group, they are a bit secretive, so it's hard to say exactly. But Petra's right, essentially. It's composed of a bunch of rich, powerful people and media figures—almost all male, and white—who peddle capitalist visions of bliss and make secret deals with each other to ensure their power is not upset."

InDepth nodded. "Good, er, I mean, not good. But it means our records of Earth are pretty accurate. According to the information we've gathered, there appear to be several of these kinds of groups that meet every year and have slightly different aims, but in the end, they share some of the same members. Many CC scholars think the majority of these groups also have ties to at least some state intelligence agencies."

There were gasps and guffaws around the table. "Surely you jest!" one said.

"I unfortunately do not." InDepth pushed her glasses back up her nose vigorously. "It is hard to overstate how serious the infection is down there! For example, every one of these 'intelligence agencies' exists to supposedly protect democracy from international and domestic threats. Yet none of them apparently see the obvious cases of the subversion of democracy done in the wheeling and dealing within these groups. These deals have huge implications, but they are kept secret. And, you can't have a democracy if the citizens don't know what is really going on."

Murmurs of disbelief and outrage flitted around the room.

Petra jumped in. "No, to intelligence agencies, these dealings are just seen as business as usual, even though they secretly affect official federal level policy all the time. Only when a foreign entity does something blatant, do they eventually deal with it—usually after an alternative media outlet draws attention to it.

"Speaking of, it's even worse how these intelligence agencies ignore the widespread problems within what we call the news. Heck, we know that the intelligence agencies themselves regularly ask corporate media to quash certain stories. These people at these agencies, who are supposed to be protecting democracy, refuse to recognize the suppression of very popular viewpoints—suppression by the corporate media outlets—as threats to democracy. Not long ago, one of the richest candidates down there changed his party affiliation and simply bought five hundred million dollars-worth of "free speech" in order to run for national office. Meanwhile, the corporately controlled outlets (including his own) gave tons of coverage to him and other candidates, but not to the one candidate with far and away the most grassroots donations. The reality is, that without that media coverage, candidates just can't get more popular.

"None of the so-called intelligence agencies charged with protecting democracy saw any of those things as threats to democracy."

Several in the room gasped at this. As Sharon shook her head sadly to confirm what Petra and Professor InDepth were saying, a palpable mixture of anger and sadness began to rise in the room.

Petra's energies continued to gain steam, and she kept talking with an increased urgency and seriousness. "It's that bad and worse! The basic premises of intelligence agencies are that others are not to be trusted, so they came up with the bright idea that they themselves needed to lie, steal, cheat, and interfere covertly in order to…somehow try to…promote truth and democracy in other parts of the world."

There were more gasps all around the room at this. A Wallert in a corner emitted a sort of strangled shriek of distress.

"Tis true, I'm afraid," Petra said sadly, tempering her voice momentarily in response to the Wallert's distress. "On Earth, spies are closely aligned with what we call the Military Industrial Complex. Or MIC. And the MIC mindset has always been completely infected by MMR. I mean, truly, in Might Makes Right, it is the use of or threat of force that determines who has 'power over' others. That literally is what is meant by Might Makes Right. As we've said before, any nine-year-old child can see the illogic of using force to keep the peace, but generation after generation of brainwashed humans keep funding and otherwise supporting military legitimacy. The MIC is vast and is one of the most lucrative industries on Earth."

A Kanga gasped loudly at this. "Say it's not so!" she pleaded.

"I'm afraid it is so. And not only is it lucrative, it's deadly. The most infected of humans believe that killing people to keep the peace is justified in most cases when they do it, but never when anyone else does it... There are just no words for how crazy it can get down there." Her tone showed urgency, as everyone in the room listened with rapt attention and horror.

"On top of that, the players within the MIC take obscene amounts of our tax money while kids go hungry.

"In the US, huge amounts of tax money goes to agencies with corrupt spies working for them and billions more goes to pay MIC contractors, many of whom who employ lowlife mercenaries to do terrible things such as run illegal arms, aid and abet militias, start riots, assassinate people, and probably engage in a lot of blackmail and extortion.

"They do this because their true objective is to gain power and control by any means necessary, not to protect democracy."

She sighed heavily. "These so called intelligence agencies gather information on pacifists, social justice activists, and other peace mongers! Meanwhile, they let dozens of high level criminals in administration after administration continue to be crooks and continue to hold high level offices. Hell, the leaders of these spy agencies sometimes become presidents themselves. I know my words are hard to believe, but they are true!"

"I thought they were patriots?" someone asked with a wavering voice. The crew on the GSS Prosperity were not at all used to hearing about such levels of corruption and obvious foolhardiness.

Props—But Not In A Good Way

Petra was so wound up by this point that she no longer seemed to notice the shocked and dismayed looks around her. She replied to the question of patriotism with patience for the participant's question, but her voice remained uncharacteristically serious and urgent.

"An aura of heroic selflessness is a something these spies and the other MIC goons work hard to peddle to the public. They work in partnership with the corporately owned media to promote that vision. But spies being patriots in the sense of truly working for democracy? I'm sure some actually do work that does align with those values. But that clearly is not the true aims of most senior leadership. The leaders allow some work for the common good in order to help keep up appearances. But they all just want more power and control for themselves and their friends—the ultra-wealthy. That's why they have to peddle their supposed virtue and heroism so hard."

Because Petra was already known to be quite chipper and upbeat, her words produced even more shock than they might have. "We cannot underestimate the role propaganda plays in this infection! It's huge. The media peddles softball questions to MIC spokespeople and ignores the obvious corruption.

"When certain things do get out—again, usually through alternative media outlets—the corporately owned media doesn't pursue them, instead they do damage control. They have learned how to carefully present 'controversies' about issues, or give watered-down spins on the subject as if the watered down views were 'public opinion,' knowing full well they are the ones actively shaping that public opinion. All kinds of decisions about what is and is not seen as important news are carefully spun through corporate filters, all while the parent corporations continue to shape cultural norms in other ways beyond the news."

"And in what ways do these parent corporations do that?" Captain Cabeza asked mildly.

Petra paused for emphasis "Excellent question, as usual, Captain. These same corporations also own entertainment groups. These entertainment groups have created—as entertainment—show after show of what amounts to propaganda. There are literally scores of series billed as entertainment about patriotic and righteous cops, FBI agents, loyal spies, detectives who work undercover, military law enforcement entities, and general good deeds done by the military and other aligned professions. These shows feature instances of force and violence, often being used for 'good.' And, by the way, almost all of those shows are incredibly androcentric."

Meg's energies turned snarky at this point. "How convenient for the males down there."

"So true," Petra said. "But back to the point. Then they market the hell out of these shows. Humans are adaptable and will often grow to accept and even truly like a great variety of horrid things, like these shows and…kale."

Sharon shuddered theatrically.

"With only a little prodding from marketers, humans will often consume whatever entertainment options are available. That makes the cultural norms continue to drift in the direction of seeing the use of violence and spies and military as a good thing. These shows have also gotten shockingly violent down there."

Several beings now looked a bit puzzled. A Wintonesian named Alice asked, "I thought humans were almost Semi aware? How can they not see what's happening?"

Petra regarded Alice calmly. "Well, it's a good question. The thing is, cultural norms are pretty much still invisible parts of life for most humans. The vast majority of them, especially when they think about things like violence, continuously mistake cultural norms for 'human nature,' not realizing the truly stunning numbers of options humans have at their disposal. With just one brain, humans only have the capacity to attend to a limited number of things at a time. So most accept whatever cultural norms are around them. Only when things get really unfair do they start to question how their lives are organized. And even then, they do so sort of half aware that their realities are just made up of norms.

"You have to remember that from the moment they are born, human babies start to adapt to their cultures by just soaking up whatever is around them uncritically. They learn whatever language is around them, they learn whatever customs are around them; they are taught to believe in certain things and to regard some things as important and other things as not very important."

Heads started nodding slowly.

"So here we are indoctrinated to value Goodness, cooperation, collaboration, love, respect, and we sort of assume those things are good. And the ideas work for us, so we continue to accept them," another Wintonesian said.

A Centrail named Scarface said, "Yes, but our elders also carefully tell us they are indoctrinating us. They encourage us to actively think through the values being taught."

Sharon nodded. Petra said, "Yes, exactly, humans are taught about love and fairness, too. It's just not the only things they are taught. So when their values clash, lots of times people don't even notice, and they just sort of accept both. For example, in America, the framers of the Constitution wrote 'all men are created equal' while they owned other human beings. And they were just as blind to their hypocrisy about how they treated women or people without money. They thought it was 'natural' that some humans were 'inferior,' even as they were envisioning equality.

"So clearly they were more than a bit dense when it came to recognizing their own cultural constructs. And they still are. Humans often have real trouble seeing cultural constructs as such. The most infected often revert to ideas about human nature when pressed. Sexist people or racists will often truly believe biology or human nature is at the root of sexism or racism. They don't see it as stemming from oppression."

"Wow." Meg boomed the word a little louder than she may have meant. Many beings in the room, already shocked by the ideas, startled a bit at her vocalization.

Captain Cabeza cut in at this point and directed her comments at Petra. "It is very clear that MMR stunts reasoning in humans. Our pressing issue is learning how MMR transmits, and how to neutralize the infection. This idea of cultural norms being mistaken for 'human nature' seems important. So, what I hear you saying is that, first off, some cultural norms are based in…narratives that are false. Or what amounts to propaganda. And that false narrative or propaganda effectively hides how things really work down there. Is that accurate?"

"Yes, Captain, it is. As you know, for centuries both men and women told each other than women were inferior to men—and most of the population believed or went along with this obvious lie! It was cultural-level propaganda. It's just astounding what they will believe when their fears have been triggered.

"The —current— deceits are hard for many to see, just as it was nearly impossible for many to see past the lies of male superiority. One example is millions and millions of humans believing that military might will keep them safe, and the threat of violence will somehow lead to peace.

"We all know that no aware or healthy cultures would ever allow entities like this to exist, but many humans wouldn't really understand or believe what I'm saying, because they've been so brainwashed. Hell, they still see military veterans as heroes, not victims of a massive scam."

Sharon nodded in agreement as the CC crew members looked at each other with shocked expressions.

Petra's energies flapped vigorously as she continued. "On Earth, if Sharon were to say something like 'I see vets as victims, not heroes,' in many cases she'd be shunned by otherwise intelligent and good people.

"The atmosphere for people who talk about these ideas is much like the atmosphere was for American atheists trying to get their ideas out fifty years ago. It can get downright dangerous to say these things out loud in certain instances, even in otherwise intelligent company. And don't even get me started on the lack of free speech in other areas on the planet."

Petra sighed. "I know it's hard for you all to believe, but I'm really not kidding. The most infected humans openly profess to 'know' that—a male vision of—God is on their side, so they are justified if they kill other human beings."

A Centrail angrily spluttered, "The Hubris!"

Petra sighed again. "Yes, truly. Hubris is a huge piece of it. People get so arrogant without cause. It can feel like we are living in some sort of a sitcom. Except the humans most afflicted with Hubris sometimes do rise to power, or strongly support those who are also afflicted; and then they do hideous things, so it's really not all that funny.

"Remember, MIC folks are among the in the worst afflicted by MMR. And people within the MIC have at their disposal regular soldiers, spies, and mercenaries who will kill other humans due to differences in beliefs—no matter how wrong or unjust the order is. The Hubris down there can easily lead to the deaths of innocent people."

Several in the room gasped in shock. A number of beings were visibly upset, and two Wallerts in attendance were shaking and sobbing. Intra, the Wintonesian refugee from a different infected area, had been nodding and crying while Petra spoke.

Petra looked a bit sheepish. "Of course the humans I refer to are quite sick, and I am sorry for that. But in the case of 'intelligence' workers, I feel they must be more consciously aware of what they are advocating for than most. So I hold a special wrath for them. To me, it appears that many spies consciously transmit MMR-infected mindsets, so that they and their agencies can keep their power and control."

At this, one of the Wallerts started to wail loudly in distress, and hopped out of the room. Several in the room attended to him, while others continued to exchange shocked looks. In the silence that followed, Sharon said quietly, "Unfortunately, everything Petra said is true." She said it with such sadness that the group spontaneously sent loving kindness energy to them with such force they were both stunned and unable to do anything but receive the support.

Captain Cabeza had gazed kindly at those in distress, and those that attended to them. But she reverted a more serious gaze back to Petra, willing Petra to add one last thing.

Finally, Petra flapped her energy a little and said more quietly, "An idea we have down there is that everyone is just doing the best they can, and we should try not to judge people. Most people are doing the best they can, I believe that. But I believe that many people associated with the MIC are not 'doing the best they can.' Instead of protecting citizens, they are aiding and abetting the worst elements."

She seemed to struggle a bit. "I do have compassion for them, but I also struggle with bouts of utter disgust as well, which may be obvious." With a swirling of apologetic energy she finally added, "I am sorry for harsh words against other beings."

A solemn pause ensued as Captain Cabeza nodded approvingly. She raised an arm, indicating she had something to say. Everyone looked in her direction. "Thank you for the information," she said. "And also, a sincere thanks for allowing us to understand why you hold special anger, as well as sorrow, compassion, and pity for these beings. It is indeed tragic to consider the waste of what could otherwise be fully functioning humans. A period of silence for their stuntedness and their loss of humane responses seems in very much in order."

As had been the case for several minutes now, more than a few snuffles could be heard in the room. During the silence, Sharon and Petra both marveled at how the crew had responded, so shocked at the state of things, and how willing they were to show their vulnerability, anger, sadness, and compassion about the information and towards each other. Sharon allowed a couple of her own tears to stream down her face in grief and in gratefulness for the support these beings were showing her and her planet.

Gradually the group regulated itself, and moved off from the grief.

Captain Cabeza said, "May we all grow in Goodness."

Everyone replied back with the same words, according to their own time.

Mysterious Connections Of The Nefarious Sort

After a few more beats, InDepth Looked at Cabeza who inclined a head subtly.

"Thank you, Captain. Petra's information is sobering, and quite illuminating. Truly your words have helped us see some of the dreadful effects of MMR even more clearly." She bowed respectfully in Petra's direction. "But, let's go back to the original question. Exactly how intelligence groups work with the elite business groups is a mystery. I have no real idea about what they do exactly." Professor InDepth then looked over at Sharon to see if she had anything to say.

"I'm not exactly sure either," Sharon said. "What probably happens is the members within a group vow loyalty to each other no matter what. And probably they also vow to protect everyone else involved, too. So, for example, if one of their people gets into trouble for a shady deal, another one with connections to judges will ensure that the trouble goes away. My guess is it's that simple, and that disgusting. "

"Also, you have to realize, the idea of loyalty gets carried to ridiculous lengths in what we call 'party politics' in America.

"The real truth of it doesn't matter—especially, I'd guess, as the level of Hubris rises. Loyalty is all that matters. And loyalty is quite obviously and openly used to support very corrupt actions. It's quite impressively twisted." She sighed. "It's pretty common on Earth, at least in my country, and especially lately. What it truly is, is treasonous, but hardly anyone says that out loud."

Sharon paused, debating, then decided to go

ahead with it. "I think they have taken cues from major religious groups who cultivate similar levels of loyalty. Speaking of which, a lot of these groups seem to have ties to monotheistic, patriarchal religions, as well. And the vast majority were only open to rich, white men for a long, long time—in fact, some still are male only. Like the Bohos, or as I like to call them, the Bozos."

The group was staring at her, again dumbfounded by the stuntedness of these humans. "You're kidding!" someone said.

"Oh how I wish I was! The Bozo Grove gatherings are still held within a hundred miles of where I grew up. They are still male only, and they are where many important deals are still made...even in the twenty-first century," Sharon said grimly.

Professor InDepth spoke up again. "Sharon's right. Many of the most powerful groups still exclude most people, and though they meet publicly, what they say is carefully guarded in secrecy. Groups like the Tri Lateral Commissary all have members who have vast sums of money, and those members have access to other groups who also control incredible amounts of money. That would include groups like the Calooded Group and Baneshare. These groups will say they are 'simply' private equity firms, but they regularly move money around to some very dark ventures.

"And it's true, the intelligence agencies Petra spoke about must be aware of that, but...they do nothing. That's why many of our CC scholars suspect they have secret ties to each other. Then there are these sort of activist groups like the Blitterderberg and, as Sharon calls them, the Bozo Grove group. They support the causes of the rich and powerful, and appear to spend most of their time working to keep power and money in the hands of those who already have it.

"The members from those groups then go to meet with official government groups. For example, the Camp Dullard ancillary meetings are well known. And then there are these other groups that purport to be working for the public good, like the Planetary Economic Forum. In reality, only gazillionaires attend their meetings at someplace called Davio's, so…only those most obsessed with power and control go to these meetings. In other words, the millions upon millions of people who are mostly filled with Goodness rather than ego don't actually get into the circles where the power really is; only the most infected with MMR do." InDepth paused to let that information sink in.

Sharon looked rueful. Truly her planet was a mess. But the sincere and palpable sadness, disgust, and outrage reverberating around the room heartened her. She'd unfortunately gotten quite used to armies of apologists, and rude denials from other—more infected—humans down on Earth. So to be in a group like this, that could clearly see how horrible things were, and who were honestly appalled by the actions rather than cynically resigned to them, or completely oblivious about their existences, was truly wonderful, despite the heaviness of the truth itself.

"I thought there were a few journalists among them? Aren't they supposed to report on corruption, and be part of the checks and balances there?" someone asked a bit nervously.

Professor InDepth nodded at Sharon to answer. Sharon grimaced, "The only kinds of people who get officially invited to groups like that are allies. So, yeah, there are a few lap dogs for the rich and powerful, but they peddle in propaganda, not journalism—whether or not they admit to it. Petra's right about propaganda. It's a very important piece of this puzzle. On our planet, at best, the news is just another 'for profit venture,' and what is considered news is quietly but carefully run through filters that the news outlets then deny are there. But freedom of the press clearly only belongs to those who own the printing presses."

There were fresh gasps of incomprehension. "But surely the humans know that treating news or information like a for-profit business is dangerous?"

Sharon shook her head sadly. "No, they don't."

There were some shocked expressions. Professor InDepth saw the incomprehension among the crew and elaborated. "No, it appears they generally don't, and much of the reason for that is because the news outlets don't share that kind of information! In America there are about five corporations with a lot of money and power to direct what is and isn't considered news."

More gasps were heard. The professor went on, "According to the research I've seen, several of the largest movie studios are all owned by more or less the same enormous firms that own the news outlets. Remember, one of the primary things MMR does is consolidate and expand power for a few. And it's a frightfully strong virus down there right now. Look at how well the businesses follow that theme. It's an impressively robust disease."

Meanwhile, Back At The Ranch

During the silence that followed, a Wintonesian participant looked up from a computer screen and said, "Um, excuse me, but it looks like a meeting of many men from a bunch of these groups is coming up…in a few months…for us…I mean…it looks like in less than a week, uh, in Earth time. It's going to be at…uh, it looks like…how weird…well, this seems unlikely, but it looks like it will be at a ranch in the state of New Mexico. It's sort of a mishmash between the groups. Looks like there will be dozens of these guys, and their entourages."

The Wintonesian skimmed through the information as it spoke. "Yup, it is almost exclusively white males. And what appear to be administrative people and other minions. With a bunch of bodyguards. They apparently need a lot of bodyguards. They will be gathered at a ranch, called Zed Ranch. It's going to be heavily armed."

"Why there?" someone asked.

The Wintonesian spoke up "Well, let's see... Ah, wow, this is interesting. It belonged to a man named Jeffrey E. He is dead—Goodness have mercy, it looks like he was a monster. He was convicted of several sex crimes, and given a really light sentence. And he was friends with… oh wow, look at this list of people. He had met dozens of times with heads of state, and with British royalty! He knew a bunch of famous actors, he took meetings with very influential media publishers…yeah, wow, he was up to no good…he was impressively corrupt. And there are rumors that he was somehow involved with intelligence groups. He appears to have influenced state and federal attorney generals, law enforcement leaders, and…this list just goes on. You have to wonder what he had on these guys, since he was a convicted sex offender...pedophile...himself...I mean, why would people do his bidding?"

Professor InDepth pushed her glasses back up. "Yes, that would appear to be a reasonable question. Obviously money is at work., but...the majority of those people would also have their own vaults of money, and could have withstood threats to their loss of empire. But if he held other, more overtly illegal actions over their heads, then they might be pretty compelled to do his bidding." InDepth's tone was grim.

When Sync spoke, there was an uncharacteristic graveness in her tone. "This does look ugly. Why would these men associate with such a person unless he did have some kinds of illegal information on them? I mean we don't know that for sure, but it looks pretty bad."

She swirled energy around. " I don't know how humans who value compassion and truth keep going. No wonder there's so much depression and acting out." She'd carefully avoided looking at Sharon as she said this, but Sharon felt again validated by Sync's kind awareness of how difficult things really were for humans on Earth. She wiped tears of gratefulness from her eyes.

"This is all horrid, but important information. Can you tell us more?" Captain Cabeza asked.

The young computer expert nodded. "Yes. A few minutes ago, I found a guest list for this, uh...gathering of whatever they are...at the ranch, so I cross referenced names. Like I said, many of the men invited also show up as members or participants in these other groups. I just ran the odds of this guest list to rule out coincidence that maybe these guys were randomly selected. I honestly can't even read the odds against it being coincidence without stopping to count the zeros. One, two three, four.... The odds are approximately 754 billion to one. Which sounds terrible. But according to my records, the amount of wealth that the participants control or influence is quite a bit higher than those odds. That means the wealth that will be represented in that room of maybe a hundred people will be about as much as the combined wealth of more than two billion of the world's poorest people, give or take."

The room again succumbed to a stunned silence. Sharon felt her stomach lurch a bit, as it tended to do when she thought too long about these kinds of facts.

"If this were an Earth piece of science fiction, the villains would be, umm, a bit overly obvious, wouldn't they? I mean, it would be so obviously obvious, it might seem a bit overblown," Meg said from a corner of the room. Others around the table murmured in agreement.

Petra spoke up. "Well, it's much easier for us to tell the story clearly, using our own variation of narrativium. On Earth, no one's telling the whole story. You have to realize that the same guys that will be at this meeting spend literally hundreds of millions, if not billions of dollars to keep this part of the plot line discounted, hidden, or spinning so that it seems less ugly than it is. They employ PR goons, lawyers to threaten people, and so on."

Petra flapped her energies a bit. "On top of that, humans are all juggling a million other things. They are often exhausted by simply making a living at crappy jobs in loud, polluted, and over priced cities. They are surrounded by propaganda that encourages them to shop their cares away. They have to do all kinds of chores and errands. These things add up so that egos are in charge and their souls are being purposefully silenced for huge parts of their waking lives. Most of them are too distracted to even think about these guys or the stuff they're doing."

Yet another round of gasps occurred. Someone

said, "I don't think I can take much more of even hearing about how bad things are down there! You poor, poor beings!"

There were further murmurs of agreement.

Petra said, "Thanks for the sympathy, you all. We appreciate it. But to get back to the point: A majority of humans don't even know who these guys are. Humans are busy dealing with all kinds of pressures: sick parents, endless bills, traffic jams, what to eat, how to get twelve things done in three hours. They have financial worries, and they are constantly being told that status matters, and that unless they do A, B and C, others will find them lacking. That kind of propaganda is everywhere."

She looked at Sharon. "Even the relatively secure among them become often obsessed with keeping up, rather than looking at what is happening. And so they fall for consumerism, even as they are able to identify some of it. Propaganda is a well-oiled machine down there…'in the land of the free.'" Petra waved off energy to close the subject. Sharon nodded, but didn't add anything.

Murmurs

Cabeza called for a break. The beings gathered at the meeting were obviously not accustomed to learning about the effects of MMR firsthand from survivors. They'd been greatly shocked—several times—by the descriptions of what life was like for humans on the planet.

Several members erupted into more tears during the break, and the numbers of participants consoling them meant that the break had to be extended. After three hours, including a nice lunch, the participants had regained some equilibrium and were ready to get back to work. Captain Cabeza sent a mind command to invite everyone to gather back in the conference room. As they gathered, murmurs went around the table.

"By the gasses of Uranus, we should disrupt that gathering all right!" someone said.

"And do what?" Meg asked.

"Excellent question, as usual, Meg," Captain Cabeza said, officially calling the meeting back into order. "Let's start right there regarding this gathering. It certainly looks like we've got the right group—an auspicious sign for sure. These are men heavily infected with MMR. But CC laws are clear about contact with Unaware beings. So even with Earth's permission to do with them what we want, our options are very limited. I think we might be putting...the car before the garage, is that what they say, Sync?" Captain Cabeza said.

"I think the expression is 'putting the horse before the carriage,' Captain."

The Captain's curt head give her a quick wink as another head said, "Ah, yes, that does sound more familiar."

"This ranch is in the middle of nowhere and will

be heavily guarded." The same computer expert who had told them about the meeting looked up from her screen as she said this.

"We could disguise ourselves as guards, maybe?" said a young officer.

Sharon studied the officer with interest. Wintonesians are classically humanoid in appearance, but grey in color. Sharon was getting the impression that they started out as dark grey, but faded to lighter shades over time. Regardless, the being looked fairly human to Sharon's eyes, and she mused again at how comfortably at home she felt here on the ship, and what a kind, healthy environment surrounded her. Sharon had also noticed that the walls of the room changed colors subtly along with the mood in the room. She had not noticed this in other rooms, but resolved to pay attention going forward.

Another Wintonesian has answered, "Maybe, but...we'd have to put the real guards somewhere, right?"

"Yes, but what will we do once we're down there? That's what we need to really focus on!" Professor InDepth said with a little exasperation.

"Well, we could test them all," a Centrail said. "See if there's something that makes some of them overly susceptible to becoming so infected. I mean they all were subjected to similar collective traumas, but only some of them become...so...hideously infected."

"Uh, if I may," Sharon said, "I think the little Fear Song in my BNFP might point to some of the issue. Not all of it, but...You know, the Amygdala in Overdrive song?"

Sync emanated surprise. "Our Honored Guest is right." Sync then gathered some energy and threw it somewhat playfully out into the room, as she chuckled.

"I cannot help but notice that we've held many pieces of the puzzle in our possession all along...oh my word there are just layers of synchronicity here! We overtly teach everyone there's nothing to fear, and yet we couldn't figure out that those who are more susceptible to fear are the ones spreading MMR infections on Earth? Wow, we really do keep growing in awareness every day, don't we?" Sync's energies swirled around with enthusiasm.

At that point, the ship seemed to purr for a moment, but nothing else happened. Everyone noticed, and a few Wallerts shivered in happy awareness of the synchronicity. The Captain and Sync silently conferred with each other on how to acknowledge or not acknowledge the purring. After a moment, Sync vocalized the ending line of the conscious intention for good meetings: "May we always find wonder in the singularity." Heads nodded and they all replied more or less in unison, "Praise Goodness."

A different Centrail broke the silence. "So if we do test, and we do find enlarged amygdalae or weaknesses in a similar areas that makes certain beings—er humans—more susceptible, what then? I mean, going back to the Captain's observation, we can only intervene in limited ways." The Centrails then bowed to each other and briefly turned bright green in a species-specific signal they were engaged in good faith, intentional debate.

Aside: Turning green is only possible when Centrails are acting in good faith. Centrails involuntarily turn reddish when they revert to ego-based thinking.

"Our colleague raises a good point, and one we should address," Professor InDepth said. "But I would like to also propose another avenue. It seems copious amounts of propaganda in various forms are key to keeping the MMR-infected power structure intact at this point. Force is not used as often as it was previously, but it does appear that propaganda has taken its place. Petra's already talked about how virtually all of the corporately owned sources of information purporting to be unbiased are actually engaged in serious pro-MMR agenda-setting."

As she continued, she directed her comments pointedly at Sharon to get confirmation. "Do you concur with that assessment?"

"Yes," Sharon said. Now her voice took on some of the same urgency they'd heard earlier from Petra. "The propaganda is brilliant down there. It's brilliant precisely because it's so easy to miss. We've talked about the news. And please remember, even though it's clear to Petra and Emma and me, millions of other humans will flat out deny that there is bias in their favorite news sources. And then, in entertainment, the execs can just say 'Ha! We're not engaged in any agenda setting. We only produce what people want!' But many times people want it only because the same four of five corporations have spent millions and millions of dollars promoting it. And again, it's usually incredibly androcentric stuff they peddle relentlessly."

The whole room was silent for a few moments as they pondered ideas and strategies.

Meg's energies started whirring a bit. Several beings looked with interest in her direction, knowing that these were signals that she was on the verge of thinking something through. Suddenly, she unselfconsciously exclaimed, "Of course! Memes!" Her energies turned triumphant.

"Would you like to elaborate?" Captain Cabeza said with a touch of humor.

"We use the Amygdalas in Overdrive song and

create memes! Memes are so…compact. They can be seen as simple statements, not true educational tools. So the CC would be able sign onto that, wouldn't they, especially if Sharon mostly authored them, right?

"We go down there, create a UFO kind of stir at that meeting—you know, set up a bit of a media feeding frenzy by somehow disrupting or messing up a meeting of the rich and powerful. Get people to pay attention to it. I don't know, maybe we could create a huge tornado there or something. Anyway, we get the people's attention by messing with this meeting. Then directly after that, we could create a whole bunch of memes showing how silly MMR is. And link these guys to it, and the whole idea of MMR. We create pictures of MMR infections: certain political leaders, brutal military destruction, armed white supremacists, you know, the most infected folks, and then underneath we simply put the words 'Amygdalas in Overdrive, It's when our IQs take a dive!' Then we somehow get them to go viral, you know, make them so popular that they come up everywhere."

Sharon spoke up. "And we could pair memes up with a novel I've been working on! I could incorporate some into the novel, too."

Captain Cabeza threw all five heads back and exclaimed, "Right, so you are proposing we fight their propaganda with our own propaganda. That's fitting! And it's not going to hurt anyone. I love it!"

Sensing the badly needed lighter tone and willingness in the room to pursue this idea, Professor InDepth said, "Let's just go with this right now."

Preppers Gonna Prep

Over the next few days many memes were produced, but the hard work of figuring out how to infiltrate and disrupt the meeting safely took much more time. Luckily, the crew had about three months to get ready.

Sharon and Petra spent many hours helping Meg perfect disguises for the crew members who would pretend to be bodyguards and assistants for the meeting's participants. Sharon and Petra also led training sessions for crew members in how to act like the kinds of humans who would be willing to work at events like this. Ship historians, as per standard ship protocols, captured the trainings, with all their successes and mishaps. Various situations were slated to be fashioned into entertainment and/or instruction for CC members to view in the future.

Planetside practice runs were essential pieces of the planning. Each crew member spent at least six hours planetside passing as human. The way the crew members had to behave towards other beings made many quite upset, and more than a few became physically ill. Meg created supplies of anti-anxiety and anti-nausea pills to help with this issue. A few volunteers dropped out due to not wanting to mimic the actions of the MMR-infected enablers. A few more dropped out after their practice runs, and went into recovery periods. They were replaced by those on the long wait list for the mission. The crew members were quite invested in the mission, but it was still quite difficult for them to act so callously. So they swallowed medications as needed, and practiced for many hours. By the time deployment actually came around, everyone felt pretty good about the crew's ability to fool the humans who would be attending or working at the meeting.

The reconnaissance work of the terrain they'd be going into fascinated Sharon. In roughly the middle of Mr. E's ranch, there was a very large and opulent mansion. The ranch took up several hundred acres in a rural area of New Mexico, and was almost completely surrounded by another large, privately owned ranch, owned by one of the lesser known figures involved in the activities of these rich men. In total, several thousand acres of land were privately owned between these two multimillionaires. This privacy would —under normal circumstances—enable the attendees of the upcoming meeting to meet in complete privacy, and with several layers of security. But the numerous levels and kinds of security measures were easy enough for the CC computer whizzes to detect and work around.

On the two ranches various outbuildings and shops dotted the landscape. There were two landing strips for airplanes, a couple of large hangars, and five concrete helicopter pads. There were also a few modest houses and shops, where people who presumably worked for the multimillionaires lived. Plans were drawn up for temporarily disabling the humans that might be found in these places.

The crew also studied the layout of the mansion and its several guesthouses. On Earth, all of the major GPS providers block off access to satellite images of high value or sensitive properties in their mapping applications. But aboard the ship, getting a precise layout of the ranches, the assorted buildings, and the main mansion was all rather easily accomplished due to a bit of eleven-dimensional physics that allowed three-dimensional holograms of the buildings and nearby terrain to be recreated shipside. This allowed for very realistic practice drills aboard the ship.

Dodging the security checkpoints would be quite easy since the crew would be directly transported to their assigned locations within the ranch, without having to drive, hike, helicopter, or otherwise physically traverse the exposed desert terrain.

Shipside, post-mission quarantine protocols were set up and readied. Intra, the refugee from the Solarium of Onychomycosis, also known as S.Ony, headed up the committees working on projects related to this. Volunteers down on the planet the longest would be at some risk of contamination by MMR, so arrangements were made for recovery programs. As was usual in the CC, thinking ahead to the wellbeing of the crew was the foremost consideration. Intra and the other quarantine committee members planned enjoyable recovery and post-mission quarantine activities, complete with popular live music acts, food and festivities, and entertainment. They worked hard to try to develop a way to make the quarantine period as enjoyable as possible. They also developed contingency plans in case some crew members became ill and did not recover as fully as hoped.

Other committees worked on the educational materials aspect of the mission. Crew members studied marketing and propaganda to help them understand how information currently 'went viral' on Earth. There were numerous debates on how to best to spread the message about both the infection of MMR, and its roots.

Denial Is Not A River In Egypt

During the planning, Sharon, Emma, and Petra held several large informational meetings. At one of them, Sharon told the crew that, as a psychotherapist on Earth, one of the hardest parts of her work was helping people break through their own denial. She explained that the concept of denial is most commonly paired with addiction, especially to drugs and alcohol. She said a few knew that denial was at work in other addictions, too, such as gambling and anorexia. But Sharon pointed out that most people did not realize how pervasive it was in other areas of life.

Sharon said the same mechanism seemed to be in play for a fair percentage of folks regarding religious and political beliefs. She shared her own observations about how this extended to those deeply afflicted with MMR-infected kinds of beliefs such as misogyny, racism, and homophobia. Infected humans would deny they were racist or misogynist or homophobic, and would rigidly stick to 'defenses' of their beliefs in ways that made no logical sense at all. Elements of denial seemed to hold true for many who held beliefs about military necessity and economic systems built on MMR principles. People blindly supporting such systems routinely dismissed the ills the systems caused in the same ways that alcoholics dismiss their own liver cirrhosis. She also shared that some folks appeared to be in full denial about the actions and suitability of some political 'leaders.'

The planning crew worked hard on how to break down denial. This part of human psychology was quite difficult to deal with precisely because of this issue:

Almost universally, Sharon explained, the humans most afflicted with denial are in denial about being in denial. "Nothing's ever easy down there," she'd sighed at the end of her explanation.

Indeed, adult human minds often become so riddled with thinking errors that they come to believe outrageous things without batting an eye. But uninfected children often initially have a hard time understanding some of the most horrible behaviors that adults resort to.

Sharon shared her own story about being a child and learning about war. She described how an older brother had first told her about it, and her horror upon learning that people willingly learned how to kill other humans. She was even further appalled to learn that the world had bothered to come up with rules for how to kill people, in something humans called 'the Geneva Conventions.' As a child, she couldn't imagine why they bothered to come up with rules for how to kill or maim people "humanely" instead of just figuring out how to not kill each other—after all, she already knew that resorting to violence was a shameful thing.

She told the crew that it was at this point when she—as a child—knew that something was making people sick. She knew people were meant to be loving, and that life was much better when people were kind and happy. And that something must be terribly wrong with humans if they still engaged in war.

She shared how disillusioning it was to realize tens of millions of people apparently went along with the idea of war, and that millions of them had organized their lives around being in the military. She also shared her lifelong puzzlement about how millions could buy into the idea that those willing to kill other humans were especially brave or even heroic.

The crew were shocked by anecdotes like this,

but Sharon, Emma and Petra took pains to further explain that a good number of people really did believe warring was somehow part of "human nature," and not a sign of extreme illness.

As a young adult, when she had learned that some men and their families profited immensely from war mongering, she had gotten very stuck in hating these people. So as a way to try to get unstuck, she tried to figure out what the heck was wrong with them.

While studying power in college, she wondered at how people so blithely attributed some people's obsessions with power to "human nature." She knew her own human nature didn't share these same obsessions, nor did the people she most liked and respected seem to have obsessions with power. So she studied and searched for some time before really putting certain ideas together.

She took care to mention that since she also lived within the cultural norms, it took her years to do this. But this was how she'd eventually come up with ideas that squared up with what the CC called MMR. She further saw how MMR stayed undetected due to denial, and had become convinced that trauma was what really started whole cultures headed towards infection.

Sharon, Emma, and Petra also taught the crew members about their firsthand knowledge of the many good points about humans. They shared how many millions—really, billions—of humans could see through the MMR, given half a chance, and that most could still access at least some of their Goodness. They spoke about the efforts that had already been made on the planet to recognize how people had historically been 'carefully taught to hate' and how terrible most people now realized that was.

They further pointed out that nowadays the

majority of people were not actively taught to hate, but that because of the generations of oppression, certain groups had privileges that were often hard for them to see in themselves. They also pointed out that many people still focused more on males, and males themselves tend to listen best to other males—a fact which the crew found especially disheartening, given that the larger members of species the universes over were known to be the most susceptible to falling for "logic" based on MMR arguments.

Nonetheless, Sharon pointed out how the majority of humans already consciously know—and certainly that all small kids know—that love is love is love. Their task was to help humans embody the love and to stop the forces that tried to mold children and adults into accepting in false beliefs about superiority in whatever form the sense of superiority took.

Pathways to Cures

It was easy enough for the crew to see that one of the most difficult aspects of MMR is its ability to infect beings unknowingly. Infected humans often have no conscious idea that their mindsets are horribly distorted and diseased by Fear-based thoughts. They often become quite defensive or go fully into denial if the subject is broached that they may have an infection.

Figuring out how to mitigate denial while propaganda was still being pumped out to humans would be difficult. So the crew focused on the concrete advances that had been made, especially in the last couple of hundred years.

The crew members spent many hours trying to decipher the exact mechanisms by which the many advancements in unlearning and recovering from MMR had taken place. During this time in the preparations, many articles were written, and theories put forth both by crew members and by Sharon, Emma, and Petra.

Aside: Those may be available for humans to peruse at later dates.

Several crew members thought that the humans' forays into computer networking were helping. Sharon and Petra were more neutral on that theory, because of the ways propaganda could also be distributed via networking, but did concede that norms could spread more quickly in any direction due to the influence networking.

Their talks were quite popular throughout the ship. During many social hours, it became a favorite pastime for different beings to impersonate Petra's chipper voice and quote various lines such as: 'Computer algorithms in the hands of MMR-infected corposrations are really quite like strong hooch in the hands of troubled teenagers. On the one hand, most teenagers do live through their most reckless escapades. But some don't. And the damage they do in the meantime!'

For their part, Sharon, Emma, and Petra made extensive efforts to impress on the crew that it is often that the most oppressed humans, whether due to color or gender or other qualities, who really galvanize advancements towards equality, since they generally have little to gain from MMR mindsets.

The crew determined that when enough humans could access compassion and see the perspective of another group, official policies and cultural changes seemed to follow. Compassion and awareness seemed to be key.

The crew also studied why, throughout the planet, women seemed to be less invested in MMR in general. It was obvious that women were endowed with less power down on Earth. So they knew the downsides of MMR thinking much more intimately.

But women also seemed to provide more thoughtful leadership when they did break through barriers. The committee members intensively studied why this might be. They determined that part of it, of course, was due to women, on average, being physically smaller than men, so they more intimately knew that might does not necessarily make right.

They thought another reason was due to the way women were socialized to be women. Their socialization allowed them to show compassion towards others in more situations, and that kept them (generally) a little closer to their souls.

Consults With The CC, Or: It's All Up To Sharon

Several consults with CC officials were held to find ways to work within CC laws to "seed" ideas, but not overtly teach humans about the disease the CC knew to be MMR. Finally, they came up with a compromise that seemed promising. It was determined that Sharon— a native human—could start off giving the initial explanation about MMR. This was a relatively easy sell, since she'd already mostly written a book about it. She would finish it, and then she, or more likely a few crew members, would try to get that book distributed widely on the planet.

Earth herself was also consulted during the preparations. In the end, Earth was hopeful, if a bit skeptical, about the final plan. She communicated that regardless of the outcome, she was profoundly grateful for the help from the CC, and said she would do all she could to hold off using the radiation and to protect the crew.

She mentioned that she was hopeful that many of her most aware humans would enjoy Sharon's book if they got access to it. The problem was getting the book into many hands.

In an unusual move that was nonetheless authorized by CC officials, Earth adopted twenty-six crew members who would stay down on the planet after the initial mission deployed the approved memes and stories. The crew members would stay in human form and would be considered humans for the entire time they stayed planetside—which was anticipated to be about two Earth years. These crew members would not be part of the crew who stormed the ranch, so their training would have a different focus from the majority of the crew had volunteered for the mission.

More information will be released by the CC regarding these crew members' heroic actions, over time.

Part 4

A Little Help From The CC

As part of the efforts to create a plan for Earth, a call for submissions went out to crew and passengers alike. The call was an invitation to submit essays, stories, poems, or other written ideas for consideration to try to help humans on Earth learn about MMR.

Quite a number of beings aboard the ship responded. It took many hours for Sharon, her elements, and a committee of MMR and humanoid experts to get through them all. At the committee's final meeting, Sharon said she had been brought to tears several times by the compassion the writings universally contained.

Some of the writings were clumsy attempts by beings trying to convey their thoughts in languages that were not anything like their own. Others were more successfully composed, but began and ended with perspectives so different from how humans lived on Earth that they would not make much sense to the humans infected with MMR. But even in those, Petra, Emma, and Sharon witnessed the heart-centered meanings of the writings —and they also saw how the beings conveyed their thoughts with sincerity and patience. The lack of rancor and bitterness was quite striking to the trio, caught as they had been in the disagreeable ways humans tended to write down on Earth.

In some of the writings, the love and compassion were so evident that the good energies almost jumped off the page and hugged the reader. Even in the most unusual entries, the lack of anger and bitterness caused Sharon and Petra to reflect on just how much they had also been affected by the anger and frustration that surrounded them on the planet. Many of the pieces were quite eloquent, and Sharon allowed her heart to soar at the beautiful ways the aware beings conveyed the universal concepts of love and peace, how wise their words were, and how kind.

They were so kind.

Representin' For The CC

Several thousand beings had taken their seats at an event to announce what was going to happen to the five essays that the committee, headed up by Sharon and her elements, felt would be the most compelling to humans. Due to the numbers of beings who wanted to attend the event, it was held in the largest auditorium on the ship. Sharon found herself nervous about speaking in front of so many wonderful beings. But her speech of thanks and the announcement of how the writings would be incorporated into the plan to help combat MMR on Earth were important things to convey, and she would try to communicate with as much grace as possible.

Everyone had gotten As Neededs that contained the final five essays, so they knew which essays had been chosen. The part they didn't know, though, was how Sharon would translate them into her own words.

Professor InDepth opened the event. InDepth spent a few minutes updating the audience about the progress on the general plan to infiltrate the meeting of infected men on Earth. Except to marvel at how naturally InDepth thanked various committees without pointing out individuals, Sharon had tuned out a little. But, all of a sudden it seemed, Professor InDepth was no longer speaking, and the applause was dying down. With a small hiccup of anxiety, Sharon got up and willed herself to walk confidently towards the speaking area. Once at the speaking area, she relayed her thanks and the plan, sticking closely to her notes so she wouldn't get off track.

"Thank you, Professor InDepth. When we first arrived here on the GSS Prosperity, I was overwhelmed and very confused. But I always felt safe and well cared for. As a human who had been living on an infected planet, the sense of feeling safe and cared for by everyone around you—unfortunately—is not always a given. And for far too many, it is instead a very rare occurrence. So, because of that palpable sense of safety and care, the shock at being pulled up into a spaceship was far less disorienting than it might otherwise have been." She paused a beat, and added with a small grin, "And the calming medications helped greatly, too." The auditorium erupted into laughter. "Thanks again for them, Meg!" she added after a beat.

"Since coming aboard your wonderful ship, Emma, Petra, and I have learned so much from you all about what love and kindness really are, and how expressing kindness in everyday actions really does make so much of a difference in the quality of life. It's hard to describe how impactful it has been. When I first heard your regular meeting prayer, I was so touched, I cried. It still moves me a great deal. To you, it may sound like a small thing, but to focus on kindness and Goodness as a consciously explicit intention before all work meetings is something that the disease of MMR takes away from beings that are afflicted with it." Here she paused, and recited the meeting prayer:

"May we work well together and prosper. May we find meaning to better all our lives. May we become aware of the answers we are seeking and better all our lives. May we be guided by Goodness. May we always find wonder in the singularity." Sharon bowed her head slightly as she intoned the last sentence.

The audience in the auditorium intoned "Praise Goodness" more or less in unison.

Upon their response, Sharon teared up and had to shake her hands up and down in front of herself for a few seconds, a curious signal many humans emit when they feel greatly touched. After a moment, she was able to continue.

"Now, on to the entries! We want to thank you all so much for your efforts. We have been told that it would be considered rude include the names of the individual authors of the pieces at this event, or at any time going forwards, as that could possibly detract from the sense of community effort and cohesion that has been so evident. So we won't do that." She paused and chuckled before adding, "I must say not naming the authors individually feels a bit odd to me, as a human, even as I can see the solid reasoning for the custom.

"Please do know this, though: it was a true joy to read all of the hundreds of writings you all, both crew and passengers, contributed. We are humbled by the amount of love and loving-kindness you have shown to us and the humans down on Earth. Our words of thanks seem so inadequate in the face of your generosity, well wishes, and frankly fantastic ideas about how humans can rid themselves of MMR. We struggled mightily in trying to decide among so many fabulous ideas. Know that we are forever in debt to you all for your kindnesses. Thank you, and may we all grow in Goodness.

"Now, how we're going to use these writings. We've already gotten approval from the CC for how we're going to use the writings, and we are so excited to share this news!" She paused dramatically. "So here's the deal. I will be able to incorporate your writings—word for word—into the so-called fictional story I have been writing about MMR. In other words, I am writing an almost completely factual account of our call for submissions here on the ship. But I'm writing it as if it were a piece of fictional subplot in my story. That way your words will be preserved, but it will appear as though I will have written them as part of a science fiction story. So because I am presenting your words as if I wrote them, the CC says it's okay to use your aware words exactly as you wrote them! Do you follow me?" Sharon asked the crowd.

The audience responded with laughter and applause. "Kind of a nifty way to show the layers of individuality within the singularity, isn't it?" With the applause not dying down, Sharon had to shout her final words of thanks, and she bowed a few times in a sign of respect to the audience while they continued to whoop and applaud.

Just as Sharon was getting desperate to get off the stage, Sync spoke up. "Ah, that is a wonderful use of creativity for us all! Thank you so much, honored CC member!" Sync boomed out above the din. Her energies conveyed great amusement. Relieved, Sharon retreated from the stage. Sync let the energetic applause go on for a little while longer. Then she took over the emceeing for the next part of the meeting.

"Thank you so much, honored CC member. We are most pleased to help and support you, your elements, your planet Earth, the billions of humans, and trillions of other species that live on your planet. And we are honored to attempt to support your individual bits of consciousness in becoming ever more aware of their places within the singularity."

Sync paused here for a moment until the applause quieted completely down. "Without further ado, and in no particular order, our own Captain Cabeza will present the entries the selection committee felt would be the most successfully deployed down on Earth."

Excited applause punctuated the room as the auditorium darkened and a large screen appeared on the stage. On the upper three-quarters of the screen, Captain Cabeza appeared, preparing to read each piece out loud.

The audience knew they were in for a treat as her heads and dermatil all began to engage in complex and graceful choreographies. On the lowest quarter of the screen, the writings themselves appeared, scrolling by in English, the honored member's native tongue, as the Captain spoke them. Cabeza was off to the side of the stage, visible to all. She was doing the readings in real time, but the lighting effects and camera angles were polished, as if all involved had practiced the choreography for weeks in advance.

Cabeza began by saying, "It is my great honor to read these writings to you today. Thank you so much for your efforts and attention. Our first entry is about intentionally creating cultural norms—something humans don't yet do down there on the planet."

Several in the audience gasped or exclaimed at the statement. Cabeza acknowledged them with a raised hand. "Exactly! It is shocking. And my understanding is that's one of the reasons why this piece was chosen, to help nudge humans towards the ideas that they can, and indeed, really must, learn to more intentionally be aware of and intentionally create their cultural norms."

She cleared her throat: "The first entry is called

Cultural Norms Are Built By All Of Us!

People are formed by literally millions of bits of cultural pressures around them. Just about everything around us has been created by humans—our chairs, the cups holding our coffee, our computers, our electoral systems, and our economic realities.

We are socialized to respond in certain ways to these bits of culture. When we respond, we are helping to create, sustain and evolve cultural norms. But the norms we create are not the essence of who we are as human beings.

Instead, cultural norms are constructions that fulfill some of the needs of the times and the places where they are formed. They can be likened to the buildings humans create. And just as some buildings are constructed in better ways than others, some cultural norms are healthier than others. This is a fact of life.

The analogy is very apt. Cultural norms serve to contain meaning for us in much the same way that buildings help us shelter and organize our lives. Buildings help us feel secure when they are well built, pleasing to be in, and efficiently designed. Cultural norms serve us best when they are pleasing for all, and help us all get our needs met efficiently. We need to realize that, just as we have intentionally developed building codes for greater safety and efficiency, we can and need to become more intentional about building cultural norms that are respectful and helpful to all.

Buildings and infrastructures have changed greatly over time. We've gotten more skillful in terms of building them. Imagine the large cities of Earth two hundred years ago. Some building techniques have stayed the same, and others have changed considerably. Same with cultural norms. Some—like languages—have stayed more or less the same, since they serve us well enough. But other norms, such as the dynamics of oppression, for example, have changed quite a bit, just like modern lighting and our expectations about indoor plumbing have changed considerably.

It's good that norms change. They need to change as our knowledge grows and other factors in our environments change. Not to put too fine a point on it, but changing is essential to growing. Let me repeat that: It's essential, it's how we evolve. And if staying at home for a few months due to the coronavirus crisis has taught us anything, it is that we can change quickly if and when we want to or need to. The virus also makes it quite clear that it can be disastrous when we cling to old norms in certain circumstances. We can —and need to be—quite intentional and focused at certain times in history.

So just as building codes helped people develop standards about safe construction, and helped people become more mindful about creating higher standards of living, we can start seeing the need for more and more intentionality in how we recognize and create our cultural norms. As we adapt to different ways of living, we can welcome new standards and metaphorically refuse to go back to the old ways of not having indoor plumbing. We can refuse to live with exposed wiring or shoddy framing.

We can do that by refusing to return to the old, drafty, leaky, anxiety-producing ways of living our lives. We can refuse to mindlessly value convenience more than the health of our communities. We can refuse to listen to greedy capitalists who urge us to act irresponsibly. We can refuse to mindlessly pollute or allow industries to pollute.

We can refuse to take others for granted, we can refuse to value money more than other humans. We can simply refuse to put up with bullies. We can instead embrace our connectedness and responsibilities to each other. We can act with love and compassion towards each other, by checking in with our neighbors, by adhering to science based standards of safety when we interact with others, by giving a damn about others who may be vulnerable.

We can learn to intentionally embrace the new things we are all learning, right here, right now. Embrace the love that is available, right here, right now. Cherish it; let it guide your actions.

Because we are now in the Anthropocene. And we must (quickly) learn how to keep intentionally changing our norms to better fit our rapidly changing circumstances if we hope to survive for any length of time.

Cabeza paused here to signal the end of the entry. It was met with hearty applause and cheers.

After the applause died down, Cabeza cleared a couple of throats and began again. "The second entry is called:

The Shadow Side of Democracy

Party A wrote on BigBook: The Earth has entered a decline brought about by our own doing. America is a large player contributing to the decline. But this crisis isn't political. There is nothing to be gained by nationalistic or partisan finger-pointing. At this point, we must understand that the prevailing dominance of unscrupulous capitalism over social concerns is only a continuation of what the European migrants who got America started were fleeing. To me, it is one of the saddest examples of human history: a group of people who landed on a continent with an overabundance of fertility and resources and whose people were allowed the unheard-of opportunity of pushing a societal 'total reset' button. And then they fucked it up so royally. How come?

Party B wrote in reply: I believe this reset opportunity failed—specifically in America—because the founders of the country (unconsciously) held ideas of 'Might Makes Right' in addition to the ideas of democracy. The founders saw the democratic ideals clearly, but didn't see the many ways they were mired in Might Makes Right mindsets (examples of owning slaves, the horrible treatment of people who were already living on the land, the treatment of women, etc.). MMR mindsets can't help but create power and control issues. So here we are, two hundred thirty some years later, with unheard-of luxuries, still mired in MMR mindsets that will be the cause of our demise if left unchecked for much longer.

MMR also explains why folks create and maintain propaganda, and why those who accumulate power become desperately afraid of an equal playing field and fight it tooth and nail. Some are terrified of allowing true democracy…

At this point in the recitation, Captain Cabeza faltered slightly. It was clear some of the entry had inadvertently been omitted. She played the mistake off as best as she could, bowed to polite applause, and continued on with the next entry.

The Saga Of Amy G Dala

Captain Cabeza's heads performed a more complex choreography for the next piece. CC beings familiar with Nervonian culture understood the choreography to signal that a rap/limerick style poem was coming up, a favorite among CC beings. Many clapped and whooped in anticipation. But Sharon did not know this and wondered what was going on. A slow hip-hop track started up in the background as Captain Cabeza cleared several throats and stated in a somewhat deep voice, "The third entry is called:

The Saga of Amy G Dala

This story of Amy is completely true
Although her name is a bit misconstrued.

Her name may be a little bit wrong,
But leaving it this way helps us sing the song

Of Amy's trials and tribulations
Which caused the failure of many great nations

You see the fear Amy felt inside
Led to the turning of the tide

Away from grace, love, and generosity
To ideas of fear, hate, and scarcity

It is a very sad tale indeed
But to learn about it is what we need

To become more aware.

So let me tell Amy's story today
And from it we can learn a better way

In a time of yore, terrible things happened,
And in the minds of survivors big fears got
fastened

Until they were plagued with deep, dark fears
Coming from their brains' lowest tiers

One of the survivors called Amy G Dala
Still makes fear spread just like a mandala

She has a steel trap of a memory
Any small thing can trigger a reverie

Of which she is scarcely aware

Whenever Amy was triggered and spoke out,
The words that came, came in a shout!

Fear would rip all through all the air
And cause people to act in ways unfair

Trauma causes us all to react
With scarcely any regard for fact

We just want to regain some freakin' control
That is our first and foremost goal

At those times we don't think about hurt
It's only control we want to assert

Because we are unaware

So we act in many terrible ways
Because trauma has set our minds in a daze

We resort to oppressing and disrespecting
We engage in all kinds of ugly transgressing

To try to consolidate 'power over'
Humans use tricks born of brimstone and sulphur

Anyone who is frightened can oppress and attack
And accuse others of what they themselves lack

Unless we learn how to stop and think
In an endless cycle we will continue to sink

And become ever more unaware

Fear is at the root of all oppression and pain
And drives many of us almost insane

Trauma makes us all act a little crazy,
Because our thinking gets, well, a little bit hazy

In moments of fear we can't really think
Brain functioning actually does freakin' shrink

We turn to the basics: fight or flight
And our brains get stuck this way even though it
ain't right

In days of yore women turned to flight
And I'm sure you can guess, many men turned to
fight

And stayed unaware

Historically you can see this was true
And how it led to power for only a few

Because of the fears in the air
Certain beliefs became overly aired.

Certain genders and colors got far more power
And with all sorts of praise they'd be showered

While others who did so much of the work
In the shadows they'd have to lurk

Else the bullies would come along with guns
And act out like frickin' Attila the Hun

To try to keep us all unaware

Meanwhile, Amy met a man named Thalamus
A guy who seems to influence all of us

And ever since they got married
Life has always felt a bit harried.

They settled down in a town called Limbic,
Where people began to get real sick

The illness was soon called MMR
And it made people act very bizarre

But because the sickness was so very strong
They really didn't understand what was wrong

They stayed sick and unaware

And so we still live on a world that was built
Out of lots violence, oppression, and guilt

And the world couldn't help but become forlorn
As generation after generation was born

So we tried to make violence and inequality seem
normal
Even creating laws to make the lies ultra-formal

But our world has been stunted from the very
start
Because we allowed fear to overrule our hearts.

So let me say it ever so clearly
We've all paid a price very very dearly

Because we remained unaware.

The truth about Amy and Thal is simply this
It was always fear they meant to dismiss

Neither really knew how to deal
With what fear and trauma made them feel

So they tried to put it all away
And simply get on with the day

Avoiding the messy messy truth
They told themselves was civilized and couth

But this lie was made completely from fear
And the cost of it was very dear

Because they remained unaware.

The story is Amy and Thal had a son
Some say he was the only one

They taught him to never show any fear
And to never—ever—shed a tear

Even though fear is a helpful emotion
And tears are essential to love's potion

So their son grew to hate
As a way to compensate

He and his kind looked down upon those
Who let their emotions and their hearts show.

And in their hate, they remained unaware.

And so his hate grew and grew
Incredibly, he believed his lies were true

About anyone who was Other
Including women and his very own mother.

It was obvious to most that he wasn't that bright,
But he was ever so sure he was right right right.

And Amy G Dala, who was his mother
Even began to think she was Other

And she became so utterly scared of the world
That hatred for others was all she could unfurl

And so they remained unaware.

Millions of people both before and after
Knew their hearts held love, kindness, and laughter

They could see the lies of supremacy
Were reinforced by a few very doggedly

They made a lot of progress, though more was still needed
Meanwhile, the power addicted still barked and bleated

Of the dangers that would befall us all
If equality cast its 'dangerous' pall

On the very unequal and muddy playing field
Where the powerful lived and were able to steal.

But the aware started to multiply

And then one day a spaceship appeared
To one (of millions) who refused to live in fear

Our hero was actually taken aboard
Onto a ship that would normally soar

Among the aware and the awakened,
Those who lived with their love truly unchastened

By any fears that were amplified or enlarged
Due to Limbic systems that were overcharged.

And the aware agreed to sound the alarm

About the aftereffects of trauma's harm

To humans who were still unaware

These friends agreed to try to untwist
The hapless lies that do exist

On the planet of which we speak
Where circumstances were ever so bleak

Their ideas were laughed at and dismissed
Nevertheless they STILL persist

The aware know that trauma is at the cause
All sorts of issues that give us pause

In survival mode there really isn't a care
About what is right, just, or fair

Still, some stay unaware

The fearful just want to recreate power—
That's what really makes their hearts turn sour

And some still turn to greed and lies
And attribute success to war and spies

But when their propaganda fails to sell
Any of the lies it has to tell

We will all finally know:

Inequality is completely uncouth,
And that, my friends, is the absolute truth.

We hope you understand our song
And know that we all really do belong

Among the aware
Among the aware
among the aware.

The Captain bowed her heads in a complex wave to thunderous applause. When the applause died down, Cabeza smiled and said, "Thanks so much. The next piece is a bit different in tone."

Who Would Prosperity Harm?

Cabeza paused a moment and then took a sip of water. She then looked out into the crowd. "This next piece is called:

The Question of Our Time

Who would be harmed if we had prosperity for all?

So, some people insist everything is just fine. The multimillionaires and the billionaires running our oligarchies in various corners of the world insist everything is just fine. They spend billions to spread the word that there are no conspiracies—they try to convince us that the world is running exactly the way it should.

A few million reactionaries agree with them, but literally billions of people are saying no, things are not just fine. My question for all of us, but especially for the multimillionaires and the billionaires is: Just what would be so awful (seriously) if we made changes that would help others live in prosperity? What would be the ultimate harm to billionaires if they gave up a few million or billion dollars for the greater good? They'd still have more money that any mere mortal could spend in a lifetime, and could live in complete peace. That's truly what I don't get.

Understanding our unity as 7.7 billion humans all living together down on this one marble of a planet is still difficult for some to grasp, but we are one planet and one people.

To keep up with our stupendous technological advances, big changes are needed socially as well. For a million reasons, but mainly because climate change and other disasters of our own making are not going to go away miraculously, I'd like to propose we collectively bring on this big change by means of *relentlessly* asking a simple question. I propose we all ponder this question as continuously as possible:

Who would be harmed if we really had prosperity for all? Hmmm? Really, who would be harmed?

Captain Cabeza then bowed her heads. Though the audience applauded, the mood in the auditorium now took on a fierce edge as the audience contemplated the question. Murmurs circulated about how bad it must be if writings had to overtly remind the humans that these kinds of questions are the most important to contemplate.

Cabeza responded to these comments with an ad-libbed explanation.

"Yes, it is that bad down there. Certain leaders are putting kindness and wellbeing at the center of their decision-making, and it works—Goodness knows, it works. We should applaud them and hope they serve as models in the years to come.

"But unfortunately some leaders don't ever think to make these kinds of questions front and center in their policies, their ideas about progress, their news casts, or their public discourse. And the reality is there are enough of them still 'leading' to make it a hell for humans down on the planet right now.

"They argue from purely self-centered egoic states; they argue for certain ideologies, not for the common good. They argue from Fear-based mindsets, all while ironically believing themselves to be extremely clever and brave. This is what MMR does—it causes beings to see each other competitively rather than communally. It causes them to want power over each other. That's how they get so off track. They fear each other.

"And because they fear each other, they value the consolidation of power over each other. That's at the root of why they still have militaries! Militaries! Can you believe it!"

The auditorium erupted with boos and hisses and a few outraged comments.

Cabeza nodded several heads in agreement. "Obviously, no civilizations with cultural norms based on caring, belonging and a recognition of the innate interdependence we have upon each other would ever resort to military interventions. But they really have been so traumatized that a great many of them sincerely believe that might does make right.

"We can't force them to change their mindsets for the better, but the good news is it's becoming quite clear to most down there that ideas based on interdependence and connection have been overlooked and undervalued. We hope these writings will help more of them know they are on the right track when they demand new values to live by."

Applause greeted these words, and the tone lightened. Cabeza paused, patiently waiting for the auditorium to settle itself.

"The last entry is meant to give them hope that they already have made many steps towards convening collaboratively. Heh-heh, you all saw what I just did there right? The fifth entry is called:

On Earth Today

On Earth today, the love is often hidden.

The love is often misplaced. Misplaced. Even though it is everywhere. It is everywhere. But love can be patient. And it is wise. Wiser than me and my ego, that's for sure. Love is truth. It's not bound up in ego. It's rooted in a complex history, in the Earth's history, in the clouds, in space. Our hearts tell us that love is in the good, the bad, the ugly, the beauty, the chase, the indifference, and in the consummation.

The love I want to show, it's in these words somewhere. I want to let the beings in the world love each other, and prosper in loving-kindness. I do, that's what I truly want. And in these times, it seems that there are so many supposed enemies—we, in reality, are all afflicted with autoimmune diseases, like patriarchy and racism. We believe certain parts of humanity are better than others—or at least deserving of more attention than others. As if we could ever really know what directions the mystery is taking us.

The mystery moves and changes and evolves in time and space. Its scale is unfathomable—from the tiniest of nano particles to spans of space that stretch millions of light years across. Both extremes will make our simple minds explode if we think about them too deeply. We, who are born of temperate climates, we think we know, we think we are wise enough to know, but really now, that's the fiction. We know nothing. And we need to see how wondrous that really is! And not fear the many opportunities we have for awe and finding new ways to be surprised and new ways of connecting!

But, instead of wondering with cotton-candy dreams and love in our hearts, we are fearful as babes in the woods. We are lost toddlers, shitting in our diapers, trying to survive as best we can, and making messes of it. Patriarchy is an example. Militarism is another. Failed ideas born of hubris. Hubris born of profound fear of the world, profound fears about our own inadequacies. In reality, the only times we are truly inadequate is when we resort to hubris and me-first ego states. Indeed, it is directly through our hubris that we have created worlds where it is impossible for all to thrive.

Hubris kills our sense of wise knowing. We know we belong to each other. We know it, but hubris blinds us to this knowing. Fear makes us crave power over, rather than belonging with. And so we become blinded to our knowing, and become so small and so supremely misguided by our individual egoic—and Fear-based—ideas about might makes right that we resort to violence and oppression.

Others of us—the majority, I like to believe—think, and feel and believe in worlds where we live in peace, prosperity, harmony, and equality. But even as I, along with millions of others, know this, some are just as convinced that an equal playing field is either already here (ha!) or somehow wrong. How can we get so opposed to each other? How?

Men spiting women are men cutting off their noses to spite their faces—they are acting...foolishly, obviously. They are acting as an autoimmune disease does when parts of our own bodies attack other good and essential parts of our own bodies—there are no two ways about that. Autoimmune diseases are varied—from very dangerous ones like diabetes, or MS, or rheumatoid arthritis, to irritants that just make life miserable, like psoriasis. We need help. We need to cultivate attitudes of awareness that help us not react so stupidly to differences. Racist rhetoric is nothing but another (dangerous) autoimmune disease. Humans so afraid and on edge that they perceive the mere existence of other humans as threats.

Most of us can see these things and name some of these actions as acts of evil. Are they? Does evil really exist? Does good exist? Or are all acts just different options in an amoral universe composed of things so vast I can't fathom, and so small I can't imagine them either?

Does the universe lean towards good, or is it amoral? Posing that as an "either/or" question is a false dichotomy, I eventually decide. I can have both—an impersonal universe that is nonetheless based on love, love, love, love, but wherein it is still up to us tiny bits of individual consciousness to create the love, the compassion, the abundance of mindsets, the graceful ways of living, to eventually become more fully embodied consciousnesses made of intentional love. Aware and loving. We see the buds of flowers and know their true paths will lead to flowering. We can only hope that spreading and sharing the goodwill of love love love is how humans bloom. It's up to us, yes, us individually, to create opportunities for love, for betterment, for each other, with skill and grace.

Those who have been leading us are not doing that right now. Certain players, some obvious, some more hidden are creating an ugly mess out of a great opportunity, and everyone knows it. We are acting like spoiled children do when they are over-tired—we throw tantrums instead of learning from the wonder of life.

And thus we still need to fight against what some of our brothers and sisters, and their individual bits of consciousness mistakenly think is true, when they hold and espouse beliefs rooted in fear and MMR. Because our souls absolutely know these beliefs of superiority and hubris are wrong. Our souls know that these mistaken beliefs are born of ego-bound bits of fear-induced…idiocy.

Parts of me—wiser parts, I think—knows that the righteous indignation that causes me to see ill-advised actions as "idiocy," or any of us as "them" is simply a waste of time. And we really don't have a whole lot of time to continue to waste.

Parts of me are also aware that fear is easier to act upon than love, especially when we have been afraid for a long time. We must be humble enough to put our pasts down, carefully look at the baggage we carry with us, and consciously decide who and how we want to be—Fear-based, stingy, me-centered, focused on consolidating power over others and creating an utter shitpile out of the Earth in the process? Or loving and kind and generous towards all our brothers and sisters, and all the other living forms on this lovely planet?

I know what I aspire to. So let love in, let the energies swirl around gently. Make a point to seek it out, find the love, especially its more life-giving parts: the gentleness, the tenderness, the compassion, the vulnerability we need to experience in order to really feel love, and revel in it. It's right here, whether you are alone or surrounded by hundreds of people. It is in the air we breathe. You can create it in your mind. It has no color, no gender, no religion, no species, really. Its love! It surrounds us. We need to nurture it. For it is what will help us continue to survive and grow in good ways. Feel it, feel it now, right now, let it flow within you, then make it grow. Right in these few seconds. Revel in the feelings. Do this every day! Feel this every day, even if it's only for five or ten seconds of now. For love is as natural and necessary as sunshine and water.

#

As Captain Cabeza got to the end of the last

recitation, she stared out at the audience. "Thank you."

The auditorium burst into thunderous applause. To them, the words were self-evident, routine even. But as one, the audience recognized that the obvious often needs to be stated over and over and over to soothe the frightened, to help beings internalize truths, to help beings come into understanding, to help beings remember what their existences are truly made from. So they roared their approval with enthusiasm and love, like lovers encouraging each other, or like good friends showing support, or like parents encouraging their kids. Cabeza's heads all took their bows, and her many arms applauded the audience right back. This went on for some time, until it finally died down of its own accord.

While the applause was still going on, Sync asked Sharon if the hashtag symbols were used correctly for social media. Sharon shook her head, but smiled broadly, "No, but they are perfect the way they are."

Sync then thanked the Captain for her stirring performance and shared a few words of closing. The event dismissed shortly after that, with the ship's morale high, and optimism so thick in the atmosphere, it was almost as if it were a physical element. Indeed, even the ship purred a couple of times as the audience filed out of the auditorium, excitedly talking with one another, and congratulating everyone who had entered writings in response to the call.

When she got back to the Navigation Deck, OT noticed that the ship's orbital course had again righted itself from the puzzling deviation it had again taken for the past few hours. The ship's computers gave no explanations for the resumption of the original course, just as they had been silent about the reasons for the deviation. But the timing was synchronous, as the deployment back to Earth to disrupt the rich men's meeting was coming up. OT immediately informed the Captain, who was also relieved, as well as a bit curious about the timing.

Part 5

The Meeting Of Radically Different Mindsets

Or: Obligatory Fight Scene

Two days after the reading event, showtime down on Earth was upon them. Sharon was more than a bit nervous, but felt a sense of confidence from all the good thoughts being sent her way.

She was appalled at how anxious she had gotten just thinking about going back down to Earth. She did not want to be among the infected any more than was absolutely necessary, and could not seem to shake a sense of dread about it. She'd even asked Meg for a bit of calming medication to help her maintain a sense of equanimity. It helped.

She knew they'd come up with as much of an intervention as the laws would allow, and all she could do was go down and be as powerful as she could. She was thoroughly rested, and she and Petra had been briefed about how it was going so far. Because she was a native human, Sharon was also armed with a taser (manufactured on Earth of course) that she hoped she would not have to use. As per CC law, no nonnative being could use anything other than their own energies and bodies in dealing with Unaware beings.

One hundred CC crew members had been sent down a couple of Earth days before to take on human forms, then infiltrate and temporarily replace the bodyguards and assistants who were needed for the event preparations. A secret code was developed so crew members could signal to each other if needed. Their deployment had gone well, overall. Due to the extraordinary lack of interest this particular group of infected humans had in one another, not one crew member's cover had been blown so far. Almost all the reports back from the infiltrators had indicated that the humans employed by these men were self absorbed and not very attentive to anyone but those they thought had power.

Out of the original hundred crew members, seven could not stomach acting out the Callousness and Hubris levels their covers demanded. They had already been transported back to the ship. Since a slightly higher level of illness had already been anticipated, thoroughly trained backups were ready and chomping at the bits to be involved. The backups were immediately sent to replace the sickened crew members. It appeared they had all successfully been integrated into their roles full of diseased cultural norms.

The plan itself was simple—probably too simple. Sharon, Petra, Emma, and their entourage of CC crew members and emissaries would go down and create the biggest ruckus they could manage, planetside. The idea was to cause a pig show, and try to get a media frenzy going. They would attempt to broadcast the disruption of the meeting, and get as much traction on social media as possible to draw attention to how these men were plotting to continue the consolidation of power for themselves and people like themselves, that is, those who were already obscenely rich, and almost exclusively white, and male.

So it was decided (and the CC administrators approved) a plan where crew members, could—as peacefully as possible—physically disable their guards in order to prevent the meeting from going off as planned. They'd do this disguised as humans, of course.

That physically disabling guards and disrupting the meeting to prevent it from going off in secrecy was being allowed by the CC showed how serious they believed the threat to Earth to be. Earth had argued hard for a more drastic physical intervention, and had in fact originally told the CC she would be happy if they obliterated the entire ranch once all the participants arrived. The CC, of course, would not sign off on anything like that.

Sync and Meg privately told Sharon that they thought the CC had been moved by the argument Sharon had made when she said that even pacifists like herself will take physical actions for protection when rattlesnakes are coiled and ready to strike vulnerable beings.

The GSS Prosperity's and Sharon's arguments also made it clear to the CC administrators that these were the men most able and responsible for the efforts to lead the world into shitstorm after shitstorm of economic collapse, warring factions, scarcity, and mistrust. These were the men who duped entire militaries into doing their bidding, or if that failed, men who employed mercenaries who would covertly incite division and literal riots. They told the CC that these were the men who controlled entire industries and nation states; these were men who directed the financial masterminding that had been consciously raising economic inequality to staggering levels on the planet. And this ranch, owned by a notorious (and already very dead) member of their kind, was where they would be gathering.

Clearly, the men coming to the meeting all already had real blood on their hands thanks to the MMR infection that led to their 'profits first' mindsets. Because of some recent media reports, and the recent death of Jeffrey E, the timing was such that the majority did need to meet discuss how to regroup, continue with their schemes, and figure out how to handle several other current media and legal attempts to expose their nefarious doings.

Still, Sharon, Petra, and Emma privately worried that the CC plan wouldn't be enough to disrupt the well-oiled machine of world domination these men had designed.

Sharon now mused that was probably why she had butterflies the size of hummingbirds careening around in her stomach as she prepared to go planetside. The bodyguards could easily kill them all. And they might very well do that, if given a chance, since they'd been trained to be so callously inhumane.

Or they could all be arrested, and the media could spin the event in such a way that it could set back the work of millions of other Goodness-filled humans who had been working through normal channels to try to solve the problems on Earth. That's all.

Over the past few weeks, Sharon, Petra, and Emma had publicly voiced worry about whether the disruption and the subsequent plans would be enough, even if the crew members staying planetside learned how to be social media whizzes. During that time, crew members, but especially Meg, Officer Sync, and Captain Cabeza had given them pep talks. Several times they seemed to imply they had some other information that they could not divulge that led them to be more optimistic about the plan. They'd been quite upfront about not having proof, but said they had several indicators that led to them believing the plan would 'almost certainly help spark enough movement down on Earth to make a positive difference,' as they put it. These talks had helped. But still, Sharon, Petra and Emma all noticed that none of them had ever gone as far as to say they were certain the plan would work well enough to cure the MMR infection.

Crew members had learned that the most

important players were scheduled to arrive at the ranch before the bulk of the other participants. The most important (and not coincidentally, the most afflicted) dozen of them would be meeting in a few Earth minutes to agree on and finalize the details of the larger meeting's agenda. Forty more CC crew members had been sent down to Zed Ranch four Earth hours ago to subdue and replace the personal bodyguards for the earliest arriving participants.

In CC time, things were moving both interminably slowly and very quickly. Finally, after months of planning, Sharon made her way to the transporter area of the ship.

OT was at the controls for these important maneuvers. She and Specialist Shelley were getting last minute details set up to transport Sharon to Earth. Sharon stood at the mark in the transporter area. The goal was for Sharon to appear at the height of the disruption for dramatic impact and to minimize the length of the fight scene. The crew had already begun to create a ruckus, and were engaged in physically subduing the heavily afflicted humans at the ranch.

Sharon was now listening carefully to OT's vaguely Scottish accent. "Uh, Sharon, it looks like it may be getting a little rough down there. Be careful!"

Sharon nodded. Her mouth was dry, and though they'd shrunk in size a bit, she still had quite a rowdy bunch of butterflies flitting around in her stomach. She faked a confident pose and gave a thumbs-up signal.

OT was now saying, "Okay, all controls are reading good and green. Get ready, everything is looking good, Sharon." As the last indicator light turned green, OT said, "It's show time! You will be planetside in four, three, two, and one!"

Sharon suddenly manifested in a room. Chaos

surrounded her in the form of honest to God hand-to-hand combat between women and men. Surprised at the gritty physicality of it all, she shouted, "What the hell?"

"There's no time, Sharon, watch out!" a woman yelled. The woman tossed a metal pipe towards Sharon who neatly caught it. She raised it as she turned. Danger was almost upon her; there was no other recourse. She dodged and put all her power into the pipe as she swung it as hard as she could as a huge hulk of a man lunged at her. The bat engaged with a sickening whap as it hit him on the side of his head near his neck. He instantly fell away with a yell. Sharon's stomach lurched, but she held the pipe up high again.

"Just look out for any man, Meg's turned all of the ship's crew in this room into females, so we'd be able to tell who's who!" another woman cried.

Thankfully, there appeared to be a majority of women in the room. Right next to her was a man in combat with two women. His backside was to her. Still holding the pipe tightly in one hand, she pulled out her taser with her other hand and went in to tase his back. He went down quickly. Several women pounced on him to immobilize him. Three more men engaged in other battles with other crew members went down in rapid succession. One of them looked dead.

The man Sharon had first felled had been the last commander in the room to be defeated. Seeing his face clearly for the first time, she immediately recognized this reviled world "leader." He was moaning on the ground, barely conscious. Danny Issa-ass, another political monstrosity, was motionless nearby; she wondered if he was dead. Then she saw another motionless form and recognized "Junk Bond" Jammy Dimondista. A feeling of elation at the sight of these two figures came upon her, unbidden. She immediately felt revulsion at her own elation. There was blood trickling out of the other world "leader's" nose.

The women were clearly winning the battle. Sharon saw several women filming the scene, surrounded by cohorts keeping them safe. The men still engaged in combat began to realize they were fighting a losing battle, and their movements became more tentative almost simultaneously.

"Surrender and you will not be harmed!" one of the women roared. The men slowed their attempts further, but did not fully stop posturing and feinting.

"Hands up in the air!" roared another, a taser in her hands.

At that point, six gunshots rang out in rapid succession. The women scrambled towards the shooter, and the gun was easily wrested away from one of the bodyguards. Miraculously, the shooter had only grazed two women, who had been able to dodge more substantial damage from the bullets, quite literally, due to the differences in time perception. Luckily someone had taken video of his cowardly act, and the women's heroic tackling of him.

Finally, as yet another man fell to the floor, the remaining eight or nine stopped fighting, fear showing in their faces. No words were exchanged for a long minute as the men stood with hands in the air.

Then guns began appearing in midair until there were close to four-dozen hovering high above the humans, at inaccessible points in various parts of the room. They were being rounded up, magically, by some invisible force. The guns then, as one, disappeared from sight. Meg had practiced this trick for quite some time— reverse manifesting is quite difficult to do. She sent them to one of the rovers where they'd be retrieved later. CC scientists would study them before destroying them.

The women acted like this sorcery was a common occurrence, which freaked out the men still standing. The CC members had purposefully surrounded the men in ways meant to show they would use force if needed. But it was somehow also clear that their first preference was to remain nonviolent. The men warily regarded these strange women. For a couple of moments it was quiet, except for heavy breathing born of effort, and the groans and gasps of people who had been injured. More women had begun to fish out cell phones and began recording the events, as had been planned. Technically they could do this, since there were real humans involved, even though the crew were not native to the planet.

During that first silence, two of the men gave each other eye signals and, seeing an opening, they tried to grab a small woman. Multiple women dove for the men and immobilized them.

One woman strode over to the closest man. With a look of utter distaste, she used the time-honored Vulcan nerve pinch on his neck (which many humans have mistakenly thought was fictional). He gasped as he fell, but was silent afterwards,. She then strode over to the other man, now screaming for mercy, and repeated the action. "Fools," she muttered. The males still standing seemed frightened again, but no one moved to harm them. Several began to bow their heads in a sign of surrender as they raised their hands higher.

There was a scuffle a few feet away from Sharon as a man (who looked a lot like a particular PM who will remain unidentified) gathered what little wits he had, and began to raise himself to his feet with effort. "Bitch," he said as he lunged at Sharon when he was about halfway to his feet. Sharon easily evaded him and kicked him in the leg, resulting in an audible pop. He fell to the ground again, howling in pain. No one else moved, though a few of the women winced in sympathy for his pain.

In the meantime, Sharon's very human levels of adrenaline had kicked in. Her muscles and all but a small sliver of her mind reacted of their own accord as her mind exploded with anger and she got ready to kick him again. She stopped herself at the last moment and kicked in a wall nearby. As the drywall broke, Sharon lunged towards him, but again veered away and this time punched a large hole in the same wall in one swing. So this is what adrenaline unleashed felt like!

After she dusted her now bleeding hand off, Sharon turned and roared down at him: "You, sir, are a stupid piece of utter crap! You are a disgusting and miserable human being because—and only because—you have been made deathly ill by a cultural disease. You are infected with MMR. As a result, you often act like an utter fucking moron! Do you hear me—you act like a fucking moron because you are a fucking infected victim of a fucking disease. You are a pathetic victim of it!" Her hand bled a bit, but she didn't notice. Sensing the razor thin edge Sharon was on, Meg, who was in a nonmaterial mode, discreetly pumped some calming medicine into the air.

Sharon took two breaths and with great effort composed herself enough so that she did not attack him. Instead, she looked around and encompassed all of the surrendered men in her glare. Cell phones kept emerging. Sharon knew she was being recorded from many different angles. Pointing her finger dramatically at the men, one after another, she shouted, "You're all infected with a disgusting affliction born of fear and trauma!" A few of the men flinched. Even with the medicine, she was close to being out of control, and rage was evident on her face.

"This disease has stunted men as humans, it has stunted women as humans, and it has endangered the entire fucking health of the planet! And yet, despite our better judgment, we have been working hard to save your sorry ass lives," she spluttered at them. "Most humans have been trying to just live life as best as they could, while vile, stunted beings like you act like disgusting, entitled brats!"

She looked with disdain at the same polarizing political head of state who was lying on the ground, and viciously kicked a wall again. More drywall crumbled. "Fuck you idiots, just fuck you!" she shouted. "You are so infected by your Hubris, your Greed, and most of all your fucking Fear, that you sincerely have no fucking idea of how goddamned sick you are. But you are.

"Part of me agrees with the Sidis and believes it is a mistake to let you asshats live, but we are committed to nonviolence. Many of us doubt some of you will ever recover from the disease." She glared meaningfully at the head of state as she said this. "But we can and will neutralize you so you won't continue spreading fear and inequity to everyone. Prison will be a great start, and when the authorities get here—the real authorities, not your asshat cronies—we'll hopefully see that happen."

Turning her gaze towards the rest of the room, she continued. "It may prove to be our folly to show compassion in this instance." Upon uttering those words, she found she still had rage coursing through her veins. So angry she couldn't form more words, she kicked another wall several times in a row, very near to another man's head. Some part of her heard him whimper. "You whimper once, asshole, do you have any idea of how much pain you have caused for others?" she roared. "For fucking years?"

Another part of her heard both Petra and Emma

urgently tell her to, "Calm your ass down!" Meg sent another dose of calming medicines, and eventually Sharon regained some control. She rather theatrically shrugged and continued speaking, with a little less venom.

"But alas, we are committed pacifists, so our intent is, for now, that you will live." She paused and threw up her hands. "But you are idiots! You fucking attack us! Us! The people who bring you compassion and nurturing! Us, the people who love you simply because you are somewhat sentient beings! You attack us because of these pathetically stupid ideas you have all been brainwashed to believe. You are all morons about power and status."

One of the men looked up at this, trying to comprehend what she was saying. She directed her next words directly at him, hoping that this time she would be able to stay more under control by latching on to some connection of some sort. By now at least three dozen cameras were trained on Sharon. "You are acting like idiots because you've been socialized from fucking trauma-based reactions! Don't you see? You believe the world is dangerous, and so to mitigate that danger, you think you have to have power and control over every fucking thing in sight. Like that would ever be possible." She sighed heavily. "Trauma is the real problem! Trauma! You were afraid. So you developed these stupid ideas about having power over every group of people, and over the Earth herself—as if." Here she paused. She clenched and unclenched her hands and took several long slow breaths, rage still evident in every muscle.

"As if might could ever possibly make right! So yeah, that part is fucking called patriarchy, of course it is, and it's fucking disgusting, but the patriarchy was born from trauma. Fear and trauma are at the roots of your stupid Might Makes Right thinking, your idiocy, your ridiculous beliefs that you are superior to others! Trauma!"

The man who had looked up, lowered his head again. Sharon saw this and strode over to him. As she did so, the group of women surrounding him parted to allow her to address him at close range. Petra was urgently telling Sharon to call up compassion and use it now damn it!

The man was white, with green piercing eyes, probably about 5'11", in his mid-thirties or so. He had broad shoulders and was in good physical shape. Good-looking, if one were into that gender, Sharon thought absently, as she continued to try to calm herself. There were beads of sweat on his face, and he was still breathing a little hard from combat, and maybe from fear. His dark hair was cut very short, and stubble was visible on his face. He was very much a good-looking, average Joe kind of man. Sharon reached out and lifted his chin, forcing him to look at her. He did so with fear now quite evident in his eyes.

Still holding his chin, she said, "We don't hate you!" she said these words loudly, forcefully, but she managed to say it without rage. "We don't! We fucking hate some of your actions with every last fiber of our beings, but we don't hate you. We know you are sick, ill, stunted by your ignorance, stunted by fears you don't even allow yourselves to know about. Stunted by your denial. You have been stunted by traumas that aren't even yours, traumas that were handed down to you. We know this. We know this." Sharon paused, allowing the words to sink into the man's mind, into the whole room.

The man stifled what sounded like a sob. Whether his emotion was due to her mercy or to his understanding, or both, she wasn't sure, but she flashed a serious smile at him and in a softer voice continued.

"Dude! We had feminism! We learned to be humans again, like we were meant to be. We learned to let go of the fear. We thought of our socialization in terms of oppression, and it was. But it was more than that, it was more than that. And we couldn't see it. No one really could because we'd all been so brainwashed.

"Fear-based reactions infected the culture. When there's danger, we all jump into fight or flight mode. Women were taught to be afraid, but men were taught to respond with attempts to control, no matter what. Humans have been on high alert for hundreds and hundreds of years."

She paused for breath here, still holding the man's face in her had. He nodded very tentatively.

She allowed herself a small smile. "Women were taught to be the keepers of the flight responses. Men were taught to use the fight responses. We got stuck in them. They became unhealthy. They became really, really unhealthy. Your fight responses are as detrimental to life and the planet as the flight responses women shed during feminism."

She paused and looked into his eyes. He looked back without a challenge, anger, or contempt. His expression indicated he was even comprehending what she was saying. "For sixty years we thought the disease was patriarchy, and it was. But it was also deeper than that. The disease is caused by fear. Trauma causes fear, it causes all people to run and hide, or scramble for power and control for the rest of their pathetic lives—all out of fear!

"Fear is the real driver. Fear causes people to try to control and oppress others. Fear causes people to believe they have to build empire, to become greedy, to engage in preposterous ideas of defensive pre-emptive strikes. Fear is the real motivator behind every last one of our bids for power over others, our attempts to bully. All of the traits, all of the ugliest traits we can imagine, the ugliest traits that humans can possess? They are born of fear! Your bosses are the most Fear-based humans around!"

The man nodded at this, trembling a little. Sharon let go of his chin. He continued to look at her in some amazement, some understanding evident on his face. Sharon chuckled a little and glanced at the larger room for a moment before returning her gaze to him. She said nothing for a long moment. Finally she addressed the entire room, loudly, authoritatively, and with compassion.

"Feminism helped us, but it didn't help you guys enough. Men are still trapped in these trauma-based ways of being men. Believing in might makes right, being infected by that kind of brainwashing." She paused one last time and said, "We got over our fears, and it is past time, boys—way fucking past time—for you to get over yours!" At that, she reached out and tenderly caressed the man's chin as he lowered his head, nodding and sobbing softly.

One beat later a woman roared, "Such truth! A moment of silent contemplation is in order here. Thank You!"

In the split second of silence that followed, Petra tsked, and said rather loudly, "Ah, jeez. That won't do! That's just not what a Semi aware human from this planet would say right now."

"Seriously, Petra?" said Sharon. "The cameras are rolling. We need the help here."

The woman who had uttered the words looked crestfallen. But she nodded anyway; she could hear the truth of Petra's words, even as she was embarrassed and hurt by them.

And then, a split second after Sharon wished for help, Meg and Sync manifested as human *chingonas* (English translation: bad asses). And what goddesses they appeared to be! Meg took a stance, coolly snapped her fingers, and stopped time for everyone. In reality, it was an effort that took some of Sync's help as well, but Sync did not appear to need any recognition of this. At the snap of Meg's gorgeous holographic fingers, all movement in the room froze except for Sharon, Petra, about five of the lead females, and Meg and Sync.

Sharon didn't even notice this amazing bit of 13D wizardry—truly, stopping time wasn't an easy trick, even for 13Ds. The move was a major bit of "holy shit!" level competence. A big-assed miracle. But both Sharon and Petra ignored it. Instead, Sharon said urgently, "Is it possible for a do-over here? The shout of support really didn't sound like what a human would say during a video that would go viral."

Meg replied with a tsk and an eye roll. Sync gave her a serious look, they muttered something between themselves, and Meg quashed the response. The unfrozen CC crew waited and kept guard while Sharon, Petra, Meg, and Sync conferred in urgent tones on what would be a more appropriate response.

Finally they had agreement. They relayed the new phrase to the CC guards. Then Meg, in a massive bit of concentration, rolled back time on all of the cell phones recording the moment. "And maybe we could adjust a couple of the cameras for better angles?" Petra whispered earnestly.

At that, Meg glared at her. "Would you like me to also sing a song while I do that, and then change costumes before I unstop time?"

Petra cooed a small, embarrassed apology.

Sharon bowed deeply, but kept her mouth shut. Meg then winked, and said, "Lucky for us all, I like you," to Petra, and then pointedly looked over at Sync. Sync swirled a bit of encouraging energy around, and they conferred again. After a pregnant pause, Meg swaggered around the room and made some adjustments to the placement of cameras and lighting. Sharon and the other women helped. As energy fanned about her, some part of Petra muttered quietly to Sharon, "Goodness, Meg looks hot."

At that, Sharon laughed out loud, breaking the tension a bit more. Once they'd all fiddled enough with the cameras and both DDDs had adjusted the lighting, Sharon got back into the same pose she'd been in during her speech. She looked at Sync and Meg. Sync looked around one last time to make sure everything was all right, then locked eyes with Meg. Meg nodded once and snapped her gorgeous fingers again. "Action!"

The scene picked up right in the middle of Sharon's speech about cultural illness, the universe, and everything. Camera shots of men sobbing, Sharon looking glorious, and women looking both fierce and compassionate.

The room came alive with a wild energy bordering on chaos. Sounds and movements swirled around them all as Sharon again said with great feeling, "Feminism helped us, but it didn't help you guys enough. Men are still trapped in these trauma-based ways of being men. Believing in might makes right, being infected by that kind of brainwashing." She paused one last time and ad-libbed a little, "We need to take back our cultural norms and consciously turn them into aware and compassionate norms that truly serve us as a species. We've got to learn to be vulnerable again, as a species, and shed our ego-based Hubris, as a species. We got over our fears, and it is past time, boys—way fucking past time—for you to get over yours!" At that, she tenderly caressed the man's chin and he lowered his head, nodding and sobbing softly.

And then, a shout went up from the crew. "Right on!" The shout was picked up and turned into a chorus. The chorus was loud and clear. "Right on, right on!"

And the cameras kept rolling.

What's Next

Dozens of law enforcement officials descended onto the ranch after a series of strange events took place. A few anonymous calls were made to 911, and because of the importance of the location, and knowledge among law eforcement about the meeting, law enforcement and EMTs were dispatched in great numbers to the ranch.

Once there, the responders began trying to piece together what had happened. It was soon obvious that many bodyguards, henchmen, and security professionals had been surprised and disabled.

While the EMTs and fire department personnel called to the ranch were focused on the safety of the individuals, the leaders of virtually all of the security and law enforcement agencies were furious at the security breach itself. They rather belatedly focused in on the actual health and well-being of the dazed and confused people they found at the ranch.

In their defense, the scene at the ranch was worthy of concern. Not just one or two, or even six or eight professionals, but dozens of bodyguards, ranch employees, and even a few secret service officers were found unconscious and tied up in various places around the ranch. None appeared to be seriously harmed, but when they regained consciousness, they were uniformly befuddled about what had happened to them. Many claimed their doppelgängers appeared in front of them with a few women, and then the next thing they knew— here they were. Though there were some with a few bruises, most of these humans only suffered slight headaches and confusion that seemed to just extend to the circumstances from the past few hours. They all professed to know nothing of what had occurred.

The first responders kept as much of that

information out of the media as possible. What they had found was truly stunning. In addition to dozens of highly trained bodyguards all having been disabled, there was evidence of a chaotic encounter of epic proportions. In the main ballroom, several men were injured, and four, including two high-profile politicians and a very powerful financial banker were dead. But just as with the other security personnel and ranch employees, all the people they found in the mansion were unsure about what had happened. Every on-site security camera had either been unobtrusively disabled or showed nothing out of the ordinary. They later found one audio recording, but that is a tale for another day.

While even more law enforcement officials were still arriving at the scene, several social media sites started receiving multiple recordings of events that had taken place at the ranch. By the end of the day, there were dozens of these videos. Some videos even originated from the men's own accounts, though most were uploaded by individuals who claimed to be associated with something called the CC.

The videos were so weird that a number of them went viral almost immediately. Among these videos were many confessionals made by the vilest of the men. They were all filmed in the mansion at the ranch and made within a couple of hours of each other. The PR goons and lawyers took the confessional videos down quickly, but enough copies and screenshots were made that they were still widely distributed. And many other videos still stayed up on accounts to show there'd clearly been a large-scale disruption by a group of women.

Within hours, all social media sites were spreading related clips and posts. Videos of the fight scene, and a wild speech about a thing called MMR, inundated all the major social media platforms. Most of the posters indicated they were 'spiritually related' to the hacker group Anonymous. As would be expected at this late stage of MMR infection, many of these videos have since been taken down both by authorities under the auspice of 'national security,' and by threats from the lawyers representing the multimillionaires shown in the videos. Comments clearly made by bots or sock puppets infected other sites. But numerous copies still exist and are keeping the topic of MMR active in some corners of the internet.

Back at the ranch, law enforcement officers found several sets of papers that they at first mistook as a script of some sort. The papers were all copies of notes from a planning meeting, and a manifesto of sorts—in draft form.   Of course these were left behind purposefully by the CC, but that was unknown to the responders.

As would be expected, the various intelligence agencies kept this information as hidden as possible. But our sources on the inside say that some in the intelligence communities actually appear to be moved by the manifesto.

Several social media posts and videos referenced 'The Manifesto,' and by the next day several copies of the actual document were circulating on social media as well, though not as widely.

Because there are a few handwritten points that are difficult to decipher, a typeset copy of the entire document will follow.

An Urgent Communication From Other Beings In The Known Universes

Also Known As: The CC Manifesto

Greetings from the CC! We are your friends. We'd love to chat, but there is urgent business to attend to.

Main Task: Humans need to achieve a basic understanding of how their whole planet has been infected by MMR. They also need to understand how MMR works and how it harms them. We hope this will help all who read it on their collective journey to awareness.

Please remember: The boundaries between propaganda, education, and entertainment are sometimes thin and porous, a point we (both as consumers and producers of information) need to reflect on again and again, if we are ethical.

MMR 101

What MMR is: It's an all-encompassing mindset about how people see the world, their tribe's place in it, and what human nature is like. It is a Fear-based mindset that grows out of knee-jerk reactions to fear/trauma that never mature into more reasoned responses.

MMR stands for Might Makes Right and is the belief that the world is, at root, about domination—dominate or be dominated.

People infected with MMR deny, dismiss, or simply can't see all the gazillions of complex interdependencies, the give and take, the collaborative and cooperative systems at work all around them on Earth, and in the amazing examples in the space beyond their planet. They believe the vast majority of life can (and should) be arranged into rigid hierarchies. As if! MMR is a pervasive belief system that poisons the thinking processes in otherwise intelligent people. We are very sorry you are infected with this disease and wish to help.

MMR infection is strikingly similar to the mindsets people develop in PTSD: People with PTSD believe the world is a dangerous place, they don't trust others, they believe danger is at every turn, and they try to control everything they can. They often believe that grabbing all the power and control they can is the only thing that will keep them safe. In both cases, people will often do a great job of unconsciously creating the worlds that they believe to be out there. PTSD generally afflicts individuals. MMR afflicts both individuals and entire cultures.

In MMR, people and cultures do not trust Others, so they (seriously) **fear equality**, assuming they will be harmed if they do not dominate Others. MMR cultures by definition cannot create conditions that allow for peace and prosperity for all!

MMR becomes taken for granted—like eating with a fork or in other parts of the world, with chopsticks. We forget we learned to do this, that it isn't a part of "human nature." All around the world, cultural assumptions feel natural and become utterly taken for granted because we get so used to them. And they can be hard to see, like air, or more to the point, germs themselves. MMR infection is the same.

MMR is a psychologically based autoimmune disease. Make no mistake, MMR will kill off virtually all of the species it infects if unchecked, including those at the top of the hierarchies.

In MMR mindsets, people become deathly afraid of showing any vulnerability, and often grow to fear and disdain compassion, seeing it as "weak." Seriously!!

This is very dangerous, because back in reality, compassion and vulnerability are necessary ingredients for life-affirming emotional states and for making wise (and mature) decisions about all sorts of things, both on personal levels and in the larger world.

MMR is at the root of: **all forms of oppression. Every last one.** Truly.

'All forms of oppression' includes racism, sexism, colonialism, **the destruction of the environment** for resources and profit, homophobia, genocide, religious persecution and religious belief in exceptionalism, empire building, exploitative relationships, wealth inequity, educational inequities...and on and on and on (so backwards!).

MMR infection is 'power over' not 'power with.' MMR infection is what causes power to become corrosive. All oppression is caused by humans who have been heavily infected by and stunted from MMR. You cannot have oppression without MMR infection.

But it gets worse. Some forms of MMR stay more on the down low: MMR beliefs get cozy with our egos and show up in our status symbols. We become egocentric through all kinds of stuff, from clothes and jewelry, to cars, to the trips we take, or the cool places we go to be seen. MMR motivates some folks to "need" a big screen TV or throw the perfect party. Or be "alpha" in social situations. MMR is at work in our excessive focus on popularity and gaining likes on social media; it's there in contact sports, and in other highly competitive endeavors. Basically, it's what motivates us to be seen as enviable, rather than doing things because they are right or interesting. Because MMR gets in so tight with our egos, it often makes appearances in even our closest human relationships—especially between men and women. Even in healthy relationships, truly healthy ones, it will make small appearances. It's danged hard to recognize in the moment because of how heavily infected Earth is and because of how Earth cultures have trained human egos to stay in defensive mode. But we can learn to recognize it a lot better and stop it before it gets worse.

MMR is the special sauce that keeps the unwoke, unwoke. It's what keeps many of us only half woke, and it's still stunningly hard to avoid falling into on twenty-first-century Earth.

But there's good news, too. Like anything else, we can learn to kick MMR's ass (to use its own terms, lol). It is susceptible to more than one form of kryptonite. Some things that defeat MMR are: presence and receptiveness, openness, playfulness, self-awareness, vulnerability, and compassion. There may be other antidotes as well, but those are the most important ones we, in the CC, know about right now.

Creating Cultural-Norm-Making Salons

Hopefully this manifesto and the videos of the Zed Ranch Disruption will spur humans' interest in finding out about MMR. If we could, we would offer more support. However, this Manifesto and a few other acts are all we are allowed, due to CC laws.

Our suggested plan: When our communications have successfully reached a few hundred brave humans, Cultural-Norm-Making Salons seem like they'd be a natural next phase. The CC hopes they become a thing for humans. Humans might want to spice up the names a little—maybe call them 'Norm Changers' or something. We envision them to be like old school rap groups (which were used by people before rap was rap), also known as "consciousness-raising groups." These were big in the early 1970s. People joined them who were looking to expand equality, prosperity, and civil rights for all. For real, dudes and dudettes.

Here are some ideas about what Cultural-Norm-Making Salons could look like:

1) In the beginning, the groups/salons should focus on learning about MMR, and its relationships to fear and trauma.

2) Groups should help people become better at recognizing MMR in social situations, educate others about the issues, and be places where people could brainstorm tools to reduce the infections on the fly.

3) Groups should then work on ways to lessen the flow and impact of propaganda and other MMR-born tools. The CC hopes other humans will create and release books, animated short films, publish manifestos, and general buzz around the information pertaining to the affliction of MMR.

Threatened By The Spread Of Knowledge

Like any other equalizing actions, some (scratch that: all) efforts to educate humans about MMR will be seen as to quite threatening to folks who have the very worst infections (kind of like how people get defensive about certain topics and don't want anyone talking about them).

◆ Those who are the most infected by MMR will likely be the greatest barriers to humans regaining any sense of health. They are the true carriers of the disease. But they are still human, just effed up and out of control. Just know their actions will probably get more and more ugly as they see their power over others fading.

◆ They will also likely be in denial about being infected with MMR. Have you ever noticed that people in denial are almost always in denial about being in denial?

◆ Who are they: Humans with deep MMR infections are those who attempt to influence the public by demonizing other people, those who buy elections, those who are (or vote to retain) obviously corrupt and immoral people (y'all need to vote), those who actively seek to oppress others, those who do not act out of compassion for others, and those that stoop to violence or other acts that violate trust. Some of the infected are super rich. Some of them just follow leaders who are infected—you know the racist folks always looking for a fight? Yeah, that's MMR in action.

For the most part, the **worst infected** are only a small minority of people; although, everyone's a little infected right now (sorry, but that's how we get better: by being honest about where we can grow).

Those most sick from the disease think equality is a thing to be feared, and they do actually FEAR it (they will never admit that, though). They must be humanely neutralized—that is the end goal. The phrase 'humanely neutralized' has very specific meanings and limitations within the CC, see the definitions document at the back of Paloma's book for further information.

Current High Risk Factors

First, MMR is already everywhere. It's infected our business and political systems. This is going to make it hard for healthy interventions to gain traction. So we won't dwell on this, except to point out that it is propped up by **propaganda** in many forms that are currently not recognized as such. We will talk more about the various forms of propaganda in a moment.

Second (with our deepest apologies to the millions of good men out there), males are in charge within many institutions on Earth. This is—quite frankly—pretty problematic at since males (being larger, on average, than females) are naturally more susceptible to MMR. How could they not be?

Another reason why men are more susceptible is due to how males are socialized to aspire to power and wealth and avoid vulnerability and compassion. That is not to say that men cannot be effective healers, not at all.

But we must be honest enough to recognize that on average, men think more in terms of MMR (alpha dog stuff), and they have more to lose from giving up MMR. Sorry, but if half the population (of any species) is spreading a deadly disease much more than the other half, you need to stop that half quick. Women (on average) are healthier in this regard. Seriously.

Recommendations Specifically For Men:

Women can do these things, too! You can come up with your own, but just know **that hardest suggestions on this short list will probably help us recover the fastest. Really.**

◆ Be very intentional about ensuring you make tons of room for and then listen to the women around you who have similar goals.

◆ We recommend all men (and especially those in leadership positions) find ways to make women your confidantes, 'go to' people, posse, and co-leaders. Make them **a majority**, not one or two, or even a few on your team. We recognize making them a majority of your team might seem impossible and unnecessary. It's not. It is about the only way we will get to the results we all want before the MMR infection kills off the entire species.

◆ Remind yourself several times a day that women (on the whole) are much more likely to be the best experts about **using kindness, compassion, and thinking about the well-being of others**. **Using these as top values is how truly aware (uninfected) beings make decisions and live life. Period.**

◆ Remind yourself several times a day that women (on the whole) have been socialized to see the world differently from men. Try to be, think, and act like a compassionate, heart-centered, warm, and loving woman. But first, make sure you shut up and listen to them. Really.

◆ Finally, defer to the ideas from the women on your team a **majority of times**. Honestly, the options they want—on the whole—may well be less sexy and less immediately profitable, but they will likely be much more practical at bringing about the changes that will make the most differences to the most people. Did we mention that MMR is responsible for all oppression?

Please note, we included these strategies rather than some vague exhortation to 'keep your ego in check and respect women.' These exhortations, while valid, are often, if not usually, forgotten in the midst of real-life conversations and decision-making. We know. We've been there, done that!

Propaganda

The history of propaganda started long before the current era, of course. But in each generation and all over the world, it exists to create and preserve power for a select few. MMR is what creates a "need" for propaganda.

On Earth, history has—up until very lately—been written and told by the victors. Humans are generally waking up to that as a fact that has hindered them, and that waking up is a huge step in the right direction. But humans are still blind to related things. For example, in America, mainstream news belongs to the billionaires. Four or five corporations own a majority of the news outlets. They generally do a terrible job of reporting on any issues that would go against their own corporate interests. While this makes sense, it's unacceptable.

Similarly, mainstream entertainment is controlled by those **same** corporations, and run by those who are deeply infected with MMR. As a result they keep pushing hyperviolent action, horror, crime, gore, androcentric, white-focused, and sexually exploitative movies, which then keep implying to us that violence is fine and only certain kinds of people should be in charge.

As Violence Declines, Propaganda Is Needed More Than Ever

Those deeply infected with MMR have always been willing to use violence to enforce their rule. The last several decades have seen a—general—decline in the actual use of violence (the state-sanctioned brutalization of certain minorities and communities notwithstanding, unfortunately). Public hangings and witch burnings are permanently on the decline (yay). There's (overall) less domestic violence and bullshit like that. So the disease has mutated a bit (as diseases tend to do).

But there are still super-infected, power-addicted folks out there. Those who already have tremendous power over others are terrified of losing the power. They are sophisticated (they are sick, not stupid) and able to sell us shit we didn't even know we wanted. They sell us a line about chasing money and fame and power.

Our world is obsessed with power and control. It's not a very healthy world, anyone can see that. We believe— no, scratch that—we KNOW that people who aren't infected by MMR aren't as obsessed with power and control. It's simply not as important to healthier people. It is important to greedy people. Think about it that way. Unaffected people (and people recovering from MMR) don't have such obsessive power and control "needs."

◆　　We need to find ways to get the point across that people who are unwilling to contribute to making society a roughly equal playing field are cowards. The reality is 2,153 people are hoarding so much wealth that they own as much as 60 percent of the world's population.[1] **So really, calling it cowardice**

---

1. Fact, Jack. See Oxfam's report on global wealth inequality from January 2020. At that time there

doesn't even begin to describe it. It's utterly disgusting.

◆ But we also have to balance that with a compassion for the millions of good people who bought into ideas about the righteousness of things driven by MMR infections. We have to help them see another story, one where they can more easily see that MMR exists and creates lasting and ongoing harms to millions of people. We have to help them see they were duped, without guilt tripping them for the harm they've done while they were infected. Kind of like how alcoholics in recovery have to acknowledge 'yeah, I did all that' in a way that's healthy enough for them to stay sober and do good stuff.

A New Age Might Dawn

We think the vast majority of people want to find ways to recover from MMR .

(Another handwritten note here points an arrow to that sentence and says, 'But getting over the hump of avoidance due to discomfort, Hubris, and simple ignorance is a mighty big hurdle.')

Propaganda is the catalyst that exposes the person/culture to infection. It's the cough that spreads the germs. Fear is the germ itself that can infect people. Fear is also (unfortunately) the primary emotional signal that any being's survival instinct pays the most attention to when it is triggered.

---

were 2153 billionaires in the world with a combined net worth equal to that of several billion—with a b—people. https://www.oxfam.org/en/press-releases/worlds-billionaires-have-more-wealth-46-billion-people

Fear can be easily triggered. When that happens, symptoms of MMR can appear. Fear and trauma naturally causes fight, flight, or freeze reactions. Because facing fear head on can be so scary (!), people can get stuck in primitive reactions (like becoming control freaks or super aggressive). MMR does pretty much the same thing, but on a cultural level.

The reality is, MMR clings in the minds of humans with a stubbornness that surprises those less afflicted by it.[2]

Aside: stubbornness of the infection also may be what was meant by the Eagles' song lyric 'A new age is dawning on fewer than expected.'

Proposed End Goal

To create environments that allow for sustained Thriving for all humans, and the natural flora and fauna found in the environments around them.

To Thrive, souls need to be heeded in pretty danged near every situation. Souls are the wisest parts of us. Each human possesses one. They are wise because they are kind, compassionate, generous, nonviolent, loving, insightful, and funny. This is what they want humans to know about them. Full stop.

Souls need to be listened to so they can help humans recreate the kinds of environments that allow for them and all other souls to flourish. Given a bit of latitude, they can and will create systems that make it easy for **all**, not just some, beings to Thrive. Fear-based thinking where egos take over are the main problems

2. Our follow up will be more specific about who is likely to be the least afflicted by MMR on infected planets. We will be carefully recording findings from Earth as our efforts proceed there.

that souls face right now that prevent them from being better heard and listened to on Earth.

Instead of listening to their souls, humans infected by MMR have 'ego first' orientations. Self-interest rather than the common good is how folks think in MMR. They also develop an all or nothing mindset where attainment of goals "by any means necessary" become normal. After all, the underlying Fear that drives the mindset of MMR is survival. Any humans who are (consciously or not consciously) in survival modes are simply not going to be focused on fairness or sustainability.

Therefore a very important piece of the end goal is to reinstate the legitimacy and need for compassionate, heart-centered reasoning in decision-making, and recognize and eradicate the 'me first' mindset that is so prevalent in MMR-infected cultures.

Our Aftercare Plan

FYI, twenty-six brave members of the CC have volunteered to remain on Earth and will be working to ensure these ideas get planted in the minds of millions of women and men who might be in positions to understand and further spread them. You will be unable to determine who these crew members are, as they are indistinguishable from regular humans, although we will let you know that they will all be manifesting as female, due to women's propensity to be less infected with MMR. If you want to try to follow their leads, we suggest you pay extra attention to, and act on anything kind, compassionate, generous hearted women say in the coming few years. In this way you will be able to join us in the quest to help humans rid themselves of the MMR infection and replace it with compassion and loving kindness based awareness.

We don't know what the outcome of this fight will be, but everyone here at the CC hopes for the best. We'd like to encourage humans to please use their Goodness (and privileges) for good. Also, please be aware that Earth has other means for regaining health for herself, but if she has to use those means, it won't go well for the humans.

Lastly, we wish to support humans in being compassionate with themselves. If you, dear human, have previously been fooled by propaganda which tells you relentless striving is awesome, and subtly reinforces that profits are more important than human lives, or if you have gotten caught up in beliefs about "rationality" and have downplayed compassion towards others, or if you have dismissed claims by those who have suffered inequities or have characterized those working for justice as lawlessly misguided, and possibly even evil people, do not despair. This is what the propaganda has been designed to do. This propaganda has been cultivated over several centuries. It has been well funded, widely distributed, and the propaganda creators have been highly skilled. The uses of fear, acceptance, authority, and trust have been carefully cultivated, and skillfully used against you. Please remember, literally billions of dollars have been spent to program humans. Thousands of strands of cultural norms have been crafted to support erroneous beliefs in the superiority of some over others.

All humans are molded by millions of bits of cultural pressures, and you are not to blame for believing the many cultural level lies that were skillfully constructed. But they have been exposed now. We hope you can gather the necessary courage to act according to your newfound understandings. We wish you well, and send more love than you can ever imagine.

Our ambassador ship, the GSS Prosperity will

come back for a follow up visit in 3 CC weeks (which is equal to 699.3 Earth days).

*

That ends the document, and thus we come to the very end of this CC-sponsored celebration of a being's first travels into the known universes and Semi awareness. We'd like to take the time (lol) to remind readers that MMR is a real infection in the known universes, and we hope humans take this cautionary tale very seriously. The rest of the story is playing out in real time on the planet, and it is too soon to tell what the outcomes will be.

Spell It Out: What About Sharon and Petra?

Sharon, Emma, and Petra chose to remain on the GSS Prosperity in order to continue to work on healthy solutions for Earth and to recover from their prolonged exposure to MMR. They have regained the ability to be appropriately heeded when they say common sense things, but the ability—currently—is limited to areas within the CC, and with the help of allies on Earth. It is hoped that their words will become known down on Earth as well.

Further epilogue-ing: The GSS Prosperity—as is customary—will provide a publicly accessible update directly after the follow-up visit to Earth. We hope you share our desires for a positive outcome for Earth, and invite all sentient beings to review the report. We hope you find ways to take concrete actions to eradicate MMR in as much of your sphere of influence as possible. Finally, send good energies to the planet and its beings (including the humans), if you are able to do so. The CC's report will manifest in 2022.

MMR Sucks—Also Known As An Afterword

I originally gathered my thoughts and wrote much of a nonfiction book about something called Cultural PTSD. Some aspects of the theory (such as it is) are definitely not news, but some aspects are ideas that I still haven't seen talked about elsewhere—at least not where I've looked, and I have been looking.

But instead of presenting a nonfiction pseudo-academic theory that would most likely get filed in potential audience's minds as either 'crackpot thoughts written by a non academic,' or 'looks really heavy and boring,' it eventually dawned on me that science fiction might be a great way to get the ideas across.

Also, I don't have a PhD. In these early years of the Anthropocene, still mired in MMR and the never-ending hierarchies it produces, the reality is that not having the correct initials behind a name substantially discounts or even taints theoretical models in the nonfiction world, no matter how correct the ideas themselves may turn out to be. Luckily, the same story is not necessarily true in fiction—see what I did there?

So, here we are. Careening between fictional beings, and some pretty accurate descriptions of dystopic bits of our real lives in the early days of the Anthropocene are some thoughts- some of which are emphatically not meant to be tried at home. I do not condone violence, or anything like the story told in Armagettin', for examples. But I am interested in what would happen if we could somehow envision a world without greed. And I do think we need to find more effective ways to stop those who resort to corruption and violence- and recognize that they do make up a frightening percentage of folks who chase after "power over."

Anyway, in between these thoughts I've also thrown in both real and bogus science, some personal angst, and various puns and references for spice. But even in fiction I can't seem to avoid drifting into annoyingly pedantic tones from time to time; I am aware (lol), and I apologize for those times. I also apologize for any and all other weaknesses in the writing. The Appendix that follows is a quick overview of the original theory—and though it isn't terribly humorous, I wouldn't mind if the ideas were more widely disseminated in the world, ya know?

I also want to note here that some of my favorite parts of this book are located in the definitions section that follows. Though the terms are defined in CC terms, they have a lot of real-life applications and would make great starting places for real life discussions about intentional norm making.

My hope for writing this is that people enjoy and share this book, and those who feel called will really become Norm Changers and start Norm-Making Salons. I'd also be greatly pleased if some people create animated videos, memes, or other modes of expression to help spread these ideas.

Why? Because MMR is real, and we are all infected by it. We cannot continue to use MMR-infected thinking in the Anthropocene and expect to survive. In other words, it's late, and we all know it. It's a crapshoot. Most days I'd be happy if Earth took the radiation. But my sister has a kid I'm pretty fond of, so for his sake, and for the millions of other truly wonderful people like him (including you, dear reader), I think we should keep working to create the kind of world where we are all able to Thrive.

Namaste,

CJ.

Appendix 1

Cultural PTSD: A Quick Introduction

The theory of Cultural PTSD is meant to address general cultural norms writ large—norms we all are familiar with, as citizens of Western cultures. Though this theory takes a lot from ideas gleaned from intergenerational and transgenerational trauma, it's different. It says we are all living within cultures that appear to contain many elements that are similar to the symptoms that people with PTSD typically have.

That is not to say that we have all been exposed to trauma or are having our own individual bouts of PTSD. Rather, the theory shows how many of Western civilization's most entrenched cultural norms, values, and assumptions are similar to those of people who have PTSD. And because these PTSD like responses are at the cultural level, we are all affected by those cultural norms, values, and assumptions, regardless of our personal histories.

There are four major points to the theory of Cultural PTSD, and two more about recovery from the problem. They are:

1 Human history abounds with trauma.

2 The (enormous) extent of the impact from these traumas on our current cultural norms has not been consciously recognized by most people.

3 We have cultural-level symptoms very similar to those found in individuals with PTSD.

4 PTSD seriously impairs people—by definition. Cultural norms born of fear and trauma symptoms also seriously impair us.

5 PTSD is treatable. Cultural PTSD symptoms are treatable as well, once recognized as such.

6 We need to recognize our cultural symptoms and treat ourselves at the cultural level.

CulturalPTSD.org goes into a little more detail on these points (as well as some others).

There are several dynamics that are crucial to help further explain the theory:

Power and Control Are Normal Needs

Woven throughout the theory—and central to it—is the notion of power and control. How humans acquire, use, and respond to power has been at the heart of many Western sociological, anthropological, and psychological theories. Indeed, having a sense of power and control is a basic human need, and negotiating power in one way or another is a central task in life, whether we are consciously aware of it or not.

Trauma Is About Loss Of Power And Control

In the aftermath of trauma, power and control issues often become central —for very understandable reasons. Not only does personal power and control vanish during traumatic events, but the traumatic events themselves tell us that frightening and bad things can and do happen when people do not have power and control.

A compelling argument can be made that the primary need people have for the first days, weeks, and often months after experiencing real trauma is to try to regain power and control—by any means available. Regaining a sense of power and control in healthy ways takes time. It also takes work to recover from trauma, work lots of people don't know how to do, or are not supported in doing. The reality is things often go wrong in recovering from trauma—we often get stuck.

As a result, power and control issues are common for people with trauma histories, and these issues persist, often for decades after the trauma events.

Trauma Leaves Us Uneasy With Vulnerability

In the immediate aftermath of trauma, an immense sense of vulnerability pervades us. Our primary tasks are to manage that vulnerability, try to regain some sense of meaning about what happened, and regain some power and control over our lives again. Understandably, as we try to piece our lives back together, we become unwilling to knowingly place ourselves in more vulnerable states. **This is a normal reaction, but it needs to fade with time**. Unfortunately, that doesn't always happen. But not only is the road to vulnerability rocky under the best of circumstances, but up until very recently, showing vulnerability in Western cultures has been actively discouraged, especially for males. That fact has deep implications for the whole of Western culture.

We Need To Experience Vulnerability To Experience Other Life-Affirming Emotions

Several essential life-affirming qualities **require** some level of vulnerability. When carefully deconstructed, it becomes clear that a certain amount of vulnerability is always present when people experience and express qualities of compassion, generosity, trust towards others, and collaboration. See the definitions section for fuller list of the various qualities that vulnerability makes possible or blocks from happening (really, it's eye opening). A lack of ability or willingness to be vulnerable leads to difficulty in experiencing those emotions, and they become undervalued in individuals and eventually in the culture at large. At the same time, personal quests for power and control remain large, and tend to produce emotions such as ruthlessness, status, and competitiveness, and these in turn become more valued.

Any Threat Of A Loss Of Power Gets Confused With Survival Needs

It cannot be overstated: When we (as humans) feel we may lose personal power and control, we act in primitive, survival-based ways. In the face of even small to moderate amounts of uncertainty, much less traumatic circumstances, I'd argue we usually react with our survival instincts driving us, not other modes of reasoning. We especially do so when we are unconsciously triggered or unaware that we fear a loss of power. As humans, if we are not sure where or what the threat is exactly, we tend to overreact to everything. It takes practice for most of us to not go directly into survival mode.

In survival mode, no humans (none, nada, zip, zero) are focused on fairness, the rights of others, or long-term strategies. We are focused on survival; we get primitive, defensive, crazy even. We also tend to get extraordinarily self absorbed, to the point of not even seeing others as fully human, much less truly considering their needs thoughtfully. In these ways many humans have found (and continue to find) ways to rationalize terrible behaviors with relative ease. It's important to note that these dynamics happen on the individual level and on cultural levels, only at the cultural levels, they are more easily hidden from awareness. History and current examples abound of rights being trampled by certain groups of people, and then those groups further "not seeing" the validity of complaints about oppression.

Oppression As Normal Power And Control Needs Gone Awry

Behavioral health clinicians know power and control needs are often skewed in people with PTSD. At the cultural level, discrimination and oppression are obsessive and often desperate attempts to gain power and control for some groups at the expense of others (witness the extreme levels of cruelty in some political acts in numerous countries). Western history is chock-full of examples of extreme inustices where obsessive quests for consolidation of power have led to horrific outcomes for entire groups of people, up to and including genocide. Colonialism, racism, religious fervor and persecution, sexism, homophobia, and class and economic inequities are some of the most common ways people have tried to consolidate power historically. We are most definitely still reeling from those effects.

The theory of Cultural PTSD hypothesizes that many of these dysfunctional cultural norms originally formed from assumptions, behaviors, and beliefs of people who were attempting to deal with trauma in their lives and communities in the best ways they could.

This theory is in no way justifies or is an excuse for egregious actions, but is instead an explanatory theory, illuminating precursors to conditions that produced the kinds of oppressive beliefs and actions that are still stunting us.

In other words, cultural dynamics like xenophobia and ethnocentrism, and things like discrimination, oppression, and empire building, are strikingly similar to the fear-based beliefs individuals hold (and the actions they take) when they are in the grips of PTSD or unprocessed, trauma-based reactions.

Our Cultural Level Problems Are About Power And Control

Think about any or all hot button social issues. They boil down to disagreements over the use of power and control. Who gets to determine the proper amount of control over environmental regulations, tax policies, abortion, gun control, labor rights, corporate and small business hiring practices, military funding, and the like often get quite polarized and emotional. Cultural PTSD Theory says this polarization is precisely because these issues are, at their cores, about power and control, which some of us then mistake for threats to survival. It must be noted, that whether or not a specific policy is an actual threat to survival is not the point (think in terms healthcare for all—not really much of a threat, right?). It is the perception of a threat that triggers (often unconscious) fear. That (often unconscious) fear then propels a person or group of people to fight like hell against any supposed threat.

Limbic Systems Triggered By Cultural Contexts

Many thought leaders link current cultural malaises to a culture filled with violence, economic insecurity, and very real and pressing environmental issues. We've learned a lot about the roles our limbic systems and amygdalae play in making us worried and more susceptible to fear mongering. We know fear sells, and are starting to come to an understanding about how to deal with that.

Cultural PTSD helps further explain the ease by which our fight, freeze, or flight systems are and already have been activated. It also shines light on our cultural tendencies to conceive of aggression, oppression, and other forms of violence as "normal," if not desirable.

Trauma changes how people see and behave in the world. Unprocessed trauma often leads to large, lifelong changes in behavior in individuals that can substantially reduce their quality of life. Conscious work has to be done to recognize and modify that behavior. The theory of Cultural PTSD says very similar dynamics happen on cultural levels. It is simply unrealistic to expect that our earliest repeated traumas from things such as disease, flood, famine, and predators wouldn't affect us on cultural levels.

Reenactments of Trauma

While it may seem perplexing, and can be exasperating to those witnessing it, common dynamics for trauma survivors who haven't yet experienced healthy recovery from trauma are to reenact or perpetrate trauma on others, or put to themselves in situations where traumas will be repeated. This seems to be true especially if they were subjected to early trauma. But the facts are: it happens. For example, those who witness domestic violence as kids are more likely to be in abusive relationships as adults—both as perpetrators and as victims. As horrible as it sounds, trauma can easily get normalized like any other bit of culture.

Cultural PTSD says that as members of a group

react to life in traumatized ways, they may easily normalize pretty ugly behaviors, such as consciously oppressing others (even within their own groups and families), in order to gain more power and control. Within even a short period of time this can lead to cultural shifts where violence and oppressing others becomes accepted and then normalized by large portions of the population. It also can become largely invisible because it is normalized.

Cultural Level Mindfulness For The Anthropocene

In these early years of the Anthropocene, we are in the midst of learning how to apply metacognition or insight-oriented thinking to our cultural lives. We are beginning to become mindful at the cultural level. In the past few decades, we've made amazing advances in becoming more culturally insightful. We have become more cognizant of how we think about and treat numerous groups at the cultural level. This includes seeking justice and acceptance for groups oppressed by traditional socio-economic factors such as race and gender. It also includes a deeper understanding of a whole variety of other factors, such as how colonization affects how history is taught, and how our cultural institutions themselves become oppressive, among other issues. But we are, as a species, still in the beginning stages of learning how to actively deconstruct our cultural contexts.

Cultural PTSD is an important next step in the recognition of how our cultural norms are skewed in certain ways. The theory helps us understand how profoundly both our personal and political levels of life are affected by these (often hard to discern) dynamics.

We have generally conceived of and addressed

many social problems as separate problems. Cultural PTSD theory says that the majority of our problems broadly related to oppression (including climate change and capitalistic norms of scarcity) can be better understood as interrelated symptoms born of unprocessed trauma reactions that have been codified into cultural norms and assumptions that we all live among.

Conclusion And Evolution

The strategies of trying to consolidate 'power over,' and the accumulation of wealth (as proxy for power) at the expense of others are strategies rooted in survival, and are due to dynamics originally born from trauma and fear-based thinking which over time turned into accepted cultural norms. While we have survived as a species by using these strategies widely, the majority of us have become quite aware that these strategies are—at the very least—greatly hindering us in the Anthropocene.

At worst these strategies will continue to do the kinds of things they have done historically: directly lead to the deaths of millions through callous acts such as genocide, slavery, and inequities with regard to access to resources like food, water, shelter, healthcare, and education. These legacies will continue if we remain as blind as we have been to their true roots.

Trauma by definition changes how people see the world and approach life. Humans have suffered through immense amounts of trauma. We have developed cultural norms born of fear and trauma that have created systems of oppression and inequity, and lead to unnecessary suffering for all of us. When individuals recover from trauma, it changes their lives, and indeed saves lives.

We need to become more aware of these cultural dynamics, and nimbler in our collective abilities to change from these old fear-based and survival-oriented strategies, to more proactive, collaborative, and compassion-based strategies, policies, and actions in order to navigate the Anthropocene successfully.

Definitions

(Curated Specifically For Sharon

During Her First CC Year)

As Needed: A specific type of mind command and a subgroup of what are commonly called 'accessible mind commands.' As Neededs are written forms of communication created and placed exclusively by BFDs (see **BFD**) that provide information on a given topic. As Neededs are unobtrusively placed in semi-visible holograph form until requested by any aware being who wishes to know more about the topic at hand. As Neededs manifest in fully accessible forms when a being requests access to them telepathically or out loud. They are typically rendered either as printed word or in video form. The compacted semi-visible form that hangs out in space can be compared to hyperlink buttons on Earth internet pages. The being focuses on the holograph and requests to access it, again either telepathically (see **mind command**) or using vocal chords.

aware: (The word is not capitalized, except at the beginning of sentences) Official designation for beings who have attained certain levels of awareness (see **awareness**). Compare with **Newly aware**, and **Semi aware.**

awareness: (This word, when used as an official CC definition or construct, is never capitalized, except at the beginnings of sentences—it has no need to be capitalized, it belongs just as it is). Awareness is the state of truly understanding, respecting, and acting in accordance the idea that 'everything is connected, beautiful and divinely a part of us.' Nothing more, nothing less. We are all still growing in awareness. Awareness is the essence of belonging. The CC is comprised of all of the aware beings who exist in the known universes, and 'actively aware' beings are its administrative agents. The first and most important aspect of the ability to become aware is a willingness to experience vulnerability (See **vulnerability**) usually expressed in the form of curiosity. In fact, a being must be vulnerable (at some level) while in the state of awareness. See also **curiosity**. Goodness (see **Goodness)** is both a cornerstone of creating the state and a quality encompassed in the definition of awareness (but of course Goodness cannot manifest unless vulnerability is present).

BFD: A type of 11D being called a Biological Firmament Designer who creates and manifests fully functional matter based items for 3D beings. Items may be used for all sorts of purposes. Sometimes these Biological Firmament Designers create adjunct parts of themselves. Think of these creations as something like children that do not grow up. The best known of these creations are Bio Fuel Dispensers, also known as Bio Food Dispensers. When referring to the 11D being herself, the important distinction is referring to them as a Designer, rather than a Distributor or Dispenser or any other D word.

Aside: The GSS Prosperity's own in house BFD

is named Meg, and she is charming. In Meg's case, she is also a manifestation of the Black Feminine Divine.

A few examples of creations include: Biological Fuel Distributor, Building Feature Duplicator, Bio Form Dispenser, Book Facsimile Distributors, and Big Facsimile Disc (in honor of Disc World which is, of course, part of the known universes). These terms can all be used more or less interchangeably for your purposes as a newbie, but they are specific designations and the creations are all slightly different. To be on the safe side, we suggest you just refer to them all as BFDs.

CC: Stands for Convening Collaborative. The Convening Collaborative is the name of the governance entity for the singularity of aware beings in the known universes. It's a huge governing body, and almost universally loved by CC members. All aware beings are automatic members, which gives them certain rights and responsibilities. All automatic members are invited to join as active members. The vast majority do. Active members pledge to strive for Goodness. Striving for Goodness is the main foundational reason for the existence of the CC and, not coincidentally, for its astounding success.

Chingona: A type of hominoid species, very closely related to humans, but unlike humans, all Chingonas are aware.

Also, a term of respect and admiration. When referring to the species, the word is sometimes capitalized and sometimes not—like Humans or humans. Either is correct, but capitalization is less common and a more formal designation. Chingonas originally inhabited three separate planets within a far away, well-functioning solarium called Zapatis, but are now found throughout the known universes, since they like to travel. They are intuitive, fierce, highly intelligent, full of Goodness, and do not take any bullshit.

Because of their wonderful reputations, their species name became a term of highest respect for any being engaged in brave and love-based acts. When the word is used as an adjective, it is generally applied in the feminine form without capitalization, or, less frequently as: chingone or chingonx.

Consilience: Similar understandings coming from various separate (lol) fields of study or sets of data. Evidence from various quarters that lead to similar conclusions.

An example for our purposes: Political science recognizes something called MMR, feminism calls it Patriarchy, and Cultural PTSD might see it from a trauma-based and cultural transmission angle. In the CC's definition of consilience, though, it's important to be aware of incomplete consilience, which is the most common form. That is, each field may recognize the same dynamics but from different angles, and come to significantly different conclusions, thus losing some strands of importance about it.

An example: Blind humanoids working in different fields might discover through their separate studies in touch, smell or sound that there is a large being in the room. The recognition that there's a being in the room is consilience, but the problem with it (and again, one that is much more common than scientists like to admit) is then each scientist might study a different part of the being, and thus understand it as something quite different from what it fully is. If one of the scientists then becomes more famous than others, the large being in the room that an omniscient narrator would know to be an elephant might be described as a being that is sort of like a soft leathery blanket, due to the blind scientist only being able to touch the elephant's ear. Another might describe elephants to be like snakes, due to studying the trunk, or a third might perceive elephants to be like trees after exploring its legs. The entire understanding would be lost for some time, even though some consilience had been first recognized. Moral of the story: Even when there is consilience about something, there will be larger truths still hidden from understanding. See **Singularity**.

Curiosity: Requires vulnerability. Whole-hearted interest in finding out about something. The basis by which we truly learn and deepen our understanding about life, the universe, and everything. A foundational ingredient, and the bedrock for awareness. Required tool for decision-making for truly living in compassion and wisdom.

DMU (Dark Matter Universes): Universes composed of dark matter, as it is known to 3D life forms in the MU. Compare with **MU**. Not much more can be written about these universes for you, Sharon, during your first year with us. Trust us, the concepts needed to understand DMU are just too unusual for most humans (even you) to understand, as they do not abide by things like matter.

Aware beings in the MU live within the constraints of matter. Therefore they share more or less similar

1) Conceptions about matter (officially called Debris in the CC, see entry for **Debris**),

2) Conceptions of space, and along with that, the existence or lack of gravity, and lastly

3) Beliefs in 'Time,' a concept that, for lack of a better term, is simply a made up construct, very useful, but quite an arbitrary thing, much like base 10 mathematical systems.

Aside: Curiously, almost all matter-based life forms tend to hold beliefs about Time.

None of these ideas apply in the slightest when we define the DMU using official terms. See? Very tough nut to crack for humans (and actually for most Semi aware MU life residing in single-digit dimensional forms).

Debris: This is the CC's official term for what you call 'matter.' Nothing more, nothing less. Instead of your quaintly poetic saying coined by Dr Sagan, 'We are all made of star stuff,' we, in the CC officially say, 'We are all made of Debris.' To you that may sound a bit…lowly. But once you understand more of the CC ideas, we think the connotations you have about the word Debris will change. Capitalizing the D in Debris is customary.

Fear: (The word is capitalized almost always within the CC to connote its definition as a significant state of being to be accepted and transcended). A state where the being believes there is danger of some sort. Fear can manifest as the being feeling physically threatened. Or, in Unaware or Semi aware beings, a state of believing (or merely suspecting) that the being's basic understanding of reality is in danger (of being seen as wrong or inadequate) in some way. Fear is a basic response to life (much as love is, see **love**), so some reaction or response will follow if a being senses a need to go into a fear state. When the survival instinct is (often unconsciously) triggered, Fear almost always results—unless the being becomes aware enough…of its own reactions. Common reactions: Fight, flight, or freeze. Often immediately induces Hubris in Unaware beings, especially when MMR infections are present in the rest of the cultural milieu.

Goodness: (Unlike most other positive CC concepts, this word is capitalized when used in CC terms—the reasons for this are complex). Goodness is a basic building block upon which awareness rests. Goodness and awareness are inextricably linked. It is a being's capacity for honesty, agreeableness, compassion, empathy, and ability to work within a collaborative in a multispecies (Tribe) environment for the common good. It is almost fully encapsulated by things such as human concepts of altruism, but needs to include the Chingona-based idea of the 'loving bad-assery' or a mamma bear's fierceness.

Goodness is most commonly manifested by such things as a being's eagerness and ability to stay true to their role as a public servant. It is manifested by any actions that come from a spirit of being truly invested in furthering the common good, whether through grand actions, or more usually by simply living as a justice-oriented, kind, and compassionate being.

Goodness is comprised of goodwill and every being is endowed with some, as it is inextricably linked to the survival instinct found in all beings. Unlike Fear, which is the 'avoid' aspect of the survival instinct, Goodness is the 'approach' part of the survival instinct. It is the willingness to further explore and actively search out ways to belong and flourish within a multi-systems-based environment.

True Goodness is distinguished from Fear-based adaptation by use of complex reasoning. At higher levels, it still can be difficult for matter-based beings to distinguish between Goodness-based motivations and Fear-based adaptation motivations, but it is much more of an issue for those who are Unaware. All beings, once aware, continually grow in their understandings of awareness due to the persistence of difficulty in determining actions that are truly Goodness based.

Growing in Goodness/awareness can be defined as continuing to refine the distinctions and continuing to choose to live and act with more Goodness (compassion)-based actions and values—and with as much mindful awareness as possible. Goodness-based strategies are often consciously chosen (with awareness). In contrast, Fear-based adaptations are often quite reflexive and tend to be adopted and repeated unconsciously.

Hubris: (This word is almost always capitalized within the CC). The state of arrogant certainty that often veers into a denial-level presumption of being correct in the matter (or matters) at hand. Defensive certainty about one's own beliefs, and belief in one's own correctness of understanding are almost always accompanied by a diminishment of ideas that are not of one's own. Falling victim to or displaying Hubris (and subcategories of it, such as 'being a bore' or '_____splaining') is most often not a conscious state. It is a symptom of illness.

Some less destructive forms of Hubris, however, are conscious. Ego Bound Judgments resulting in short bouts of Superiority are examples that most Semi, Newly, and aware beings experience as PFFFs. As long as these bouts do not become too routine or disheartening to the being, they remain almost completely harmless, and will not affect Goodness levels.

Attempting to ascertain whether or not a victim is consciously engaging in Hubris or is unconsciously displaying it is difficult, and has not been proven to be helpful in eradicating it—which should always be the end goal.

CC guidelines recommend that aware beings who encounter Hubris in infected individuals act with charity and grace, but move to **chingona** states when necessary. For even if the being is consciously engaging in Hubris, they are most certainly suffering within the stunted confines of their Fear-based worldviews. Those stuck in the kinds of 'power over' mindsets that MMR produces are obviously not able to fully connect with or understand others.

Hubris is a primary function (primary symptom) of MMR. And yes, the derogatory terms mansplaining, whitesplaining, straightsplaining, and other forms of splaining are manifestations of Hubris that are unfortunately very well documented among humans on Earth.

The state of being infected by (unconsciously held) MMR beliefs inevitably leads to Hubris in at least some areas. Hubris and awareness cannot coexist. Hubris is directly (but not entirely) caused by the fear of vulnerability (see **vulnerability**), which blocks beings from learning. Complex cultural systems based on Fear-derived values are always in evidence in areas where Hubris is found. Hubris is always a symptom of illness, usually MMR. Indeed, MMR is almost always accompanies the most troublesome and persistent forms of Hubris.

Humanely neutralize: The most extreme process by which the CC uses its sanctioned powers to render a being harmless to its self and others. Often involves a lifelong quarantining of those who have presented a consistent danger to the well-being of others, and who appear to be acting from persistent levels of Hubris. Beings that need to be neutralized should be treated humanely, but their actions should be fully and carefully monitored, and their actions restricted to such an extent that they do not have the means to harm others. Beings who need to be humanely neutralized for long periods of time are generally far too Hubristic to consider self-harm, but measures taken to ensure the beings do not engage in preventable self-harm are also encapsulated within this definition.

Aside: Measures are in place to support any CC member who is temporarily incapable of accessing enough Goodness to act within the CC's general expectations of conduct. Extensive support is available and freely given to those who are suffering emotionally or unable to use good judgment.

(The) known universes: Official wording within the CC for all known universes (lol). While Earth perceives 'a universe' and some humans have brought into awareness ideas related to the possibility of parallel universes, the CC is aware of gazillions of universes, and is comprised of members from almost all of them. This also includes gazillions of un-verses, which exist in the dark matter realms.

love: Awareness. Nothing more, nothing less. In Unaware, or Semi aware beings, or in areas where MMR infection is present, this basic 'approach' aspect to life is often seen as both scarce and profoundly dangerous, and thus only allowed in very specific and fetishized ways. The concept of love in these instances is skewed to only encompass certain 'objects of affection' and tends to be intensely felt in ways that result in phrases like 'lovesick' and 'afflicted.'

Compare with your Earth's Dr. Barbara Fredrickson's theory of love. Seriously, she's got it pretty much right. She defines love as heartfelt connection, nothing more, nothing less (which can, of course, be seen as awareness). To her, many connections of love are fleeting—sharing a smile with a stranger, laughing over dinner with a friend, chatting for three minutes with a hiker about the beautiful day and the trail conditions ahead. Some love connections are short term, a connectedness with a coworker, or a sporadic relationship with an acquaintance, seen only infrequently. Fredrickson's theory of love does not relegate love only to a long-term, romantic commitment to another. Not coincidentally, Professor Fredrickson's theory of 'broaden and build' is quite analogous to the expansion of the known universes themselves, as well as to the continual broadening of awareness among all aware beings.

Lunctus: Shared communication between and among souls. Though not all souls are Lunctus, a majority are. Shared communication can occur between souls attached to various types of species, and in some cases across species. Resonance fields are related (see **resonance field**), but more focused on the resonance with the ideas or concepts at hand, rather than the relationships between the communicators.

Matter=Not: This is a style of ship that is suited for use in both 3D Conventional and Dark Matter Dimensions. It is currently cutting edge technology due to being powered by both Quarks Inverted (see Quarks

Inverted) and dark energy, making each ship an animate being in certain ways, as well as a transportation device. Aside: The GSS Prosperity is a Matter=Not ship designed to perform a variety of generalist duties for the CC. Usually it performs at least a couple of functions on any given assignment. For example, it often functions as a medical unit or wellness enhancer, a research and exploratory ship, and as a simple tourism vehicle simultaneously. However, its most common assignment involves assisting with special projects such as setting up, tearing down, or providing transportation for large scale celebrations, art installations, and building projects.

MIC: (Obscure reference to Earth-based phenomenon, stands for Military Industrial Complex—always capitalized. Note this phenomenon is most definitely NOT found among ANY aware cultures). On Earth: Can refer to 1) An obscene conglomeration of interconnected humans (all deeply infected with MMR) employed by corporations who seek to profit from war and other might makes right kinds of (destructive) scenarios involving violent exchanges of 'power over' others; or, 2) Interconnected enterprises (run by individuals deeply infected with MMR) that create, distribute, and profit from weaponry and other (usually deadly) forms of so-called defense tools. It must be noted that there are those employed by the MIC who believe they are doing good work and are cognizant of the dangers of the MIC, but they are outnumbered, and fighting a losing battle for peace (see what we did there?).

mind commands: Not capitalized unless at the beginning of a sentence. The main mode of communication between members of the CC. Mind commands are any form of words, physical patterns, or energy that convey concepts from one being to another. They are usually sent directly from a conscious mind to other conscious minds telepathically, but can be comprised of spoken words or energy sent in specific forms. Accessible mind commands are the rough equivalent to important public signs, printed matter, and prerecorded information you are used to accessing on Earth. Also see **As Needed** for more information on a subset of accessible mind commands. Incoming mind commands are the rough equivalent of speech for humans. Mind commands are generally prepared and sent by one being, but can be received by an individual, or by an entire group of beings.

MMR: (Always capitalized within the CC). Also known as Might Makes Right. Any of several manifestations of serious (usually fatal) culture-wide, planetwide or Solarium-wide infections/diseases that cause Goodness to be trivialized and allows Fear, Greed, Callousness, and Hubris to multiply as underlying (and often unconscious) cultural values. MMR stands for 'might makes right' and those infected with it believe the life can be boiled down to the idea of 'dominate or be dominated.' Those infected with MMR are unable to grasp that systems of interdependency and collaborative interactions are far far far more common systems of how beings and ecosystems interact with each other. They believe simple hierarchies (based on the threat of violence) can and should be used to hierarchically arrange beings or other things into overall social levels of 'importance' or 'worth' or 'high or low status' (sic). This ludicrous idea then replicates itself throughout various parts of the infected culture, much like cancer cells did in many humanoid forms.

Relationship to awareness (see **awareness**): The act of evolving into awareness requires that beings shed the belief that MMR is ever legitimate (or useful) as an underlying value for how to value things or lives or how to live life. In many ways, the primary nature of awareness is the profound lack of MMR.

Power structures based on MMR assume a 'power over' (sic) value about the nature of power. Compare with the much more common (among aware beings) conceptions of power as an inherently shared or symbiotic dynamic, a.k.a. 'shared power,' or 'power with,' or 'interconnection,' or 'interdependence,' or 'reinforced and strengthened through collaboration,' or most often 'belonging.'

Within MMR mindsets, power is seen as a resource to be used by one being (or group of beings) 'upon' another. By using 'power over,' beings can and do attempt and often succeed in imposing their will (often unilaterally!) on others or on the situation at hand. Violence (sic) or the threat of it is known to regularly occur in order to force the 'power over' aspect of the dynamic. It is the threat of violence or sanctions that is the ultimate root basis of MMR.

While thankfully rare within the known universes, MMR has been quite tenacious as a disease where it has struck. It is believed to be responsible for the vast majority of die-offs among beings that fail to make the transition from Unaware to aware beings. And fully 99.8 percent of violent outbursts waged throughout the known universes are caused by either MMR or naked Fear.

MMR is always fueled by Fear. Curiously, those afflicted with MMR, will almost always deny their actions have anything to do with being Fear based. Beings infected with MMR are usually unaware they are infected in addition to being Unaware beings.

Though there is no known cure, recent understandings have come to light that explore the issue of MMR as a disease born of unprocessed trauma reactions (unprocessed trauma reactions understandably tend to be Fear ridden and focused on regaining power (over) and control (over) by any means necessary). It is hoped that these new understandings will lead to effective interventions that can finally cure MMR.

MU (Matter Universes): Universes composed primarily of Debris and Space. Time is also available (and almost always applied) in these Universes. Gazillions of combinations of Debris abound in the known universes. In many, but certainly not all, of these universes, certain areas exist where Debris and QI (Quarks Inverted, also sometimes called life forces) combine. When Debris is infused with Qi (in specific combinations, of course) life forms are brought into being.

Newly aware: The term Newly aware is used for those who are awakening for the first time, or are still opening to awareness and attempting to make meaning (sic) of the totality of the singularity. Fully aware beings know that they cannot grasp total understanding of the singularity. But the term Newly aware is applied to beings who (for years or even decades) try to comprehend all (as if). The term is not derogatory, only descriptive. Many aware beings have periods of being Newly aware. The N in Newly is always capitalized. Compare with **aware** and **Semi aware.**

Oumaumau: From a human perspective this was a curious asteroid with a strange shape that appeared to human astronomers in 2017. It was actually the GSS Prosperity cloaked as inanimate Debris to avoid detection by humans. Aside: Oumaumau's monolithic appearance is not that different from how a human appears to other humans as a monolithic entity. Humans are made up of a complex system of electrically charge bits of matter that are "human," but they also host a bunch of separate beings in the form of bacteria and microbes, who all live within the larger "human" shell. The real difference between Oumaumau's inhabitants and the simple organisms that live within individual humans is that all beings aboard the GSS Prosperity/Oumaumau are aware.

PFFF: Stands for Personal Feelings as Fluctuating Forms, self-explanatory.

Resonance Field: A 10-dimensional space currently unrecognized as such by humans. A nonmaterial (dark-matter based) emanation of feeling that evokes real understanding and compassion. A resonance field is a field of shared understanding and empathy for the ideas at hand with others (who may or may not be physically present). For example: If you are among the many humans who knows Emily Dickinson has spoken directly to you as you've read her words, then you have experienced a resonance field with her. Often preceded by deep interest, deep listening, and feeling with. Is a field of understanding, rather than a Lunctus communication (see **Lunctus**). The two are easily confused.

Quarks Inverted (for humans, this can be thought of as life force and called qi or chi): Quarks Inverted is thought to be the root building block in the dark-matter dimensions. Describing anything from dark matter realms is kind of tough, but we'll give it a go because the social history is entertaining. The term is used in the singular form, despite quarks always grouping together and being referred to as plural quarks. Confusing we know, but it is what it is.

Quarks themselves (very, very small particles of matter) were brought into awareness about 45,000 light years ago—yes well before what you quaintly call (a) Big Bang, in a currently inaccessible part of what you call 'the' universe. The being who brought quarks into awareness was an ancestor of the famous 11D philosopher Spacias (records of the linage survived by a complicated eleventh dimensional process, but the actual name of the ancestor has been lost to antiquity).

Aside: Many, many light years later, a direct descendent of Spacias was thought to have brought into awareness the entire concept of color as well (a type of 7D entity, thus the confusion between auras and souls among some humans. They are similar).

Anyway, Spacias's unnamed ancestor was known to be a bit, how do you say it in your language— a bit of a player, and would organize massive parties in certain corners of the known universes. Those parties produced new forms of being. You call them nebulas, and most nebulas produce star nurseries. The idea of these parties hung on and was replicated in all subsequent incarnations of the known universes. Obviously, they exist in the current ones. In your universe, these areas are still producing new entities today, and your astronomers on Earth have correctly identified a few of them…really a great achievement for an Unaware 3D species.

Quarks Inverted can "decide" to go through a process we call Migrating to manifest in the Matter

Universes. Migrated Quarks Inverted (MQI) is often just referred to as Quarks Inverted or as qi in the world of matter. You, Sharon, are familiar with qi, or sometimes known as ch'i as a name for the life force energies within animate beings. Though there is a lot of misinformation out there about MQI (among humans anyway), CC's best science tells us that it necessary for animation in the material worlds. It is the ingredient which charges matter (Debris) with animation, thus germinating a chunk of (inanimate) Debris into a living entity.

The way QI manifests in its migrated form as qi are not easily understood by humans, nor communicated very effectively in this dimension. But know this: your (Earth) scientists not understanding it, or dismissing it out of hand is a large problem. In fact, we consider it to be a primary issue that leads to humans not successfully making the transition from Unaware to aware beings- (as referenced elsewhere, the majority of human timelines end at the year 2047).

What is qi? Qi manifests as electrical impulses certainly, so we'll call it that. But know that within qi there are magnetic fields at work as well, along with other fields you are Unaware of since they 'reside' in the dark matter realms. As you know, electrical impulses are not thought to be animate in the material world. However, when the Quarks Inverted "decides" to Migrate into the world of matter, a small amount of residual dark matter collides with matter. If certain kinds of radiation and light are also in the vicinity, the whole conglomeration transfigures into that specific kind of energy (qi) that produces animation in the matter realms.

Lastly, may we say that the moment of transfiguration produces a spectacular sensation for those in the vicinity, much akin to a wildly successful release of sexual tension buildup in humans.

In pursuit of exactly that kind of sensation, many higher Dimensional beings actively seek out places in the known universes where the levels of that kind of radiation and light are such that the transfiguration to qi is easily accomplished. The Horsehead Nebula is one of the most famous of these places.

Semi aware: Partially aware beings. The term is not derogatory, merely descriptive. Describes those who struggle with the belief that awareness is everything and everything is nothing, but still a part of a real thing, part of the singularity. Semi aware beings tend to revert back to defining reality through their egoic concerns, and think of it as absolute. They do this out of beliefs that egos are more real than the singularity they are a part of. Semi aware beings have moments of transcending their egoic beliefs, but the transcendence is often only fleeting, and they spend the majority of time in Unaware living, missing out on the love that is always around them. Semi aware is also used to describe those who have experienced some awareness, but are not (yet) convinced that awareness really is the answer. This skepticism can, of course, be functional in certain instances, such when beings need to remain in egoic states in order to survive for short periods of time.

Aside: Research has determined that where MMR is present, beings often need to stay in egoic states for long periods of time in order to stay safe or 'make a living.' This keeps them ensconced in the Semi aware state. The S in Semi is always capitalized. Compare with **Newly aware** and **aware**.

Singularity: The field of consciousness, connection, and life that is what we are all born into. It permeates all dimensions, both matter based and dark matter based. Different beings perceive and understand life and reality in different ways within this field, yet it is all connected. It is the ultimate elephant in the room, but, as egoic-based beings, we are all only able to understand and describe very limited aspects of said elephant at any one point. **Newly aware** beings seek to try to fully understand singularity. **Aware** beings know it is futile and completely unnecessary as well.

Thriving: The naturally optimal state of being for all beings living within a given ecosystem. Fertile environments where the strengths, interests, and propensities of the animate life forms within the environment are aligned with the environment in such a way that all are in vigorous and sustainable good health. Think of children when they are flourishing: they love to learn and play, and they feel love, both as a recipient and a giver of it. They feel safe in their communities and accepted as members of them. This is what the environments on healthy plancts allow for all their citizens, all of them.

Trauma: A kind of experience that profoundly changes social norms, behaviors, beliefs, and assumptions in many arenas of life. Trauma affects individuals, families, cultures, and entire planetary trajectories. It is thought to be at the root of MMR, since a loss of power is always at the root of trauma (after all, MMR is, at its most basic, a warped and conception of how power is organized). Trauma is the experiencing of an event(s) or situation(s) where a being's sense of safety is profoundly threatened. To be considered traumatic, the event must trigger the survival instinct in the being, and also disrupt previous levels of functioning in the being. Aside: Trauma can be normalized by cultural values and assumptions to the point of rendering the trauma invisible to virtually all beings who operate solely within the constraints of the culture. See Paloma's essay "What is Trauma" within the book *Cultural PTSD* for a fuller explanation.

Unaware: Designation applied to certain beings or species with certain (very low) levels of awareness. This is fairly small subset of the gazillions of known species in the known universes. Unaware beings are those with the theoretical ability to conceive of universal awareness, but are not able to do so due to personal egoic blocks. At the species level, many among a species may be aware, but if the most influential among their species are not, and the species as a whole acts in ways that render the species as a whole, Unaware, then the species is designated as Unaware.

The Unaware are ego-bound beings that have some sense of self, but no real sense of their fundamental interconnectedness. Unaware beings are self-centered, self-absorbed, and tend to act primarily from Fear-based impulses. The state of being Unaware is much like early adolescence. It is a developmental stage where the singularity (see **singularity**) can be grasped, but belief in it cannot be accepted. And yes, many humans, especially those most infected with MMR, are in this developmental state, Sharon.

The state of being Unaware is considered the most dangerous time of evolution for any given species. This is because beings can (and do) collectively extinguish themselves during this phase. Many times extinctions occur due to heavy MMR infections in leadership while many in the general population are not heavily infected. Unfortunately, in most MMR related certain diseases and infections there is a marked tendency for the beings who are demonstrably the least suited to be healthy leaders to covet and go after leadership roles the most.

Humans in the current timeline (as well as several other ones) are in this rare subset of being at risk of extinction due to their own Hubristic and supremely misguided actions. This is directly due to the MMR infection. The U in Unaware is always capitalized.

Aside: As stated earlier, Unaware beings actually are a small subset of beings. Life forms generally begin at instinctual levels of awareness (these species are often described as nonaware). Earth examples include beings such as bacteria, primitive plants such as algae, and other animated life forms that lack complex brains. These beings simply function without any sense of self or differentiation. Many of these species evolve to become aware on a planetary level (many plants and animals seem to have a sense of being interconnected with their planetary environments). However, these species are still considered nonaware at the universal level. The method by which nonaware evolve into being able to theoretically become fully aware at the universal level is not yet fully understood.

Vulnerability: A feeling state of great importance. Necessary and primary ingredient needed to attain awareness and support Goodness. The state of vulnerability is the state of being able and willing to not use defensive tactics when encountering life. Synonymous with 'openness' in many ways, but with the being's implied acknowledgement that some surprise and even danger—could—present itself by acting with open engagement. Openness is a willingness to share, and vulnerability is a willingness to share a bit more openly (lol), combined with an undefended willingness to be affected (at the heart level) by the act of sharing.

A certain (sometimes very small, but nonetheless present) amount of vulnerability is needed for all of the following life-affirming qualities to exist **in their pure** forms:

Deep learning ('tis true), Goodness (see **Goodness**), openness (of heart) and openness to experience, trust, love, collaboration, cooperation, ease, empathy, sympathy, true benevolence, gratitude, equality, egalitarianism, goodwill, true companionability, true kindness, true fondness, true affection, warmth, loving kindness, compassion, respect, mutual understanding, perspective taking (ability to see things from other perspectives—a.k.a. have insight, have deep understanding), interdependency, sharing, reciprocity, true generosity, the ability to flourish or thrive, altruism, true happiness, true delight and pleasure, willingness, warm-heartedness, unguardedness, gentleness, heart centeredness, true partnerships, true communion, camaraderie, mutuality, fellowship, mercy, tenderness, true courage, courage to act out of wisdom, diplomacy, statesmanship, curiosity, wonder, awe, and, importantly, humor, and playfulness. It is truly sad to think of how many things humans miss out on when they refuse to feel moments of vulnerability.

Due to deep infections by MMR mindsets (now understood to be born of unprocessed trauma reactions), this word is popularly understood by humans in completely negative terms such as: conquerable, unsafe, defenseless, assailable, susceptible, unguarded, under attack, unprotected, undefended, threatened, endangered, comprisable, under fire, insecure, dangerous, or undefended (all taken from Synonyms.Com). It is easy to see why it is so Feared, when vulnerability is defined solely in these ways.

True wisdom will never be found by those who are unable or unwilling to experience being vulnerable. Being undefended is essential to attaining awareness. Currently the CC is exploring ways to help humans relearn pathways to encountering life without using defensive measures (where defensive measures are not needed, of course).

Wealth Inequity: A symptom of advanced MMR infection on many planets. Wealth Inequity is a measure of how much the wealthiest on any given planet have in relation to their poorest inhabitants. On Earth, as of January 2020, the 2153 billionaires in the world have more wealth than 4.6 billion poorest people on the planet according to Oxfam's 2020 report. (Note from CJ: This is a horrifyingly real statistic. Find a summary of their analysis at https://www.oxfam.org/en/press-releases/worlds-billionaires-have-more-wealth-46-billion-people).

Miscellaneous As Neededs:

Debate About BFD Offspring:

Various scientific research communities argue over whether the BFD creations of smaller BFDs are inanimate objects with sophisticated AI, or actual beings who have a unique variation of consciousness. These smaller BFD creations are bits of reality manifested from the same stuff as all reality is ultimately manifested from: electrical impulses. Electrical impulses combine in certain ways to produce varying densities of matter comprised of varying proportions of elements, mixed at certain temperature and in specific ways.

And creations such as the Bio Fuel Dispensers had been given electrical impulses and networking that certainly resulted in something very close to thought. They also have the abilities (and the programmed imperatives) to create their own items from those same basic elements that they acquire and stockpile in certain dimensions. But they only produce thought in response to requests from other beings. Unlike the 11D beings who created them, they never initiate any independent explorations, or other manifestations of free will associated with fully animate beings.

Proponents of the idea that the creations are fully animate beings point out (rightly) that in the vast majority of cases, most animate beings spend a great deal of their time simply responding to their environments as well, and only engage in independent explorations under certain circumstances.

It should be noted that most BFDs (including the GSS Prosperity's own Meg) consider their creations to be more like inventions rather than offspring. But BFDs also exhibit quite a lot of tender affections towards these inventions. This may or may not be significant, as high levels of Goodness result in all beings developing tender affections towards all other things in their surroundings.

Amygdala In Overdrive Teaching Song: Some Variations

Amygdalae in Overdrive
Keeps nothing but Greed and Fear alive

Amygdalae in Overdrive
And suddenly it's okay to deprive
Others of their rights

No It's Not,
No It's Not!
No It's Not!

Amygdalae in Overdrive
Afraid of equal playing fields
They hide behind their riot shields
Too afraid they will not measure up
They become utterly corrupt

Amygdalae in Overdrive
Worried they will not survive
They steal from others and deprive

People of an equal share
So shortsighted and Unaware!

Amygdalae in Overdrive
Afraid of equality
They turn to depravity
To hide their fears
They use taunts and jeers

Avoid Amygdalae In Overdrive
So that Peace and Love will always Thrive

*

May we all learn to live in Peace, Prosperity, and may
we ALL Thrive. Praise Goodness

.